Parade of Horribles

Parade of Horribles

Rhett DeVane

Writers4Higher
writers hold the key to change.

Parade of Horribles
© 2017 Rhett DeVane
All rights reserved

Date of first publication: March 21, 2017
Published by Writers4Higher
Tallahassee, Florida, USA

Cover design by Elizabeth Babski, Babski Creative Studios
Cover photograph by Rhett DeVane

ISBN: 978-0692860403

Library of Congress Control Number: 2017904493
Writers4Higher, Tallahassee, FL

Printed in the United States of America

Dedication

For those people who live in fear and separation.

And for those earthbound angels who strive to make the world a kinder and more open place.

May we all live to see a time when we can live in peace.

Acknowledgements

Rhett wishes to thank the following people:

My family. All of you, by bloodline or by heart line.

My Chattahoochee friends. You are always there to answer questions.

My critique author friends: Donna Meredith, Peggy Kassees, Susan Womble, Hannah Mahler, Gina Edwards, and Pat Spears.

Elizabeth Babski for her excellent graphic design and friendship.

Editor extraordinaire Gina Edwards. You make me look good, hon.

Adrian Fogelin, for her expert guidance, encouragement, and friendship.

Patricia McAlpine, MSW, LCSW, for superb advice and a great title.

My Fiction Among Friends Retreat compatriots.

Patsy Harrell, Lana Radke, and Randy Harrell of the Salty Dawg Pub and Deli.

Billy Austin and Darrell Gibson of the Rutabaga Café.

Darin Jones, owner of Designs by Darin, for his expert floral designer knowledge and friendship.

Sergeant Joanna Baldwin of Tallahassee Police Department, in charge of the Special Victims Unit.

Officer Cathy Kennedy of Tallahassee Police Department: lifetime friend and consultant on law enforcement issues.

Captain Scott Lee of the FWC for information on rabies in wildlife.

James Houston, friend and beta reader.

My network of old and new friends, near and far.

My patients. You have been there every step of this journey.

My faithful readers. Without you, I would have little motivation.

My muses. They leave at times but always return bearing fresh torment.

And to God and this expanding universe for allowing me the pleasure of creation.

Chapter One

A cell phone text alert chimed—to most people, a sound as ordinary as breathing.

Jake Witherspoon rested a bouquet of sweetheart roses on his worktable. Had to be his life partner, Jon "Shug" Presley. Few people had his personal cell phone number.

Across the room, Jolene Waters, his partner in business, glanced up from a towering pile of invoices. Her fiery hair stuck out in comical tufts. Reminded Jake of a banty rooster.

He wiped moisture from his hands onto a Dragonfly Florist apron and picked up the phone.

Could be Hattie, but she'd already phoned him this morning and besides, rarely texted. Could be Elvina, with yet another question about the sunroom she was adding onto her house.

He picked up the phone. Not Shug's number. Or Hattie's. Or Elvina's. Or anyone in his limited directory list.

hi babe your hot what u doin

God knows, Shug would never write *you're* incorrectly. Wouldn't chop words to skeletons either, or stoop to lazy text-English. And jumping Judas on a pogo stick, didn't anyone use punctuation these days? Couldn't imagine Elvina Houston calling anyone *hot*, especially not someone forty years her junior, and gay.

Best to stop the idiot on the other side of that *babe* before they embarrassed themselves for something beyond poor language skills, or heaven forbid, sent some naked selfie.

"Wrong number," he dictated to the device.

I think you said wrong number. *Is that correct?* the female automaton answered.

"Yes."

Okay. I'll send that now.

Freaking amazing, this technology stuff. Jake lifted one corner of his lips. His best heart-friend Hattie called the lopsided smile his "signature Jakey grin."

"What'd you say?" Jolene said.

"Sorry, hon. Didn't mean to interrupt you." He thought about sharing the *babe* text with her, but she had her paper-pusher face on. Thank God for her. He detested the business end of things. Jolene was such an organization freak, she barely had to break a sweat come tax time. Left to his own, he would sooner pitch the papers into a shoe box and let the accountant sort it out.

He laid the phone down on the worktable. No time for some stranger's tomfoolery. Not with three festivals and the holidays looming. People tended to die around this time of year . . . those casket drapes and funeral sprays. And it wasn't only the kinfolk of the dearly departed clamoring for his services. Christmas brides with their momzillas demanded attention. And end of year parties? Not complete without flowers. Oh heavens no.

Shouldn't grouse about having a successful business, especially in a place the size of Chattahoochee. A town with two stoplights. And a state mental hospital on the main drag that accounted for the majority of the population. He could be back in New York, living in a cramped one-room. Or in an alley. Or dead.

A shadow fell across the flowers on his worktable. Jake froze. He looked toward the front door.

A man. A giant. Peering through the glass, his beefy face a black, undefined mass outlined by two large cupped hands.

Jake took a couple of steps back, tucked himself behind the threshold leading to the storeroom.

"What are you doing?" Jolene asked.

Jake looked away from the entrance to Jolene's desk. She watched him with a combination of *you're on my last nerve* and *do I need to worry about you?* When he shifted his gaze back, the man was gone.

"Nothing." Maybe one day he could spot a stranger and not think he was going to be beaten senseless.

He moved to the worktable. Beneath the clump of roses, plumosa fanned out like a verdigris fern spider web. The baby-blanket pink rose petals drew him in. If he could only spare the time, Jake could stare at a single bud until he fell inside it, lost in the intricacy of color and form. Safe.

Beauty shifted his thoughts from his overreaction to that large man. And from the pain he lived with—for a moment. His damaged left leg throbbed, a hateful heartbeat. Jake shook it. Sometimes that helped the muscles relax.

There should be a phone app for pain management. Those tech geeks had one for everything else. It would come in handy right about now, with PiddieFest weekend coming.

Too bad Hattie's late Aunt Piddie hadn't lived to witness these new smartphones. It would've assisted her with the latest gossip. Of course, Elvina had put one of the first generation cell phones into the casket with Piddie, at the viewing, before Piddie's earthly body was turned to ash and crumbles of bone. Wonder if that phone got turned to ash as well . . .

The phone chimed. Another text.

Wont you bad

What the hell? He clenched his teeth. Somebody playing a joke? It wasn't funny. He keyed in the answer this time. No need to really aggravate Jolene.

He resumed arranging the roses and plumosa. And ruminating. Floral design came so easy after so many years, his mind could go off on tangents while his hands stayed on task. Where had he been before some weirdo *wonted* him bad? Ah, yes. Piddie's ashes. Jake pushed aside the image of those crumbly "cremains"—what a bizarre term.

He'd rather remember Piddie Davis Longman as she had been in life: the matriarch with her signature lavender beehive hairdo. That lifted both corners of his lips. Oh, how he wished he could talk, actually talk, to Piddie, hear her voice.

Jake snugged flowers into place, spun the dish around. Tilted his head to check for symmetry.

So much had changed since his elderly friend left for her "great beyond." Not just cell phones. Everything nowadays morphed at blue-hot speed. Jake struggled to keep up.

Somewhere in the little frame house on Morgan Avenue that Piddie had bequeathed to Jake, a storage box held a growing slush pile of outdated tablets, phones, and laptops. Wouldn't it be lovely to push *delete* for that. Except for Shug's first mobile phone, a flip-top brick that reminded Jake of an overstuffed Star Trek communicator. That one, he'd keep.

Note to self: find that box and recycle some of them. When you have time. Right.

3

He turned his head toward the rear of the shop. Could store a box or two back there.

Jake reached for another bloom then paused. Perhaps he could slip a few canisters of Shug's festive decorations into the donation pile, too.

"Christmas. Lord help me through it," Jake mumbled under his breath.

Jolene shot him the stink-eye. "Tell me you aren't already stressing about the holidays."

"You don't live with Shug." Jake took a deep breath, let it out. He stood, arms akimbo, glaring at the floral arrangement as if *it* were somehow responsible for the eight Christmas trees waiting to take over the house. And that didn't count the two new ones Shug had bought on closeout, end of last year, one meant to hang upside-down from the ceiling.

Except for the soft click of computer keys, the shop grew quiet, until Jolene started to hum.

Jake threw up his hands. "Tell *me* that's not *Rudolph the Red-nosed Reindeer.*"

She glanced up from the monitor. "Huh? Yeah. Suppose it was. Hey, blame yourself. You brought it up."

As if she needed encouragement. Jolene was known to hum carols in July.

"You used to like Christmas," she said without looking away from the laptop.

"Still do. But the last couple of years, the commercial muckey-mucks have worn me out." He stopped long enough to catch a breath. "Every year, they cram fah-la-lah down everyone's throat earlier and earlier. I won't be surprised if people start to order jack-o'-lanterns filled with poinsettias."

She chuckled. "But your yard is always the talk of town, with all of the lights."

"That it not *my* doing."

"Can't be that bad, Jake."

Jake shoved a rose into the arrangement so hard the stem bent. "Crap." This time of year brought out the cussing man in him.

He couldn't tamp down the mounting rant. "Blow-up figurines will wheeze to life on our front lawn. Small wonder we don't torch a trans-former." He whirled the arrangement, stabbed in another rose. This one didn't break under pressure. But he might.

Like Hattie's goofy, optimistic self, he adored the fall. Pumpkins, baskets of russet and golden mums, cinnamon-scented everything. Bring them on. Thanksgiving? Also grand, with lavish Southern dishes shared with the people he called his heart-family.

"Of course, we'll still have a live evergreen. Why miss the opportunity to scatter my gleaming hardwood floors with spiked needles that poke through even my thickest socks?"

Jolene pushed back from the desk and crossed her arms.

Elvis, Shug's Pomeranian, used to eat the dang needles then yak up the sludge later. Jake's chest felt heavy. God, he'd miss that old dog's green puke this year. He truly would.

"I even have to put up with a rosy-cheeked Santa toilet lid cover. Hell of a place to rest my own butt cheeks while I put on socks."

Jolene's lips twitched into a grin. "Sounds like *some*one needs a vacation."

"Where would I possibly fit in a vacation?" Oops. That sounded more harsh than he intended.

"Maybe it's time to shift some of your responsibilities."

He huffed out a breath. "Right. Like some fool would volunteer." Who besides him could pull off two huge events in less than three weeks? "I've already handed over the fall carnival to a committee."

The text alert sounded. *Seriously?* He snatched up the phone.

Got to have u

You moron! **Wrong number.**

Jolene groped for the pencil she'd stashed behind one ear. "My, aren't you Mister Popularity today?" She made check marks on several invoices.

He scowled. "Hardly."

Jake slipped the phone into his apron pocket and picked up his pace on the Welcome Baby basket. He filled in the blank spots with fern, and pink and white sweet peas. The sweet peas—real name lathyrus—added for their color and enchanting scent, fresh, but not overpowering. No baby's breath fronds. So common.

He turned to take the finished arrangement to the wheeled delivery cart. The text chime chirped again. He set the basket down, palmed the phone. Another one? His heart fluttered.

You cute.

Different number. Same bad grammar. At least this one had a period at the end, and a capital letter at the start.

5

Jake thumbed in the reply. "People really should double-check before they hit send," he said.

"Don't ya know it." Jolene nodded without looking up. "I hate those robocalls, too. I even went to that Do Not Call website, registered my number. Fat good it did. I get solicitation calls most every day. Especially political."

"'Tis the pre-election season." Jake frowned. "Politicians. And they say *gays* are a threat to society."

Jake selected a cane from a long line of hooks, one of eight fall-themed walking aides. If he was going to limp the rest of his life, might as well make a fashion statement. Elvina—head of Chattahoochee's little-ole-lady hotline and the social engine of the Triple C Day Spa and Salon—had this one created especially for him. Carved wooden handle, fall leaves shellacked onto the shaft. Tacky enough to charm. Sturdy enough to help him balance.

Since the hate crime that had nearly cost Jake his life, he had amassed two hundred and twenty-eight walking canes, if Hattie's last tally could be trusted. Sister-girl tended to exaggerate. She was one to talk, with her fifty million refrigerator magnets. And those rocks both she and her sister collected.

Should get rid of some of his canes, but couldn't. Each reminded him of a few more steps away from that horrible night in '99. The night two teenaged cousins, Marshall and Matthew Thurgood, wrecked this shop. Then one of them wrecked him.

"I'm heading out for a couple of deliveries." He loaded the rolling cart. "And I have to make a quick stop by Elvina's house, talk with Bobby before he installs the sunroom windows."

"Oh, joy. Better you than me. That guy can be so prickly."

"Get past the redneck bluster, and he's not a bad sort." *Besides, I adore Hattie and her family, so Bobby comes with the package.*

Jolene tapped figures into the laptop.

"Want something from Mary-E's while I'm out?" he asked. Hattie and Bobby's middle sister Mary-Esther owned and operated the Wild Rose Diner a couple of blocks down.

"I would really, really like a muffaletta." Jolene twisted her lips. "Nah. Better not. I brought a salad from home. I can barely squeeze into my pants now."

"Okay, Joe-gee. Ding me if you change your mind." Jake pushed the cart toward the back door.

The phone chimed. Jake paused by the rear entrance, at the same spot where his blood had pooled that awful evening over fifteen years ago, painted over when Hattie and a handful of his townspeople had cleaned and repaired the damage to his West Washington Street shop.

Unknown caller.

This time, the downy fuzz on his nape prickled when he read the words.

Looking at u

Bobby Davis used a rubber mallet to tap a board into place. He switched to a hammer for the nails. This part of being a handyman was easy. Dealing with women like Elvina Houston, not so much.

He heard a car motor idle, then shut off, followed by the slam of a door. In a moment, he watched Jake Witherspoon trundle across the side lawn. Little dude even walked with a swish. An accomplishment, given that bum leg of his.

" 'bout time you got here, Fruit Loop," Bobby called out through the opening where one of the sunroom windows should be, would be, if Elvina wasn't being such a flaming pain in the ass. "Beginning to wonder if I needed to send out the pansy posse."

"Good to see you, too, Scarlet-neck O-Hairy."

Bobby watched Jake decide which pile of construction debris to gimp around on his way into the sunroom. "Nice *Gone with the Wind* reference, Jake." Every time Bobby thought he'd come up with a dang good jab, the little dude-ette topped him.

Jake cocked his head, winked. "You inched up a notch, Bobby Davis. Didn't know you could read, much less would catch the literary Scarlett O'Hara twist."

"What you get for jumping to conclusions, I reckon." Dang, it was a book *and* a movie? Bobby spotted a nail head jutting from one cross-beam and used his hammer to tap it in. "I'm actually thrilled to see you."

Jake rapped sawdust from his leather loafers with the tip of his cane. "Suppose there's a first time for everything." He flashed white teeth. Bobby considered making a comment about him laying off the bleaching products, but lost enthusiasm. The back and forth might go on for a while, if Bobby didn't nip it. The two had been known to swap quippy insults until folks wished they really didn't like each other enough to bother.

Sometimes, Bobby inwardly cringed, thinking back to how he used to mistreat his sister's best friend in school. They called it bullying now, had support groups, talked about it on TV. Not like back in the day when everyone figured it to be a natural part of becoming a man. Hanging with his gaggle of goofballs, he threw out *faggot* and *fairy* and *pansy*, and other coarse jargon he could no longer call to mind.

Now, a lifetime later, he and Jake exchanged verbal punches without bothering to put on the padded gloves. But it was different. Somehow.

"What's up with the theatrics, Brother Bubba?" Jake asked. "I'm a busy little bee-queen, so please *do* try to give me the abridged version."

Bobby sifted his thinning hair through his fingers. "Elvina is driving me to—" He stopped himself before saying *drink*. Sobriety was hard-won. He couldn't bring himself to use it as a joke. He tipped his head toward one window casing. "Standard size, right? You'd think this wouldn't call for heavy thought, much less a consult with a dang decorator."

"Wait." Jake held up a stop hand. "I thought 'Vina had settled on double-hung. I spent endless hours poring over pictures, explaining windows until I wished homo sapiens had never moved from caves."

"She's been online, researching. Now, she wonders if jalousies might be more fitting, given this," Bobby punctuated his words with fingered air quotes, "1940s bungalow style of house."

Jake closed his eyes and let out a sigh so exaggerated, Bobby wondered if his entire body might fizzle onto the cement subflooring.

"I know. I know." Bobby slipped the hammer shaft into his weathered leather tool belt. "I tried to reason with her. Told her the double-hung would be much easier to keep clean, not to mention more energy efficient. But you know how Elvina gets."

Jake's cell phone chimed a chirpy little ditty. Probably some show tune. Jake glanced at it and bit his lip. Dude's features usually looked happy-go-lucky, even when the circles under his eyes said he hadn't slept in a month of Sundays, but not today. It was beyond Bobby how Jake could keep going full-tilt, given his insomnia. Guess anyone who'd been beaten nearly to damn death might have trouble closing his eyes for long.

Bobby understood the vigilance that kept Jake up nights. That was the kind Bobby had to hold onto to keep himself from walking into a liquor shop, or even down the beer aisle at the Stop-N-Rob convenience store. He had once heard one of the mental patients use the word *lurkies* for the fears that stalk a person.

Lower your guard and the lurkies'll get you.

The text alert sounded. Again? Bobby geared up to get on Jake for being the popular little cheerleader girl.

The look on Jake's face stopped him.

Chapter Two

The Hill, Monday, late morning

Hattie Davis Lewis started the day as she had every morning since she'd moved home to Chattahoochee, slouched in her late father's butt-worn rocking chair on the shady front porch of "the Hill", their old family farmhouse.

She nursed a mug of strong, black coffee and ignored the rolled *Tallahassee Democrat* on the table by the rocker. Seemed in the past few years, the news covered nothing but murders, terrorists, wars, and pathos. All that could wait. At least until she was awake enough to take it all in.

Folks knew not to bother Hattie for thirty minutes after she bumbled into the bright country kitchen for her first cup of go-juice. Holston and Sarah Chuntian understood the routine. Break her no-speak rule and pay for it.

Other than that teeny, tiny flaw, Hattie considered herself a decent human.

As assuredly as if her parents still lived inside this home built by her father's hands, Hattie sensed the protective presence behind her. The last place on earth she'd planned to be when she left the cocoon of Chattahoochee for college was where she ended up.

Hattie felt safe, as much as a person could in these days. Jake loved living in town, but she preferred being three miles out of the city limits. Country living had its benefits. Peace. And the permission to sit on this porch, sipping coffee until her teeth were furry. And she'd be hanged if anybody tried to snatch that away from her.

She rocked and looked down Bonnie Lane. Though a thick stand of trees stood between her and the neighbors, they were there if she needed them. Her older brother Bobby had moved to the land a couple of years after their mother's death. His wife Leigh, son Tank, and daughter Amelia lived with him in the log home huddled in the forest on a separate driveway off the main lane. Close enough. She could make out one corner of the other house, a modest ranch-style dwelling near the state highway. Old family friends, John and Margie Frasier.

None of the families crowded each other. Hattie liked that, too.

She twisted sideways and slung one leg over the rocker's arm then used the big toe on the other foot to coax the chair into a gentle back and forth rhythm. No matter how hinky life became at times, rocking soothed her.

For the past few years, her family—heck, the entire town—had settled down. Little dramas, always. Births, deaths, marriages, divorces. But nothing as deeply disturbing as Jake's abduction and assault back in the late '90s. Years ago, she reminded herself.

Almost dull now. Hattie pinched herself for having the thought. Dull was *good*.

The family's canine sentinels flanked Hattie, one on either side, helping her guard Bonnie Lane. A red-tailed hawk swooped into a clump of broom sedge halfway to the Frasier's house. Captain Davis woofed once, a deep bass typical of German Shepherds. Ensign Lewis jumped to his feet and yapped.

"Settle," Hattie said in a firm voice.

Best to nip it before the smaller dog turned the morning calm into a full-blown bark fest. Ensign tended to get swept up in his watchdog role. Unlike Captain, the pint-sized hound wasn't enough of any one breed to figure his parentage. Hattie guessed Jack Russell and Chihuahua, with Cocker Spaniel mixed in. Of the two rescued dogs, Ensign possessed the bravest heart. Little dog syndrome times ten. He might not be able to reach higher than an interloper's calves, but those would be chomped to a bloody mess. Anything to protect his pack.

Hattie pulled two dog biscuits from the pocket of her shirt, a threadbare red tartan flannel that had once belonged to her father, "Mr. D." She doled them out to Captain and Ensign. Captain munched his with relish. Ensign gulped his down then watched Hattie with eager eyes.

"All I have." Hattie showed her empty hands. When she wiped them on her shirt, Captain and Ensign settled back into their sentry positions.

"Mom?" The screened door behind her creaked. "Safe?"

The dogs scuttled to their feet, tails wagging. Hattie glanced over her shoulder and gestured to the rocker next to hers. Suppose a cup

11

and a half was enough coffee. She could interact with her teen. Besides, this kiddo was easy-peasy, compared with the horror stories others told of their thirteen-year-olds. Good thing Sarah Chuntian didn't share her adoptive mother's gene pool. Hattie had been told she was somewhat whiny at Sarah's age.

But she and Holston would never know about Sarah Chuntian's lineage, since the baby had been left in a reed basket on the stoop of a Jiangxi province orphanage. Still, Hattie figured the mother had loved her newborn, enough to wrap her in a soft, handwoven blanket amid handfuls of wild daisies. Hattie still had the fragile scrap of paper found attached to the baby's simple clothing. The Chinese character for the word *chuntian*—"spring" in English—had been artfully scripted on the curled rice paper.

Sarah plopped into the adjacent rocking chair and ruffled the fur around Captain's ears. She leaned down to give equal time to Ensign. A snippet of ribbon corralled her waist-length ebony hair. Captain Davis settled between the rockers and Ensign Lewis sat at Sarah's feet.

"You sound better," Hattie commented. "If you go through today with no fever, I think you can return to school tomorrow."

"Yeah, sure."

Not like she'd have to coax her. The kid loved school. Always had. Sarah would drag herself there with full-blown flu, if Hattie allowed it.

"I've been researching," Sarah said.

"Ah." No big surprise there. As soon as Sarah Chuntian had touched that first laptop, technology sucked her in. Now, she was the family computer guru. Good thing too, or Hattie wouldn't know half the capabilities of her new smartphone. The one it replaced—until Sarah shamed her into trading up—had been smarter than her. Even after coffee.

Computers. Hattie fought a rash of worry. Predators lurked every-where. Used to be, the crazies you could see merited scrutiny. Now, she and Holston had to hone their senses for the invisible threats, too.

Sarah held up a sheet of copy paper printed with five bordered columns. "I compared the top three compact SUVs. Cost, owner satis-faction, safety, price, projected dependability."

"Wow. Didn't realize you were interested in cars."

"Heard you and Daddy talking." Sarah's features transformed from serious to smiling. "Mom, the way you keep vehicles, the next one will probably be mine one day."

Oh fine. Yet another fresh concern. My kid, behind the wheel, surrounded by enraged, texting wackadoos. People drove like sprayed cockroaches, especially over in Tallahassee.

"I'm not even sure if I want to sell," Hattie lowered her voice to a whisper, "Betty."

Sarah rolled her eyes. Guess that one teen mannerism couldn't be avoided. "Seriously, Mom? Not like she can *hear* you. She's parked out back."

Hattie paused to take a sip. Hard to let go of this particular superstition. Inanimate objects—especially ones built to serve or protect, like cars, boats, and houses—possessed distinct personalities. Hattie mentally tabbed the names of the autos in her life: Sally, Jenny, Bonnie Blue, Miz Scarlett, Rosie, Pearl, and Betty. She started to tick off the boat names, but Sarah interrupted the daisy chain.

"Like, I know how you love Betty. And you still can see Pearl every day if you want, but—"

"Pearl is in *very* good hands. Your Unc Jake babies that little gray truck, even more than I did."

"Okay, so Betty is still a good car. But don't you wish you had a back-up camera and collision avoidance . . . a GPS? Betty's not *connected*, Mom." Sarah tilted her head. "And we can find Betty a good home."

"I guess." Hattie rocked. Sipped again. If heaven didn't have good coffee, she'd have to reconsider her—as Jake so lovingly put it—*white-bread behavior*, and head the opposite way.

"Consider practicality. Betty is a 2001, with nearly two hundred and fifty thousand miles." Sarah Chuntian leaned forward and fixed Hattie with intense, exotic eyes. "Ever thought she might be ready for semi-retirement?"

Who was the parent and who was the child? Often, Sarah switched roles so seamlessly, Hattie missed the transition. Born wise. And kind. She hoped Sarah stayed that way through the rest of her teens.

Hattie took a breath, let it out in an extended sigh. She slugged the tepid coffee. Winced. Maybe she'd install a microwave on the porch. Better yet, move the coffeemaker out here. "Perhaps you're right, baby."

"Fantastic." Sarah tapped the paper. "I have contrasted the Honda CR-V, the Subaru Forester, and the Toyota RAV. Those are the top three in our budget range, unless you want to spring for a Mercedes?" She raised her eyebrows and one corner of her lips lifted.

13

Hattie shook her head.

"Figured." Sarah handed her the spreadsheet. Not a letter or number out of line.

The child's room appeared as neat as every written project she'd done since she could hold a pencil. Would she be an accountant? An engineer? She had an extensive collection of feathers, small animal bones, and other natural findings. Maybe an ethnobiologist.

Hattie glanced at the paper. Sad, the top three were imports. Anyone with half a brain knew most modern automobiles claimed a patchwork lineage, parts from here and yonder, assembled in Canada, the U.S, and Mexico. Hard to be an American car snob when the world grew smaller with every heartbeat.

"Okay, honey. Let me wake up a bit more and I'll go over these figures."

Sarah stood. The dogs jumped up again, alert, tails held aloft. She looped one arm around a porch column and swung around it. "May I walk down to Unc and Aunt's? Tank and I want to play this video game. Unc Bobby's home, but he's getting ready to go back up to Miz Elvina's."

"Sure." Hattie stopped rocking. What could it hurt? Both of the kids had the same cold, at the same time, and both were nearly well. Happened so often, she and her sister-in-law had grown to expect it. "You and your cousin seem to be spending a lot of time online. Who are you playing with, do you know?"

"People from all over the world," Sarah answered. "Mom, don't freak."

Hattie thanked the stars for Bobby's son Josh, nicknamed Tank for his stocky build. He and Sarah were like brother and sister. They had shared cribs, playpens, and scraped knees. And germs. Tank watched out for his cousin as if the job of protector came with the boy-cousin role.

"Okay. But you'd let me know if anyone acted weird, right?"

Sarah nodded. She pulled another whirl around the column.

No reason at all to distrust her. It was the kooks Hattie worried about when she woke up in the wee hours and dragged out the concerns. "Suppose I'll get your daddy to ride over to Tallahassee with me sometime next week, test drive a couple of these vehicles," Hattie said.

Sarah started toward the edge of the porch then turned around. "Actually, Daddy said that he didn't want to . . . um . . . cramp your style."

What a lily-liver. She'd rib him later.

Hattie loved the man to the edge of the universe. Still couldn't believe someone as honey-hush gorgeous had chosen *her*. Plain old her. "Go." Hattie waved a hand. "Don't keep your uncle and cousin waiting."

Her daughter flashed even, white teeth. They might spend a fortune on computers and years of college, but at least the dentist assured Hattie braces wouldn't be something they'd have to finance.

Not that money was a huge issue. Between Holston's book royalties and her massage business, they did all right. She would do anything to care for her kid, and keep her safe.

Sarah sent her the love-you wink and wave. Then she walked away. Hattie watched her daughter's easy, loping gait. Captain Davis marched beside her. Ensign Lewis remained on the porch. Split dog-duty. A few feet from the house, Sarah halted, spun in the opposite direction, and trotted toward the back yard, Captain trailing behind.

"Where're you going?" Hattie called out.

"Forgot to feed the Chick Flicks," Sarah called back.

"Remember, grab the rooster jabber for Hendrix!"

Sarah waved twice—*yeah, yeah*—and disappeared around the side of the house.

Hattie slung back in the rocker, cradled her cup, and smiled, thinking of the nickname her daughter had created for the chickens. That kid loved animals as much as computers. Good thing, 'cause the Chick Flicks were some of the most unattractive fowls Hattie had ever seen. For some neurotic reason, the chickens plucked out each other's feathers, until the whole flock looked like wounded, hardcore head bangers. The fresh eggs were wonderful. Ugly didn't hurt them.

And that dang rooster! Handsome, but affected. Had to be the wackiest critter to ever strut a coop. If they had a chicken ward uptown at the state mental institution, Hendrix would deserve admission. The only sane way to enter his lair was wielding a stick long enough to poke him if he decided to rush you, which he usually did. Spurs hurt. Hattie had the scars to prove it.

She reached down and rubbed Ensign's head, got a slobbery lick in return. As much as she loved the dogs, she missed the serene company of a cat. The strays that had wandered onto the Hill shortly after their old cat Shammie crossed the rainbow bridge seldom ventured toward the house, and never inside. A few days back, Hattie had noted a newcomer, a young butterscotch tabby. Fat, or more likely, pregnant.

The Hill provided a draw for the lost or abandoned as it had when she and Bobby were children. She'd watch and wait, coax the feline to become friends. If a litter of kittens was in their future, Hattie could choose one for a house pet and find good homes for the rest. Then she'd get the mama cat spayed.

By that time, Elvina might like a kitten. She often commented on how empty her house would seem when Buster was gone. That Tomcat was over twenty years old. He couldn't last forever.

Hattie slugged the last of her coffee. Time for a refresh, sans the dregs. And call for car-shopping reinforcements.

Jake jumped when the phone sounded with the Lone Ranger ringtone.

"Stop with the freak out. It's only Hattie." He took a moment to breathe and lower his shoulders. How were all the crazies getting his private number? Already ten texts this morning. Plus a couple of garbled voice messages. Low, creepy male voices. He swiped the screen icon to answer, "Morning, Sister-girl."

"Hiya, Jakey."

He put the phone on speaker and checked the time on his watch. "Early for you to form coherent words."

"Funny. I've been up for nearly an hour, thank you very much." A pause. "What'cha doing?"

"Fiddling with flowers, as usual." No need to tell her that he was also shooting out of his skin every time the phone alerted. "What's up?"

"I need your help."

Didn't everyone, right now? His text alert sounded again. Ignore it. "Fall décor? Parenting advice? What?"

"Car shopping."

Jake placed the cut mums back into their water vase. "Ah, Jeez O Pete. Didn't see that coming. I must be slipping."

"I want to ride over during the week, when Tallahassee's not such a zoo. Maybe, tomorrow? Rumor is, Holston won't go with me, and Sarah will be in school." Pause. "Pu-leeeease, Jakey?"

When in the pluperfect hell could he carve out time for this, on top of everything else? But this was Hattie, and he'd row across the Gulf of Mexico in a hurricane for her. Nobody had ever stood beside him like Hattie, during childhood when the other kids harassed him for his shyness. Not when he returned to town and some launched insults behind his back, or more often, to his face. And when he lay in the hospital for weeks, broken, Hattie's was the first voice he had heard. She had rambled on and on, recounting funny and poignant scenes from their mingled pasts. Words meant to lure him back from the abyss.

"I will go with you on one condition." His stomach grumbled. Had he even had breakfast today? "We stop for lunch at the Salty Dog. I am giddy over the mere thought of their grilled Rueben."

Dead air. "Sister-girl? You still there?"

"Yep. Um. Can we take Pearl? I'll buy lunch and pay for gas."

"Is Betty ailing?"

"Nope. She's as faithful as always. I can't bear having her watch me shop for her replacement."

"As I recall, you bought Betty on a whim, put the down payment on your Visa. Unlike you, really. You usually take decades to make a decision. Surprised you want to actually shop around this time."

"A woman can switch things up from time to time, Jakey. And there's the other issue. I will *not* have Betty end up on some used car lot, deserted, for *any* person to buy her. She's like Pearl, and I can't imagine leaving her with a possibly abusive stranger."

Jake chuckled. Bless her, she grew so attached. "Good news. A couple of days ago, Jolene mentioned how she's looking for a reliable secondhand vehicle. Bet she'll snap Betty up in a heartbeat. Go online and check out the Blue Book value. Give me a figure."

His text alert beeped. Jake flinched. Forced himself to relax. "Tomorrow, Sister-girl. I have to tend Mother's grave, so I can't leave real early. Be ready by ten. Pearl and I will scoop you up. Bring your checkbook, or in your case, Visa."

"Okey dokey. I owe you big, Jakey."

"No debt between friends, doll." If there was any debt, he owed the balance.

As soon as Hattie ended the call, she heard Captain's baritone bark. The tone changed, amped up a notch: his danger alert. The chickens cackled, too.

Ensign scuttled across the front porch and dashed toward the back yard. Hattie set down her empty cup and followed, walking at a fast pace at first, until she caught sight of the drama unfolding next to the chicken coop. She broke into a run.

Sarah held the rooster-jabber stick in front of her. She danced back a few steps at a time, matching the direction and speed of the snarling raccoon at the business end of the stick. Behind the fence, Hendrix screeched and hurled himself against the wire. The chickens squawked.

"Sarah," Hattie yelled. "Stay as far away as you can! I'll grab the gun!"

Holston had left for his writing haven in the Triple C. No time to call Bobby or the neighbors.

She wheeled around and rushed to the house, into the master bedroom where she entered the code to unlock the gun cabinet. She grabbed the rifle, checked to make sure it was loaded, then tore through the house and out the back door.

She reached a spot a few feet from her daughter. Slobber dripped from Captain's mouth, his staccato barks mixed with growling intakes of breath. Both dogs barred their teeth. Ensign lunged forward, circled, lunged again. She lifted the rifle, steadied it. *Breathe. Take time to aim.*

"On my signal, haul buggy fast as you can toward the tree line." She forced her voice to come out even, though what she really wanted to do was scream. "One. Two. Three. Go!"

Sarah whirled and peeled off. The pitiful animal lined up in Hattie's rifle sights staggered. Strings of foamy spittle sprayed from its mouth. Hattie sent up a quick prayer:

Living so close to nature, her father had made sure she and her brother could shoot. Only targets, of course.

She held her breath, sighted. *God, don't let me hit the dogs.* She squeezed the trigger. Once. Twice.

The raccoon collapsed. The Chick Flicks lost what remained of their tiny minds. Hendrix ran in circles, flapping his wings.

Hattie lowered the barrel. Then she cried.

She heard the sound of an engine behind her and turned. Bobby's battered pick-up rumbled up the lane, pulled around the side of the house, and skidded to a stop. Exhaust billowed in its wake. Her brother burst from the driver's side, not bothering to shut the door. Sarah barreled toward Hattie then body-slammed her in a tight hug. The dogs circled the raccoon carcass, barking.

"Heard the shots! What in the blue blazes?" Bobby sucked in a lungful of air. His brows knit together when his gaze landed on the furry heap. "Ah, shit."

Hattie set down the rifle then rubbed her hands up and down Sarah's back. "You did good, baby." She glanced up at Bobby. "Yeah." Tears blurred her vision.

She watched the breeze lift the dead animal's fur. Raccoons were some of her favorite creatures, with their little bandit faces and animated movements. When she was a girl, Mr. D had found a couple of newborn 'coons abandoned in the woods, their tiny bodies nearly chilled to death. Hattie named them R.C. and Moon-Pie, put them in a shoebox, warmed by an electric bulb. She fed them. They grew bigger and more annoying. They lived in her mother's sewing porch until spring, when Tillie put her foot down.

The raccoon that lay bleeding in the dirt could be one of their descendants. Her spirit sank with the thought.

"Heard someone shot a rabid skunk not far from here, last week," Bobby said. "Raccoons are rabies carriers, you know."

She'd have to catch the new butterscotch tabby soon, take it— her?— to the vet for a rabies vaccination.

"Know how you hate to shoot anything, Hattie, but you did what you had to." Bobby tipped his head toward the house. "Best get me a garbage bag. I have some old gloves in the truck."

Thank goodness for Bobby's years on the Florida Fish and Wildlife Conservation Commission. Though Bobby had retired, he'd know where to take a suspected rabid animal. They'd cut off the raccoon's head to confirm the disease, though its disturbed behavior and the fact it had faced down humans in broad daylight settled it for Hattie. Sad. The cute little critter didn't deserve such a horrible end. Crazed with a disease that scrambled its brain, foaming at the mouth, desperately thirsty. Then shot.

Bobby glanced around and picked up a fallen oak branch. He walked over and prodded the dead raccoon. "Good aim, Sis. Looks like both shots landed mid-body. Had you hit the head, it would've been useless to the lab grunts." He cast the stick aside and shooed the dogs back. "Remind me to never get on your bad side."

Hendrix gave one last elaborate crow and flap. The Chick Flicks went back to pecking the dirt.

"I came out to fetch my caulking gun for Elvina's sunroom, but that project can wait until tomorrow. I'll give one of my FWC buddies a buzz, get this to the lab."

Hattie rubbed a hand across Sarah's hair. "Go inside and fetch your uncle one of those heavy duty, black leaf bags." When her daughter was out of hearing range, Hattie said to Bobby, "Yes, I hated to kill it, but I'll pick off anything, or any*one*, who tries to come after somebody I love."

19

Chapter Three

Triple C Day Spa and Salon, Monday afternoon

Elvina Houston tapped a quick text to a friend in North Georgia, then slipped her smartphone into her jacket pocket and entered the hair stylists' suite, a manila folder tucked beneath one arm. The jabber of women's voices met her.

The quiz she'd copied from her last counseling session was going to light her coworkers up, or at least make them think about themselves a little more. Elvina wasn't much for all the self-help mumbo jumbo, but her counselor lived and breathed the notion of self-examination. Might as well share free what she'd paid to learn.

Going to a therapist was a habit, after all of these years. Started with a grief counselor after Piddie died. Now, a family therapist for what the new counselor called "garden-variety neurotics." The gab sessions kept Elvina's blue spells on a tight leash. That, and good drugs.

She stood at the threshold between the expansive salon and the reception room with one palm held firm on the mahogany trim. Since her broken ankle back in '08, her balance was a tad off. By golly, she needed to make herself use a cane during the daylight hours. As much as she'd like to stand back and observe, her legs bothered her when she did too much for too long. She slid into the room and took a chair. Still a good spot.

Elvina took stock of the mannequin heads in the room. Two lined up next to Mandy's work station mirror with their lofty wigs held in place with T pins. One, cotton candy pink. The other, gray with blue highlights the same shade as the spider veins on Elvina's legs.

Head stylist Mandy Andrews held a silver silk butterfly in her left hand and a rat-tailed comb in the other. Still impressed Elvina, even after all of these years, how that comb seemed like a natural extension of Mandy's arm.

The second hairdresser, Wanda Orenstein Brown, perched in her stylist's chair with a Styrofoam form clamped between her bent knees. The wig balanced on its rounded crest glowed an ungodly shade of lavender. "Who made that weird stuff in the fridge?" Wanda asked.

"That's Jake's kee-noah and wild rice salad," Mandy said.

"You say that *keen-wah*, Mandy. Not *kee-noah*," Elvina corrected. "You're pronouncing the second syllable like God's arc builder." Someone had to keep these gals straight. And the whole town straight, for that matter.

Mandy toggled the pointed end of her comb to separate two stiff gray curls and then fastened the butterfly. "Whatever. I said it like it's spelled on the recipe card Jake left on the counter. Q-U-I-N-O-A. Kee-no-wah."

"I hate that!" Wanda jiggled, always in motion. Her red hair surely fit her personality. So did the clipped accent. Let Wanda spit out a handful of words, and anyone who'd been born and raised in the South would know she wasn't.

"How can you say you *hate* that rice, Wanda?" Mandy said. "Have you even tasted it? Kind of crunchy, with dried cranberries, feta cheese, and those tiny green peas." She held up a pointy finger. "And some sort of dressing. Balsamic maybe. Oh, and shredded carrots, too." She used the same finger to air-dot the end of the list. "It is G, double-O, D, Good!"

"No, I *meant* . . . don't you hate it when words sound totally different from how they're written." Wanda rotated the wig form to check it from all sides. "Like gnat. Should be *gee*-nat." She puffed out a breath. "But no, it's *nat*. Besides, I don't need my food making me feel stupid."

Elvina tamped down the smile tempting her lips. Wait for it. Someone would snatch the bait and drag it to the bottom of the pond.

"You can accomplish stupid without any help. That what you're saying?" Mandy flashed a grin.

There you have it. Dependable as hot biscuits melting butter. Some things Elvina could count on.

Wanda fired Mandy a quick dagger-eye, then asked Elvina, "Do we have any of those little pipe-cleaner bumblebees left?"

"My desk. Left side, third drawer down," Elvina answered. "Y'all have to slow up at some point. Got two more cards of butterflies and a handful of those glittery gold spiral coils Jake had me order last week. That's it."

Wanda used one foot to spin the stylist's chair. She set down the wig form and scurried from the room. Elvina swung her legs out of the way in time to avoid a collision. Some days, working with Wanda was like waltzing with a tornado.

"I swannee." Elvina pursed her lips, shook her head. She felt her own beehive quiver. She wore it every day, not slapped on for some festival. "That gal. If I had a pinch of her zippety-doo-dah, I'd feel twenty years younger."

Make that thirty years. Elvina had to remind herself she was just plain old. She'd pass for mid-seventies, thanks to quality makeup, current fashions, and hair fixative products. Folks would fall out if they knew she smeared hemorrhoid ointment beneath her eyes each morning to shrink the puffy bags. The internet—what a wealth of life hacks.

Elvina pulled her shoulders back and sat up straighter. Lordy, aging gracefully proved to be a tiresome hobby. Add that to sorting details about births, deaths, illnesses, anniversaries, and every imaginable community drama, plus her duties at the helm of the Triple C, and, well, it was a good darn thing Elvina could keep up, at any age. But someone had to do it. She'd throw a punch, if one more person asked her when she planned to retire.

Wanda swept back into the room in the same fashion she had left and the conversation didn't miss a beat.

"Don't know about you, Wanda," Mandy said, "but I'll heave a relieved sigh when this PiddieFest weekend is over. It was enough when it was only one dance party, but stretching it to three days is stretching *me*." Mandy jerked her gaze toward Elvina. "No offense, 'Vina. You know I loved Piddie Longman as good as anybody."

"None taken." Elvina stood and moved through the room, lining up the extra chairs, squaring the occasional tables. She rearranged a stack of women's magazines. Top one promised *lose 15 pounds in two weeks* on page 21 and a *decadent chocolate torte* recipe on 42. Goodness gracious. No wonder most women were bat-shit crazy.

The beehives for PiddieFest lined up like colored ice cream cones. Elvina's spirit sagged. Dear God, she missed her best friend. Shake it off, old gal. No time for getting maudlin.

While folks in this salon and for several counties around loved Piddie's memory, Elvina still thought of her longtime friend as very much alive, no matter Piddie wasn't wearing her earthly suit anymore.

"I know what you mean by feeling overwhelmed." Wanda plopped down in her chair. "I'm running around like chickens with their banshees cut off," she added in her best Southern voice imitation.

"That's either 'chicken with its head cut off,' or 'running around like a banshee,'" Elvina corrected. "We have to work on your Southernisms, hon. You tend to marry them together."

Wanda wiggled her fingers. "I *do* try." That, said in perfect New Jersey. Or, what Elvina thought of as New Jersey-esqe, given that she'd never visited the state and all she knew came from TV sitcoms, and Wanda.

Mandy puffed. Her wispy bangs lifted. "All I know is, two large events in one month was already one too many. The Madhatter's Festival gets bigger every year, too. Was it five thousand in town last year? Now, with PiddieFest the week before it." She blew out a breath. "Poor Jake. He's lucky to take time to whiz."

"PiddieFest was Jake's idea, remember," Wanda said. "I think it's a hoot, honoring someone that way. Melody had to order four times as much Kiss-of-the-Harlot red nail polish. Everyone is asking for it."

Elvina returned to her chair and sat down. Ah, yes. That Harlot red, Piddie's favorite shade. Elvina chuckled. "Used to drive Evelyn wild. 'Can't fathom *my* mama painted up like a common streetwalker,' she'd say. More than once I heard Piddie tell her there was nothing common about her, that she would 'paint red across her bare behind and waltz down West Washington Street if she heard anymore guff.'"

A ripple of laughter rounded the salon and Elvina allowed herself to chortle as loud as the others, even though it was unseemly to laugh at your own funny. Somebody ought to put them on reality TV. Like Southern Kardashians, with plenty of excitement but none of the divorce rumors. Actually, come to think of it, more like Duck Dynasty with better hair. And no camo. Most days.

"Back to what you were saying about Jake—he spreads himself way too thin." Mandy plugged the final butterfly into the towering mass of curls then moved the foam head aside for another, this one with a mint green wig.

"How many more do you have to style?" Wanda asked. "I'm finally down to the last two."

Mandy wiggled one hand over the pale green hairpiece, as if she could conjure up the next outrageous fashion. "This one, then I am done, in every way. I've seen so many beehives, I'm seeing them in my sleep. Had mashed potatoes yesterday at Mary-E's place. Found myself staring at that pile of taters, wondering how it would look with four shades of cheese and a curl of bacon on top."

"Y'all need to speed it up. I got a quiz for all of us," Elvina said.

"Oh. Jesus Peas," Wanda said.

"That's *Jeez O Pete*," Elvina said.

Wanda circled her eyes, but didn't talk back.

Elvina studied the line-up of finished wigs. None of them could come close to the original owner's tower of hair. Piddie had been a short woman—a smidge over four feet—before old age snatched back a few inches. Elvina and Mandy were the two living souls who knew the deep truth: half of Piddie's curls had been an add-on, dyed to match. Some things were strictly no-tells. Elvina would take Piddie's secret to her own casket, along with her cell phone, of course. Good enough for Piddie, good enough for her, though Elvina's was a newer model.

"Jake came up with the idea for PiddieFest after I told him about this thing they have up in Baltimore, HonFest." Wanda puffed up her chest.

Guess it was okay if she took a *little* credit.

Elvina snuggled back into the tone-on-tone director's chair. Times such as this, early weekday mornings at the Triple C, provided a rare chance for the coworkers to slow the pace, actually talk. Not like Saturdays, when Elvina did good to take a pee break, had to order out lunch and eat it at her desk. The womenfolk depended on the Triple C for the most current gossip. The menfolk gathered their intel uptown at the Borrowed Thyme Bakery and Eatery, or at the Ace Hardware counter, not nearly as high drama as the Triple C's version.

"I *do* worry about Jake," Elvina said. "He looks hang-dog tired, here lately." Jake never appeared totally rested, not since that Thurgood boy beat the tarnation out of him. Of course, that boy had fatally shot himself later. Such sad justice. And the other kid, the boy's cousin, served prison time for his part in the whole mess.

"Shug stopped by for a cup of *my* coffee, earlier today," Wanda said. "He was on his way to one of his hospice patients in Sneads. He told me Jake's been tense. Like he's ready to jump out of his skin."

"Jake tends toward theatrics. It'll pass," Elvina said. "I told him adding events to PiddieFest was stretching it. But did he listen? Noooo." She smoothed her skirt, plucked a stray clump of hair from the hem. That geezer cat of hers was shedding something awful.

"He signs on for *everything*," Mandy added. "Worse than Sheila Bruner, the queen of all volunteers, used to be."

And Sheila Bruner had tried to kill herself. Not everyone was privy to that fact, either. Something chilled Elvina's shoulders, crept up her neck. She shivered. Piddie had called the edgy sensation "a rabbit running over your grave." Supposed to mean something bad was coming.

Elvina checked the time on her gold watch, the one Piddie had left her. Still ticking, like she was. Though some days, the timepiece lost a minute or two, like she did. "Where in the world is Melody?" Elvina asked.

"Right chere!" The nail specialist sluiced into the salon. The chain bling on her designer purse clanged in time with the tap of her high heels. She stowed the handbag—suitcase to Elvina's thinking—in a drawer of her work station. "Sorry. Tried to get here earlier. J.T. woke up in the middle of the night, throwing his pure guts up."

Mandy made a face and tsked. "Stomach flu is making the rounds."

Add cold and flu season to Elvina's pot of concerns. Holes in the schedule didn't serve the business and it was up to her to spackle them best she could. Plus, she hadn't taken time to get her flu shot.

"No, don't think it was a bug, more like what-all J.T. wolfed down at Mary-E's place last night." Melody bobbed her head for emphasis.

"Food poisoning?" Wanda asked.

Melody's mane of blonde danced when she shook her head. "Nah. All of us ate the same thing and we're fine. J.T. gets carried away when he eats fried food. He had two heaping plates of fish, and those Cajun hushpuppies and French fries, too." She gestured with one finger. The nail shade, Coral Dreams—same one Elvina preferred. "And apple pie. With two scoops of ice cream."

"Bet he's got gallbladder problems," Elvina said. She prided herself on her amateur doctoring skills. Who needed a medical degree, as long as you had the internet? Of course, you could think you were dying for sure, if you read too much. Not that she ever did.

Melody dismissed Elvina's diagnosis with a hum. "J.T. seemed fine this morning. I fixed him some soft-scrambled eggs and dry toast. He went on to work at the station. Chief of Police is a demanding job, what with all the meanness nowadays."

And we're surely not immune to bad folks. Elvina pushed thoughts of the evil that had stirred her town. All that nasty hate crime business belonged in the rearview mirror. Other than the occasional disorderly drunk or minor theft, the town eased through time. She rapped one fist on the chair's wooden arm, to jinx any bad luck.

The Triple C's sole massage therapist slipped into the room so quietly, Elvina jumped when she noticed her. "Lord Almighty! I wish you'd learn to make a rustle, Stef. You're good as a ghost."

Stefanie Peters shrugged. "Guess it's a habit."

Elvina pulled a quick head count. "Woo-hoo! Evelyn! We're waiting on you to take my quiz!"

"In a minute!" a voice echoed from the room adjacent to the reception area.

"This test of yours won't take long, will it?" Mandy asked. "I may be finished with the wigs, but I have a boatload of other stuff to do."

The snick of the back door stalled the conversation. Jake Witherspoon hustled into the salon, a basket of golden and russet mums in his free hand. He slid the flowers onto Mandy's counter.

Wanda stepped over and cradled one of the palm-sized blooms. "Beautiful!"

Jake chose a seat, lowered himself, and hung his cane on the chair's arm. "They *are* especially delightful this year. I have the delivery truck full, ready to set them into place in Piddie's plot."

Good, that would add some color to her day. Each morning, Elvina visited the small, square garden at the rear of the mansion where part of Piddie's ashes rested. Unless she was too sick to get out of bed, Elvina never missed a visit. There was that *one* time after she broke her dang ankle looking for her cat Buster in the dark back yard. Stupid armadillos and their diggety holes. That episode had set Elvina back several weeks.

Given Elvina's history of depression, the grief counselor had suggested the one-sided chats as a way to help Elvina deal with Piddie's death. Too bad heaven didn't have cell phone towers. They could call each other. Elvina doubted Piddie would cotton to text messaging. Spoken words were so rich, no need to tag a sentence with a silly emoticon.

The visits helped her feel less untethered. Elvina figured Piddie enjoyed it too. Heaven and all of that glorified perfection had to grow tiresome. As far as Elvina could surmise, that realm had no TV, radio, or internet.

Evelyn breezed into the room, stopping so abruptly, her short-bobbed, brown hair swung like a curtain. "Did I miss anything? I'm swamped, what with orders starting to come in for my holiday line."

And there was another thing to thank the Lord for: fashion design. With Evelyn Longman Fletcher all caught up in ELF-wear, her custom-made clothing for women and children, she didn't have time to cook. Piddie's daughter didn't inherit a talent for the kitchen. Evelyn was locally famous for her bad casseroles.

Beside her, Jake fiddled with the cane, twirling it on its rubber tip, tapping it in rhythm, until Elvina reached over and stilled the motion.

"So . . . what's up with this precious little pow-wow, 'Vina?" Jake asked. His cell phone chimed. He glanced at it, blanched, then stuffed it into his pocket.

Elvina opened the manila folder. "I have this great little quiz." She handed a stack of papers to Jake, motioned for him to pass them around. She pulled a bundle of pencils from her skirt pocket and dealt them out.

Jake looked at the stapled packet. "Busiest time of the year, with PiddieFest, the Madhatter's Festival, the fall carnival, and every other event imaginable pressing down on me, and you want me to take some silly test?" He riffled the pages. "It's a book! Really? And 'Vina, we still need to discuss your window selection before Bobby makes me want to hurl myself off the Jim Woodruff Dam."

Elvina waved his comments aside. The windows could wait. "This only takes ten minutes, tops. It'll tell us what our weaknesses and strengths are, so we can understand each other better."

Mandy scraped a hand through her hair. "Goodness, 'Vina. We already know way too much about each other after all of these years."

"Sounds like fun to me." Melody tapped her coral-painted lips with the eraser end of her pencil. "Look, it classifies you into animal categories. Otter, golden retriever, lion, or beaver."

Wanda readied her pencil. "I'm in. I could use a laugh."

Jake's text alert rang again. He checked the message, paled, keyed in a reply.

What was up? The boy certainly had more than his share of things to stress about. That leg of his would make men twice his size weep for mercy. Hope he and Shug weren't in a tiff. Not that she fully understood homosexuality. But people were people and love was love. Jake Witherspoon and Jon Presley were two fine people. And the world could use all the love it could get. Sure had enough crazy people willing to blow themselves up, to kill others and spread fear.

Elvina would wedge the reason from him later.

27

No one spoke for a beat until Jake said, "What the hay. I could use the distraction. What do I have to do?"

"Check the little box by one word on each line. Pick the one that best fits you. I'll tell you how to score it when you get to the end," Elvina answered. She could usually coax them into following her lead. "Don't overthink it. Go with your first response."

A few minutes later, after her scoring instructions, Jake announced, "I'm a golden retriever."

"Otter," Mandy said.

"So am I." Wanda chuckled.

"Beaver," Stefanie added.

Melody looked at Jake's score. "I'm a golden retriever, too." Her head bobbed. "I *love* those dogs."

Evelyn finished tallying her columns. "I'm a beaver. Almost a golden retriever, but more so a beaver."

"What are you, Elvina?" Mandy asked.

"Pit bull," Jake quipped before Elvina had a chance to speak.

"Funny." Elvina twitched an eyebrow, waited for the tittering laughter to quiet down. "I'll have you know, mister smarty pants, I'm a born leader." She thumped her chest with a thumb. "*I* am a lion."

"Close enough," Jake said.

Elvina summed up the character traits. Lion: good at making decisions, goal-oriented, strong and direct, but sometimes bossy.

"Amen to that," said Jake.

"Otter: social, open and positive, but has trouble with discipline. Beaver: organized, creative, yet often too perfect. And Golden Retriever: loyal, accommodating, and calm, yet not assertive enough, and needs to be loved by everyone."

"Sure seems to fit us all," Mandy said.

"Especially the *perfect* part," Evelyn added.

Jake stood with the aid of his cane, balanced for a moment. "*I* have work to do." He pushed his lips into a lopsided pout. "Still can't get over that I'm a golden retriever. Why not a wolf, or maybe a fox? They're strong and cunning. Even a mixed-breed canine like the ones Hattie takes in. At least a mutt can overcome anything." He paused. "I'd settle for a Pomeranian."

The truth dawned on Elvina. So, *that* was why Jake seemed sad around the eyes. He and Shug had taken it so hard when little Elvis went to dog heaven, a couple of months back. Elvina figured they'd get another dog, but so far not.

Melody smiled in her sweet way. "Goldies are adorable, Jake. And gentle." She gestured with a well-manicured hand. "And faithful."

"Oh, I *do* like them. Like all dogs." Jake wiggled his shoulders. "For sure, I *am* quite golden with a swishy tail, but I'd like to think I was likened to a breed with a little more bite than bark. That's all."

His cell phone alerted. Elvina noticed how Jake's face flashed annoyance and something else. . . . Fear?

Chapter Four

Bobby smoothed a line of clear caulk, wiped the applicator tip with a clean rag, and leaned back to check for flaws. He might have led a life filled with imperfections, but anything he built with his two hands fit together so well it might as well have appeared by magic. Boards, seams, corners—all, homogenous and aligned. If only he could've snapped his own life into shape with the guide of a chalk plumb line and laser level.

At least his last six years had been as close to balanced as he could manage, thanks to the appearance of his missing older sister Mary-Esther, a pivotal event that had forced the raw pit of buried anger and guilt to the surface.

He'd spent hours at AA meetings, blended with a string of appointments with a therapist, crawling around inside of his head. Imagine him, Bobby Davis, sitting on some shrink's couch, pouring out his guts, sobbing like a girl, then piecing the shards back together until his soul now felt almost as sound as this sunroom he had created for Elvina and her sorry excuse of a cat.

He heard Buster's loud calls echo from inside the house. Poor critter. Whenever Bobby was around, the cat was either underfoot or searching for him. He ate as if someone might snatch away the bowl. Still, Buster looked skinnier by the day.

When Bobby first started the porch two weeks ago, the old geezer had padded onto the concrete slab, eyeing Bobby with a combination of suspicion and disdain. So sorry to disturb your peace, buddy boy.

Days passed. The framework took shape and Buster decided Bobby was worth his attention. Each morning, Buster found a spot in the midst of Bobby's tools and curled up for a nap. Eat, sleep, eat, sleep.

What a cushy life. Envying the cat on that account, Bobby learned to work around the lump of nappy, yellow fur.

By the second week, Bobby carried a handful of soft, Elvina-approved Whisker Lickin's in one pocket. Couple of pieces for Buster first thing, a few when he broke for lunch (along with chunks of Bobby's sandwich meat), and some more at five when the autumn sun faded. The cat could use the extra calories.

Bobby had always been a dog person. Mostly hunting dogs. The one he had now, Stick, was a blue-tick hound. Stupid as a stick, hence the name, but spot-on in the woods and so loyal, he was often annoying. But cats, they were different. Came to you when it suited them. And it usually didn't. Except for Buster. Bobby couldn't move without stepping around him.

Buster reminded Bobby of himself. Banged up from too many long nights of brawls and carousing, wise in the way of practiced fools. Hard *not* to like him. Had to give the old Tom credit; he was still on this side of the dirt, notched ears and broken tail as proof of his tenacity.

From inside, Buster's screeches elevated to the panic level. Where was the old furry fart? Like Bobby, Buster had full run of Elvina's house, but usually stayed on the porch. Bobby set down the caulk gun and searched out the cat, found him staring at a living room wall like he was watching a video. Bobby picked him up, careful not to squeeze too hard. Poor critter felt light as air. He carried him to a bed fashioned from the rags he kept at every worksite.

"Need to get you some of those Chinese herbs Hattie rattles on and on about." He lowered Buster to the makeshift cushion. "Your mind is leaving you as fast as your get-up-and-go." With one finger, he roughed up the fur around Buster's ears until a deep purr rattled the cat's chest. Bobby trailed the other palm down the animal's back and felt the knobs of his spine beneath the dull coat.

Thing about aging animals: when they reach the end of the gangplank, they lose interest in grooming. Either become barrel-chested as hearts slow, or grow sapling thin. Eyes cloud. Hearing dulls. Bobby recalled a couple of his deer hounds that had even developed dementia. Wandering, crying or barking at nothing, stumbling into obstacles. Until they could no longer eat, or move. Come right down to it, people act much the same when the years grab them.

He cried like a damned fool every time one of his pets died. Nothing ripped his insides like having to say goodbye to a faithful friend.

Bobby continued to scroll his palm over Buster's head and down his back.

He wiped the shed fur from his hands, spoke in a low tone. "Bubba, your mama's gonna be the end of me, yet."

Buster opened one eye a slit. Closed it.

"Now she's quibbling about the damn flooring. One minute, she's sure she wants tile. Next, she's certain she wants carpet. Yesterday, she texted me about wood plank." He danced two fingertips around Buster's ears. The cat attempted a meow, managed a low grunt. "I told her you'd like carpet. Warmer for your feet. Muffles noise better, too. Since this isn't a screened porch, mildew won't be too much of an issue, though you pitching up hairballs might be."

His cell phone vibrated. Bobby silenced the ringtone every morning as soon as he arrived. It seemed to annoy Buster. He palmed the device, checked the number. Jake Witherspoon. Bobby slid the answer icon to the right with one fingertip. "About time you called me back, Freddy Fruitcake."

"For your information, Mr. Beef Brisket, after I stop by Mother's gravesite, I'm on my way to pick up your dear beloved baby sister, to take her car shopping." A sigh. "So cut me some slack."

Bobby lowered himself to sit. Buster stirred then quieted. Bobby held the phone with one hand, continued to pet the cat with the other. "Are you a complete glutton for aggravation?" He heard a huff at the other end.

"*Some*body has to do it. Holston bailed, that handsome coward, and you're busy with the sunroom. Can't interrupt that, even if it's the end of all time and Gabriel's trumpet blasts. Your wife is conveniently occupied. No way Mary-Esther can break free from the diner . . . so . . ."

"My *other sister* Jake Witherspoon to the rescue," Bobby said.

"Precisely." A pause. "What's the decorator's emergency *this* time?"

"Flooring."

Another extended sigh. Bobby could imagine the expression on Jake's face. "I'll talk to Elvina when I get home from Tallahassee," Jake said.

"Good. Thanks."

"Oh, and Bobby?"

"Hmm?" He stopped petting Buster and inspected the splinter lodged in his thumb.

"Fruitcake. Really? You disappoint me." *Sigh*. Wow, three sighs in one conversation. "Not very original, Bobby. It brings to mind mental instability or maybe a horrid holiday gift, not sexual orientation."

Bobby chuckled, started to reply. He heard the disconnect beep. No way that less than stellar jibe had offended Jake. He'd come up with way worse. "Ah, geez."

He hadn't even had a chance to tell Jake about Hattie and her adventure with the rabid raccoon.

Buster lifted his head and studied Bobby with large, golden eyes. Weird, that cats didn't blink. Like they could look straight through a person. No wonder cats used to bug him, back when he hid from everyone, especially himself.

Jake slid from the Dragonfly Florist van, careful to regain his balance before stepping away from the open door.

"You can sit there and text alert all you want to." He laid the cell phone on the console. "Vibrate yourself until you freakin' blow up, for all I care."

He grabbed an antique walking cane, its handle inlaid with flecks of abalone shell. The shaft of this one was a vibrant yellow, the shade of fresh lemons and dye-flower coreopsis. Always, for the ritual pruning, fertilizing, or planting, Jake selected a cane in the shades of nature.

In the past few years, he noted how home decor and fashions had muted to blacks, grays, and mottled hues. Ignoring man's imposed view, nature continued to paint with the colors of the rainbow until the fading light forced the world to darkness.

Maybe that is why he and his fellow florists stayed so busy. People grasped for the color that stress had effectively squeezed from their lives.

He slipped a plastic bucket loaded with supplies over his arm and limped to his parents' gravesite.

"Mornin', Colonel, Betsy Lou." He set the bucket down. "I only have a few minutes, Mother. But if I don't provide a bit of care now, your spring will be dismal."

He grimaced as he lowered himself to the ground. Couldn't crouch: no way he could endure bent knees long enough to garden. The bad leg throbbed before settling into its constant backstory ache.

With a small hand rake, he loosened the soil around a rose bush. An autumn rainstorm had left the ground moist and yielding. Everything about this fall had been unusual. First, the anticipated cool snap, a reason to rejoice. Then, unexpectedly, the humid days returned, with temperatures reaching into the low nineties. Hard to argue against global climate change. This part of the South was fortunate. At least it didn't face the flooding storms and tornadoes like the neighbors to the north and west.

"The magnolias are still in bloom behind the mansion, Betsy Lou." He talked as he worked in a scoop of compost. "That ancient one you planted before I was born is bursting with blossoms big as a double fist. You should see it in the moonlight, the way it glows like it has Chinese lanterns bobbing on the limbs. So odd, for early October."

The rose bush in front of the headstone appeared dead, its thorny branches devoid of leaves. He would add new plants in the spring, after the threat of frost. Fall and winter were less work- and time-intensive. Good thing too. His to-do list was long as God's arm.

"I found this Seven Sisters vintage rose out by the old cemetery near Greensboro." He tamped the soil around the base of the bush, adding a measured amount of plant food-doctored water. "Guess I've told you that a few times, but a good story bears repeating." He chuckled low. Not as if Betsy Lou could tell him to hush up like she always did when she was alive.

Jake smoothed the ground and added a fresh layer of mulch. Didn't have to worry overlong about these vintage roses. They would grow anywhere, poor or rich soil. Still, every living thing deserved proper nourishment.

One day, when he left the planet, these roses would run wild. Since the Witherspoon plot rested next to the back border of New Hope Cemetery, no one would mind their crazed overgrowth. If Jake ended up here—the Colonel and Betsy Lou had purchased enough property for him, too—he could hover over the plants' wantonness, looking down on his final decorator legacy.

He and Shug had discussed their last wishes. Cremation for both. Memorial parties. No sappy, teary services. Both sets of ashes would fit onto one plot, if they decided to rest near his parents. Oh, wouldn't that make the Colonel and Betsy Lou twirl in their coffins? A shiver rippled his skin. *Think about living. Not death.* He shook off the gloom and resumed the recital of the roses, as he did most times when he came to groom the graves.

"This other one, I found on a back Alabama road near Dothan. Piddie has a gravesite by a little wooden church up there and Evelyn and Hattie wanted to go visit, so I tagged along."

Jake smiled so wide he felt the muscles crimp his skin into the twin dimples everyone found so adorable, so they said.

"Actually, it's only a grave marker up there, what Piddie called her *vacation grave*. But, I told you that. Cracks me up every time. I like saying it—vacation grave."

Jake chuckled. Such unlikely comrades, Piddie and Betsy Lou. Piddie had been the only reason his mother had stayed in limited contact with Jake after he fled for the anonymity of New York.

"The blooms," he touched the thorny branch, "will be yellow. The kind of color that pops out at you. Piddie loved yellow, so I thought you might, too."

Jake shifted his bad leg to alleviate the building cramp then shimmied a few inches to reach the next shrub. Why he felt the need to chat defied reason, but he did it every time he came here. No matter which direction Betsy Lou had headed when she lifted away—up or down, depending on how the earthly scorecard read—his mother was surely not in earshot.

"This Confederate Rose looks like nothing 'cept a few woody sticks now, but it will show itself, come summer. I got the cutting from a nice lady in south Georgia, when I attended the Mule Days Festival last November."

Jake shook his head. "I know. I know. Doesn't fit me, does it? Your thin, white, gay-boy son amongst all those beefy redneck farmer types. You'd be surprised how well I can get along with them, thanks to Bobby Davis."

He troweled the soil around the stick-bush. "Remember those drives we used to take, Mother?"

●●●

The convertible's top is always down when Betsy Lou Witherspoon drives. Jake's late father had never liked the smear of the breeze on his cheeks. Certainly, The Colonel didn't condone his wife's passion for purloined shrubbery. Since The Colonel's death, Jake and his mother are free to take to the country highways in search of adventure. And they both relish the wild wind.

His mother's lips glow, slick-fuchsia. Her dress is deep red, tied with a polka-dot lime green belt. A silk scarf in pale blue floats around her head. The shades don't complement each other. Betsy's color choices never do. Jake is accustomed to the eccentricity and would feel uncomfortable if his mother appeared otherwise. People whisper the word *colorblind* behind cupped hands, but Betsy Witherspoon is so wealthy she can wear a feed sack tied with sisal rope and folks will smile and nod as if she picked it up in Paris.

"We're in such good luck, my baby boy!" His mother flips the sun visor down and checks her lipstick in the clip-on mirror. "Actress told me about a little black church cemetery near Mount Pleasant. One we haven't visited!"

Actress Monroe is the maid and cook for the Witherspoon family. The wizened, portly black woman is the kindest person in six-year-old Jake's world: soft, with pillowy, pendulous breasts—the kind of motherly female who hugs little, mostly ignored boy-children tight and bakes teacakes at least once a week.

Jake's stomach rumbles. In the frenzy of his mother's departure, breakfast was forgotten. Only a cup of black coffee and a cigarette for her. Actress had clucked disapproval when she pressed two napkin-trussed cookies into his hand before his mother tugged him from the mansion. Jake slips one of the cookies from his pocket now and nips bites, careful not to scatter crumbs.

"Just when I thought we had scoured every single, solitary church-yard within an hour's drive"—his mother whams the steering wheel for emphasis—"one comes to light right under our noses."

They ride for a few minutes. His mother whips a turn onto an even narrower road.

"These black folks have little churches tucked back everywhere." She jams the cigarette lighter button with the tip of one bright finger-nail. When it pops out, she uses it to fire up a Kool. Why she calls the cigarettes *cools* doesn't make sense to Jake; the tip glows red hot when she sucks in.

"I do believe that if there're five families, they throw up a sanctuary." Her words puff out with smoke signals.

Actress once old Jake that going to worship is a person's way of talking directly to God himself. So what if they have more places to call the Big Boss?

Betsy Lou stops the convertible with a jerk. His head snaps for-ward, back. A cloud of dust curdles in the car's wake. "Look!" She waves in the general direction of a rickety split-rail fence at the rear of a half-acre cemetery. To others, the thicket might appear to be poison ivy or Virginia creeper, woody vines good for no purpose. To his mother, they hold treasure.

"Get my pail." She snuffs her cigarette in the overfull ashtray and sweeps the scarf from her head. Careful not to tread directly on a grave, Jake walks behind his mother to the edge of the clearing. The bucket bangs against his leg.

"I wish they were in bloom so I could tell the color." Betsy Lou drops a towel on the pine-needle carpet and kneels. He sets the pail beside her. Since the way she sees color differs from his and everyone else's, he wonders why she's concerned with the hues. He knows not to ask.

Once she is engrossed in selection and clipping, Jake slips away.

The double door with its curls of white paint is unlocked. Jake glances around and steps inside. Rows of wooden pews line up on either side of the single center aisle. A boxy podium stands at the end. A cross draped with a length of deep purple fabric hangs on the wall behind it.

The hopeful light of early spring filters through eight, six-paned windows. He slips into one of the pews. The timeworn wood feels slick beneath him. Jake breathes in the cool silence.

The simple building is so different from the plush-carpeted churches in town. On the infrequent occasions when he and his mother attend, Jake senses the reason: *to be seen*. On some basic level, he knows the members of this little church come for another reason: *to see*.

The door creaks behind him. He jumps.

"What are you doing?"

Jake scuttles to his feet and faces his mother.

"You have no business in here! What would folks think? Get to the car, and make it quick. I've got a hair appointment."

Jake doesn't talk back, keeps his face blank. No use working up an excuse, not after he's stepped outside of his mother's steel boundaries. He ducks his head and rushes toward the door.

"Clearly, you don't belong in *here*," she spits out when he passes.

He wishes he could tell her; he doesn't feel as if he belongs anywhere.

●●●

Jake palmed the soil and mulch into place around the final bush and dusted his hands on a damp rag. He rose with the help of the cane. After gathering his supplies, he faced the grave.

Feeling that same hollow disconnect he'd had as a small boy.

Years after the wild rose escapade, when he came home, the prodigal son returning from the mire of New York to lay his mother in her final resting place, Jake had discovered Betsy Lou's secret rose garden. Like the mansion, the grounds had fallen victim to neglect, but tucked deep behind overgrown hedges, he had found a well-maintained row of vintage climbing roses.

Through it all—the denial of truth, his expulsion from home, the years of stilted, infrequent communication—his mother had maintained the one true thing she and her son shared.

He turned from the gravesite and made his way back to the truck. Hattie waited, and the present overrode the past, for now.

Chapter Five

To Hattie, Tallahassee felt at once familiar and foreign.

Even before she attended Florida State University, her family had burned a trail to the capital city at least twice a month to shop, attend various medical appointments, or visit friends in the hospital. She could recall a time before the malls, when only the main streets had more than two lanes. Now, the scramble of humanity took her mind off killing that sick raccoon.

"Amazes me every time I'm over here, how much Tallahassee's grown." Jake jerked the steering wheel to avoid an aggressive driver attempting to share his lane.

Hattie released her breath and unclenched her hands. "That moron in the red Charger didn't even look!"

"Don't know why I let you talk me into taking Apalachee Parkway. I detest it." Jake blew his horn at yet another wacky driver. "And so *not* a direct route between the car dealerships."

Hattie tucked the printed estimate for the Subaru into her purse. "I know, Jakey, but I love coming this way." She patted his arm. "Thank you, thank you, thank you."

"Gee, a triple-header gratitude gush. Not like we've both *never* seen the Capitol." He glanced to his side-view mirror and blended back into the center lane.

Hattie got such a kick out of seeing the state buildings at the crest of one of Tallahassee's seven hills. The historic center structure with its domed cupola and graceful, timeless lines perched atop the rise. The Old Capitol had been slated for demolition to make way for its glitzy replacement, until the public pitched a collective hissy fit.

She lifted her gaze to the modern edifice centered immediately behind the old capitol building, a twenty-two story high-rise built in the '70s. Nothing odd about that; the present pushed the past aside everywhere she looked. The crowning, and damning, touches were the two lower, matching, round-topped buildings flanking either side of the tower. "The Prick of Florida" and its sidekicks stood proud at the crest of Apalachee Parkway. Nothing in any of the other states came close to The Prick, and it was well worth the detour.

Hattie cranked down her window then rolled it back up, enjoying that her former old truck Pearl had turn handles rather than electric switches. Should be cool and crisp by now. But it wasn't. Sheesh. "This was the main spot where we took newcomers, back when I lived over here. Canopy roads, the downtown parks, and this final highlight. Cracked them up every time."

Jake joined her in a chuckle. His phone chimed from its position on the dash. He threw it a quick, snarky glance. "Wish I'd shared those years with you, Sister-girl."

Hattie noted his attitude, the subtle shift at the end of his sentence. Merry to melancholy. What was up with that? Maybe those two messages were Shug. Were they having a tiff?

"Oh, but we're sharing it now," she said. "That's what counts. I totally get why you left. If I was gay, with a mother like Betsy Lou . . ."

"Betsy Lou was only part of the problem," he said. "When I was eighteen, I didn't as yet have the balls to stand up to small town ridicule, excuse the somewhat obvious references to our esteemed New Capitol."

Things had changed since the late '90s, but had they really? Hattie still snipped an occasional jibe aimed at her best friend or his partner. After Jake's assault, the anti-gay rhetoric had quieted for a bit. Lately, the Supreme Court's decision in support of gay marriage nudged that mean-spirited beast.

Hattie clenched her teeth, recalling an incident the past week. One of Hattie's massage clients had commented on how she couldn't abide the thought of two men or women sharing a legal bond.

"Suppose certain men in this town will wish to marry." The woman had shifted her eyes toward the end of the building Hattie shared with Jake. "Not telling you what to do, dear, but I'd not allow *my* child to associate with such. Bad influence on our innocent youth."

The implication that Jake Witherspoon or Shug Presley—Unc Jake and Unc Shug to Sarah Chuntian and Bobby's two kids—would *ever* harm a child had sent Hattie straight to furious. Her face heated up now, thinking about it.

Who had been by her bedside after the cancer surgery, urged her to give Holston a chance to capture her heart, and stood with a bouquet of flowers, welcome home banners, and mounded boxes of disposable diapers at the Tallahassee airport when they arrived from China with baby Sarah? Jake. Who had helped her ease into the family homestead, decorate, and make the old place their home without deleting its former occupants entirely? Jake!

And don't even get her started on Shug Presley and the way he went out of his way to help anyone who remotely looked needy.

Though Hattie made it a rule not to discuss politics or religion with anyone outside of her family and close friends, she had made an exception for that meddling, condescending woman.

Hattie had forced her voice to remain calm, to drip sweetness. Southern females developed that talent starting at birth. Melted sugar coated harsh words much better than piss and vinegar. Most times, their real meaning didn't sink in until a beat later.

"Well now, marriage aside," Hattie said, "I'd rather *my* child have the influence of two gentle gay men—men who do everything for this community and spread nothing but kindness and love—than some holier-than-thou hypocrite who polishes a church pew on Sunday and stirs up mean the other six days of the week."

Hattie had relished the ripple of emotions passing over the woman's features: sanctimonious, to puzzled, to offended. Bingo. Doubt the woman would make another appointment. Okay if she didn't.

"This trip to 'The Prick' has been fun, but can we eat?" Jake interrupted her thoughts. His cell phone vibrated. He shot it a look, sighed. "All of your car haggling has given me a beastly appetite. I know the Dawg's not exactly on the way to the Honda place, but then, neither was this enchanting side tour. I'll even pick up the tab. Consider it an early birthday present since I haven't taken a second to buy anything for you, not even a card. I am such a rotten friend."

"You came with me, good enough. Besides, if I get a new ride, it can be my birthday present, to myself."

Hattie entered the Salty Dawg Pub and Deli first; Jake, Southern gentleman, held the door. She raised a questioning eyebrow and Jake motioned to the last booth close to the front plate glass windows.

She slid into the simple wooden booth, allowing Jake to take the *gunfighter's seat*, the position with his back to one wall and an unobstructed view of the room. When she and Holston dined out, her husband did the same thing. Was it a protective male instinct? Jake's wariness bore a deeper meaning, she supposed. Wonder if Jake and Shug tossed a coin to decide who sat where when they ate out.

The Dawg occupied a narrow space, with one long bar, two dining areas dotted with booths and tables, a small dance floor, dartboard area, and a pool table. Wonderfully dark, cool, and cavernous. And it had the best dang burgers in town.

The server appeared. "Hi, Jake, Hattie. Good to see y'all."

Another point to tip the scales in favor of local joints. Sure, she *was* a mushroom Swiss burger with sweet potato fries, but she was *also* Hattie Davis Lewis, loyal patron. Hattie regarded Jake. Definitely, a grilled Reuben on rye with fries and a co'cola. The server didn't bother writing down their spoken order, only nodded and scampered off. She'd probably fall out dead if either of them ever ordered something else.

"So, what's up with the text messages?" Hattie asked. "Your phone has vibrated so much, I'm surprised it's still in one piece."

Jake dropped his gaze to the table where his smartphone performed a jiggery dance, as if on cue. "Nothing, really."

"Has to be Elvina on a rampage. That's it, right? She's still stressing over that stupid sunroom. About to drive Bobby nuts." She laughed. "Wouldn't be a long trip." She paused. "Sometimes, she calls him ten times in one morning."

He swiped the screen. The jig stopped.

"Whoever that was must've crawled on your bad side. You didn't bother reading it."

Jake slid the phone toward the condiment holder and tented it with a folded paper napkin. "I think some drunk, bar-fly coed has given my cell number out by mistake."

"Huh?"

The server delivered Jake's co'cola and Hattie's iced water with lemon. Jake took a sip. "For the past few days, I've gotten texts from different numbers." He swished a hand. "Whoever they're trying to reach must be young, cute, and hot: all adjectives I've read repeatedly. Though I am not young, I *am* hot." He pinched his lips together. "Or, at the very least, disarmingly cute."

"Have you tried blocking the numbers?"

"Too many."

"Called your provider?"

He shook his head. "Plan to. Haven't gotten around to it yet."

Hattie sensed the weight of the upcoming festivities pushing down on her friend. Everything he touched had to be glorious and perfect.

The phone buzzed. Jake snatched it up and tapped the screen. "There. I silenced all notifications."

"How annoying."

"Yes." One nod. "'Tis."

Hattie slurped her iced water. "What does Shug suggest?"

"Haven't told him."

"Why not?"

Jake fiddled with a cuticle. "Because he'll say I'm turning it into my usual parade of horribles." He perused the paper menu as if he didn't have it memorized. "Let's talk about something else." He fixed Hattie with a stare. "Except for rabid raccoons, please. More of the gory details won't mix with my lunch, or yours for that matter."

In minutes, the food arrived. Steam curled from Jake's sandwich. He used a knife to flip over the top layer of bread. Hattie did the same with her sesame seed bun. Maybe she could manage to hold off shoving it into her mouth until it wasn't still cooking.

"So, you and Shug plan on getting married?" Hattie asked.

"How many times are you going to ask me that?" Jake dabbed a fry in a plastic cup of ranch dressing. He shunned catsup. Hattie had tried the ranch dip once, didn't care for it.

"You know how I love a good wedding." She squeezed a generous swath of catsup over her sweet potato fries then created a moat around them.

"Gah, Sister-girl. Why bother ordering fries? Tilt your head back and squirt the stuff directly into your mouth."

"I like catsup." She took a dripping bite and wiped a napkin across her lips.

"You passed *like* at least a cup ago," Jake said. "Obsessed is more appropriate."

Hattie ignored the comment. So she had passion for things she loved. "*Are* you?"

"Am I what?"

"Getting married?"

He gestured with a fry. "Do we need to? We've been together for over fifteen years. Can't see the reason for a legal ball and chain."

"Thought you and Shug would jump at the chance."

"Nice to know we *can*, but not imperative that we *do*. Does every straight couple marry? And half of those who do marry end up divorced." He sipped his drink. "Some of our friends feel differently. Practically rushed the Clerk of Court offices in June." He hesitated. "Not ruling out that we won't take the step someday, but . . ."

Hattie forked two errant mushrooms back into her sandwich, took a bite, moaned. So messy, so good. "But?"

Jake tapped his chin. "You've got a little . . ."

She wiped melted Swiss cheese from her chin.

Jake reassembled his sandwich and sliced the Rueben into fourths. What a neat freak. He took a delicate bite. Melted cheese blended with hot Thousand Island dressing oozed from the sides. She resisted asking for a small taste.

He dabbed his mouth with the edge of a napkin, chewed, then answered, "It's as if people think of me and Shug as the poster children for homosexual males."

"Now, I don't think—"

"Let me finish." He held up a hand. "Neither one of us is in the closet. Shug might pass for straight, but me?" The same hand swished. "I could wear flannel and spit tobacco and any fool with half a brain would pick up on it within seconds. I can't abide people who hide behind a curtain. People know me and Shug are a couple. We don't flash it around or try to convince anyone differently from the way they chose to believe. We're private people and, for the most part, fairly boring." He paused. "Some folks don't care. Others tolerate us. Why give the radical ones a reason to blow up and show out?"

"So you're scared to do it?" Hattie wallowed a fry in the catsup.

"You can't be openly gay and not hold some degree of . . . anxiety." He looked down. Trailed his own fry in the ranch dressing.

"Right." Hattie dropped her fry and reached over to brush his forearm with her fingertips.

She tasted a metallic tinge on her tongue. Same thing happened every time she allowed herself to think of the night the Thurgood kid brutalized Jake. Stepping into the open back door of the Dragonfly Florist. Into a puddle of her best friend's spilled blood. Dear God.

Some memories cemented into her mind and refused to leave.

Hattie jerked back her hand, grabbed the catsup-laden fry, and stuffed it into her mouth to stop the sensation.

Jake's smile didn't make it to his eyes. "Why I love you dearly, Sister-girl. You get me. You always have."

Parade of Horribles

Jake trailed the shiny new Honda CR-V Hattie had bought after lunch. As soon as she laid eyes on it, Jake knew: the compact SUV would make its new home on the Hill.

"Lookit!" she had said, pounding his shoulder to a pulp. "It's milk chocolate brown!"

Besides catsup, Hattie Davis Lewis was a pure fool for chocolate, though she preferred the dark variety with sea salt. Jake was surprised when she hadn't chosen the darker brown vehicle on the lot. Jake favored the mocha tone, but kept his lips shut. Wasn't *his* new ride.

He'd never owned a virgin vehicle. In New York, why bother with a car, virgin or otherwise, with public transit readily available. When he returned home after his mother died, he took over Betsy Lou's Lincoln Towncar. Driving that overblown lorry was like navigating a curb ditch with a cruise ship. Took an acre to turn it around and a parking slot sized for a tour bus.

No matter. The Lincoln, the mansion, and every piece of family belongings had to be sold to pay off his mother's barge of debt.

Secured on its dash clip, his phone played the theme from *The Lone Ranger*. Fitting, since she drove like a mounted sheriff pursuing a bank robber. If Hattie could make a car rear back on two wheels like the old Western hero's horse, she would.

Except for today.

"Yes, m'love?" he answered. Great thing about the smartphone. It automatically went into intercom mode when he was behind the wheel.

"This is so very cool. I dialed you using Bailey's Bluetooth!"

Car already had a name. That fast. Bailey, Hattie had explained to him and the poor beleaguered salesman, because the auto's color reminded her of the shade coffee turned when she mixed in Bailey's Irish Cream. Add to that, Bailey White was Hattie's favorite Southern author. Both were sound enough reasons, he supposed.

Good thing Hattie hadn't allowed her monkey mind to roam to other things associated with the color brown. The poor SUV could've been named *dog poop*.

"Sister-girl, you need to stop diddling with the steering wheel buttons and concentrate on your driving."

"I am!"

Jake heard the XM radio volume rise and fall, rise and fall.

"This is the best birthday present I have *ever* bought myself! Sarah is going to adore all of the gadget stuff, when she inherits."

Jake let off the accelerator to allow space between his truck and the bumper of her new car. "Hattie, my dear, you are driving like a narcoleptic slug. At least go the speed limit."

Smart move, opting for State Highway 90 over the interstate. Those truckers didn't cotton to erratic slowpokes. "I have so little time to do so much," he added.

"Bailey is my *love*," she crooned.

Lordy, what a sap. Jake patted the steering wheel. "I know, Pearl. She cast you aside for Betty in '01, now Betty's in the rearview mirror, too. Don't you worry, sugar. I'll take special care of you. Drive you until your little headlights dim and your wheels fall off."

Admit it. You're as big a sap as Hattie. Maybe more so.

"I did not cast Pearl aside! Take that back."

Oops. Forgot I was on speaker. Good thing Hattie wasn't easily offended.

"Snatched back. You are absolved."

"Let's cruise by the Triple C on the way home, Jakey. I want to let Bailey meet Holston and the crew."

Jake eased off the accelerator again. What was another half hour, when he was already so behind, he was tailing his own shadow. "Have to get there first. Hang up and drive."

"Oh, all right, Donnie Downer. Where is that disconnect thingy? Let's see . . . oh, here it—"

His phone beeped once then went dormant. Guess she found the button.

Jake smiled. That poor, poor salesman. Fellow looked as if he'd been pummeled by a Goliath by the time Hattie signed the final paperwork to transfer the tag. Had to give Sarah Chuntian kudos; her spreadsheets saved them all from Hattie's usual indecisiveness. Hattie was a typical Libra. The gal could weigh options for hours, until no one really cared which way the end decision fell, as long as it fell.

Maybe he'd drop by the Honda dealership next time he was in Tallahassee, take the fellow a nice bottle of Merlot. Good for everyone that Hattie kept a vehicle for years. Chances were the guy would retire before she walked into the showroom again.

Allegiance must be a Davis family trait. Jake recalled Mr. D and Miz Tillie. Never showy folks, and they traded vehicles only when necessary. Bobby drove a faded, rust-pocked pick-up. Mary-Esther still had that van she'd lived in for months before she showed up in

Chattahoochee. All of those vehicles could qualify for those antique car tags.

Loyalty had its perks. Once a Davis decided you were worth friendship, she—or he—would hair-lip hell before allowing harm to that friend, even if that friend was made out of metal and plastic.

The phone asked in its automated voice: *You have a text message. Would you like to hear it now?*

"Yes." For the love of Pete. Was Hattie using the car to text now?

I know what you are. The voice paused. *Would you like to send a reply?*

Jake's chest squeezed. "No." The word came out so soft, the phone didn't respond for a few seconds.

Sorry. I didn't get that. Let's talk later.

Chapter Six

Tuesday evening

Jake thumbed through the antique wooden file box. Piddie's instructions for that killer baked artichoke dip had to be in here somewhere. Yes, Elvina had inherited Piddie's treasure trove of trusted recipes, a fact she gloated about. She assured Jake he would be next in line for the collection. What Elvina didn't know was that Jake had found this cache of handwritten index cards stuffed behind some old fig preserve jars when he first moved in, and he wasn't going to tell her. Betcha a million bucks Elvina didn't have the artichoke recipe. Hah!

He could make a similar dish, go online and google some random instructions, but Piddie's dip was always such a hit, served hot and gooey, with crisp pita chips. Perfect for the PiddieFest kickoff party at the Woman's Club.

The cell phone rested nearby, atop the microwave. Silenced. Not even on vibrate. Jake didn't have to look to know at least thirty text messages waited. And if he looked at any of them long enough, he saw menace. Share those fears with Shug, and his partner would no doubt carry on about how Jake had snatched up the director's baton for the Parade of Horribles' marching band.

He heard the back door open. Feet stamped and the door closed. Jake glanced at the Felix the Cat kitchen wall clock. Its ball eyes rolled side to side, opposite the direction of its swinging curlicue tail. Eight thirty p.m. What a long day. His partner had left the house in the wee hours.

Shug entered the small kitchen, leaned down for a quick hug and kiss, and walked two steps to the refrigerator. He rummaged. "Where's the tea?"

"It tasted a bit off. I poured it out and bleached the pitcher." Jake located the dip recipe behind the dessert divider tab. Wow, he was truly slipping. "I'll make fresh, if you want. You usually don't do caffeine this late in the day."

"This'll do." Shug pulled out a Diet Coke, unscrewed the cap, and took a swill. "I need it tonight. I am so behind on paperwork, I may be up until breakfast."

"Welcome to my world." Jake took a deep breath. He couldn't recall the last time he had slept more than a few hours at a stretch. Normal. Or his version of it.

Early in their relationship, he and Shug had agreed to leave the day's hassles at the door. Both of them had enough pain racked up in their pasts, before they decided to share their lives. If you dwelt on bad, it would swamp you. Shug understood this. Jake did, too.

Jake initiated a ritual where each would "hang their worries" on the evergreen shrub next to the back steps. Symbolic, but effective. Not so good for the plant. It failed to thrive no matter how much care and fertilizer Jake lavished on it. Guess the constant drape of troubles took a toll. Now, he and Shug simply stamped their feet before entering, as if doing so culled the day's dirt and aggravation from their shoe soles. Nature be blessed, that shrub bounced back. The rubber mat didn't seem to mind collecting their muck.

Shug pulled out one of the vintage aluminum-frame chairs and slumped into the shiny red vinyl cushions. The skin around his eyes looked bruised and his brown eyes didn't shine with their usual good humor.

"Rough one?"

Shug nodded. "Still gets to me, sometimes." His partner rarely spoke of his hospice work. Beyond the privacy rules, Shug held his patients' last days sacred.

Jake waited for Shug to continue. He focused on the recipe card, pale blue flowers printed around the edges. One of Piddie's originals. He noted her lacy, loopy script, the small grease smudges from her buttered fingerprints. His throat constricted. At times, he missed Piddie terribly, more than he ever did Betsy Lou.

Maybe it was the impending PiddieFest, seeing all of those magical hairdos, eating comfort food, and hearing endless stories about Piddie, that made him remember his aged friend, her wisdom, her compassion. Why couldn't everyone look through a person's exterior to the honest core and drop the need to judge? Piddie could do that.

"Not that I don't love what I do," Shug said. "With the elderly, I feel as if I help them make peace, sometimes. But not the others . . .

the kids, or the people who are adults, just barely . . . with children left behind. Those stab me." Shug balled up a fist and thumped his chest.

Jake had fashioned numerous funeral flowers and coffin drapes, seen the deceased, painted up to look as if they only slept on those silken pillows. But he had never touched a body, not even The Colonel or Betsy Lou. Didn't ever plan to, either. The idea that someday, someone would handle his cold remains made him shiver.

Shug had held the hands of the dying, he told Jake. Their skin cooling as hearts slowed then stopped. He had washed soiled bodies of sweat and expelled fluids before the family had to experience that reality of death.

Wasn't always a clean, neat ending, like they showed on movies and TV. How Shug did his job without falling into a deep depression amazed Jake.

"We should plan a getaway," Jake said. Enough about death and darkness and sad shit that made him want to fall on a kitchen knife. "Doesn't have to be far off, or exotic, or expensive. Let's pack up Pearl and drive." He shoved back from the table. "We can leave now. The heck with it all."

Shug drank his cola. "Good as that sounds, maybe later, after the holidays." He closed his eyes, took a couple of deep breaths. "Actually, I need to talk to you about something."

Oh no. Jake forced himself to breathe. One more issue and he would strip and run screaming naked to Georgia. For real.

"One of my patients—the lady in Marianna—is close to passing over." Shug opened his eyes and looked at Jake. "First of all, let me say, she gave me permission to talk to you about this. She is the most impressive person, a retired English teacher. We've had long talks, until the last couple of days when she couldn't speak without great effort. She asked me for a special favor. I couldn't agree to it until I spoke with you."

Jake sat back, crossed his arms over his chest.

"She has this little dog. A pug. Named Juliet. The woman has no children and no one in the family to take it. Her husband died last year, heart attack."

"Shug, I—"

"I know it's not been that long since we lost Elvis. And we've talked about getting another puppy, someday. But Jake, this little dog has so much personality, and is over twelve years old. If Juliet ends up in a shelter, who's going to adopt her?"

It had been lonely around here without the tip-tap of dog feet. Those nights when Jake felt so detached. While the world rested. When he could hear Shug's gentle snores. The song of crickets in the shadows. No matter what ungodly time of night, Elvis had kept him company.

"When can Juliet move in?" Jake asked.

Shug's face lit with a genuine joy that sent a gush of love pouring into Jake's chest. It warmed away the cold pit of uneasiness from the stress, and those stupid texts.

"There's another thing." Shug's expression darkened.

What? Was the pug a biter or one that peed on rugs with abandon?

"My sister called today." Shug froze in place.

Jake scraped his memory for the names. Shug rarely referenced his family. "Genevieve? Sue Ellen? Marcie? Lois?"

"Genevieve."

Oh for the love of all things sacred. Not *that* sister.

Of all of Shug's siblings—he had six—Genevieve was the most harsh, the only one Shug had bothered to relate any backstory. When Shug finally decided to open up about his sexual orientation, long before Jake came into the movie, she had lost her ever-loving mind. Denied she had a baby brother. Spread the venom in his hometown until the mention of his name came with "the look" and a raised eyebrow.

Oh yes. *That* sister. The spit dried in his mouth.

Of course, that was *after* she rounded up a baker's dozen of zealots bent on "curing" her brother.

Though his other sisters and the two brothers had stayed in touch occasionally with Christmas cards, Shug hadn't been back to his birthplace since. Had he even crossed the Alabama border? Not that Jake knew of.

"Genevieve wants to come for a visit," Shug said after a pause so extended, Jake thought he surely imagined he had heard Shug speak her name at all.

When Jake didn't reply, Shug continued. "I know what you're going to say, but she seemed like she really needed to reach out. Things have changed in the past few years, I think. *People* have changed."

The Parade of Horribles morphed into a riot.

"She'll arrive on Thursday. She wants to stay here." Shug's left eyebrow formed a question.

In the middle of PiddieFest. With the kickoff party, Piddie's Inner and Outer Beauty Contest, and the PiddieFest Ball. "Here?" Jake swirled a finger. "As in *here*?" He used the same finger to point down.

Shug dipped his head in a slow-motion nod. "Genevieve says she has something important to say and it *must* be in person." He knocked back a slug of cola like it was a fifth of Jack Daniels and he hadn't had a drink in decades. "I offered to put her up at the B and B, but she insisted. Said she was the 'emissary for the family' and needed to 'immerse herself in understanding,' or some such."

Jake felt the blood leave his face.

Wednesday, September 30th, the wee hours

Elvina Houston strolled down Morgan Avenue. Two a.m., a time when most folks yielded to dreams. She would gladly give in to either if she could only sleep. But no need to begrudge insomnia. And no reason to allow age to steal her favorite form of exercise. Thanks to the folding hiking poles Hattie had given Elvina after she recovered from the broken foot, and the fancy LED headlamp Jake found at Lowe's, Elvina could still enjoy her nightly meanderings. She wore her cell phone on a belt clip.

Every evening, she fell dead out in her easy chair, Buster in her lap, the six o'clock news out of Tallahassee blaring. Elvina slept like the dearly departed, for sixty minutes, no more. She might catch forty winks here and there. Why was that, you reckon? Old people seemed to require less sleep, or maybe they didn't want to waste any hours on a pillow when so little time remained. Could pop a pill, she supposed. But she hated to add anything else to her chemical soup. During her blue spells, back before medication leveled her out, Elvina would take to her bed for several days straight, emerging stick-thin and haggard. No, she'd take sleep when it came, for as long as it stayed. Life sure was a series of trade-offs.

Every day at half past noon, the television in the salon was tuned in to her show, *The Young and the Restless*. She smiled, thinking of what Piddie had called it: *The Young and the Rest of Us*. No way could Elvina miss an episode. Every woman in town, even some of the menfolk, watched the daytime drama then talked about the characters as if they were kin. Because of her phone duties and managing the busy schedule, Elvina missed important details of life in the fictitious Genoa City. Good thing she had the DVR and her new big screen LED television at home, and that she could play it twice since she usually dozed through it the first time.

Elvina admired that Phyllis Neumann character, with her fiery red hair and personality to match—or was she an Abbott? Hard to keep up, since the characters married and remarried each other so they could throw a party. If Elvina was a few years younger, she'd color her own hair and get all up in everyone's business like Phyllis. Elvina huffed. She was already in the know about most everything that went on in Gadsden County and some of the surrounding burgs. All she needed was the flaming hair to go along. She could *so* be Phyllis.

A CPD cruiser slid by, slowed. A hand waved from the driver's side window. Elvina returned the greeting. The white Ford Taurus with POLICE slashed in blue letters down the side sped up, turned at the next intersection. Wasn't the Chief. He drove a black Crown Vic. Now *that* was a car to be reckoned with—like the Feds used to drive.

Oh, those police people didn't fool her. Not one whit. Every night, one of the officers on patrol passed by at least twice, keeping watch over her. That J.T. Mathers had tried his best to get her to forgo her walks, or to switch times to the daylight hours. Why should she give way to advanced age? No reason. And besides, she had known Chief Mathers since he was a tow-headed little snot-nose. Age trumped rank.

Furthermore, night was the best time to keep up with her townspeople.

Elvina made her way through the neighborhoods, hugging the curb. No need to worry with a flashlight for the spots not illuminated by streetlights; the headlamp lit the way and kept her hands free for the hiking poles. She especially liked the small lamp's flexible strap: pink camo-print.

Darkness revealed more than the light of day. Elvina caught snippets of conversations, saw the lights of those who shared her affliction. After years of nocturnal roaming, Elvina knew what vehicles belonged, and which ones didn't. Hedges couldn't hide every indiscretion. The streets had a thousand eyes. But none as watchful as Elvina's.

When she passed Piddie's old house—only two doors down from hers—she noted two lighted windows. One would be Jake's. He didn't sleep much either. Poor thing. She could text him right now and he'd fire back an answer. The other window—the small back room where Shug had his computer. Guess he was as swamped this time of year as everyone else.

Funerals kept Jake busy with flowers and Elvina busy with the casserole committee and attending the bereaved. Sad, when folks got so sick then died close to the holidays. Was a hot time for suicide, too. Couldn't let down her guard, as she'd done once not long ago. Four women had nearly committed the unspeakable act, right under her nose.

By golly, that sort of thing was not going to happen again on her watch. No sir-ee.

Chapter Seven

Wednesday, September 30ᵗʰ, morning

Jake's kitchen smelled of homemade "veggie-dump" soup, Piddie's invented use for the small amounts of leftover beans, peas, squash, and other cooked vegetables stored in the freezer. Fast, easy. Add some chicken broth, a couple of cans of diced tomatoes, whatever meat he had on hand, spice it up, and let it simmer. Heat up some rolls, maybe throw together a cheese board.

He wondered if Genevieve was wheat or dairy intolerant, or just plain intolerant. His offerings would have to suffice. What else did one fix for a relative on short notice, when work and life equaled a spinning dervish?

Jake's doorbell sang out. The advertisement had stated it was supposed to mimic *Hello Dolly*. Sounded more like a sickly parrot on a bender. Jake held up a wooden spoon, stalled mid-stir. Red-tinged broth dripped from its rounded edge. He settled the crockpot's glass lid into place and the spoon onto its rest.

"Jon! She's here!" Jake called out. He was more than rattled. Other than the brief time after he and Shug had first met at Tallahassee Memorial, when Jake read Shug's given name on the laminated identity tag, *Jon* had been reserved for off-kilter moments. Jon, I've sliced my finger and I'm bleeding out, or Jon, there's a roach the size of an antelope in the cupboard, or Jon, your infamous she-devil sister is *here*, standing on our front porch!

"Can you get it?" The yelled response echoed from behind the bathroom door. "I'm on the toilet." Shug never said "on the john." Inside joke.

Perfect. Sacrifice the hapless golden retriever to the fiery-eyed she-wolf. Every hint of spit left Jake's mouth. He took a sip from his cold mug. Now he'd have leftover coffee breath. Jake dismissed that worry. Doubtful he'd get close enough for Genevieve to catch a whiff.

He shrugged the kitchen towel from his shoulder, checked the front of his shirt for splattered soup spots. He pivoted, grabbed his cane, and started toward the front of the house. Less than twenty steps total, more if he shortened his stride. On the way past the hall leading to the small bath, he leaned in and said, "Okay, but you *so* owe me."

Jake noted the open front window a beat too late. The piece of dry toast he'd managed to nibble for breakfast threatened to resurface. That window allowed fresh fall air in, and let those last words to leak out. Oops. Jake closed his eyes for a moment and pressed between his brows, at a spot Hattie had touted as a pressure point to snuff a blooming tension headache.

The doorbell sang again. And again. And again.

That's it. He'd snatch it out and buy one that simply went *ding-dong*.

"Come-ming!" Jake called out in the lightest voice he could manage. Too bad he wasn't actually a golden retriever. Everyone liked those dogs.

The door stood between Jake and Genevieve. Jake held the knob for a beat too long.

The doorbell rang. Jake didn't care if he never heard *Hello Dolly* for the rest of his life. He pulled his shoulders back. *You are a proud, gay man. You can act your way out of anything.* Internal coaching: he had resorted to it often to survive the aftermath of the assault, used it most mornings to coax his knee to move. *You can do this.*

Jake swung open the paneled door. A squat woman waited on the other side of the screened door. Genevieve Presley Alcott. No need to second guess the name. Her initials were monogrammed on her paisley red Vera Bradley handbag. First thought: *she looks like someone's somewhat overdressed grandmother.* Second thought: *Red Riding Hood had mistaken the big bad wolf for* her *kindly, sick grandmother.*

"Well, hello. You must be Miz Genevieve." Jake held the screened door ajar. "Please come in. Shug, Jon, is in the—. He'll be out soon."

She stepped through the threshold as if entering a portal to purgatory. A rolling bag with a tethered tote the same red print as her purse trailed behind her. Also monogrammed. Even odds, she had the glass case and cosmetic bags, too. A woman can never have too much Vera Bradley. So he'd heard.

Jake cast a quick glance toward the driveway. Late model red Toyota Corolla. Had to be a rental. She must've flown into Tallahassee.

From Shug's sketchy details, Jake pegged Genevieve as more of a Cadillac or Lincoln sort. Something big, flashy, and for sure, not foreign.

Strike two against Jake and Shug, besides being gay. Jake drove a Toyota truck and Shug a Toyota Prius. Nothing, one man had recently assured Jake, screamed liberal like a Prius.

"May I take your luggage to the guest room?" Jake asked. Genevieve didn't speak, only pushed the bags toward him. *So, I'm the glorified bellhop. Alrighty then.*

Jake passed Shug in the hall. "Your turn."

"How is—"

"Seems human." Jake continued down the hall, whispering on his way past, "Though I can't swear to it, as she has yet to speak."

Jake parked the Vera Bradley tower next to the bed, technically, in his room, where he spent a few hours on the rare occasions he actually slept in a bed. No need to share space with Shug, when Jake couldn't capture sleep for himself. Jake generally favored the recliner in the cramped living room, the only place he could get his bad leg into an almost comfortable position.

He swept one last spot-check glance around the bedroom, the tenth time in less than as many hours. Nothing glaringly homosexual, not that there ever was. Crisp, scented linens. Wedgewood blue and yellow theme. Cheerful, cozy. Crystal water pitcher and matching glass on the bedside table. A stack of folded towels, topped with lemon verbena guest soap. A bamboo tray with pens and buttery yellow stationery, and a remote. A phone. Small flat screen television.

Better than the Hilton. And Jake figured his cooking could outshine any B and B's chef.

Jake heard the Presley reunion in the living room. Genevieve's throaty Southern voice, the kind that confirmed she had smoked her ration of Virginia Slims. Shug's precise replies. He was clearly in his polite, nurse mode. Calm, approachable, non-threatening.

A mosh pit of emotions could loom behind a hedge of civility.

Jake cut through Shug's bedroom to reach the kitchen. Soup needed a quick stir, though he had checked it minutes ago. He'd bring out a tray of iced water with lemon and put on a fresh pot of Kona coffee. Surely she drank coffee.

Anything to be a good host. And appease the grandmotherly pit bull in the living room.

Jake halted the dog analogy train. Pit bulls weren't bad dogs. He'd met one or two of the gentle lugs with tails that could sweep a coffee table free of knickknacks with one pass. Perverse owners were to blame for creating the dragon-jawed monsters that made the headlines.

Genevieve resembled a pug. She had the same smashed-in face. Since their future adoptive animal child belonged to the breed, Jake didn't want to use that comparison either. No, he'd not liken Jon's sister to *any* dog.

Jake stirred the soup. He reached in the drawer for a smaller sampling spoon, dipped a scant amount, blew on it to cool. Then he tasted. *Umm.* Never knew exactly how veggie-dump soup would turn out. Different every time, given the eclectic blend. Thank you, Piddie, this one was excellent.

Now, where was he? Oh, the correct association for Genevieve.

Insect. Something that ate its kin. Praying mantis? Nothing as cuddly as a dog.

"Black widow," Jake mumbled. "Oh, better yet, a brown recluse."

A squat little arachnoid with venom so potent it could eat a hole through to the muscle, with one teensy bite. Jake pictured an oversized brown recluse sporting a Vera Bradley tote. He clamped his hand over his mouth to keep the giggle from turning into a guffaw.

Hattie inched forward, careful of sudden movements. She slid two aluminum pie tins heaped with canned cat food next to a water bowl. The good stuff, at nearly a dollar for a tiny can, necessary to make friends with a feral feline.

She had left Captain and Ensign inside the house with fresh chewy bones. The two black and white cats—Oreo and Tux—accepted the lumbering shepherd and his mouthy sidekick. The new yellow-striped juvenile did not.

Tux head-bumped her forearm, a cat greeting, then hunkered down to the food. Oreo, the petite female, appeared a moment later. More than likely these two were from the same litter. Only a guess though, since she'd not seen the mother or litter mates.

Hattie scooted back a couple of feet and sat cross-legged. In a few minutes, a movement caught her attention: a flicker of butterscotch fur then a set of wary, yellow eyes watching from behind Holston's John Deere riding mower.

"C'mon, c'mon, baby," she cooed. Animals needed to become accustomed to her voice first, hear the peace in the sounds she made.

Hattie's patience and the little cat's hunger would pay off. Hattie had been an animal charmer since childhood, learned everything she knew from Mr. D. "Get down on their level so they don't see you as a threat. Keep your voice low. Let them come to you." Her daddy knew the tricks.

Hattie smiled. Good thing a person's mind had a magical way of recording snippets of the past; she could hear the big man's whispered advice, as if he sat beside her now, waiting to make friends with the tabby.

The little cat slipped from the shadows and hugged the barn wall, moving in a crouch. Move. Stop and watch. Move. Stop and watch. Hattie averted her gaze. Direct eye contact made animals wary. She wouldn't like some stranger staring at her either.

The phrase *stranger danger* popped to mind, a little ditty she and Holston had repeated to Sarah Chuntian so often, it came out like a parental mantra. Eat your vegetables. Sit up straight. Look both ways. Brush your teeth. Stranger danger.

How sad, to live in a time when parents had to view everyone as a potential threat. When she and Bobby were kids, the farmhouse's doors were seldom locked, never during the day, and at night only when the years passed and her mama and daddy had to pay attention to one fact: the world was changing.

Guess I should be happy Sarah and Tank are involved in video games. Hattie took a breath and released it. The kids weren't running the streets with some gang, ripe for any creep lurking nearby.

Used to be, no one dared enter a house or a car uninvited. You didn't lock auto doors either. Her daddy often left the keys in the ignition. Who wanted to carry keys around all the time? What a nuisance.

She thought of Bailey, still sparkling from her initial bath yesterday afternoon. Second vehicle she had possessed with an automatic alarm system. Pearl didn't have one, and Betty, the last SUV, had, but Hattie never used it. Bailey locked and alarmed herself if Hattie walked off with the key and forgot. Pretty cool. But, like the other personal safety measures, sad that they were necessary.

Hattie snuck a glance toward the striped feline. The tabby, now less than three feet away, crouched, eyeing her and the two cats lapping the food from the tin farthest from Hattie. She shifted her gaze enough to watch from her peripheral vision. The second pie tin rested less than a foot away.

"C'mon, baby." Hattie made a soft clucking noise with her tongue. Wished she could speak feline. Her foot cramped. She shifted. The tabby dove behind a stack of bagged fertilizer. Well, shoot.

Oreo lifted her head and trilled. She ambled over to Hattie for a head scratch then sat down and bathed her own face with a spit-damp paw. Lick, lick, groom. Repeat. For sure, Oreo and Tux were far more fastidious than Captain and Ensign. If the dogs lucked up on something curling with maggots, they would roll in it and then trot up to her as if they'd hit the putrid perfume lottery. At least that washed off. If a disgruntled, and very alive, skunk crossed their paths, there wasn't enough soap or home remedies on the planet for detox. She'd tried them all.

Tux finished his meal and joined her and Oreo. Hattie gave him equal ear-scratch time. He bathed. Afterwards, the three of them sat and watched the tabby inch forward. Who needed reality TV?

Oreo trilled again. The tabby answered with a clipped meow. So, Hattie wasn't the only one trying to make friends. The little feline stood and walked to the pie tin. It looked at Hattie for a long moment then crouched to eat.

Sarah had already named the creature: Sunny, because it reminded her of lemony morning light. Could be a boy or girl name. Hattie lifted a brow. No. *She* was clearly pregnant. No stray with an inconsistent food supply had that much extra padding around the midsection. Could the vet give a rabies vaccination to a pregnant cat without harming the developing kittens? And how in the world could she keep the mother safe until after the kittens were born, if so. Not so urgent, normally, but with the recent incidents of rabies, things were different.

Note to self: call and ask for expert advice. Or she could google it, like Sarah did. Who knew how much of that online information was reliable?

Hattie reviewed her plan. Step one: *establish trust.* Step two: *draw the animal to her.*

Oreo brushed her arm. Tux stood and joined them. Hattie petted Oreo with one hand and Tux with the other. Only a matter of time before she'd share affection with Sunny, too.

Step three: *capture.*

Wednesday, slightly before sundown

Jake stopped the Dragonfly Florist van at the red light. Jeez O Pete. Two signals in this town and he managed to enjoy at least one of them every time he left for a delivery. He considered turning left, as he should.

Instead, when the light flipped to green, he drove forward. Less than a quarter of a mile later, he veered south onto the road to the Apalachicola River landing. The initial Genevieve infestation pushed him. That and the line-up of text messages that seemed to billow more every day.

If he didn't take a moment to himself, he'd ignite. And then who would head up the festivities?

He should inspect River Landing Park for muddy spots after the recent rain. Had to do that before the PiddieFest beauty contest and dinner under the oaks.

Add that to the list. For later.

He parked the van on a section of cracked pavement. Used to be an important road. Now, it lead nowhere.

People weren't encouraged to venture onto what remained of the Old Victory Bridge, but some did. To make out. Smoke weed. The police swung by the area when they could, on weekend nights. The Chief of Police's budget had been stretched so thin, patrolling the vestiges of the past was not a priority. Plus, the barricades and fence kept people from going onto the old structure. In theory.

Jake had never bumped into anyone else here. The end of the bridge was his sacred space. Even if he had to break the law and scale a padlocked chain link fence with his bum leg.

He switched the cell phone to mute. Could leave it in the van, but what if his leg gave out and he couldn't manage to drag himself back and over the fence? Or if someone followed him?

He'd never been down here at night, only when the sun tipped the trees and spilled onto the aging concrete.

Jake grabbed his cane and a small flashlight, shut the door. He walked around the concrete barricades and scaled the fence in his improvised, jerky fashion, then navigated past clumps of brush that had sprung up between the cracked asphalt. Given a few more years, wild would overtake tame, thumb its nose at man and his attempt to pave paradise.

The scent of the marsh draped over him, an aroma so fixed in his soul, he'd die if he had to be away from it for too long. Back in New York, Jake often dreamed of the river's perfume.

He strolled, taking in lungsful of air. His shoulders relaxed more with every step. From here, Jake could sense the river, a swishing sound. The bridge curved above a thick stand of hardwoods and a palmetto swamp. He thought of the trees as one organism, the watchers. They were here when he came into the world, and they'd be here after he left. The thought both reassured Jake and made him sad. Life was too damn short.

The span ended with an expanse of fence stretched across the jagged edge where the bridge had been severed on the east side of the river. Beyond, a drop-off to the roiling Apalachicola. He walked to the fence and curled one hand over the steel horizontal bar.

Upriver, the Jim Woodruff Dam funneled the waters collected from the Flint and Chattahoochee rivers by Lake Seminole, then selectively spewed that water through its gates. Before the assault, Jake used to spend time alone on the shores of the lake. The memory of that night left a permanent stain.

The section of the river sweeping beneath the jagged edge of the old bridge boiled with swift eddies that fought against straining boat motors.

No telling what it would do to a person.

Chapter Eight

Wednesday evening

Hattie wormed the tip of one finger beneath her styled blue beehive and scratched. Heaven help her if she ever lost her own hair. How could anyone wear a wig every day without going stark raving mad? Her cousin Karen, Evelyn's daughter, had to wear one, after she had the breast cancer chemo. This wig gave Hattie new appreciation for what Karen and so many others had endured.

She looked around the Woman's Club hall and smiled. Had to admit, it was giddy fun seeing the somewhat reserved females of Chattahoochee decked out in towers of hair and glitter. And the outfits! Outlandish. This year, picking a winner would be hard.

The PiddieFest Kickoff party drew in more locals every year. Soon, they'd have to find a place larger than the Woman's Club. Piddie would be proud.

From the curb, the pristine white building with dark green shutters appeared more genteel family residence than clubhouse. On either side of the entrance, rows of azaleas and dogwood trees lined the cement walkway. In the spring, the fuchsia and white blooms transformed the simple building into a Southern showplace. Since neither usually bloomed in the fall, Jake's helpers had hauled in bales of hay, pumpkins, and fall foliage.

Inside, the expansive hall teemed with costumed partygoers, save for a scattering of less-abled seated in ladder-back chairs along the walls. The blend of floor polish, air freshener, and a hint of cinnamon joined the scents of warmed cocoa from the chocolate fountain, coffee, and a host of finger foods. If buildings held memories, this one hosted the gentle ghosts of time-honored casseroles, laughter, and fellowship: the kind of place Piddie had loved.

Wanda stepped up to their group. "Have you seen Pinky?" The dragonfly ornaments in her scarlet beehive jiggled. Perfect, that the New Jersey native's wig was as vibrant as her natural hair. "That husband of mine has turned into a social animal. Imagine." Wanda scanned the room.

"He was over by the punch bowl last I saw him," Hattie said. "Hard to see with so many people crammed in here."

"My husband is all nutted up," Wanda said.

Elvina's penciled eyebrows arched. "Nutted up? That's a new one."

Wanda's lips, painted to match her mound of synthetic hair, spread wide. "Good, eh? Admit it, 'Vina."

"Reckon so," Elvina said in a flat tone.

As close to praise as Wanda would ever get from Elvina Houston. Hattie pinched her lips tight to avoid grinning. She should pull Wanda aside, offer an *atta-girl*. No. Wanda might gloat and that would really get Elvina fired up. Elvina liked to be the one to invent a new funny. For sure, she'd never concede to a Yankee. How many decades had to pass before some Southerners let go of all of that? Hattie reached over and grasped Holston's hand. She happened to love her Yankee.

Holston lifted her hand and kissed it. Heat flashed through her body. Her head itched worse. Didn't help any that the weather wasn't committing to fall, as it should. The last week had seen temperatures near ninety. Absurd. A few azaleas were blooming in her yard, and she'd spotted a scattering of flowers in the hedges lining the Woman's Club entrance. Poor plants. As confused as the rest of nature.

The hall's AC strained to chill the air. Too many hot bodies. The rest of the wigged women around Hattie glistened with sweat. She looked at Holston. His cheeks were ruddy. Bet he'd rip off that coat and bowtie later.

She spotted her older sister Mary-Esther bopping between the kitchen and food tables. They exchanged waves. Mary-Esther looked more like their deceased mother every year. A bit unsettling, but at the same time, comforting. Too bad Mary-Esther couldn't join the fun, but her catering business had really zoomed. The tables strained under the weight of platters and pots—from Piddie's Southern fare, to Mary-Esther's Cajun dishes. Plus, the yummy artichoke dip Jake had provided.

"Pinky brought some of our homemade scuppernong wine and that stuff's potent," Wanda said. "You know he rarely drinks. Maybe a beer when it's *real* hot and the beer's *real* cold." Wanda's gaze continued to roam the crowd. "A glass of merlot with dinner, but only one. He had a couple of good slugs of our vintage and now he's acting like a pure fool."

Mandy chuckled. She took a sip of her punch. Judging from the way she swayed, Hattie figured she had spiked *her* mug, too. "Pinky Green? As shy as that boy is? He blushes down to his toenails, trying to say hello."

Add to that, his red hair and skin pale as a newborn piglet's. As Hattie recalled, it had taken Pinky two months' worth of weekly haircuts to work up the nerve to ask Wanda to dinner. Good thing Wanda was no nonsense, or they'd still be holding hands, and for sure, not married.

"Have you found out about that crazy-fied raccoon?" Mandy asked.

"Not yet, but we're pretty sure it was rabid." Fresh worry attacked Hattie. "The dogs are vaccinated, and the barn cats, but one little stray cat is not. And, she's obviously pregnant. I'll try to keep her safe until the kittens are born. Then I'll have to find homes for them and get her to the vet."

"You should take one of the little ones," Mandy said to Elvina.

"I don't think Buster would cotton to such," Elvina said. "Much as I'd love a baby kitty around. I'll spread the word after they're born and weaned, help you find homes." She patted Hattie's arm. "Haven't seen your brother and Leigh. They coming?"

"Bobby's wiped out, trying to finish up your sunroom. He plans to get started again, first thing tomorrow morning," Hattie said. "Then he has to focus on building ten new vendor booths for the Madhatter's festival, ones they can break down and reuse every year."

"Hate that he missed this on account of me." Elvina frowned.

Hattie waved a hand. "Bobby would rather watch paint dry than attend a party. He'd have to put on a suit. We'll be lucky to get him into one when he's laid up in his casket." She didn't add, *Bobby might be tempted to sample that homemade wine.*

"Bull's the same way," Mandy said. Her words slurred together. "He had to put on a sport coat tonight and you'd think I'd asked him to wear a straight jacket."

They laughed. The reference, perfect for people who had lived most of their lives sharing the spotlight with a state mental institution.

"Sarah Chuntian and Tank are happy staying with Bobby and Leigh," Hattie added. "Playing some video game. Leigh and Amelia are busy making cookie dough to freeze, for the carnival at the end of the month."

"Y'all know that woman who came in with Shug?" Elvina asked.

Heads shook around the circle. The women's hair adornments danced.

"Must be some relative," Hattie said. "Favors Shug a little." Odd, Jake usually shared everything with her, but they had both been so busy lately. She'd seen him bouncing between the food tables, directing events, and scowling at his cell phone at regular intervals. Poor guy looked like he was ready to keel over, or jump out of his skin.

"Can't imagine who it'd be. Shug's family tossed him aside years ago." Wanda narrowed her eyes. "Hateful people. How could they do that to such a kind-hearted man?"

"Whoever she is, she's staying at Jake and Shug's. I spotted the car in the driveway." Elvina motioned toward Mandy. "Plus, Jake had Mandy scrambling last minute, making the woman a wig for this party. Has to be someone special." Elvina tilted her head toward Wanda. "You and Shug are close. You should ask. I have to teach you how to get important information."

"If Shug Presley wants to tell me, he will," Wanda returned. "*I* respect privacy, Elvina."

Wanda scores a point. Whoa. Game on. Everyone's gaze shifted to Elvina.

"The Bible says we should love our neighbors as ourselves," Elvina fired back. "Hard to do if you don't know what they're all about and what they're up to." She lifted her chin.

Wanda huffed and walked off. The crowd parted. Closed ranks. No worries, the two would make up later and resume the ongoing jibe-fest. They were as much fun to watch as Bobby and Jake. Pure foolishness.

Hattie took a sip of the punch. Piddie's recipe. Lime sherbet, pineapple juice, and something else . . . club soda or ginger ale? Good, no matter. She toasted Elvina with a lift of her cup. "You and Aunt Piddie surely stuck to that particular Biblical edict."

"We certainly did. And you'd all be better off if you paid more attention to what all goes on behind the scenes." Elvina rotated her head to the right and gestured. "I can't put my finger on it, but something about how that woman is acting, asking such personal questions, doesn't sit well with me."

Mandy's smile only worked on one side. "Maybe she follows your philosophy, 'Vina." She cast a wink to the rest of the group then blinked as if her eyes weren't in focus. Good thing she wasn't the designated driver. Hattie glanced around the room. Where was Bull? Hope Mandy's husband wasn't with Pinky Green, hitting the home brew. His wife was getting goofier by the second.

Elvina didn't flinch. "No, Mandy. I can sense when someone is genuinely interested. That woman"—another head nod—"is as fake as Carla Jensen's boobs." She motioned to a woman two clusters over.

Everyone in the tight circle laughed, even Holston. Carla's breasts were high, huge, and bank-financed, a fact the young woman boasted to anyone who admired them a beat too long.

Chapter Nine

Bobby snugged the four-foot plank into position and snapped the connection. He sat back on his tucked legs and admired the flooring. Unbelievable, how much the laminate mimicked real heart pine. Another half-hour, tops, and Elvina's sunroom would be complete. And he could take tomorrow morning off.

Let Jake handle Elvina Houston from this point. Bobby had served his time.

Good thing Elvina had left for that dumb PiddieFest kick-off party. Because of finishing up this addition, he'd wormed out of that, this year. Still, Leigh would insist he don a tux and drag him to the ball.

Tomorrow, he could hand over the decorating piece of this project to the fuss-butt flit. *Hey, remember that one.* Jake couldn't top it, for sure. Nah, he probably would.

Left up to Bobby, furnishing the room would be mindless. He glanced around the addition. Throw a leather recliner and end table with room enough for a glass and a remote in that corner. He swiveled his head. And a high-definition TV in that one. One of those little electric woodstoves would be a cozy add-in. A room-sized rug to keep kitty and human feet from the chill of winter since Elvina had opted for laminated wood flooring. Done and done.

"But nooooo," Bobby said aloud in sing-song, "Jake'll want window treatments and upholstered chairs and all sorts of geegaws." He looked toward the rag bed where Buster napped. "Don't fret, buddy. I managed to put in a word on your behalf, since this room *was* built for you. Jake's ordered a fancy cat bed. He messaged me a picture. Got a freakin' ruffled canopy over it. Sorry, little dude." Bobby shook his head and snapped the next plank into place. "All I know is, when I die, I'm gonna come back as a house cat. Lay around all day, eat, get pats on the head." He glanced toward Buster. "You ain't saying much.

What, cat got your tongue?" He chuckled. Hattie wasn't the only one in the family who could pull off a pun.

Bobby paused. Studied the slumbering lump of fur. Old Tom must not feel good. Didn't want the treat Bobby had put down earlier. Meowed a couple of times like the devil was chasing his dreams. *Reckon I'll call Elvina, give her a heads-up, after I lay the last board.*

He returned full attention to the flooring. Something soft brushed his elbow. He jerked. Bobby whipped his head around, expecting to find Buster wobbling beside him. Cats were like phantoms; they could slip up on a person. But Buster hadn't shifted an inch, still curled up in his bed of rags, without a canopy.

Just his imagination playing tricks on him.

Twenty minutes later, Bobby stood, checked the quarter round trim for gaps. All good. Elvina would brag about this room, post pictures on her Facebook page, on Pinterest, too. He'd probably end up with a line of women begging him for a sunroom. Who needed flashy advertising when he had the Mouth of the South in his corner. Bless her.

He gathered the soiled rags, bits of wood, and his tools. One last pass with a dusting mop and the room would be ready for unveiling. Too bad he had to disturb Buster, but those other rags had to go, too.

He crossed the room. "Sorry, bubba. I have to ask you to vacate."

The cat didn't move.

Bobby bent down and touched Buster's head. He looked closer. No rise and fall of the cat's midsection. He rested his palm on Buster's fur.

Nothing.

"Ah no," he said, his voice barely a whisper. "Why'd ya have to go and die on me?"

Chapter Ten

Thursday, October 1st, early morning

Hattie held a fingertip to her lips and pointed to one darkened corner of the barn.

"What?" Sarah Chuntian spoke in a low tone.

"Shhh." Hattie motioned for her daughter. Oreo and Tux settled down to their plate of cat tuna. Somehow, Oreo managed to eat and purr at the same time. How was that possible?

A low form shifted in the shadows. Hattie heard Sarah's intake of breath. The yellow-striped cat stood and walked toward them. The animal paused for a beat, eyeing Sarah, then strolled to the second food plate and lowered her rotund body to eat. Her belly rippled on one side. The young cat shifted positions and resumed her meal.

"Did you see that?" Hattie asked.

"Yes." Sarah nodded. "Means she is close to having the kittens."

Hattie swiveled her head to regard her daughter.

"Gestation for felines averages about sixty-six days," Sarah added, "though it could be as little as fifty-six. We don't have any way to know how long she's been pregnant."

"Doing your research, huh?" Hattie said. Her kid was for sure born old.

Sarah tilted her head. "Where will Sunny have her kittens?" She gazed around the barn.

"I piled some old soft towels in a spot behind the John Deere. She seems to favor that place, and we won't be using the mower anytime soon. Hopefully, she'll have them in here and not outside where the hawks and other predators can get to them."

"Can we lock her inside until she has the babies?" Sarah asked, then quickly added, "No, she'd freak."

"And bolt out the moment we cracked a door." Hattie thought of the deceased raccoon. "Better to let her come and go. She's generally inside, anyway. And Oreo and Tux are keeping good company."

Hattie dragged up a bale of straw for the two of them to use as a bench. They sat in silence, watching Sunny eat. She thought of poor Buster, hoped Elvina had gotten some rest. Losing Shammie had crushed Hattie, and Elvina was more attached to Buster than she'd let on, Hattie bet. As soon as the vet's office opened, Hattie would take Buster's towel-wrapped body for cremation.

Elvina needed a kitten. Now Hattie had to drum up other adoptive parents. Quick, from the looks of that belly.

"Sure you don't want to enter the Little Miss Piddie contest? I have an extra wig for you." Hattie looked at Sarah. The bright orange hairpiece would complement her skin.

"I'm a little old for that, Mom." Sarah pulled an eye roll to accompany her reply.

Might as well get accustomed to that gesture. Maybe Sarah would stop by her mid-twenties. Someone should provide parents with a timeline. Give them hope.

"Okay, baby." Hattie reached over and pushed a hank of dark hair from her daughter's eyes. "If you change your mind—"

"Won't."

Hattie's spirit wilted. This would be one moment in a long string of moments. Her child was growing up. She wasn't ready to let go.

Best to watch the cats and will the tears to suck back inside. At least she'd soon have a litter of kittens on the Hill. Something to cuddle. Something needy.

Oreo and Tux finished their meals and stared at Sunny. Sarah held out one hand and curled her fingers. "C'mere," she cooed. The two older cats sauntered over and allowed Sarah to pet their heads. Sunny backed away from the empty plate. She sat and regarded them.

Hattie clicked her tongue, held out a hand, palm up. "C'mon, Sunny."

The tabby stood, considering, before walking a few steps. Hattie touched a spot between the tawny ears. Sunny jerked back and eyed her. Hattie didn't move. Sunny took a step, meowed. Hattie extended her hand and again trailed two fingertips across the stripes between Sunny's ears.

"Smooth moves, Mom."

"More than one animal charmer in this family."

Sunny leaned into the head rub before shifting to Sarah for equal time.

"It's about establishing trust," Hattie said. "Trust is so *very* important."

Elvina dipped the tea bag a couple of times, checked the shade of the brew, then lifted the bag from the steaming water. Third cup of green tea this morning, but she needed as many antioxidants as possible today. Last evening had proven worse than any she could recall since that moonless night she snapped her ankle in the armadillo hole, trying to get that dang cat out of the fight he'd gotten himself into.

When last evening was all over, when Hattie had wrapped Buster in a clean towel with a promise to take him to the veterinarian's office as soon as it opened, when Bobby left, when she had finally shoved Jake out the door with a line of reassurances—Elvina had walked for nearly two hours. The police cruiser passed her three times, then J.T.'s black Crown Vic.

There were no secrets in Chattahoochee. By solid dawn, her phone rattled with text messages and voicemail announcements. At least one member of Elvina's trusted casserole brigade would no doubt show up later at her house with a covered dish in hand. As if she had an appetite. But that's what a person did when she learned of a death in a friend's family. Trotted out her best, comforting dish, preferably one with enough melted cheddar on top to clog up every artery in a person's body, twice.

She looked down at the soggy teabag, its thin paper as pale and translucent as her own skin. Hope all of this tea wasn't staining her teeth. Her dental hygienist would pitch a fit and fall in it. Too bad she couldn't mix the leaves into brownies, like those marijuana dope fiends did. Come to think of it, chocolate was supposed to help a person's sagging spirits, too.

Mandy stepped into the Triple C's kitchen. Not her usual chatty self. She poured a mug of coffee, took a sip. Still not a peep from her.

"I wish you'd all quit tiptoeing around me." Elvina added a generous dollop of tupelo honey to her cup, stirred.

"You don't have to act like everything is normal, 'Vina," Mandy said. "I know you feel like your heart's been ripped clean out."

And Mandy did understand, being a fellow animal lover. Surprised she hadn't come over to the house as soon as news reached her.

After Buster passed, J.T. had stopped by the house when he saw the collection of cars. J.T. would've told Melody as soon as he found out. Then Melody probably burned up the lines phoning Mandy and the rest of the Triple C crew. News spread like ripples from a stone cast into still water. Usually, Elvina was at the epicenter, initiating those waves. The fact others could be trusted to watch over Chattahoochee reassured her, in a fashion. After she was no longer on this side of the dirt, someone would be able to step up and carry on the tradition.

"I don't have time to yield to a sinking spell." Elvina discarded the limp tea bag, dried the counter with a paper towel. The stainless steel sink needed a good scouring. Lime deposits circled the fixtures. She pulled her phone from her pocket, tapped in a reminder to pick up some of that special cleanser they'd been out of for a few days. Used to be, she could make a mental note. Good thing the phone would tweep to refresh her wilted memory.

"We understand if you need to go home." Mandy had such a sweet tone to her voice, a lump threatened Elvina's throat.

"Nonsense and never mind. There're still things to do before the PiddieFest Inner and Outer Beauty Contest." Elvina didn't add, *Home is the last place I want to be right now.* No need to get overly maudlin. Gotta pick yourself up. Get on with it. Elvina replayed Piddie's last words left for her on a cassette tape: "Go ahead and grieve, but don't go trying to crawl into the grave with me." Elvina had lived through losing her dearest friend Piddie. She could, by golly, get beyond losing a scruffy alley cat. She took a sip of tea.

Poor old Buster. He was on his way to the cat crematorium by now. Could've dug a hole in the back yard. Bobby had offered such. No sir-ee. Wasn't going to happen, not to one of her own. Didn't matter Buster had no pedigree, the old feline deserved more than being worm food. His ashes would come back to her by next week. She already knew what she'd do with them. Soon as she asked proper permission.

"Well . . . if you're sure, but we can let the phones go to voicemail if you need to leave." Mandy extended one hand then withdrew it when Elvina looked at her.

"Wish everyone would stop being so dang nice." Elvina felt an instant stab of remorse after Mandy's expression sullied. That gal was no good at hiding hurt feelings. Showed in her eyes. "Not that I don't truly appreciate all of you." Why did the proper words fail Elvina so easily anymore? Given a couple more years, she'd do good to grunt and point.

Mandy didn't reply, only offered a sad smile on her way out of the kitchen. Probably heading to Evelyn's sewing room, for one last nip-and-tuck fitting before the PiddieFest Ball.

Last year, the gowns were as spectacular as the wigs. Since mid-August, Evelyn had been busy as a fly in a butter bowl. As soon as the master seamstress completed outfitting most of Chattahoochee's women for the ball, she would start with her holiday line. At least sewing kept Evelyn from entering one of her weird concoctions in the bake-off.

Elvina took a few moments to finish her tea then used the back door to exit the mansion. My, it would be nice if the temperature fell a few degrees. Poor plants didn't know whether to shuck leaves or bud.

She passed by the koi pond, stopped to check the mint patch. Fresh sprigs sprouted from the woody stems. Too bad. First frost would nip them back. When it came. If it ever did. Overhead, the squirrels chattered and lunged from one pine to the next. Buster might have "crossed the rainbow bridge," as Hattie liked to put it, but there would never be a shortage of tree rats to keep her company. Elvina had given up trying to pin individual names on the animals. Unless one had an odd patch of hair or some physical deformity, one squirrel looked like the next.

Pots of russet and yellow mums lined Piddie's memorial garden. Jake hadn't had time to scoop them from their pots and plant them. He should hire help, but he wouldn't. Said gardening relaxed him. Insisted on scooting along on his behind with that bad leg stretched out straight in front of him. Brought tears to Elvina's eyes every time she saw him do that.

Elvina settled onto her bench. Two squirrels lunged from the pine tree and landed on the opposite end. Those first raw months after Piddie passed, Elvina had used mounds of peanuts to lure the skittish rodents from their lairs. Now, she figured they handed down the info on an easy snack to their offspring, soon as they drew their first breaths.

The moment she had stepped from the mansion's back steps, the scouts scampered to meet her. The rest would follow shortly.

For sure, the squirrels at the Triple C were not shy.

She doled out two peanuts. Both animals squatted and nipped the shells to confetti. On the ground, three more of their kin joined her audience. Elvina threw a handful of nuts to them then brushed her palms of shell dust.

"Mornin', Piddie." Elvina spoke aloud, as she always did. Used to be, they'd lock a person up for talking to no one. Not any longer, in these days when folks were doing far, far crazier things: shooting into crowds, strapping on bombs and blowing their fool selves up.

"Guess you've already spotted Buster, as he left *here* yesterday evening. He wasn't a saint, but I reckon all pets go to heaven. Even at their worst, they are better than most of us."

One of the squirrels inched closer, watched her as if it understood.

"Grief is a funny thing, Piddie. It never truly leaves you be. It lurks. Waits until you lose another loved one, whether it's human or animal, and here it comes with a shadow wide as the Milky Way. Settles over your heart . . ." She rested one hand on her chest. "And you feel it all again, every one of those times you hurt before."

Bad thing about living to the senior years: too many had left her. Her husband Clyde, the dear man, then Piddie, the dear friend. Last few years, Elvina had attended numerous funerals and visitations; they had become her main social functions. She owned so many black outfits, she could be a funeral director. Add to that a call tree of women ready and willing to fire up their stoves and bake cakes and casseroles for the bereaved families.

Wouldn't have it any other way. Back when she and Clyde lived in Miami, they barely knew their neighbors. You could die and rot, and no one would be the wiser until the fumes fouled their backyard barbeque.

Clyde had been her love, her life partner. But Piddie had *saved* her life. She remembered the first time she met Piddie Davis Longman. Elvina was pushing an empty buggy down one aisle of the IGA. Skinny as a junkyard dog. Having one of her "blue spells," when she barely had the energy to get out of bed, much less eat. She had looked up from her meager list to see a short woman with hair bigger than life, standing beside her. Piddie stuck out a hand, introduced herself, and struck up a mostly one-sided conversation. By the time the two of them reached the checkout counter, Elvina had a cart full of groceries and the scoop on most everyone in town. Come to find out, Piddie lived only two doors down from her on Morgan Avenue.

That began a friendship so ironclad even death couldn't drive a nail through it.

Elvina would never forget the woman who threw her a lifeline. Who *could* forget such?

"I wonder, if you'd mind me spreading Buster's ashes here, Piddie. Since that close encounter with the armadillo hole, I hardly venture into my yard." Elvina glanced around her. Though the gardens were dormant, the peace of growing things offered comfort. "I come here every day. I could visit both of you. Now, I won't throw him all over your plot. I can put him in one corner. Don't reckon he'll take up much space, being so little and all."

The squirrels watched Elvina. She huffed and pitched out another handful of peanuts. Little mooching opportunists. *Her* little mooching opportunists. Might as well own it.

"I knew Hattie was a softie. She came running as soon as Bobby texted her about Buster. Bobby was shook up about it, too. He and Buster had become fast friends. But you should've seen Jake. That boy fell all to pieces. Took two cups of chamomile tea to get him calmed down. Guess it took my mind off myself for a bit. Strange since Jake didn't really ever cotton to Buster, not like he did that uppity Persian Hattie used to own."

Elvina tilted her head back, closed her eyes, and took a deep breath. Opened them again, to the cloudless blue sky. Why was heaven always in that direction? Seemed, when she sensed the gentle presence of Piddie, it was all around her.

Not somewhere far away. Not down. But not up either.

Chapter Eleven

Friday, October 2nd, morning

Hattie stood on the bank of the Apalachicola River. It had been such a dry summer, the banks extended far into the water and only a deep channel proved navigable. Not good for boat propellers or inexperienced operators, but great fuel for the hot debates between the upstream urbanites sucking resources and the Florida panhandle people and Gulf aquatic species that depended on the supply of fresh water.

Suppose that was the way things worked out. One man used and the next man went without. Learning to share toys back in kindergarten should've taught them all a valuable lesson. It had not.

The earthy scent captivated Hattie. Wet sandy soil mixed with the underlying tang of decaying vegetation. When she shifted her head to look upriver, she caught a whiff of fish. Probably a bed of bream in one of the eddies below the Jim Woodruff Dam. She recalled the spot. Mr. D headed there when the water was right, before putting downstream. Her father had known every deep hole and sandbar on the Apalach.

"Daydreaming, Sister-girl?"

Hattie dragged her attention from the waterway and aimed it toward Jake. "My family spent so many hours on this old river when I was growing up. Pity I don't come down more often."

"You're like me. Never have the time." Jake dislodged a rounded river rock with the tip of his cane—this one, purple sparkly. He lined up the tip with the rock, aimed, and teed off. The rock landed with a thunk. The wavelets blended into the current.

Hattie faced Jake. "We used to *take* the time. If nothing other than to drive to this landing and stare at the river. It's less than a mile from downtown." She turned back toward the wide waterway. Behind her, the parking lot was filled with empty boat trailers, most connected to trucks worth more than three of her little Honda. With the unusual warm weather, the fish would be hitting solid. The anglers had no doubt awakened before dawn. "Have we grown into such old farts, Jakey?"

"Sister-girl, it's not about being *old*. It's about time. It's speeding up."

True. Aunt Piddie had always maintained that life zoomed as soon as there was more runway behind you than ahead. Sarah was a young teen. Before Hattie and Holston could blink, their daughter would graduate from high school. Move out. Go to college—FSU, hopefully, or Piddie's ashes would whip into a whirly-gig. Sarah would get married, have children . . . Oh good Lord, she'd be a grandmother! She could practically feel her cells dying. Hattie halted the thought conga line before it danced to her own funeral.

"Speaking of time . . ." Hattie tipped her head back, toward the stage. The *Pageant Posse,* Jake's label, flitted back and forth, arranging the backdrop, checking the sound system, and babbling instructions to a covey of lesser minions.

Usually, Hattie detested beauty contests. Often happened that way when a woman wasn't born with stunning features or a hot body. Why judge someone based on looks, anyway? Reality rested beneath the crust. Hattie figured she had plenty of that.

"Is our little Chinaberry coming today?" Jake asked. They made their way toward the center of pageant activity.

"Nope. She's beyond all of this now. She's at a friend's house playing some video game they've all gotten hooked into. Said she was putting the final touches on a project for school, too."

"Kiddo studies all the time. Glad she's finding at least a little time to play. No harm in that."

"Hmm. Suppose." Hattie smiled. "Heck, look at us. We're like overgrown kids ourselves, with this PiddieFest thing."

The PiddieFest Inner and Outer Beauty Contests weren't the typical display of superficiality Hattie associated with such pageants. The Junior Piddie contestants were judged on written essays on a limited list of subjects, involvement in school civic clubs, and input from a select committee of teachers. Boys could enter, and had, but the majority of young contestants were girls. By festival time, the competition narrowed to seven finalists, an honor in itself. The deciding votes rested on a five-minute or less piece written by each contestant.

For the adult contest, held before a large dinner on the grounds, the entrants ranged from early twenties to the nineties, all female, decked out in PiddieFest finery. In addition to wearing their costumes, the contestants had to rack up hours of community service and provide homemade comfort food for the communal dinner. Most local men considered themselves masters of the grill, but wouldn't be caught dead parading around in a beehive and sequins. Though, for the inaugural year, Jake *had* donned a scarlet wig and matching gown to play M.C. He had been prettier than most of the women, Hattie recalled.

"I'm pleased as punch about the women of color who have entered this year," Jake said. "Thanks to Lucille Jackson. She broke the ice."

"As it should be. Everyone knows my aunt spent as much time in the Morningside A.M.E. church on Wire Road than she did at First Baptist. She had friends of every skin color and nationality. Reverend Jackson's wife was top on that list."

"Piddie maintained that little wooden church had a direct hotline to the Almighty. Said they spent time worshiping Him and not putting on a show with fancy trappings." Jake paused. He pulled out his phone and checked it.

Jake did that a lot, especially here lately. Hope she didn't get as attached to her cell phone. One day, people wouldn't know how to look each other in the eyes, or talk. Sad.

He slid the phone back into a pocket in his coat. Good thing men didn't have hot flashes. With this warm weather and that formal wear, *she'd* melt down for sure. Heck, she couldn't recall the last time she had dressed up, worn pantyhose. The dang seam always ended up catawampus, with one leg pinched like it was in a sausage casing.

"You won't believe who entered last minute," Jake said.

"Who?"

"C'mon, guess."

"The first lady of Florida? Bride of Frankenstein? Mother Mary's first cousin? Oh, wait . . . Meryl Streep?"

"All, superb conjectures." Jake bumped her shin with his cane. "Better."

Better than Meryl Streep? Hattie couldn't fathom such.

"Shug's sister. Genevieve." Jake grinned.

Those dimples of his, combined with blue eyes that held deep mischief and empathy—if he was a straight man and she wasn't already married to the hunk of the century, Hattie would eat him up.

For today's festivities, Jake had surely put on the dog. White tux and tails. Purple cummerbund and bowtie. Matching cane. Hair slicked back with some shiny goo that made him look like gay Elvis on a Disney cruise. Hope that boot-black rinse he'd put on his hair would wash out. Perfect for the effect he was going for, but Hattie preferred his usual frost-tipped sandy brown. Went better with his freckles.

"Shug's sister is not so bad, eh?" Hattie said.

"Surprising, but true. Genevieve dashed over to the Goodwill in Tallahassee and threw together an outfit. Of course, she stands not a ghost's breath chance of winning since we know little about her volunteer work or, for that matter, anything about how she spends her time in Alabama." He checked his watch. "She and Shug will be here in a half-hour, along with the other contestants."

"What about the recipe section of the contest?" Best part of the PiddieFest Inner and Outer Beauty Contest was the food. The tables stood ready: two for salads and appetizers, three for main courses, one for vegetables and bread, and three for desserts. Add to that, tea so sweet it would make her teeth ache. So much for dropping a few pounds over the summer. This dinner would take care of that and start off the season. Then Halloween candy. And Thanksgiving. And Christmas. Oh, and mimosas on New Year's Day.

"I turned the kitchen over to Genevieve this morning. She whipped up some pumpkin and cranberry muffins with streusel topping that will pitch you into the throes of blind rapture. Make your mind wish it had a thesaurus full of synonyms for *yum*."

"You and Shug are remarkable, Jakey. How you could open up your home to that woman after all she did to him."

"Family is family, and don't we put up with much more from relatives than anyone else? Guess everyone deserves a second chance, Hattie. Judge not, and all of that Biblical jazz."

Music blared behind them. Something with trumpets and way too much bass. God-awful. Jake huffed. "Why they put Ed Ledbetter in charge of sound this year purely defies me. Man's so deaf, he couldn't tell Ella Fitzgerald from Frank Sinatra."

Jake stood to the side of the stage, awaiting the final ballot count. Seven children faced the crowd, smiles and makeup gummed on their faces. He adored the Little Miss Piddie portion. Nobody did Southern sass as good as a kid under ten. Far as he was concerned, every one of them deserved a tiara and a winner's sash.

His cell phone vibrated. Let it be. Ignore it. Easy to see why counselors called technology an addiction.

The device had alerted five times since he arrived at Chattahoochee landing, and it wasn't even noon yet. The heavy smut-text traffic usually started in mid-afternoon and extended until midnight. He scrolled down the list. The first four, typical. Your hot. Want you. Call me. Hey baby. The last one made his breath flutter.

Gone get what I see.

Jake jerked his head to level. More than a hundred sets of eyes stared his way. Could it be someone here? A person with an agenda, stalking, waiting?

For the sake of all things sane, son, shake it off. *Of course the audience is looking at you. You're the host with the most. And besides, you look fetching in a tux.*

Was that one guy with the camo-print hat glaring at him? Before the assault, Jake would've never entertained such a notion, especially not to give thought to an actual criminal act. Every homosexual lived with walls—as he did. Not to hide. Rather, to block the pain from others' scorn.

Does a human being deserve to be despised because he has red hair, or she doesn't wear a short skirt and makeup? To be hanged from an oak limb for the shape of his nose?

Some people especially disliked gay men. Saw him as a rote representative, a scourge of decent society. A threat to hearth and home.

Years back, one particular person had fantasized waylaying him in some alleyway and binding his feet and hands. Lashing him to a tree. Picking up a baseball bat to swing and swing and swing. Until the blood blurred his vision and spilled on the black dirt. Until he wished for death.

That had been one teenager's twisted dream turned into reality. And Jake's nightmare.

Jake shivered. His bad leg throbbed.

Why anyone would consider *him* a threat . . . enough to focus such venom? Could it occur twice in one lifetime? Odds were against that. Odds were against being struck by lightning, too. Still, it happened. And some poor folks got zapped a second time.

Jake chided himself, shook off the shroud. Paranoia got him nowhere at blinding speed.

And that *no*where was not *some*where he wanted to go.

Elvina watched the woman with the green beehive. Unease crawled down her spine and inched up her belly. Piddie said the devil did that, made a loop. If she was wise, she'd heed the warning.

Minding everyone else's business took her mind off her own. Too dang empty right now without Buster.

The crowd thinned to a handful. Leftover food went home with the cooks. Jake looked like he was ready to drop in his tracks. Still, he hobbled between the grounds and stage, directing the cleanup committee.

Tomorrow would be as hectic as today and run well into the evening. Elvina should go on home, rest up before the formal ball. Not like she could load chairs or move those heavy pots of greenery next to the stage. Her empty casserole dishes were already in the Oldsmobile. She leaned against the vintage car's trunk, content, for now, to observe this feisty interloper who had blown into town in a subcompact rental.

Things didn't appear from out of the blue. Not *good* things. What was that one saying of Piddie's? Elvina tapped her temple to loosen the memory. *Good things simmer, but bad boils over.* Genevieve with her coy ways didn't remind Elvina of something thoughtful, something cooked slow. No, she was a boiler.

Shug's sister had put on an outfit and sashayed across the stage like she'd been in Chattahoochee all her natural life. Of course, she didn't stand a rat poot's chance of winning the Inner and Outer Beauty Contest, no matter how many voted for those muffins.

The woman had such a poetic name, Genevieve. Reminded Elvina of castles and knights in armor atop snorting steeds. Genevieve accompanied Jake and Shug, like she'd been cast in a supporting role. Elvina studied the way that toad of a woman moved, as if she planned every gesture, every lip twitch, every lingering eye contact.

But to what end?

Humans came with an agenda. Some evil, some good, others merely self-serving.

Elvina switched her observations to the Jake Witherspoon Show. Yesterday, he had sobbed like an orphaned toddler over Buster. Nearly fell out on her new sunroom floor. Sucked in air like he was starved for breath. Sensitive, sure. Jake wore his feelings as obvious as the cane he chose for the day.

What was making him so twitchy? Had to be Genevieve.

Give it to her, those muffins were sumptuous. Who would've thought dried cranberries would taste good with pumpkin. Genevieve had even offered to share the recipe. Elvina didn't give away the secrets of her tried-and-trues. Especially the recipes Piddie had left for her. Still, Elvina wasn't ready to list the woman's cell phone number in her *favorites*. It'd take more than pumpkin muffins to make *that* cut.

Guess this Genevieve might be a good sort of person.

Piddie whispered in her ear: *she's not*.

Friday afternoon

Hattie leaned back to inspect Bailey for streaks. The wet sponge dripped clots of soap foam onto her bent knees, reminding her of that unfortunate raccoon. The guilt over taking a life haunted her, and would for some time. As a parent, she had done what she had to do, she reminded herself for the hundredth time.

Shouldn't be washing this car again. But Bailey had a film of river landing dust across her lovely chocolate paint. How could she and Holston pull up in their glitzy finery and expect Bailey to wallow in dirt?

Hattie dipped the sponge in the wash bucket. She'd get past this sense of new-ness soon. New things became old things too fast. Not like she swapped vehicles every two years like some people. For now, Hattie relished Bailey. She zeroed in on the tire, intent on erasing the brake dust and road oil from the fancy spoke wheel. Needed that old toothbrush she kept beneath the kitchen sink.

"Mom?"

"Crapola!" Hattie jerked, nearly fell backwards. "You scared the beejabbers out of me!"

"Sorry. Thought you heard me."

Hattie stood. Stretched her back. One wheel left, then she'd use the chamois to buff off the water droplets. "Grab the hose and rinse behind me. I'm nearly done."

Sarah picked up the water hose. Palmed the nozzle lever.

"Resist the urge," Hattie said.

"What?" Sarah flashed her most innocent smile. Hattie recognized it.

"I know you want to—"

Sarah aimed the spray nozzle in her direction. Let out a *whoot!* Then squeezed.

Hattie squealed. At the last second, Sarah shifted position and directed the sharp jet at the wheel with the soap residue. Hattie laughed. The kid could pull a U faster than a stunt driver.

Sarah let off the trigger, motioned with her head. "What's this?"

"Did I miss a spot?" Hattie dropped the sponge in the bucket. Soap bubbles flew.

"No. Look."

Hattie leaned down and joined the inspection of the back bumper corner. Oh no. A place where the paint was chipped. Not a big spot, but still. . . .

"You can get touchup paint, right?" Sarah said. "Unc Jake fixes scratches on Pearl all the time. Can't even tell they're there afterwards."

"I guess. Oh, shoot and dang!" The actual nasty words in her head almost cleared her lips.

Hattie pulled a quick visual measurement. About three feet from the ground. This spot on Bailey's bumper was at shopping cart level. How did it happen? She'd had the car less than a week! Oh yeah, she'd stopped by the Winn Dixie in Quincy for a few things. Bingo.

That's where they hid in waiting, those car dingers. Didn't matter if she positioned Bailey within a moat of buffer slots. By the time she came out, a cluster of cars would surround hers. As if she'd had some wonderful inspiration for her actions and, heck, they should all gather around her.

Maybe this wasn't a total misfortune. Good came from bad all the time, Hattie believed. Now, she wouldn't stress as much. Wouldn't park two counties over when she went to Walmart or to the grocery store.

There she went, turning a blemish into a blessing. No wonder Jake called her *Rebecca of Bonnie-brooke Hill.*

"Mom? Earth to Mom."

"Huh?"

"Can I stay at Olivia's tomorrow night, while you and Daddy are at the ball?"

"Sure. If it's okay with Olivia's parents." Hattie paused. "Wait, aren't they attending the ball, too?"

"Not like we *need* a babysitter. We're thirteen!"

Olivia lived two blocks from the rec center. Both sets of parents would have their cell phones. Had to admit, the kid was right. Time to loosen the vise grip a notch.

Chapter Twelve

Saturday, October 3rd, morning

Jake pulled the bubbling breakfast casserole from the oven. The scent of melted yum filled his nose. Not a difficult recipe—he couldn't recall where he had gotten it—but rich with sausage and eggs, and gooey with sharp cheddar cheese. What was not to adore about a dish he could prepare ahead of time then slide it straight from the refrigerator into the oven? Whip out a platter of fresh cut kiwi and pineapple and, voilà, a meal any redneck gourmet would relish. He made it a few times a year—during long, exhausting weekends like this one, and always for Christmas morning. Even people who claimed to detest grits begged for the decadent recipe to use for holiday guests. They didn't call it the "Season of Light" because food had half the calories.

"All of these years, and I've never had grits in a casserole." Genevieve sipped her black coffee at the kitchen table.

That first morning, he had made the mistake of offering sugar and cream. She had launched into mind-numbing detail about the evils of devil sugar and her lactose intolerance and the ensuing diarrhea and distress, until Jake could barely eat his bagel. Genevieve had obviously decided he was worth speaking to, a mixed blessing at best. "But I like the ingredients," she added, "so I am open to tasting it. Can't be from Alabama and not adore anything with grits in it."

Shug walked into the kitchen, neat in his work khakis and button-down blue oxford shirt. He'd slip the pressed lab coat on later, if necessary, but Jake knew he preferred to visit new hospice patients and their families in something less formal and intimidating. Most had reached their fill of starched medical folks.

"Where are you heading to so early of a morning, Jon?" Genevieve asked. "Certainly you aren't working today."

She refused to call him Shug, though their mama had coined the nickname *Mama's Little Sugar Monkey*, shortened later to *Shug*. Hardly anyone called him Jon, not even his hospice patients.

"I'd think it being a Saturday and with the ball this evening . . ." Genevieve tilted her head, gave a little shake. Her hair didn't move.

"I have a patient that is not doing well. Death has no set hours or days of operation, I've found."

"Must be a difficult job, ministering to the dying. Though, I am so proud and impressed you chose such a fine line of work."

Shug's sister sat ram-rod straight. Reminded Jake of the Dowager Countess on Downton Abbey, except that he loved that character Violet Crowley, *and* Maggie Smith.

"After making it through leukemia at sixteen, it seemed only natural for him to go into nursing," Jake said.

"Suppose I was born for the profession. Mama used to say I was always 'nussing' something." Shug grabbed a mug, poured coffee, and added cream and sugar. "I switched to end-of-life care when floor nursing turned into more administration and mounds of paperwork than direct patient care." He glanced at his watch. "I'm on my way to Marianna as soon as I eat a quick bite." He took a sip then regarded his eldest sister. "Too bad you can't stay another night or two. I have truly enjoyed your visit, Gennie."

He pronounced his sister's nickname with a G initial sound, Jake noted. Like Guinea pig. Jake had never heard Shug call her by the shortened version and could count on one hand the number of times he had said her full name.

Jake turned away to give the two a bit of privacy. Hard to accomplish in a galley-style kitchen barely big enough for two people, much less three.

Soon, there would be another small dog to join the kitchen pinball game. Could be later today, if the woman passed away that soon. Jake was pretty sure she was Jake's patient today. Here they were, cozy and healthy, getting ready to sit down for a nice breakfast, and a few miles away, others were not as fortunate.

"My flight leaves Tallahassee in the morning. I *will* get to see you again before I have to leave?"

"I really can't say." Shug took the seat at the end of the table. "You never told me what you wanted to talk about." He paused.

Jake shucked the oven mitts. "I'll let this cool a bit." He turned to leave the room, but Genevieve held out an arm to stop him.

"I want you to hear this, too, Jake."

"Okay. Sure." Jake picked up his cup and slid into the chair opposite of Shug.

"But let's eat first," Genevieve said. "I can't stand another moment, smelling that casserole. I'll deal with the aftermath later."

Had to be heavy, if she wanted all of them to digest it with a full stomach. Plus risk what Piddie used to call the "galloping epizootic." He should've planned a meal without the dairy products, would've, had he not been so tugged in a gazillion different directions and remembered that fact about his—wow, he stopped himself short of calling Genevieve his sister-in-law.

"It will only take me a moment to toast the bread." Jake stood.

Scratch the hope of having his partner at the ball. He couldn't tally all of the times over the years Shug had to work, especially since he started with hospice. How selfish, that he'd feel aggravated. But he did. A little. Jake stuffed his disappointment in a different spot from where he kept his worries. No need to make it into an issue. He had quite enough of those, thank you.

He plated generous squares of the Country Sausage and Cheese Grit Casserole then garnished with the fruit. After he placed the butter dish and homemade blueberry and blackberry jams on the table, he dealt a half of a toasted English muffin to each plate and served.

They tucked into eating with few shared words. Only moans. If Jake hadn't won Shug's eldest sister over with hospitality and grace, his cooking was definitely adding the whipped topping, regardless of the dairy additions. In moments, all three plates held only crumbs and small curds of cooked egg.

Shug sat back and patted his stomach. "That was incredible, as usual."

"Yes it was," Genevieve said. "Perhaps you can bring it for our brunch, at the big Presley family reunion next month. Seventh of November. In Birmingham, of course. It has more places for events, yet is not that far for those of us still at home."

The only sound: the plastic click of Felix's tail, keeping a timed beat.

"Oh," Shug said.

"You'll both come, of course." Genevieve glanced from Shug to Jake.

"So, this is the news you bring," Shug said. "How delightful."

Jake took note of the blend of tender emotions and shock coloring Shug's face and warmed a bit more toward Genevieve. The remaining churlishness he felt about attending the ball without Shug dissipated.

"Actually. Part of it. I have two very serious reasons for reaching out to you, Jon." She cleared her throat, took a deep breath, and smoothed the front of her dress as if any wrinkles might interfere with the telling. "First, I am sad to say, I have been diagnosed with pancreatic cancer."

The statement hung in the air, fouling the fragrant steam lifting from the remaining casserole.

"Oh, Gennie." Shug reached over and rested a hand across his sister's. Probably the first time he had touched her in over thirty years.

"Let me finish." Her eyes glistened. If she cried, Jake would fall apart, too. He couldn't abide a woman's tears, even a woman like Genevieve. Though, he had to admit, she wasn't the hate-slinging monster he had expected.

"I'm having surgery next week at UAB hospital in Birmingham. It's a research facility, so I figure I'm helping others by having my treatments there. They will remove some pieces, to try to slow the cancer."

The Whipple Procedure. Jake knew that one, from others who had fought this particular aggressive form of cancer, and from Shug's clinical description. Removal of the head of the pancreas, part of the small intestine, the gallbladder, and sometimes a section of the stomach. Not an easy surgery, and it only bartered a little time. Cancer had a way of hiding, dancing back after a period of grace. It always led the rumba and didn't let go.

"I *am* realistic, Jon." Genevieve focused on Shug. The gathering tears had disappeared. "I know surgery won't cure this." When Shug opened his mouth to speak, Genevieve grasped the hand he held over hers and gave it a squeeze. "Don't. It might buy me a few months, a year at best. I am ready to go to my reward."

Jake expected Shug to jump up and fold his sister into one of those comforting hugs he so freely offered. He didn't. Perhaps too much time had slipped past. His life partner held so much inside. Instead, Shug's face transformed into the placid expression Jake had seen whenever they bumped into a family member of a hospice patient out in public—in this case, an obvious shroud against pain.

"You said you had a couple of things to discuss, Gennie. Is there more?"

She withdrew her hand and curled it in her lap with the other one. "Yes." She looked at Jake, then Shug. "I came here to see for myself how you two live. Oh, I have heard so many stories these past couple of days, of how both of you help people, how you do and do for the churches here, and it is clear that these people think highly of you."

Jake waited. The tone of her voice suggested a *but*.

"Why, you have a lovely home. And I can plainly see you are nothing more than housemates. You don't sleep in the same bed, and I've not seen the first sign that you are carrying out carnal leanings toward each other. Oh, knowing this does my heart of hearts so much good!" She bobbed her head once. "That's why I *believe* Brother Jessup's groundbreaking treatment will work for you, without fail. If you leave soon, you can be cured and eased back into our family in time for the reunion."

Shug's face grew pale. "Treatment?"

"For your homosexual affliction, of course." She held up her hands, pressed them together as if in supplication. "I have prayed for years to find someone to bring you back into the flock, Jon. As the head of our family since Mama passed, it is my Christian duty. I know it was your illness that turned you from the right path." She shifted her gaze to Jake. "And you are most worthy of salvation, too, Jake. I see that with my own loving eyes."

When Jake looked at his partner, his heart stuttered. He'd read the phrase "his face crumbled" in novels. Now he fully grasped the validity of what he'd considered a frilly literary device.

"This *treatment* . . . ?" Shug said.

"I have witnessed it, Jon." Genevieve separated the prayer hands, turned them into waving halleluiah hands. "It only takes a couple of weeks, a month at best for the," she paused for emphasis, "hardcore deviants. Brother Jessup runs the retreat. You check in and stay there on the campus. 'Total immersion in the spirit' is what he calls it." She bent her wrists and wiggled her fingers. "It's like he sprinkles godly dust on you, and you turn from your evil ways. Why, this past summer, a convert married a member of the opposite sex, in our own little church. Praise be!"

She motioned to the rest of the house with a roll of her head. "Though, Brother Jessup will no doubt think it best for you to consider different living arrangements afterwards. To keep you from the temptation of your former ways."

For the first time in as long as Jake could recall, he couldn't open his mouth and reply. He wanted to. To scream. Scratch that superior look off her face. Pitch his coffee on her stylish casual ensemble.

Jake didn't shift his eyes toward Shug. But his peripheral vision told him his partner was stone still.

How could he and Shug have been so bamboozled? Jake stared at Genevieve with dry eyes. She had gushed over their every word, commented on the rose garden, the way Jake had decorated the cottage in vintage patterns and colors.

And what about that tower of photo albums in the living room? Shug and Jake had sat with Genevieve last night, talking her through the years she and Shug had spent apart. They had purposely omitted discussion of Jake's brutal beating. For sure, that wasn't in the pictorial history. Genevieve had shared recent shots of his other siblings, too. Their children. Grandchildren. A large, smiling family with features similar to the man he loved.

Shug pushed his mug aside. Stood. "I am very saddened, and quite concerned, about your diagnosis, Genevieve. I will not, no, *cannot*, deny who I am."

Her bottom jaw dropped open.

"Nor," Shug continued in a voice so modulated and soft, Jake marveled at the self-control, "will I submit Jake or myself to this miraculous," Shug paused, "*treatment*." He picked up his empty cup and plate and carried them to the sink. Jake noticed the slight tremor of Shug's hands.

Jake heard the thump of his own heartbeat in his ears. The lingering scent of melted cheddar now made his stomach lurch. The clock's ticks rang like gunfire.

Shug ran water over the soiled dishes. He turned to face them. "I am who I am. As you are who you are. Mama understood."

Genevieve pushed back from the table with such force, the utensils jittered. "Mama wasn't one with God. Not like me and your family, and Brother Jessup."

The muscles above Shug's jaws pulsed. Jake braced himself for a shouting match, because surely this was heading to an all-out throw down. If he wasn't such a golden retriever, he'd bow up, take control. Couldn't.

"Our mother," Shug wrung out the dishrag, "was the most deeply spiritual person I have ever known." His movements slow and precise, he draped the rag over the faucet to dry. "She might not have attended church regularly, but she lived her faith with every breath. I can recall the hours she spent praying over me when I was battling leukemia. And I remember the depth of her love and acceptance, too."

"She was deluded then, if she accepted such an abomination." A line of spittle formed at the corners of Genevieve's lips. The word *accepted* had unfurled with such distain Jake felt it hover in the air between them.

"Mama might have had some faults, as we *all* do, but neither delusion nor judgment can be listed among them." Shug patted his hands dry, folded the towel. "I have to go to work." He took two steps, picked up his white jacket and folded it over one crooked arm. He hesitated beside Genevieve's chair. To Jake's shock, Shug rested a hand on her shoulder. "I hope your surgery goes well. Please extend regrets to the family, as *we* will not be attending the reunion."

Shug shut the back door behind him: a soft snick, same way he did when he came in late from work and didn't want to make noise. Jake would've banged it hard enough to dislodge the Visit Florida plates Piddie had collected over the years, sending them to the floor to shatter into a million, garish shards.

What could Jake add? Best to follow Shug's lead and resist the urge to draw blood. For certain, anything that came from his mouth would be neither civil nor blanched of emotion.

Genevieve stood, moved to pick up her plate and mug, then jerked back her hands.

Shug's eldest sister left the kitchen. Jake crept behind her, watched her pitch her belongings into her Vera Bradleys and slam the front door behind her without saying a word.

Saturday evening

"Moses on a motorboat!" Jake rummaged through the wooden cigar box that was supposed to corral his limited jewelry. He wanted to pick it up and hurl it across the room. "Where are my cufflinks?"

Devil's fingers moved it. Actress used to say that whenever he mislaid things as a child. Jake felt a little sorry for the devil. He got blamed for everything. Suppose that's what you got for pissing off the Big Guy.

Trick was to outthink the devil. How he figured he could do that, when he hadn't had the savvy to outthink Genevieve . . . *Stop! You do not have time to muckrake.*

Jake slammed the box lid shut and snorted from the room. At least Shug's sister was gone. Now, if he could find the dang cufflinks and fake his way through the final section of the festival, maybe he would find time to have a nervous breakdown.

He searched through the junk drawer in the kitchen. Not a likely spot, but given the pace of the last few days, then . . . Jake thought of Shug and hurt squeezed his heart. If Jake felt this dismal, how was Shug handling it? He hadn't come home last night. Jake wasn't a suspicious sort, or he'd fantasize about some smutty tryst. Shug in someone else's embrace. Actually sleeping side by side afterwards.

Nah. Shug would never do that. Never crush another person. Like his sister had crushed him.

Actually, his partner *had* a mistress—shouldn't they coin a gay male term for that, *mister-us*? Jake privately referred to this interloper as *Anubis*, after the Egyptian guardian of the underworld, the one sent to usher souls to the afterlife. Anubis called Shug at any hour, on his personal cell phone, and Shug would rush to be wherever Anubis summoned him. But the bed was one Shug sat *next* to, not languished *in*. And Anubis didn't embrace Shug, only the one in waiting.

At least Shug has a mister-us I can live with, until Anubis comes for me. Jake stopped digging in the junk drawer long enough to consider the twist. Would that make their relationship into a love triangle?

Heavens to Betsy, the more stressed he felt, the crazier he became.

Jake shoved the drawer shut on the clutter of junk, and his mind shut from the mental diarrhea. He moved to the bathroom where odd things sometimes stowed themselves on the cabinet over the toilet. He froze in place to give his exhausted brain long enough to make good sense. Even the devil wouldn't put a pair of ruby cufflinks in a place where they could inadvertently plunge into the toilet, right? He checked the cabinet anyway.

Saint Anthony, Saint Anthony, come around. Something is lost and needs to be found. He mouthed the saying. Not his, heavens no. He was raised Southern Baptist, and they didn't have saints, only a boatload of martyrs and miserable sinners. Hattie's sister, Mary-Esther, had taught him the little ditty about the angel of lost things. Unlike the rest of his heart-family, she'd been reared Catholic. Jake wasn't above sucking up to someone else's favorite heavenly helper. No sir-ree.

Jake jumped as if Saint Anthony had jabbed him with a holy finger. He shuffled to Shug's bedroom and opened the ornate silver box on the bureau. Dead center, his ruby cufflinks. That Saint Anthony was *good*. He didn't care if the Baptists believed in him or not.

How in the blue blazes the cufflinks had ended up here, he'd have to figure out later.

The entire day had been one discombobulated mess. Starting it off with a heart-wrenching family falling-out set the tone. Jake reviewed the scene, and the last couple of days, to ferret out where he might have picked up on Genevieve's nature. No clues. She was a taker masquerading as a giver, the kind that tripped Jake up, every darn time.

After Genevieve stormed off, Jake had scoured the kitchen to help him calm down, then stubbed his toe bloody—the foot of the bad leg—on the way to shower. Pearl had a dead battery and the jumper cables were in Shug's Prius. Yes, you *could* jump-start a hybrid. More likely that Jake might need them, but why take the chance when Shug often went to such out of the way places?

Bobby to the rescue. Parts store. New battery. Problem solved. At least, *that* one.

Then Elvina called with a crisis at the rec hall. The toilet in the ladies room wouldn't flush. Bobby left the parts store—he had followed Jake to make sure he made it—and zoomed to help Elvina. Good dang thing Bobby knew plumbing *and* building.

Helped to have friends like that.

Then Mary-Esther's big oven caught on fire. Filled up the Wild Rose Diner with smoke and the fire department swooped in. No harm, save for a defunct appliance, some extinguisher foam, and a world of stink. Jake called around, found five women willing to host cake layers in their own ovens. Mary-Esther could coordinate the rest. The PiddieFest Ball without a tower of cake as impressive as the wigs would've been a true disaster.

On to the next catastrophe. Hattie called, hot as a box of matches, about some chipped paint on Bailey's back bumper. Jake reassured her: he could and would fix it, just not right now.

"If you stand here piling entries into a disaster diary, you will *never* make it to the rec hall," he directed to his image in the bureau mirror. The reflection had circles under its eyes and needed some color on its cheeks. At least *it* wasn't leaving him text messages.

The digital alarm clock by Shug's bed read: 7:30 p.m.

His cell phone calendar alert would've told him that, if the volume wasn't turned off.

"Sheesh!"

Hattie inched her fingers behind one ear and scratched as discreetly as possible. Hard to be subtle when you're wearing a green beehive wig. Not like she'd stick out in this crowd, though. She had to shift positions every few minutes to see past the hairdos to the stage. Reminded her of a picture she took back in one particular artsy phase, lying on her belly with her Canon aimed at a cluster of fire ant hills. PiddieFest was almost over. A few more hours in this cap of torture and she could pitch it in a closet, or into the trash.

"Quit pawing at your head, Sister-girl." Jake bumped her arm. "People will think you have bugs."

She quit and didn't bother flicking disapproval his way. Best Friend would go off on some tangent. Then Dear Brother would chime in.

"And Hattie loves bugs, right?" Bobby said. "Betcha my bottom dollar there's a roach big as my fist up in that pile of hair."

Great. Now they'd launch into some gross discourse with her as the nucleus. Probably creepy, bug-related skin conditions. Handsome Husband Hunk was at the drinks' table getting them both a glass of merlot, so he wasn't here to defend her.

Her scalp was *really* starting to itch now. Maybe Sarah could stand the thought of bugs, but *she* couldn't.

Bobby and Jake high-fived. The fist-sized roach comment was original, for Bobby.

Okay, so she *had* called on Jake or Bobby upon occasion, before she married Holston, or since then, when her husband was out of town and disaster loomed. Florida cockroaches were freakishly creepy and huge, and they'd fly right at her face. Spiders could kill you. For real.

"Good crowd this year," Hattie said. Maybe if she got the two idiots sidetracked, they'd drop this bug business.

She shifted to view the rec hall. Jake had done an excellent job of decorating. No surprise there. The plain wood-paneled room looked like a cotillion on growth hormones. White Corinthian columns, greenery, gobs of flowers, and a scattering of linen-draped tables. The band members wore white tuxedos, like Jake, only Jake had accessorized his with a red bowtie and cummerbund. And ruby cufflinks. And red shoes. Cowboy boots at that.

Across the room, Hattie spotted Mary-Esther zipping toward one of the food tables. Unreal, how fast she could move in a purple-spangled gown and matching wig. Hopefully, after this weekend, they could schedule some quality sister time. Shop. Eat. She'd even let her sister drive Bailey.

The lady in front of them pivoted toward their group. She eyed Hattie, taking a little too long to check out her wig.

"Bet your bug-hair makes it onto the front page." Jake tapped his black and white cane for emphasis.

Yep. It sure would. Didn't matter if she and Holston danced circles around the couples already on the time-polished floor. Or if her banana pudding gained her points in the dessert category. She could strip to her skivvies and pantomime Madonna. All anyone would recall from this evening would be the purported infestation of her PiddieFest wig.

"So much for my dreams of wearing the tiara and gilded sash." Hattie included her brother and best friend in the stink-eye. "You do realize," she tipped her head toward the woman who had checked out her ensemble, "*that's* the editor of the *Twin City News.*"

"And she's been right there for a good while. Sister-girl, you could overlook Jesus." Jake positioned his cane front and center, then swayed side to side, a gay Gene Kelly.

She'd slug him if he broke into some bug-related show tune. Was there such? Probably.

Bobby exchanged glances with Jake then laughed. "We knew it was the head of the paper, right off. Right, Tootie-Fruitie?"

"You betcha, Red Neck-erson." Jake side-shuffled to the left a couple of steps, side-shuffled back. A flicker from one of the mood lights hit his eyes and they twinkled. "And enough with the *fruit* references already," he fired toward Bobby.

"Gosh, Jakey. Aren't you the animated one tonight?" Hattie said. "Figured you'd be close to flat-lining by now."

"I'm running on borrowed bling," Jake sang.

Hattie didn't have a clue what that meant, an allusion to borrowed time? His eyes looked a little glassy, but she knew Jake seldom swallowed anything stronger than an aspirin. When his leg really acted up, she could take one look at him and know; the skin around his eyes turned grayish white. Even four days after the assault, when bruises had stained every section of skin not covered in bandages, Jake had pushed aside the morphine pump and asked for plain Tylenol. Said the heavy-hitter meds made him wonky.

The band played an old rock standard and half of the tux and gowned people flanking their small group moved to the dance floor. Jake bopped his shoulders to the beat.

Hattie loved to see Happy Jake. At times, when she was between massage therapy clients, she would pull up a stool next to his workstation, watching his nimble fingers turn vastly different blooms and greenery into a homogenous arrangement. At the same time, they picked apart life in Chattahoochee. Jake Witherspoon knew as much about this town as Elvina.

Happy Jake came out then. But not this electric, fizzy happy.

Something Hattie's mother once told her niggled her: *When you run up against a person who's having too high of a time, really piling it on, they're most likely heading for a fall.*

Hattie and Jake talked about everything. *Every* little thing. Jake knew her secrets and she knew his.

"Jakey, are you—?"

"Am I what ? Charming. Fanciful. Handsome?" He bounced his head, keeping the beat.

"No, I—"

"Witty. Enchanting. Devilishly adorable?"

"Of course, but I . . ."

"Sister-girl, you don't know the half of it." His lips smiled, but it didn't make it to his eyes.

Hattie leaned over and said into his ear, "Tell me what's going on."

"One day. Not *now.* There's *way* too much *now.*" He planted the cane and boogied around it like the Maypole Queen. Graceful, in spite of his leg. "This *ig-mo*'s gotta go. Just saw Elvina walk in. She has the final vote tally." He took off toward the band stage.

Now Hattie was really concerned. Jake only used his coined word for a blend of *ignorant* and *moron* when he was near his personal boiling point.

Holston joined them, handed Hattie a glass of wine. He studied her. "Did I miss something? You okay?"

"What makes you think I'm not?"

"That crease you get between your eyebrows."

Hattie reached up and pressed down on the spot. Had to quit that or she'd have a permanent line. She stopped the wrinkle prevention and waved the hand. "I'm fine."

"You may not be when I tell you what I found out from Olivia's mother," Holston said.

"Bet Courtney's uneasy about the girls." Hattie took a sip of her wine. "I am too, a bit. But I suppose I have to loosen my grip a little. They are growing up, or so our daughter so often reminds me."

Holston took out his car keys. "But the girls are not at their house, apparently."

"What?"

"Matt doubled back to pick up something Courtney left behind. No sign of Olivia or Sarah. He just texted Courtney." He pulled the keys to Bailey from his pocket. "You can stay here if you want. I'll help Matt look for the girls. They can't have gone far."

"I'll get Leigh. We'll head out, too," Bobby said.

"No way you're leaving me here." Hattie slugged her wine in one quick gulp. "Let's go."

Chapter Thirteen

Bobby pulled up next to the black Crown Vic and rolled down his window. "Any luck?"

The Chief of Police shook his head. "Nope. I've worked a six block grid within walking distance of the house."

"Crap. Hattie is freaking out. Holston says he's doing his best to drive and keep her from completely losing it." He tapped on the steering wheel and glanced through the windshield, scanning the pools of light around the streetlamps. Other than one of the town's feral cats that appeared briefly before slipping into the shadows, nothing moved.

"Unless they're with an older kid with a car, they can't be too far away," J.T. said.

Bobby would like to believe that, but these days, who knew what kids were into? Creeps were only a click away. Waiting to pounce. And especially on young girls. He gritted his teeth.

"Wish that son of yours was with them." The Chief shifted his car into gear.

"Yeah, you and me both." Though Tank was a peaceable sort, his son had a warrior side if something threatened him. For sure, Tank looked out for his cousin.

"I'll make another round then swing by the river and lake landings. Call me if you see anything," the Chief said.

Bobby nodded. Like the Chief, he knew the hot gathering spots for teens. Been there enough during his growing up years. He rolled up the window, but thought better of it and rolled it back down. Wasn't like it was chilly. Plus, his adrenaline was off the chain. The fresh air would do him good.

When he turned a corner a few blocks down, Bobby caught sight of two figures in the distance. He accelerated sharply, and the old pickup lurched forward. The figures disappeared. Maybe his eyes were playing tricks.

He slowed when he reached the spot. Cruised by. Nothing. Had a hunch. He gunned the pick-up and drove forward for a block. When he was out of sightline, he stopped and parked, killed the noisy engine. Got out. He thanked himself for finally giving into Hattie's snarky remarks and greasing the door's hinges. Otherwise, they would've sang out in their distinctive metallic screech.

Bobby crept through the dark, careful to avoid the streetlights. Hope none of the dogs on this block were running loose. He hesitated a few yards from where he had seen the two figures. Then he stepped behind a thick hedge and waited.

He heard them before he saw them. Two young female voices, giggles, a louder laugh then shushing sounds. Of course they wouldn't want to be caught walking the streets, would duck passing vehicles. Bobby felt his insides ease, felt proud of his niece for her cunning, and at the same time, became one pissed-off, protective uncle.

The two girls walked alongside the curb in front of him. Bobby stepped out. Sarah jumped and grabbed for her friend. Olivia squealed.

Then both of them put on relieved faces, shifted to quivering, angelic smiles. When Bobby didn't mirror their happy-face act, the nervous grins turned to thin lines.

"Well, well, well." Bobby moved from the grass to stand beside them on the pavement. "Looks like y'all need a lift back to where you are *supposed* to be. Maybe I can keep your parents and Chief Mathers from locking you up and throwing away the key." He almost laughed when he noted their wide-eyed expressions. "You *might* get off restriction before you're thirty." Bobby motioned toward the pick-up with a nod and the two hang-dog teens slogged toward his vehicle. "If you're lucky," he added, walking behind them.

Sunday, October 4th, the wee hours

Jake pushed through his back door. The empty house echoed his steps. Times like this when he was so tired that breathing proved an effort, he wished he and Shug were hermits. No social obligations. No dying patients. And neither of them would have to drag home late . . . He consulted Felix for the time . . . Make that earlier than chicken-thirty. Two a.m.

He slid his keys and cell phone onto the kitchen table. The text alert light blinked. Stupid smiley face. He wanted to take a permanent marker and shade over that section of the screen. Should check the messages. Shug probably had left one or two.

No. First, he simply *had* to get out of this monkey suit.

He ambled into his bedroom, shucked the tux coat and cummerbund, then loosened the bowtie noosed around his collar. The ruby cufflinks, he placed in the wooden box, where they belonged. Five minutes later, he wore what Shug referred to as his *queen-at-rest attire*: lounge pants, t-shirt, and the soft, moose-hide slippers he had bought years ago on an Alaskan cruise. He swapped the formal cane for one with a carved duck head.

Jake stopped by the bathroom long enough to pee and wash his hands and face before moving back to the kitchen.

Might as well fix a cup of lavender tea. Good for stress relief. No way he'd attempt sleep, though he was tired enough it might actually happen. Jittery tired.

Since nobody was around, he chatted to himself. Heck, if he could blather to his dead mother, why not?

"Everyone loved the ball, don't you think?" He pulled out a tea bag, put water on to boil. "Mary-Esther's cake was a smash. The band was perfect." Jake grabbed his favorite mug, chunky white pottery with **Gay is the New Black** printed on one side. Where Hattie found this stuff . . . And where *had* Sister-girl and the whole Davis/Lewis crew gotten off to? He had sought them out after announcing the contest winner only to find them gone. He'd call her later, after she'd had time to have her ten cups of coffee, and give her a ration of grief for leaving the party without saying goodnight.

"I was glad to see Lucille Jackson crowned. She is the epitome of Piddie's spirit, with all she does for town. And she surely can outshine any cook within fifty miles." Jake watched the pot, willed the water to boil, tapped his cane. He could use the microwave. It was faster. Seemed wrong.

Jake looked around the small room. Most people nowadays had massive kitchens, so spacious a person could walk himself to death preparing a meal. He adored this spot, thought of it as the heart of the house. He closed his eyes and breathed in the signature aroma. No matter how many times he scrubbed, the ghost from years of fried food hung in the air, along with an overlay of cinnamon, perhaps browned sugar. Not unpleasant. Actually, comforting.

In his mind's eye, he saw Piddie seated at this very table, cradling a cup of hot coffee, a platter of warm teacakes in front of her. He'd lost count of the hours the two of them had spent discussing life after he returned to town. Picking apart his childhood for clues to who he had been and anything Piddie could tell him about the years he had spent in exile. Through Piddie's eyes, he glimpsed Betsy Lou, the ugly and the good. Yes, there *had* been some good.

He opened his eyes and checked the water. Tiny bubbles formed at the bottom of the pan. In less than a minute, the surface rippled. Hot enough. He poured the water into his cup, added the teabag. The heat released a pleasant herbal scent.

The cell phone mocked him. Touch me if you dare. Can't handle it, can you? C'mon, pick me up. See what I have in store for you.

Jake pulled out a chair and sat down. When he swiped the screen, the smiley icon indicated thirty messages. He scrolled until he found one from Shug. **Will try to be home before sunup. Been crazy here. Miss you.**

His eyes filled with tears. He blinked them away. If only he could share this runaway texting issue with Shug, he'd feel better. Surely. How could he, after that awful scene with She-whose-name-shall-not-be-spoken?

Like a rubber-necking motorist drawn to a car wreck, Jake sifted through the remaining messages. Some, he answered with the routine *wrong-number.* Others, he deleted without bothering.

I know what you are

"Oh, do you now?" he said to the phone. "And what is *that?*"

Should he be keeping a written record of the texts and the numbers? Yes, it was annoying. Beyond belief annoying. What good would it do, to keep a list?

"I don't have time to waste on this." He pressed the button to put the phone into rest mode. This week, he had two committee meetings about the upcoming Madhatter's Festival. Though he had a solid group of volunteers awaiting his instructions, he still had to be there to send the teams off into their different directions. Hopefully, Bobby had finished the last of the booths.

He did not have a wealth of hours to trace every number, even if he *had* saved them. Or to call them and ask who they were and where they had gotten his number. Maybe he could eke out a few moments to contact the cell service provider, see if they could do anything. He'd be on hold for hours. Forget that.

Left alone, most things worked themselves out. Piddie had told him that so often he could hear her words in his mind.

Outside the kitchen window, something thumped against the house. Jake jerked. Sounded like a big something. His heart hammered.

"Stop with this already, you big weenie!" He considered grabbing a flashlight, going outside to check for boogers. It was probably nothing to worry about. He dipped the tea bag up and down, removed it, and added a generous swirl of tupelo honey.

Every noise amplified. Felix's plastic tail clicked. The old house spoke in small creaks. Jake turned one ear toward the window. Was that the thump of footsteps, twigs snapping? He wished he *was* a golden retriever—good natured or not; at least a dog would bark, run toward the sound, something . . . But he couldn't move.

Silence rang in his ears. The back door knob jiggled.

Jake's breath caught and held. His heartbeat thrummed. How many times had Bobby told him and Shug they needed to buy a weapon? Like he could actually point a gun at any living creature and pull the trigger.

The back door swung open. Jake jerked so hard, the teaspoon danced on the table.

"Haa-low!"

Relief sucked the scared from him.

Shug walked into the kitchen with his arms wrapped around a bundle. Jake jumped up. A dog with a mushed-in face peeked from the edge of the blanket and regarded him with watery brown eyes.

"Honey, we're home," Shug said in singsong. "I tried to call you earlier." He stepped closer. His partner sounded cheerful, but the puffy bags beneath Shug's bloodshot eyes told Jake differently.

"Meet Juliet." Shug tipped his head downward.

The dog curled her upper lip into a snarl when Jake reached over to pet her head.

Chapter Fourteen

Monday, October 5th, morning

Hattie stepped through the entrance of the Wild Rose Diner. A wall of good scents hit her nose. The cooked onions and bacon took the lead, followed by the more subtle layer of spices, warm sugar, and fried food. Though her appetite had disappeared along with her good mood, she might work up some enthusiasm for Cajun something.

After coffee. Lots of coffee.

Most restaurants had evolved over the years, not allowing a customer to choose a seat. Not this one, even after her sister took over the reins and changed the name. Hattie walked to the first booth on the right next to a long plate glass window facing West Washington Street. Over the years, she had sat in this booth so often with family and friends it should have a dedication plaque. Or at least a deep impression of her behind.

Monday mid-morning, a great time to sit herself down and let the world flow around her. The bacon and eggs group had vacated. The lunch bunch wouldn't show up for at least another hour and a half.

She stared from the window at a twentyish guy in camo print. He leaned against his shiny black pick-up and worked a toothpick between his teeth. Couldn't hear the animated discussion he was having with the blonde woman in the SUV parked next to him, but whatever it was, his lips curled up every time he stopped talking and she started. Both of them looked too young to have teenagers. Thus, the easy smiles.

A few cars and trucks paused at the signal light before continuing east or west. Most through traffic chose the interstate rather than Highway 90. Too bad. So much of the genuine color of any area blurred at seventy miles an hour. The older Hattie got the more she relished the back highways. Why was everyone in such an all-fired hurry, anyway? To get somewhere. To grow up.

She switched views from outside to herself, and studied her hands. Working hands: calluses, muscled from hours of massage therapy and gardening. Chicken-handling, dog-petting, people-loving hands. Not the sort that tolerated fancy acrylic nails. Still, she should take a few minutes to hedge the cuticles. They were out of control.

"Hey, gal," a familiar female voice said. "Don't usually see you out and about this time of a morning."

Julie Nix, veteran server, stood by the booth. She had to be nearing seventy, but still worked every day, except some Sundays. She never had to write down an order, but she did—she had once admitted to Hattie—to make some customers feel more at ease.

Julie slid a white pottery mug with the imprinted Wild Rose Diner logo in front of Hattie and decanted coffee. She didn't bother to offer cream. "Holston joining you this morning?" she asked.

"Only me."

Julie hummed low in her throat. "You look a mite tender. Had an interesting weekend, as I understand."

Tender. A good way to put it. No need to pretend to be chirpy, or that Julie wouldn't know the latest. This café was nearly as good for local intel as the Triple C.

"As Mama used to say, 'Life can get somewhat tiresome at times.'" Hattie wrapped her hands around the mug. Holding it soothed her. She took a sip. Nothing beat coffee fresh from a professional grade machine. The water heated to the proper temperature and released the full flavor of the roasted beans. Mary-Esther never scrimped on quality.

"Can I rustle you up something to eat?" Julie gestured to the bright-colored menu on its clip, though the server had to understand, Hattie knew it from memory.

"No thanks. Only coffee. For now."

"Good enough then." Julie set the thermal carafe on the table. "I'll tell your sister you're here. She's in back, finalizing plans for the Madhatter's Festival booth." She turned, started to walk away, but then swiveled around. "You and Stef going to have your seated massage chairs set up again this year?"

Hattie pinched the bridge of her nose. Her sinuses were dealing her a fit these past few days. If only the weather would quit jerking from warm to cool and back. "Suppose we will." Add *that* to the list of things crowding her mind. "This time of year, days kind of slam into each other."

"That, they do," Julie said with a sigh. "Save me a spot, if you will. I'll need it after standing in our booth, dishing up gumbo all day."

Hattie nodded. Julie headed for the kitchen. The swinging wooden door danced in her wake. That old door, scars and all, had been renewed with a fresh coat of teal blue paint.

She took a moment to seek out the latest changes, a Chattahoochee version of *Where's Waldo*. A row of shiny booths lined two windowed walls and Formica tables formed various configurations in the middle of the long room, same as it had in its former life as the Homeplace Restaurant.

Mary-Esther had told Hattie she understood the effects of too-rapid change. Change was easier when it went at a slow, background pace. After her sister purchased the business, she had gradually slipped her translucent spell over the historic meeting place. The comfort of the old South—cathead biscuits, fried chicken and mullet, and apple pie—meshed with a fresh attitude and a dash of New Orleans. Even the most hardcore locals now clamored for gumbo, jambalaya, and muffaletta.

Every now and then, the owner and master cook threw in a surprise: hot beignets, a low country boil, and naturally, a King Cake for the Mardi Gras season. People really warmed to that New Orleans tradition, attending the party, hoping their slice held the tiny plastic baby so they could host the next gathering. Most in town had mastered the proper technique for eating crawdads, sucking the goodie from the heads. Others took heart in the fact they could always find hamburgers and meatloaf on the expanded menu. Mary-Esther had won the hearts of the town, as she had her biological family's.

Hattie let her gaze sweep the room, from the small foyer, to the dining area and walls. Mary-Esther liked to alter things in threes. Since Hattie hadn't been here in over a month, there could be as many as six switch-ups by now.

At least, she could find three.

Okay, so the teal kitchen door was one. Where was . . . There! A shadow box with a purple and green Mardi Gras mask and beads. Used to hang in Mary-Esther's house, in the kitchenette nook.

It took Hattie several more lingering passes to pick out change number three. Bingo! Give this country girl a prize! No one except a fellow collector might spot this one—the rock hoodoo stacks on the third from the bottom foyer shelf had a new friend, what appeared at this distance to be a hunk of rose quartz as large as a fist.

Hattie sucked back the rest of her coffee, refilled from the carafe.

Only someone from around Chattahoochee would be able to list the larger changes, too. The Homeplace's sunflower-print window toppers and server aprons had switched to new patterns reflective of the Wild Rose Diner, then changed again every two or three years. Always rainbow hues. Bright. Cheerful. Like Mary-Esther. Good thing too. Julie said she and the other long-term employees had grown to dislike sunflowers after so many years.

Instead of a bland, uniform oak, the ladder-back chairs showed off in shades to complement the latest scheme. An aged-barn plank wood floor replaced the worn tile, and the wall hangings shifted from season to season, always highlighting some local budding artist. Several times, the café had hosted book signings and musicians.

Hattie felt better already, being in the place where her sister lavished such attention.

Mary-Esther slid into the bench seat opposite hers. "Is my coffee strong enough for your troubles or do I need to break out my special Big Easy blend?"

Hattie huffed out a laugh. "Is it *that* obvious?" One thing they *didn't* share: a taste for chicory.

"I can count on one hand the times I've spotted you in here on a weekday morning," Mary-Esther said. "I saw Elvina yesterday. She told me about Sarah's little adventure. Sad to say, I was so crazed at the ball, I hardly noticed people coming and going."

More of what Elvina called *community sharing*. "We had a posse out looking for her, for over two hours."

"I'm glad she's okay. Did you put her on lockdown until she's past midlife?" Mary-Esther tilted her head and wobbled it at the same time, a gesture that reminded Hattie so much of their late mother, she felt her throat constrict.

Due to a mix-up soon after birth, Mary-Esther had been primarily raised by her Nana Boudreau in New Orleans and had never met her birth parents, Dan and Tillie Davis. Yet Hattie picked up so many subtle confirmations that Mary-Esther belonged to the Davis clan.

"Sarah has to go straight to the library after school. Then I'll pick her up after my last client," Hattie said.

"Hardly a punishment. The kid's a book addict."

"True." Hattie freshened her coffee, took a sip.

"Cell phone? Laptop?"

"We need to have a way to stay in contact," Hattie answered. "But her cell comes to me as soon as we get home. The laptop is limited to her school assignments."

Mary-Esther balled up her fist and pounded a spot over her heart. "Cut off from social media. Oh, you cruel, cruel mama."

"You'd think I *cut off* her hands, the way she carried on about that." Hattie made herself take a deep breath. "Not like I can take away car privileges or keep her from seeing some boy." Not yet, anyway. "Truly, all I wanted to do today was hop into Bailey and drive. This is as far as I made it."

Mary-Esther upended the other mug on the table and poured herself a cup. She added no cream or sugar. A purist, like her little sister. Mr. D had taken his black, too. "I get why you look like you've lost your last friend in the universe. Has to be hard, being a parent."

"I . . . Wow, here I am griping about this. I'm sorry." Her sister had never been able to have children after that first failed pregnancy. Number one in Mary-Esther's line of horrible husbands had kicked her in the stomach and damaged her for life. At least she had finally landed with someone solid. Jerry Blount was a good guy.

"Don't be silly, Hattie. I'm glad you feel you can come to me." Mary-Esther crimped her brows. "Did you and Jake have a falling out?"

"No, why?"

"You usually go to him. Jake was your," she air-quoted, "*first sister,* after all." Mary-Esther chuckled. "Before I limped into town in a beat-up van."

"You make it sound like I consider you as my second choice."

"Not what I intended," Mary-Esther said. "I'm glad you came by. I welcome the break. Right now, your first sister Jake is—"

"A maniac. A wall-bouncing, but well-dressed, maniac." Hattie smiled.

"October in Chattahoochee is enough to make anyone a mess. Jerry and Bobby were up half the night, working on the festival booths. This, after Jerry helped his cousin five times removed on his mother's side rewire the kitchen here."

"Ah . . . that's right! The fire."

"It was smoke, mainly. Turns out, it wasn't the stove but the connections. Thank God for Jerry and his network of people."

"One thing about folks from around here, they're usually related to someone who does whatever you need doing."

"And Jerry knows most of the county, the ones not blood kin." Mary-Esther whipped one hand in a circle. "Good for me, good for this old place, too."

Retired from the Gadsden County Sheriff's office, Jerry was involved in most Chattahoochee events. He headed up security for the Madhatter's Festival and fall carnival.

Hattie fiddled with the salt and pepper shakers, rearranging their positions, then shifting them back. "I dearly love October, the cooler temperatures. Always been my favorite time. Though someone upstairs missed the season-change memo this year. I haven't even unpacked my sweaters. I believe the whole town will breathe easier when this dreadful summer finally gives up."

"Fall is great for business, regardless of the weather." Mary-Esther knocked back the last of her coffee. "I'm catering two bridal showers and a wedding reception, on top of getting ready for the vendor booths."

"Hang in there, sister." Hattie still thrilled to the sound of that word. Hardly a day passed that she didn't praise the heavens for reuniting Mary-Esther with her family. "Thanks for taking a break to listen to my stuff."

"Anytime." Mary-Esther stood, gathered her shoulder-length auburn hair into a small wad, and fastened it with a jeweled clip. "Oh, and happy birthday. I do plan on baking you a cake when things slow down, if they do." She huffed.

"Thanks. Some birthday, huh? I got your birthday text, along with a number of others. Holston and Sarah gave me cards this morning, and Jake is making me a nice herb garden pot but I'm just not in the mood to celebrate."

Mary-Esther twisted her lips. "Still, we're here, on the planet. Got to be grateful for the small things, like breathing."

"You're right. Of course."

"You look like you need to eat." Mary-Esther rested a hand on Hattie's shoulder. "I can't fix everything, but I *will* fix you a nice, hot bowl of my famous shrimp and grits."

Monday afternoon

Jake pulled the truck onto the grass and got out. The cell phone, he left on the dash. If not for Shug, he would pitch it into the closest trash can. Dang thing had him so jumpy, he felt like he was mainlining caffeine.

He knocked on Hattie's front door five times, rang the bell then decided to check around back. Neither Captain or Ensign had sounded the doggie doorbell. Either the gang was at the pond, or . . . He rounded the corner of the house and glanced at the carport. Bailey, her usual spotless self, sat in her parking spot. Holston was still at the Triple C.

He looked toward the barn. The Chick Flicks clucked and Hendrix patrolled the perimeter of the fenced area. The door to the barn swung open and the dogs rushed out, Ensign taking the lead. They both barked until they reached a few inches from him. Then the greeting switched to hand-licking and tail-wagging. Jake fished a couple of treats from his pocket and handed them out. At least these two canines liked him. Juliet surely didn't. He would probably have to pitch his favorite loafers. Dog pee and leather weren't a good mix.

Sarah appeared at the barn door and waved him toward her. He took his time, avoiding a few potholes, no doubt created by the troublesome armadillo destruction crew.

"Hey-ho!" he called out when he entered the dimly lit barn.

Sarah and Hattie hunkered down next to the John Deere lawn tractor. Tux and Oreo trilled hello.

"Ohmygah!" he ambled over to where they sat. "Are we—"

Hattie held a shush finger to her lips and pointed to a mound of material. Jake leaned over. In a nest of towels, a yellow cat bathed one of five rat-like creatures. One, dark grey, was half the size of its siblings.

"Guess Sunny had them sometime this morning while I was uptown," Hattie said. "Aren't they adorable?"

Jake lowered himself to sit on a hay bale. He stretched his bad leg out in front. "Baby anythings are adorable. But, yes, they are particularly cute. Suppose you'll fall so madly in love that you'll keep them all. One step closer to becoming the crazy cat lady."

Hattie shot him a look. "I'd love to keep them. Sure. Got to be realistic. Think I'll keep the little calico and find homes for the rest."

"The runt is kind of cute." Jake wanted to pick it up, cuddle it to his cheek. But no, Mama Kitty wouldn't like it. Besides, he didn't need a kitten. They had sweet Juliet.

Hattie inched back and stood. "Want something to drink? I'll get us some co'cola?"

Jake nodded. "Sure." He watched Hattie leave.

"Mom's never going to forgive me, Unc Jake."

"That's a bit dramatic, don't cha think?" He winked. "And *I* know drama. You just scared Sister-girl. Scared all of us." He picked up a sprig of hay and twirled it in his fingers. "Best you be happy you have people like your mama, and your daddy, who care enough about you to *be* upset."

"I guess. But all I did was walk over to a friend's to play our game. His wi-fi is way faster."

"Not that simple, m'lady. You were not where you were supposed to be. These days, the places one might end up are as unpredictable as a cat's stripes." He studied the mama tabby. "Maybe a bad analogy. Cat stripes make sense and line up perfectly."

"Well, it wasn't *my* fault."

Jake held up a stop hand. "Chinaberry, you must *own* it. No one can take from you what you willingly give."

"That some woo-woo saying?" Sarah asked.

Jake chuckled. The kid had always been sharp. "*My* woo-woo. Supposed to mean you have the power, in most instances, to step back and keep yourself out of harm's way."

"But . . . *you* didn't."

Was this how it was with a teenager? Poor Sister-girl. She was in for a ride. "Correct. Looking back, I would've paid closer attention to the signs of trouble, kept better watch over my actions." He paused. "Do I accept total responsibility or blame for the assault on my person. No. That's on a boy not much older than you are now, who later took his own life . . . and a cousin who went along for the thrill."

"So," she held up a matching stop hand, "you really didn't have any control."

"Perhaps. Then. But it was a simpler time, when none of us worried about danger in this small town. People left their doors unlocked, even at night." Jake thought of the cell phone texts. Another way times had changed, for good and bad.

Sarah took in a deep breath and puffed it out. The mama cat lifted her head from her kittens and watched Sarah for a beat before returning to bath time. "Guess I will never, *ever*, be allowed to leave the house."

"You will regain your mama and daddy's trust." He tapped her on the temple. "And, if you are as smart as I think you are, you'll learn not to plant yourself in situations where others can take advantage of you." Jake cast aside the hay twig. "Your parents won't be around forever, my little Chinaberry."

They watched the kittens settle in to nurse. The larger kittens squeezed the runt from four positions before he finally gained space for himself. Oreo and Tux curled up and slept. Guess the birthing had worn out the support crew.

"Why does everyone call me Chinaberry?"

"Really, Sarah? You have to have heard the story a million and ten times."

She stared him down.

"So, okay . . . Your great aunt Piddie called you that from the first time she saw you at the airport in Tallahassee."

"Chinaberry trees are considered an invasive plant," Sarah said. "A common weed."

"Ah, the magic of Google."

"It's true. I read it on several websites."

"Yes. They do tend to overwhelm, given the opportunity," Jake said. "The way Piddie told it, chinaberry trees could grow and thrive anywhere, in rich or poor soil, and they provided an umbrella of shade during the long hot summers, before air conditioning took over that role. 'From China and cute as a berry,' Piddie said as soon as she laid eyes on you. Your great aunt loved Chinaberry trees. And she loved *you*."

Sarah made a noise in her throat. Hard to tell if it was agreement.

"One person's weed is another person's flower," Jake said.

Monday, late afternoon

Elvina added three hats to the overfull basket by her front door. She stood back and admired her sparse living room: big screen, high-definition TV, recliner, small couch, and two occasional tables. This latest in a series of purges lifted her spirit.

If it didn't serve her, it went. Into the garbage bin, to charity, or to friends. As long as it was out of her way. Jake called her a *heaver*: the polar opposite of a hoarder. She might collect information and pile it into every nook of her brain, but no one would ever call her a hoarder of things.

"Surely, being a heaver is not an affliction, way I see it," Elvina said aloud, now to the ghost of Buster. My, how she missed that old scruffy cat.

When Elvina finally lifted off to wherever spirits (and her cat, and best friend, and dear departed husband) went, someone would have to clean out this place. No kids. No close kin. The house was held in trust for Hattie, Bobby, Mary-Esther, and Evelyn. She'd be dog-goned if she'd leave them a mess.

She glanced around the room, looking for anything else she might add to the basket. So much of it all meant nothing to anyone except her. The older Elvina got the less it meant to her, too.

Most days, Elvina wondered why she was still on the planet. Keeping up with her town, a huge responsibility, sure. But what good did she do, in reality?

She flipped on the TV to have some digital companionship. Her cell text alert chirped. Jake returning her earlier message, finally.

Just now leaving the Hill. What do you need?

Come by my house, she tapped back.

Can it wait? Swamped!

No.

Have to stop by my house first. Then over. If you insist.

Elvina imagined the extended sigh that accompanied his answer.

I do.

Fifteen minutes later, Elvina heard his cane rappity-tap-tap on her door. When she opened it, Jake was standing on the porch, one hand on his cane, the other holding a bejeweled leash.

"Oh, my goodness!" Elvina leaned down and spoke to the dog on the end of the tether. "'But soft. What light through yonder window breaks? It is the east, and Juliet is the sun.'"

The pug's stumpy tail wagged her entire body. Elvina reached for a head pat and Juliet gifted her with a quick set of kisses.

"Aren't you the charmed one, 'Vina." Jake gave the leash a tug to lead the dog inside. Juliet planted her feet and let out a low growl. He handed the lead to Elvina. "Here."

Elvina smiled down at the pug. One slight leash shake and the little dog followed her inside then sat at her feet after she settled onto the couch.

"You're in her majesty's good graces," Jake said as he followed. "I, on the other hand, am *not.*" He headed toward the kitchen, throwing words over his shoulder. "Mind if I make myself a cup of coffee? I'm dead on my feet and I still have so much to do."

"Help yourself," Elvina answered. Why he bothered to ask defied logic.

Juliet hopped onto the cushion beside her and nestled close. "I'm not much of a small-dog person, but I'll be danged if you're not as cute as a ladybug's dimples." She gave the pug's head a pat then trailed two fingers down her spine. Juliet rewarded Elvina with more hand licks.

From the other room, Elvina heard the gurgle-hiss of the Keurig, the refrigerator door opening and closing, and the jingle of metal against stoneware.

Jake appeared in moments, a steaming mug in hand. "You're out of half-and-half. I used the last drop." He chose the recliner and sat down. "I wrote it on your grocery list."

"Thanks." She nodded toward Juliet. "I can't fathom why you dislike this little angel."

"*I* didn't ignite this fresh feud. *She* did. I usually blend well with animals." Jake tapped his cane. "Why did you summon me?"

Elvina stopped petting Juliet long enough to gesture to the basket. "That's for you."

"Heaving again, are you? Most sane people wait until spring." He blew on the mug, and then sipped.

"Don't fret, Jake. It's only a few odds and ends, and some hats. Figured you could take them to Jolene, for those fancy Lady-Hat arrangements she makes."

He stood and moved to the basket. He rooted beneath a wide-brimmed beach bonnet for a bubble-wrapped lump. "And these?"

"The Hummel figurines Piddie gave me." If she claimed Piddie had so much as breathed near something, Elvina could pawn it off on Jake. Such a sentimental sap. But she loved him. And she didn't particularly *love* those Hummels. Too much to dust.

"But you adore them." His eyes opened wide. "Wait. Are you sick, or dying, or anything that horrible? I don't think I can take another speck of worry."

Elvina huffed. "I am the picture of glowing health, if you don't count a touch of rheumatism. Plus, after that statement, I don't reckon I'd tell you even if I was kicking down death's door."

Jake reseated the clump of bubble-wrap beneath the hats. "Good grief."

"Don't you *good grief* me, Jake Witherspoon. Small wonder Juliet hasn't warmed to you. You've been positively snarky lately."

He returned to the recliner, and to his mug. "I'm sorry. It's . . ."

"What is the matter, sugar?" Elvina pinned him with her best stare of deep intent. "Tell me."

"Nothing really . . . and everything." He took a swig of coffee.

"Probably hormone imbalance." She'd read all about that online. How men suffered as much as women, after a certain age. Not sure when a *certain age* started, but she'd bet Jake was there.

"I'm so busy, and normally, I can cope, even thrive. Business is off the chain."

"Surely that woman from Alabama didn't help your mood." She leaned forward. Genevieve had left town fast. Had to be a story behind that. A good one, if neither Shug or Jake had breathed a word about it.

Jake waved off the comment. "I don't want to discuss that."

She eased back into the couch cushions. *Give it time*, she coached herself. *It'll rise to the top and pop wide open. I'll be right there when it does.*

"Much as I'd love to sit and while away an hour or two, I have to go." He drank the rest of his coffee in two swigs. "I'm meeting Jolene at the shop. Two more deaths across the river. We're up to our armpits in funeral flowers."

Elvina pulled out her phone and tapped a reminder to check the obits. "Is Shug home?"

"Why do you think Juliet and I are keeping bad company?" Jake said. "He doesn't want her to be left alone until she's more settled in her new castle."

"And Shug—does Juliet like—?"

"Ohmygah. They're sickening. He talks to her more than to me, though mostly in Shakespearean snippets. I feel like I'm living in seventeenth century England."

Elvina looked into the pug's brown eyes. "Leave Juliet with me." She lifted her gaze to Jake. "I'd love the company. You can work without worrying." She noted the relief painting his features. "You may be a golden retriever, but I think this little one is a lion, like me. We shall get along famously."

Jake grabbed his cane and stood still for a moment. Waiting for his bad leg to work, Elvina knew. "You sure, 'Vina?"

She nodded. "I'll bring her by later, when I go out. Maybe, if she likes, we can walk together first."

"All right then." He lifted his mug and ambled to the kitchen. She heard the water run, followed by the sound of the mug settling into the dish drain. He returned, walking with a bit more pep in his step, she thought.

"I owe you big for this." His voice quivered. "More than you know."

She tipped her head toward the basket. "Take that off my hands and we're squared."

"Done. Don't get up." Jake picked up the basket, hung the handles on his free arm, then managed to open and close the door.

Juliet nestled closer to Elvina and licked her hand.

Cats weren't as slobbery, for sure, but she'd get used to that. To help Jake, of course.

Jake entered the Dragonfly Florist shop from the main street side. Since the assault, he couldn't bring himself to use the back door after sundown.

"These are from Elvina." He dropped the stack of hats on Jolene's work counter.

He slid the cell phone onto his own counter. No need to check the message list. There would be at least twenty nasty-grams.

Jolene's eyes widened. "Oh, I can use these! And one's red. I'll whip up a Christmas Lady-Hat in that one." She picked up one hat, then another, studying each from all angles. Then she restacked them and moved the tower to the opposite end of her table. "But, as much as I would love to dig in, I have funeral arrangements to do. *Death* comes first."

Jake shivered.

Chapter Fifteen

Tuesday, October 6th, morning

Hattie slipped into the barn, moving at a slow creep. Sunny had grown accustomed to humans, but she possessed a mother's instinct: protect your babies. Hattie understood.

The cardboard box Hattie and Sarah had fashioned as a whelping pen was perfect. After Sunny tested the soft blankets, she moved the litter from the soiled rags to the new enclosure. Hattie kept fresh water and a bowl of dry food close by. Sunny ate and drank at some point, though Hattie seldom witnessed the mama cat leave her charges. Keeping bowls filled for the other two barn felines assured they wouldn't steal from the new little mother.

Sunny lifted her head and meowed a greeting when Hattie crouched down. No matter how many of the kittens remained on the Hill once they reached six weeks old, Hattie would keep the petite orange tabby. A special bond had developed from shared motherhood.

"Look at you," Hattie cooed. "Day two and you already have this mama thing down pat."

The kittens nursed, their tiny paws kneading Sunny's underbelly. Soon—five days, for their shorthaired breed—they would open their eyes. The box's high edges would keep them from wandering, though they only bobbed around at this point like blind moles, and Sunny nudged them back into place if they moved more than a few inches in the wrong direction.

Hattie pulled up her folding camp chair and hunkered down with her coffee. The baby kitty show proved more entertaining than watching the world from the front porch. They wouldn't stay tiny for long. She should move her favorite chair out here. But no, when the little ones grew older, she wouldn't risk the possibility of crushing one beneath a rocker.

She sipped her coffee. Sweet peace. With caffeine.

Jake stepped out to a morning still fresh with dew. Liquid pearls dusted the grass, and he spotted several tiny spider webs, invisible save for the strings of moisture clinging to the silk. He stopped to admire the annuals, their final blooms fading, yet still beautiful.

Most people walked past simple majesty. Eyes staring straight ahead. Intent on getting to some vital destination. Piddie had taught Jake the importance of looking up, and looking down. Seeing the clouds scud across an unflawed, cerulean autumn sky, then the tiny white blooms of some tenacious ditch weed—those small pieces of perfection went a long way to cover the imperfections of humans. Training himself to notice them had pulled Jake from deep sadness after the assault. Now, it eased the tight knot in his stomach.

Yesterday, neither Shug nor Jake had remembered to check the mailbox. Not a huge deal; both received and paid bills online. Even the year-end tax statements arrived electronically. Jake counted on the U.S. mail to be innocuous. An occasional magazine, the ubiquitous preholiday catalogs, sales flyers, an offer for another credit card. A waste of trees in these days of digital coupons and commercial websites. And Amazon, of course, where anyone could order happiness with a few clicks. He continued through the yard and reached the mailbox.

Nothing of consequence ever came via snail mail. Seemed a shame, when their mailbox was such a work of art. A friend in South Florida had painted the plain black box with fanciful deco dragonflies and splashes of jewel shades. Even now, eight years later, the colors held their brilliance. Jake opened the box and slid out a short stack of papers.

He walked back to the front porch and settled onto a rocker to sort through the worthless riffraff. One legal-sized envelope stood out. Jake's breath clipped when he read the first line of the letter's return address.

M. Thurgood

Seeing the name in print stirred a low, vague thrum in his head. The longer he stared at the block script, the more the feeling solidified, until it shifted mid-chest: a prickly burr lodged beside his heart. Good thing he was sitting down.

He turned the envelope over. Plain, white. The cheap, cut-rate variety he sometimes purchased from the Dollar Store when his linen-textured letterhead stationery ran out. Two strips of yellowed cellophane tape lined the back flap. Cheap glue seldom held the seal shut.

This had to be someone's cruel idea of a joke. Maybe one of the nastygram authors. Like that particular text from last night's lineup: **Soon it will be too late for you.**

Marshall Thurgood is dead. Jake heard the statement in his mind, as if some calm entity reassured him of the fact. That boy, his tormentor, old enough to drive, yet not old enough to legally drink or vote, lay in his grave, next to his parents in one corner of New Hope Cemetery, far from the Witherspoon plot. Jake wouldn't allow himself to glance toward that section of the cemetery; he took a route that didn't require him to pass the sandy lane leading toward the deceased Thurgoods.

Marshall Thurgood was more than dead; he was *long* dead, the coffin, shut and sealed, not open before the ceremony for the clutch of mourners. Even a skilled funeral director couldn't rebuild a face ruined by a shotgun at close range.

Jake pushed the rocker into a gentle back and forth. The air touching his skin: Indian summer warm.

But Jake felt cold to his core.

He flipped the envelope over. He didn't open it. He could not.

Tuesday afternoon

The smell of simmering beef stew hit Hattie's nose as soon as she and Sarah entered the back door. Whoever invented the slow-cooker deserved a Nobel prize, or sainthood. To be able to shove raw ingredients into a pot and have dinner waiting at the end of the day, what a wonder of modern life.

"I'm jumping in the shower," Hattie said. She dumped her purse on the kitchen table.

"I'll go check on the kittens." Sarah slid her backpack beside Hattie's purse.

"Okay, but be watchful." Bobby had shared the report from the lab; that poor raccoon had tested positive for rabies. "Don't stay out there too long. You have that project to finish. It's due soon, right?"

"Yes."

"Need me to read it over?"

"Nuh-uh."

"Excuse me?"

"No, ma'am."

"That's better." Her kid *would* be polite.

Sarah spun around and headed from the kitchen. The back door banged shut behind her. Guess they'd work later on leaving a room without fanfare. One battle at a time.

In the master bathroom, Hattie took the cell phone from her back pocket then shucked her shirt and jeans. So irritating to sweat in the fall when it was supposed to be pleasantly cool. Three massage therapy clients in a row nearly outdid her clinical-strength deodorant. Tomorrow, she'd wear a pair of capris and a summer-weight shirt.

Nothing like a warm shower to melt away the day's stench. She turned the knob full to the left, waited for the hot water to reach the spout, then adjusted the temperature and stepped beneath the shower head. In seconds, every inch of her skin foamed with her favorite lemon verbena shea butter soap. Who cared if it cost six dollars a bar? Worth every cent.

"Mom!"

The pitch of her daughter's voice shattered the magic of citrus scent.

"I'll be out in a couple of minutes," she called back.

"There's another wacked out raccoon!"

Hattie blinked. Soap burned her eyes.

"It's going after Sunny!"

"Get the gun!" Hattie twisted the knob and yanked back the shower curtain. She stepped onto the bath mat. Clots of soap clung to her skin and hair.

"Hurry, Mom!"

Sarah knew the combination. The secure cabinet was more of a precaution, an extra step, for anyone else's small children. Guns had been under lock on the Hill for as long as Hattie could recall.

Hattie grabbed the soiled jeans, cursing when her damp skin kept them from easily sliding on. The back door slammed. She wiggled into the shirt. Inside out, but no time to waste.

Hattie snatched up her cell phone and dashed from the house. The scene in the back yard mirrored the one she'd witnessed before, except this time, the raccoon snarled at the little yellow tabby. The two animals squared off like prizefighters. The hair stood up on Sunny's arched back. The Chick Flicks squawked. Hendrix sailed at the wire enclosure.

The dogs circled the showdown, barking. Hattie felt as if she ran in mud. Sarah halted a few feet in front of her. Sunny yowled, a low sound that climbed in volume and pitch. Only she stood between the intruder and her kittens. The raccoon lurched forward. The two animals tumbled, teeth and claws gnashing. Hard to tell where yellow fur stopped and striped gray fur started. And blood. Lots of blood.

They spun then separated. Backed off for round two, or was it three or four at this point? Sarah raised the shotgun, rested the butt on her shoulder.

Oh no! "Breathe! Steady!" Hattie called out, still running.

Sarah held the shotgun level.

Hattie halted and watched the scene: the yellow cat, wobbling, barely able to stand; the raccoon, slobber falling in ropes, moving in for the kill; and her daughter, methodically taking careful aim. Like her Uncle Bobby had taught her.

The gun fired. Once. Twice. On the third shot, the raccoon jerked and dropped. Sunny took a couple of drunken steps and crumbled. Neither animal moved.

Hattie ran the short distance to stand beside her daughter. Sarah lowered the gun. They moved together to within a couple of feet of the two animals. The dogs circled, barking. "Don't touch." Hattie held out her arm to stop Sarah.

"But, Mom."

Stillness. The raccoon's, the tabby's. Her eyes burned, this time with tears.

"It's too late." Hattie wiped her eyes then reached out to fold Sarah in her arms. "Oh, baby." She hit speed-dial for her brother.

Several minutes later, Bobby pulled into the side yard and jumped out of his truck. "What the hell?" He jogged over to Hattie and Sarah. "I was uptown. Got here fast as I could." He followed their nods to the two lumps of fur.

The chickens had resumed their bored clucking and Hendrix his guard rooster strut. Still jittery, Captain and Ensign wagged their tails and greeted Bobby with sniffs.

"Is the cat—" he started.

"Pretty sure, far as I can tell. I didn't want to touch either of them."

"Good call, Sis." Bobby walked back to his truck and returned with a plastic bag. He pulled on gloves and moved to the two fallen animals. "Yep. Both are dead." He bagged the corpses. "I'll get this raccoon to the lab."

"You don't have to take Sunny, do you Unc Bobby?" Sarah still clutched the gun.

Bobby shook his head. "No, babycakes, not to the lab. But I can't let anyone handle her. She has that crazy critter's slobber all over her."

"Leave that bag here. Holston and I will put on gloves and bury Sunny." Hattie took a shuddery breath and blew it out. "And we have to figure out how to take care of her kittens."

Chapter Sixteen

Wednesday, October 7th, mid-morning

Hattie slumped into Mandy's stylist chair.

"Mercy, hon. You look like something the dogs dragged in." Mandy whipped a drape around Hattie's neck and fastened the Velcro closure.

"I'm surprised I'm even upright. Couldn't have had more than four hours sleep last night." Hattie puffed out a breath.

"You and Holston rocking the house?" Mandy stood behind Hattie, grinning at their reflection in the salon's wall of mirrors.

"Funny. No, I was feeding kittens, for your information." Hattie paused. "Five, at first. But one died early this morning." She figured the runt wouldn't live. But no, it was a yellow tabby like Sunny that hadn't survived.

"Kittens?" Wanda carried a load of stacked white towels into the room and plopped them on her workstation counter. "I *love* kittens. Pinky finally caught all of our barn cats and had them fixed, so I guess that's it for our baby kitties."

"Just as well, Wanda," Mandy said. "You have a dozen as it is."

Wanda hummed reluctant agreement then transferred towels into drawers. Mandy leaned the back of the chair into position over the wash basin. Hattie heard the twist of levers, the sound of splashing as Mandy tested the temperature. Then warm water coursed over her scalp.

"Jake said you had a pregnant tabby hanging around. That the one had the litter?" Mandy asked loud enough to carry over the noise of the spray.

"Yes." Hattie felt warm tears press against her closed lids. *Please don't let me cry again.* Her eyes were already puffy. "She tangled with a raccoon and it killed her. Kittens are barely two days old. Their eyes aren't even open yet."

"Nature can be so cruel." Hattie heard Elvina's voice and opened her eyes enough to see her hovering at the threshold. "Holston told me a little about it this morning when he stopped by to pick up a flash drive he needed, on his way to the airport in Tallahassee."

"Holston felt awful about leaving me with everything," Hattie said. "Heck, he took turns with the feedings last night. Every two hours, like having a newborn. Actually, four of them."

"Hope you didn't give them cow's milk," Elvina said. She tapped the screen on her phone. "Says here, that will give 'em diarrhea. They make a special kitten formula."

Hattie nodded. "Sarah read up on it online. It was too late to call the vet for supplies so we mixed evaporated milk, water, and Karo syrup like this one article advised. Warmed it a little. We used an eyedropper to put it into their little mouths. I'm stopping by the vet's office after I leave here to pick up the formula and some nursing bottles."

"Who has the kittens now?" Elvina asked.

"Margie Frazier. I dropped them by her house on the way up here. She'll cover today's shift. Then Sarah and I will take up the reigns later." Hattie allowed herself to relax under Mandy's experienced touch. "There's more to it than feeding. Have to keep them warm. Have to use a cotton ball to wipe their little behinds." She opened her eyes a crack, closed them again. "Stimulates them to pee. Usually the mama takes care of that, too."

"And one died already," Wanda said. "Oh that is *so* sad."

"Luckily, it was after I sent Sarah to bed. We buried it next to its mama. Sarah was already so wound up after shooting the raccoon."

"Wait. What?" Wanda asked.

"I'm beat, Wanda. I'll tell y'all the whole story later. I promise."

"I'll give you the deluxe head massage, hon. Consider it a belated birthday present." Mandy pressed and rolled her fingertips on Hattie's scalp. If she ever hit the lottery, Hattie'd hire the stylist to do this every day.

For the next few minutes, Hattie allowed the female chatter to roll around her. Their voices didn't make up for lack of sleep, but they helped. Mandy shut off the water and squeezed the excess moisture from Hattie's hair. She wrapped a white towel still scented from the laundry around Hattie's head and sat the chair back into an upright position.

"Didn't ask you how you wanted it cut," Mandy said. "Your regular?"

"As long as it's easy for me to take care of, I really don't care." Hattie looked at Mandy in the mirror. "Not *too* radical."

The master stylist used a wide-toothed comb to tame the snarls. "Leave it to me."

Elvina shuffled into the room and sat down. "I have an idea. Let *me* take those kittens."

"I hope you *will* take one, Elvina. But it'll be at least six weeks before I can ween them, get them to where they can eat a little food mixed with formula."

Elvina held up a hand. "Hear me out. I don't sleep much on account of my insomnia affliction. I grab a half-hour here and there, but I can't recall the last time I slept a night through. It wouldn't be a botherment at all, for me to add in feeding those little ones."

"Are you sure?" It would help. A lot. Sarah had taken to the kitten's care as if she had prior training, but she had school and needed her rest. Watching how gentle her daughter had handled them last night made Hattie proud. So what if the kiddo had broken a rule? Sarah was a *good* person. The teenager stuff would pass. One day.

"Tell you what." Elvina bobbed her head. "I'll go home when I close up the front desk for the day and set up an old clothes hamper. I got plenty of soft rags left over from when I used them for Buster's bedding." She tapped her chin. "I have a heating pad I can put in there, too. Don't you fret. I'll make sure to follow instructions about how to clean their rumps. Can't be that hard."

"Look at you, 'Vina. Never much thought of you as maternal." Mandy smiled.

Elvina brushed aside the comment. "Listen, Hattie. Being old ain't no picnic. Lots of things I can't do anymore. Sometimes, I feel about as useful as a top hat on a pig." Elvina held up a bony finger and wiggled it at Hattie. "I *can* do this. Let me."

The expression on the old woman's face warmed Hattie. Everyone needed to feel like they did more than take up space.

Wednesday evening

Elvina opened the cat carrier's wire door and removed the tiny calico first. She cuddled it to her chest for a moment, allowing her body heat to warm it.

"Are you sure about this, Elvina?" Hattie said. "It's a lot to ask."

"Don't vex me, Hattie." Elvina transferred the kitten to a basket lined with soft towels. She held the other three, one at a time, before uniting them with their siblings. Important to allow them to imprint to her and other humans, she'd read. "I have the heating pad on low, but I'll check them often, to make sure they're at the right temperature."

"This is a case of formula, and I've ordered more." Hattie slid a cardboard box onto Elvina's coffee table. "And the nursing bottles. It's much easier with these than it was with an eyedropper." She petted the calico's tiny head with the tip of a finger. "I fed them about an hour ago."

Noting the crease between Hattie's brows, Elvina said, "You need not worry. I've studied up on this online, extensively. Articles from dependable websites. Plus, I spoke with the vet tech. I have her on speed dial. I can handle the two-hour schedule."

Hattie sank into the sofa. "I have utmost faith in you, Elvina. It's not that at all. I'm at war with my daughter . . . again."

"Not taking to her earned restrictions, I suppose?"

"Sarah's mad at me for taking *her* kittens away. Thinks it's me being mean. I left her with Bobby and Leigh so I could run up here. Maybe she'll be in a better frame of mind when I get home."

Some days, Elvina regretted she and Clyde had never had children. Others, she praised the heavens they hadn't. "She goes to the library after school, correct?"

"Yes."

"Why don't you let her come to the Triple C instead? I'm planning on bringing the kittens to work so I can take care of them during the day. She can help with the afternoon feedings." Elvina held up a pointy finger. "*And* we have free wi-fi. Between all of us, we can keep an eye on her until you get finished with your last massage client."

Hattie jumped up and hugged Elvina so hard, she lost her breath for a moment. When Hattie let go, Elvina sucked in air.

"That's brilliant! Holston's out of town, so Sarah can use his office. And maybe she'll pull her lower lip back into position. She's walking around with it poked out so far, she could use it as an umbrella."

Elvina's phone buzzed. She read the message: **He must repent. Before it is too late.** What in the world? She texted **wrong number.** One thing she hated, besides random texts from unknown senders, was sanctimonious idiots. She didn't know *who* must repent or *why*, but the statement implied judgment. Probably had to do with one of the presidential candidates. Lordy, the election was a good ways off and they were already pitching dirt in the sandbox like a bunch of spoiled brats.

"Why don't you head home, hon," Elvina said. "I'll take good care of these babies. At least that will be one thing off your plate."

Hattie hugged her again before leaving. Elvina double-checked the article she'd saved on her laptop. Formula should be warmed a bit. A few ounces at a time. Every two hours for the first four weeks, then tapering to every three hours. Add this to her life resume: nursemaid to a pack of motherless kittens. That was bound to move her up a level in heaven, or at least get her past the Pearly Gates.

The runt was the first to awaken. It bumbled a few inches, crying. Elvina rushed to the kitchen and returned shortly with a filled bottle. She checked the temperature using a few drops on her wrist before scooping up the tabby. No problem with this little one. It might be small, but it suckled right away. It fed until its little belly grew round. Elvina settled it back into the basket and picked up first the gray tabby and then the black and white dappled kitten. Both fed nicely. The calico was last.

"You're a bit on the slow side, little one." Elvina held the calico to her chest, allowed it to feel her heartbeat. After three tries, it nursed. Listless. Elvina worried a little. The calico was Hattie's pick of the litter. "You need to hang in there, sugar. Don't you be giving up on me." It took twice as long as the other three, but finally Elvina managed to coax the kitten to finish its ounces. She held it for a long time until its breathing settled.

A rappity-tap-tap sounded on the front door. Elvina shuffled to open it, the calico still cuddled to her chest. Jake stood on the other side. Juliet twirled in circles as soon as she spotted Elvina.

"Oh." Jake's shoulders slumped. "You're busy."

Elvina held open the door. "Come on in. I've finished feeding time." Without waiting for an invitation, Juliet led the way. She lifted onto her rear legs and craned back her head, looking up at Elvina with eager eyes.

"Guess we know who she adores," Jake said. "And it isn't me." He reached down and unclipped the pug's leash. He walked over to the basket with Elvina. She lowered the calico into the nest of sleeping kittens. It mewled once then quieted.

"Aren't they adorable?" Jake smiled down. "I love the little runt."

"He's the perkiest of the lot, I believe. Being small has nothing to do with chutzpah."

"The least among us fights the hardest," Jake said.

Had to be a deep meaning beyond that, but Elvina didn't pursue it. Later maybe. The poor boy looked so tired his under-eye bags had bags.

"I hate to ask this . . . ," Jake started.

"Yes. I will keep Juliet for you."

"Are you sure you *can*?" Jake said.

For the love of Pete, was she so wishy-washy and old that everyone had to *ask*? "Wouldn't offer if I didn't think I could handle it. Now shoo." She waved both hands toward the door. "Let her spend the night, if you wish. Or I can drop her off after our walk."

"Better bring her home, or call me and I'll come get her. Shug would be livid." Jake started toward the door then turned around. "You truly are a life-saver."

After he left, Elvina stood over the basket of kittens, Juliet beside her. Before Elvina could stop her, the pug leaped over the edge and settled down. Juliet gathered the sleeping babies to her, one by one. Then she gazed up at Elvina. *I got this*, the look said.

"Well, imagine that." Relief settled over her. She'd asked for a purpose, now she had more than a basketful.

Chapter Seventeen

Thursday, October 15th, morning

Jake threw down his pencil and headed into the living room. Maybe music would help. He turned on the CD player. Should be Sinatra, the Eagles, or Glenn Miller in the queue. Either would suffice. Instead, *The Dance of the Sugar Plum Fairies* blared. He jabbed the pause button so hard, the player slid crossways on the shelf. He straightened it then hit the switch to move the carousel to the next CD. Frank Sinatra. Thank goodness.

Wonder when the Nutcracker Suite had oozed from its jewel case? He'd have to check later, make sure none of the other dozen or so Christmas CDs had infested his line-up. Some perky elf was for sure intent on driving him completely around the bend. That elf was named Shug Presley. The holiday music probably made Shug feel better; had to credit it with that.

He skipped the CD to selection eight, *Fly Me to the Moon*. Sinatra's snappy beat sounded, then the singer's ageless voice. Jake snapped his fingers in rhythm. If he could be anyone other than himself, he would be a nightclub crooner.

Jake returned to the kitchen table where the schematic of the festival grounds mocked him. Too bad he couldn't snap his fingers enough to really fly to the moon. Bet they didn't have festivals there. Why was this draining his last brain cell? "Answer," he said aloud to no one, since Juliet was at the Triple C with Elvina and the adoptive kittens. "The Madhatter's is *not* a little event anymore."

Thank the media for that. A mixed blessing. Anytime a newspaper writer tagged something as *quaint*, the odds tipped in the favor of it becoming not-so-quaint.

Chattahoochee benefited from the folderol. The benches and decorative lighting along Main and Washington Streets stood as proof. The Chattahoochee Revitalization Committee already had its sights set on this year's proceeds, for a water feature and walking trail. If Jake and the rest of his festival planners had their projections correct, the take-away would be sufficient for those projects and possibly the next in line.

Jake chewed on his bottom lip. "Where in this green neck of the planet am I going to fit in three more food vendors among the craft people?"

Hattie's trick of scribbling problems on snips of paper and putting them in the freezer to "chill them out" popped to mind. He tore off a scrap and jotted *issues with festival*, then crammed the paper into a plastic zipper bag. Beneath several packs of venison burger, a layer of similar bags held old and recent annoyances. One day, he'd clean them out and laugh at whatever had bothered him enough to put it on ice. He added the festival rant to the bunch and shut the freezer door. He paused a moment before dashing off another sentence: *stop those texts!* He opened the freezer and sealed the request into the bag with the festival note.

Good thing Jolene covered the Dragonfly Florist, and that no one had died the past couple of days. Jake doubted he could scrape together the energy for one more thing, even flowers.

Add to this for the past week, the dreams. Nightmares, actually. It had been years since they were so vivid.

Seeing the name *Thurgood* must've jumpstarted his latest cinematic nocturnal adventures. His brain seemed intent on reliving every blow of that bat, the metallic flavor of blood, the wild-eyed look in Marshall Thurgood's eyes. Even the pop-bang of the Fourth of July fireworks. Crowds so nearby to his horror, yet might as well have been on the next continent.

He shuffled the papers. *The Envelope* rested at the back of the pile. Unopened. Simply no time for that. Somehow, he had whiffled away the past few days, with committee meetings for this, phone calls for that. He saw Shug in snippets. Juliet spent most of each day with Elvina and the kittens.

Jake tapped the pencil eraser on his chin. Could he shift the cake competition booth closer to the stage? He sketched a dotted line. Might be enough space for two food trucks, if they parked at an angle. So glad Sonny's Barbeque had decided to join them. Jake could almost taste the tang of their special sauce on his tongue. His stomach rumbled. Small wonder. Here it was a quarter 'til ten and all he'd had was coffee.

His cell phone jigged. Could be one of the nastygram authors. A bit early in the day for them. Could be a committee member. He snatched it up and tapped the message icon.

The Cup 'o' Cakes people pulled out. Owner has the flu.

Jake released his breath. Not a mean text. This time.

Sad, he loved the vendor's red velvet cupcakes: moist, with that heavenly whipped cream cheese icing. The vacancy solved one problem. He erased their name on the diagram and wrote in *Morningside AME Fish and Chicken*. That left only one more food truck to accommodate. He might be able to move others a few feet to fit in the Rutabaga Café's booth. The town's newest little eatery served delectable food, and Jake liked to celebrate local businesses. Of course, Mary-Esther and her Wild Rose Diner crew would be there. She promised gumbo, muffaletta, and fried mullet dinners. Mary-Esther already had a prime position reserved.

His stomach complained so loud it sounded like Juliet's snores. He pushed back from the table and rummaged in the refrigerator. Leftover pasta salad. Not proper breakfast, or at this point, brunch fare, but it would do. He grabbed a fork and ate the leftovers from the plastic storage bowl. Classy.

As he stood at the kitchen window, chewing, the day took shape outside. Clear blue sky. Balmy temperature. Butterflies dancing in the fading perennials. Maybe he could load up and take this to his sacred spot on the old bridge.

He shook his head *no*. Climbing a fence with a gimpy leg was challenge enough. The thought of crawling over the barricades loaded with his planning supplies and a cooler stopped him.

"Eastbank!" he said. It was only five miles to the Corps of Engineers park. He could spread out a quilt on the hill by the boat ramp.

Minutes later, he pulled the truck beside the small building at the federal park's entrance. He didn't recognize the woman at the sliding window. "The campground is full," she stated.

"That's okay. I only want to sit down by the water for a bit." Jake handed over the three- dollar fee.

"*Who* are you visiting?" She picked up a clipboard, ignoring his extended arm.

"No one, if you don't count dragonflies and maybe the occasional egret." He wiggled the dollar bills.

"We don't allow the unregistered public, unless you are visiting one of the current campers."

Right. They had changed the rules. So much of what used to be accessible, and free, was no longer either.

"I won't be here much longer than an hour, at best. I'm *from* Chattahoochee. I've come down here *all* my life." He flashed the lop-sided Jakey grin this time, showed lots of teeth.

"Can't let you in unless you're visiting a camper."

Wow. The smile didn't work. She didn't even flinch. And she had that one line down pat.

No use arguing. This woman was obviously a stickler for regulations, only doing her job. Still, Jake couldn't help feeling a tad irritated. Maybe he'd add her to his freezer list.

He eased past the guardhouse, flipped a U-turn, and accelerated. Where to now? Not the river landing; he'd be spending enough time there in the next few days. He took a left at the main road heading toward Chattahoochee Park. Maybe he could find a peaceful spot by the public swimming area. In a couple of miles, he reached the entrance. Closed off by a swinging gate.

Well, heck fire. Again, he executed a three-sixty and retraced his route. *Water. Where can I be near water?* He took the next left to the main boat landing where the town used to hold Fourth of July celebrations. The place, less than a quarter mile from the Turkey Point overlook, was where he had suffered the worst hours of his life.

Jake slammed on brakes.

He couldn't go *there*. Not by himself. No matter that years had passed, that he had tried his best to paint good over evil. That spot still held too many negative memories.

Where can I be near water, away from crowds, and safe?

He drove back into Chattahoochee then turned west. Crazy, when he had no time to spare, to drive to the opposite side of Lake Seminole. He crossed the bridge over the Apalachicola River and headed there anyway.

Past the small town of Sneads—the "twin city" to Chattahoochee—he headed north to Three Rivers State Park. Five minutes later, he spread a quilt on a wide grassy slope with a one hundred eighty-degree view of Lake Seminole. The spot was open. It felt secure.

Overhead, puffy clouds rode the lazy breeze and quivered the pine needles. The same currents tickled the surface of the water, then brushed clumps of Spanish moss hanging like witch hair from the few hardwoods near shore. Usually, the leaves were brilliant by now: the yellow hickories, orange river birch, and the blood-red sweetgums. Not this year. They would die and turn brown, leaving the limbs barren.

Midweek. Great time to find a speck of solitude. He shared the picnic area with one small family farther down, a man and woman with a toddler who dashed back and forth from the swing set to the jungle gym slides. The two covered pavilions were barren. An older couple emerged from the nature trail and passed by, a Pekinese jangling ahead of them, straining against its leash.

Jake dumped the contents of his messenger bag onto the quilt, opened the small cooler for a diet cola. He lowered himself to sit and spread out the festival diagram pages.

There. He jabbed his pencil on the paper. Why hadn't he noticed this before? He could move the face-painter lady into the children's activities booth and free up more space. Astounding, what a splash of fresh air could do for a frazzled brain. He sucked in a lungful and held it, before allowing it to whoosh from his parted lips.

Two more sets of deep, cleansing breaths, as Hattie liked to call them. Calm the monkey mind. Soothe the sore spirit. Jake felt his shoulders ease. Even his bad leg cooperated and ceased to throb. He should make it a point to be near water at least once a week.

He closed his eyes. In the distance, the toddler laughed, jabbered something to his parents Jake couldn't understand. He picked out the ratcheted call of a woodpecker, the far-off buzz of a motor straining until the boat planed and the engine sang a higher pitch. For a few minutes, it was so quiet he could hear the underlying ringing in his ears. Tinnitus often came with age and slight hearing loss, the audiologist said. His started years back, when Marshall Thurgood took a baseball bat to Jake's head and body.

He opened his eyes and allowed them to focus on the distance instead of lines on a paper. Across the lake, he could make out the far shore, the Chattahoochee landing. Farther down, the slope of Eastbank where he would've been sitting if Missy By-the-Book could've let go of her control.

He pivoted his head to check out the dense forest surrounding the picnic area. If this wasn't a state park, he would feel anxious. No telling how many human remains rested in the backwoods of the Florida

Panhandle. Jake made it a point never to wear one hundred-percent cotton clothing. If his body every lay in a thicket, if his bones disarticulated and animals scattered them, at least some fragment of his polyester-blend shirt wouldn't biodegrade. He shivered.

A high-pitched chatter caught his attention. A pair of eagles soared overhead then turned to follow the shoreline. A boat cruised by at full speed, closer this time, disturbing the mirrored surface. A turtle head popped up, disappeared. Wavelets licked the banks. Then the watery sounds faded. The turtle head showed again, bobbing.

Jake pushed the papers aside and lay back. Only one jet contrail streaked the sky. He shut his eyes. In moments, he fell asleep.

A loud rumble jerked Jake from the sweetest rest he'd had in forever. He sat up and swiveled his head. A black, oversized pick-up truck—a diesel from the sound of the engine—crept through the parking lot. Marshall Thurgood had driven a black truck, nowhere near as shiny as this one. In the South, big, muscle trucks held big, muscled dudes. Was it slowing? He scanned the grounds. Where was the little family? Must've slept longer than he thought. No other cars sat in the angled spaces. Just his little gray truck. And this monster with its booming beat.

The cell phone vibrated, chattering against the papers. Jake jerked his gaze from the truck long enough to read the message.

Time is running out.

In the distance, a man whistled some tune. The pages of his notebook lifted in the breeze, scratching against each other. Jake heard his heartbeat echo in his ears.

The truck circled again, slowed, then headed toward the campgrounds. Away from him.

He released his breath.

Jake stood and scraped the papers into the messenger bag. He slung the cooler's strap over his shoulder with the bag. Stuffed the rolled quilt under his arm. He shuffled to his own little truck, threw himself, the cane and his belongings inside, locked the door, and cranked the engine.

Thursday afternoon

Elvina motioned with a head dip. "That one's finicky." She removed the nursing tip from the runt tabby's mouth and held him toward Sarah Chuntian. "Swap with me."

"I can do this. It's *my* cat." Sarah cuddled the calico she had already named *Patches*. Then she used her pinky finger to brush its chin and mouth. When the kitten opened up, she slid in the feeder tip and bumped it along the edges of its mouth. The calico suckled, kneading its tiny paws against her hand.

Elvina resumed feeding the runt of the litter. No problem with this one. It ate as if it would never get another chance if it didn't. At this rate, it wouldn't be the smallest for long. "How'd you know to do that?"

"Read it online."

Of course. Silly me. Elvina nodded. Obviously, a site she had missed during her own research. "At least we don't have to wipe their little bottoms, like your mother told me to do." She tipped her head toward the brood basket where Juliet bathed the other two kittens.

Elvina wasn't much of a dog person, but Juliet had shifted her affections. Then again, she hadn't considered herself a cat person either, until Buster decided he would take up at her house. She wondered if Shug might allow her to adopt the pug. Most likely not. Jake had thawed toward Juliet a degree or two, but Elvina would lay even odds that he could be swayed. Juliet still snapped at Jake, though Elvina had yet to figure a reason.

"After this, you need to get your studies done," Elvina said. "Hattie told me you had some important assignment due. You can hook onto the customer wi-fi, but don't let me catch you goofing off." She lifted one eyebrow and tipped down her chin. Supposed to be a stern look, though she had a tough time being harsh with Sarah. She could remember the little angel-faced infant Piddie had coddled. Piddie would've loved this older version, too, once she got past the teenaged mannerisms.

Sarah looked from the kitten to Elvina and then circled her eyes.

"Okay, missy. Let me underscore my main rule, in case you didn't get it the first five times I said it." Elvina removed the bottle from the runt's mouth, checked the amount. Two ounces gone. "If you roll your eyes at me, this deal is off. No more Triple C and kittens after school." She held the runt in one hand, its head elevated, and gently tapped it with two fingers until it burped. Yes, all of the online forums assured her, you had to degas a kitten like a human child.

Elvina watched Sarah. The teen's eyes shifted upward then snapped back to center so fast Elvina fought laughter. Hope she wasn't causing permanent harm to the kid's vision.

"Yes, Miz Elvina," Sarah said. The calico pushed away from the bottle. Sarah checked the ounce markings then repeated the same sequence, and it nursed again.

They grew quiet for a few moments until both swapped their charges for the other two, a plump, gray tabby and a black and white kitten. In the basket, Juliet nudged the two freshly fed kittens to her, bathed them. Then they settled down and slept curled close to her. Amazing how fast they were growing. A couple of days back, their little round eyes had opened.

"You and your mama getting along better?" Elvina asked.

Sarah shrugged, but didn't make eye contact.

What a clever way for the teenager to avoid breaking Elvina's rule. "You can talk to me, Sarah."

The teen looked up at her. Holding a kitten in one hand and a bottle in the other kept Elvina from using the zip-the-lip, throw-away-the-key gesture to add reassurance she wasn't a snitch.

"We're better. Since the kittens came," Sarah said in a low voice. "It's been almost two whole weeks. You'd think they would ease up."

"Your mama and daddy are trying to watch out for you, you know that."

"I guess." Sarah bobbed her head. "I *can* think for myself. Mama *so* doesn't get it."

It had been too many years; Elvina couldn't recall that time of life when she believed she knew everything. Suppose each person deserved to think they were the center of the universe for a few years. Before reality ripped that myth into shreds.

Chapter Eighteen

Friday, October 16th, near noon

Jake glanced up, a colored Sharpie in hand. Three more vendor signs left for the final flourishes. Good thing the other decorating committee members had done the lettering. Still, he should've long been finished! Would've been, had he not chosen to goof off by the lake yesterday, as if that had turned out restful.

Jolene idled next to the street-side door. "Sure you don't want anything?" she asked.

"No, thanks." He held up a travel cup filled with ice and diet soda. "I'm drinking my lunch."

"You're going to dry up and blow away, Jake."

He huffed out a laugh. "Maybe I'll pass out. At least I'll get a little break while I'm trying to get back up."

His business partner motioned to the display cooler. "I finished the last of the table arrangements. Should be it, unless we get call-in orders. Leave them for me, if we do. I'm caught up. Finally." Her hair stuck up like a rooster's comb. She turned and left the shop. The clang of the tiny brass bell attached to the door handle accompanied her exit.

Jake stared down at the sign. Suppose the uneven block letters had a certain rustic charm. Next year, he'd insist on having them professionally printed. At least he had won the battle to have the overhead banners redone last year, and they were still in good condition. Bobby and his crew of miscreants were hanging them today, across two spots on West Washington and over the road to the festival entrance. A simple design: a top hat with a yellow daisy stuck in the brim and **Welcome to the Annual Madhatter's Festival** in large, bold print. No mention of the festival's number, fifteen by his count. Learned that lesson several years back. A pain, to redo the big banners every year.

Bobby would get the final vendor booths set up, too, bless him. Plus plant the parking signs and coordinate last minute security issues with Chief Mathers and Jerry Blount. Jake didn't know what he would do without Bobby Davis and still found it hard to believe he would ever *think* that sentiment.

The brass bell jangled. How many times did he have to assure that woman he didn't need to eat? She was as much a mother hen as Hattie. "Listen, hon," he said without looking. "I don't want—"

His voice stalled after he looked up. The biggest man Jake had seen in this town, maybe in forever, blocked the shop's doorway. First thought: *It's Lurch from the Addams family.* Second thought: *This guy's forearm is bigger than my waist!*

Every drop of moisture fled Jake's mouth.

The man stepped toward the counter. Squinted. This was *it.* Jake knew. How he was going to die. They'd find him pummeled to hash. His blood would gather in a pool at the front of the shop instead of near the back entrance. This time, the best paramedics this side of the Mason/Dixon line wouldn't be able to revive him.

He couldn't access his cell phone. Had it crammed in its new holding pen, in Jolene's desk drawer where he didn't even have to see it.

"You the owner?" The voice coming from the hulk didn't sound like a thunder-god's, as Jake had expected.

"Yes." Jake eased from his padded stool, grabbed his cane, and forced himself to pull his spine as erect as possible. Proper posture helped assure success in any situation, Betsy Lou had often told him.

Beefy Man stuck a hand in his pocket and pulled out a roll of greenbacks, plopped them on the counter. "I need some flyers."

Good thing Jake understood, and spoke, fluent redneck. "Flowers. Yes. What may I help you with, sir?"

The man looked at Jake's cane then back to Jake, his eyes narrowed to slits. "You that feller what got beat up?"

Anyone else asked him that, Jake might've come back with some snappy reply. But his brain had gone dull and this guy didn't look like the jolly type.

"Yes." Jake cleared his throat. "I am."

"Mama told me 'bout dat."

"I see." Jake risked a quick sideward glance at the wall clock. How long would it take Jolene to pick up that muffaletta and get her butt back here? Wasn't like this guy would choke him *here,* in broad daylight, right? *Calm down.* Jake swallowed to make his throat open up. "Is there something in particular—"

"I need flyers for Mama."

Finally, something solid. Flyers for Mama. "I have some beautiful sunflowers, just in. Mums, too." Jake motioned toward the display cooler to his right. "And I always have roses. Is this a special occasion, a birthday or . . . "

"Mama passed."

"Oh." Jake's bad leg throbbed. He shifted more weight onto the good leg. "I am very sorry for your loss." And he was, for anyone ordering funeral flowers. Especially for one's mother. No wedding ring. So, probably no wife to take care of arrangements. If he had a sister, she'd be here. Men seldom came into a florist shop unless forced by circumstances.

Jake pushed the sign markers aside and picked up an order pad. "If I may get your mother's name?"

"Hildegard. Hildegard James."

"Oh no. Miz Hilde? I hadn't heard." One more indication he was stressed. He usually perused the obits every morning.

The man's rheumy eyes fixed on Jake. One of them had a heavy lid and the eye wandered and quivered until he blinked it back into line. "You know my mama?"

"Yes. I mean, if she's the same Hildegard James from out around Sycamore, I do."

The man nodded.

"Miz Hilde has ordered arrangements for her church many times. Last one, a few weeks ago." Jake tapped his chin. "Homecoming, if memory serves."

Beefy Man nodded again. Not a stickler for spoken words.

Jake moved to a narrow shelf containing a row of binders. He extracted one and returned to the counter. "I have several designs, depending on what you would like, and your budget."

"Ain't gone be in no church building."

"Graveside services are—"

"I want the coffin laid solid with flyers and big bunches to either side." He used both meaty hands to draw an air design for Jake.

Jake flipped open the binder and whipped pages to a divider tab. "Here are the casket drapes. I can—"

"Don't want to look at no pictures. You just make my mama a nice un."

"Okay." Jake shut the binder. "What colors would you like?"

The big man shrugged. Took a lot of energy to lift those shoulders.

"Did Miz Hilde have a favorite color?"

Another rise and fall of shoulders.

If Jake didn't know better, he'd swear he was on one of those "you got punked" shows. And this guy was one hell of an actor. The accent was so thick Jake had to piece together the grunts, nods, and body language to assure he was getting it right.

"Let's see, last I saw your mother, she was wearing," Jake shut his eyes a beat, to call up the visual, "pale pink, and she carried a red purse." He opened his eyes.

A smile transformed the lug's features. Handsome, in a rakish, tractor-pull sort of way. "My mama loved that red bag. Had shoes to go with it and ever'-thang."

"That shade of pink in her dress, and the red of her accessories, made her cheeks look rosy, too." Jake didn't have to force the words.

The smile wilted. The man's eyes glistened. "Make Mama somethin' purty. Somethin' she'd lack."

Something she'd *like*, Jake interpreted. Maybe he should write a Redneck to English translation book. Sell them to anyone who ended up in this part of the Deep South. "A full casket drape and two standing sprays will come to . . ." Jake figured in his head. "Four hundred."

The man whistled low. "They's a couple'a hundred there." He indicated the cash roll with a dip of his head. Jake lay odds it smelled like dope; most of the huge cash payments he had received over the years smacked of illegal vocations. Wasn't his place to judge. He was *just* the florist.

"I can accept a down payment." Jake picked up a pen. Jolene would scalp him for this.

"I'll get you the rest."

"Your name, sir?" He held the pen poised above the order pad.

"Rudy. Rudy James."

Jake managed to extract the basic contact information. "Is Joe Burns handling the arrangements?"

Rudy nodded.

He could get the remainder of information from the funeral director. "I'll do the flowers for your mother myself."

The man made a sucking noise through his front teeth. At least he had some. "How you know I'm good for it?"

"You are." Jake hoped.

"You don't know me."

"But I knew your mother."

Rudy turned, made it to the door in two steps. He turned back and said, "Thank ye."

The bell accompanied his departure. Jake blew out a long breath.

First thought: *I am in one piece.* Nothing bleeding out or hanging off at a weird angle.

Second thought: *How in the world am I going to get a casket drape and two sprays done one day before the festival?*

Third thought: *Coffee. Lots and lots of coffee.*

Friday, mid-afternoon

Bobby snugged the final support beams into place, snapped the booth's hinged edges together, then slid in the bolts. Had to pat himself on the back for this new design. The whole shebang could fold down into a manageable stack. Easy to store for next year, and the ones after.

He'd lost count of the total number of Madhatter's Festivals. Bobby barely recalled the event's namesake, Max the Madhatter—a strange, little man from back in his parents' days, one of the few mental patients with "town privileges." Every time Bobby tried to bring up an image, a cartoonish leprechaun popped to mind. Guess Max had reminded him of an Irish trickster. Too bad the real Max didn't leave behind a pot of gold. Max had died penniless and Mr. D spearheaded the fundraising effort that kept Max from ending up in Potter's Field behind the state mental hospital. Laid to rest in New Hope Cemetery with a new suit and his top hat, and a plain marble headstone to mark the spot. Everyone in Chattahoochee had loved Max.

Bobby tapped in another bolt. Wonder if anyone besides his own family would miss him once he kicked off? He'd done hours of community work, yet the drunk and disorderly game warden he used to be was the subject of more local lore than his current, clearheaded version.

"That do it, Bobby?" one of his builder buddies asked.

"I'm going to check on the fire ring, make sure we have enough wood. Go on home before your wife stops speaking to you."

"Okay. Later, dude." His friend slapped the dirt from his hands and picked up his toolbox. Bobby watched him walk back to his 4 X 4 Ford, crawl in, and leave.

Bobby stowed his own tools and strolled through the River Landing grounds, checking for stray bolts or nails, anything someone might step on. People would still find original ways to get hurt. Add in a little Jack Daniels and the odds improved. The EMS folks would be on standby, and the local doc too, though the medical tent was little more than a glorified Band-Aid station. Leigh would take a shift later, with their daughter Amelia playing junior nurse.

The fire ring stood near the water, away from trees or structures, with more than enough split oak stacked uphill. Bobby wished they'd ditch the custom, but some on the committee were die-hard pyromaniacs. The whole thing stressed Jake so much, Bobby worried the little dude might go up in smoke himself.

He circled the steel barrier, checking for anything flammable. His crew had done a fine job of sweeping aside deadfall leaves and limbs. He looked up. No overhanging moss or branches to trap sparks. As good a spot as any for a fire.

They wouldn't light it up until after ten when most of the kids and out-of-towners were gone. Times like this, Bobby missed alcohol.

He'd give anything to be able to cop a good buzz and tell fish-tales around a crackling fire. He'd hang around and listen tomorrow evening, insert an occasional lie of his own, but it wasn't the same.

A beer buzz made that wide-mouth bass bending the pole bigger than a bull shark, the woman who gave him a long look hotter than Angela Jolie and Faith Hill gift-wrapped together and tied with a bow. Years ago, in that other disjointed life, Bobby could smoke, scratch, and spit with the best of 'em.

The biggest part of staying sober was figuring out new ways to act in old situations.

Bobby turned to face the river. Adding up the hours he'd spent in his former career and the times he launched one of his own boats in his spare time, he reckoned he'd spent half his life on the Apalachicola River or Lake Seminole. Like most men his age, he could navigate the local waterways blindfolded. As stone drunk as he'd been many times, he might as well have been sightless. Bobby doubted there was any day or night—save during the worst, pissy cold of February—when someone wasn't putting up and down the Apalach.

He watched a big man steer a sixteen-foot bass boat to the landing's floating dock. Sure hate to run up on the likes of that dude in the woods, without a sidearm handy. Fellow needed a bigger boat; he looked like Sasquatch sitting in a teacup.

141

That was a good one. He'd have to share it with Jake later, show him he wasn't the only one who could create what Jake called an "original mental image."

Something about the hulk stirred Bobby's hackles. Once a law man, always a law man. The dude had as much of a right to use the public landing as anyone, and he could—up until early tomorrow morning when the city would rope off the access road. Wasn't that they worried some terrorist might slip in and bomb the festival; they needed the asphalt parking lot for the food truck vendors.

The guy stepped onto the dock, lashed the bow and stern to the steel cleats. He swiveled his head, checking his surroundings. Jumpy, for a big man. Who could *he* be scared of, and why? The giant head pivoted toward the bank where Bobby stood. He noticed Bobby a little too long.

Shoot. All Bobby needed was to get into a throw-down with some-one who looked to outweigh him by a good fifty pounds. Bobby kept himself in fair shape, no gut hanging over the top of his jeans. But this fella's upper arms were big as hams, so much that his arms didn't rest anywhere near his sides. Even from this distance, the blue ink lines and swirls showed on his biceps and upper chest, the part visible above the cut-up flannel shirt.

Bobby thought of a scene in that movie, the one with dueling banjos. *Deliverance.* Yeah, that was the one.

Disengage, Bobby coached himself. He wasn't in law enforcement now. He was a middle-aged fellow with a wife and two kids, and a wonky knee. Bobby tipped his head once, a Southern male gesture for *howdy, how you doin'* and *you go your way, I'll go mine.*

He crossed his arms over his chest, feet planted apart. The man stared a beat longer, enough for Bobby to wonder if any of his crew might still be on the grounds.

Just when Bobby figured he'd have to pray hard, or run as fast as his bum knee would allow, or scream like a girl, the gorilla man tipped his head once.

Bobby breathed in through his nose then out. Adrenaline heated his chest and crept up to burn the tops of his ears. He turned a couple of steps, enough to watch the man without showing territoriality. The dude loped to a black, late-model pick-up, backed to load the boat onto the trailer, then left in a fog of diesel exhaust.

Friday evening

Elvina settled the last kitten next to a makeshift mama-cat fashioned from scraps of furry material—Evelyn Fletcher's artful creation for when Juliet wasn't on duty. The little ones mewled for a couple of minutes before falling to sleep. She smiled. The runt never failed to squirrel his way into the middle of the pack after his belly was full.

Come Monday, she'd cart them by the veterinary clinic to have them checked over and firmly establish their sexes. Two males and two females, from what she could tell comparing information from the internet with their *down-unders*, as Piddie used to call the male/female parts of the anatomy.

The smallest kitten, she called Runt. That name would probably stick since everyone who'd met the tenacious little tabby liked it. Hattie and Sarah's calico was Patches. The other two—a female and a male—she simply referred to as Gray-Stripe and B&W. The new owners could pick their titles later. At the Triple C, Elvina introduced the orphaned family to anyone who walked in and already had potential leads on good homes.

But for the next four weeks, the kitties belonged to her and to Juliet.

She clipped the lead onto the pug's collar. "Time to get our walk. Then you have to go home to your daddies." Juliet balanced on her back legs to lean over the basket's edge. "I know, honey. It's hard to leave, but you have to go to your house at night. Don't fret. I'll take good care of them until you return to duty in the morning."

Elvina gave the lead a slight tug. The dog returned to all fours and followed her to the front door where the pug waited for Elvina to position her headlamp, grab the two hiking poles, and clip the leash onto a carabiner hanging from her belt. The smartphone, she also secured onto the belt, opposite side.

Change dictated change. Elvina could take care of four newborns and a dog, and run a spa, and still take her evening strolls. Planning was the key to life.

She checked her watch. Eleven-thirty. Plenty of time to sweep the usual route and get Juliet home. That Shug Presley was a funny one; he teared up every time he met her and Juliet at the door. Guess there was no way she'd talk him out of ownership. Did dogs have godmothers? If so, Elvina would sign up. At the very least, the two of them could continue their walkabouts. Shug was busy and Jake couldn't go far without pain in that leg. If Elvina didn't take the pug out for a bit of exercise, the stumpy dog would end up being round as a basketball, the way she wolfed down food.

Elvina turned right from her driveway then decided to take the first left. Not her normal course, but she'd heard a new renter had taken up at the old Humphrey's place. Trouble with rental houses: you never knew what sort was moving into the neighborhood. Most didn't stay long, six months to a year, depending on the lease, if there was one. Renters didn't seem to take care of their yards, not these days. Trash left out by the road, hedges and grass gone to weeds, fallen limbs scattered about. Guess when it didn't belong to you, you didn't care as much. Made the whole street look hangdog. Every neighborhood had *that* house.

"No pride these days, sweet Juliet. Simply *no* pride."

Juliet glanced up and answered with a short grunt. The pug stopped every few feet to sniff and pee a couple of drops. How Juliet stored enough water to make it through their route impressed Elvina. If *she* did that, she'd go broke buying toilet paper. Elvina laughed. And they'd lock her up for sure.

Down the block, they drew near the Humphrey's old place. A shotgun house, what they called it; you could fire a bullet through it and never hit a wall. Narrow from side to side, and long, with the front and back doors lined up. The design was considered historic, Elvina had read, but this one was an eyesore.

At night, a bare light bulb illuminated the three porch steps. The azaleas lining the walk and yard were woody and unkempt, and the live oak next to the road looked like something from a horror movie. The owners lived out of state and didn't give a rippety-do-dah, from the looks of things. As long as someone paid enough to cover the property taxes, who cared if the faded paint shucked off in peels and the shutters hung crooked? Pity. Houses needed love as much as people.

"I oughta buy that place and fix it up," Elvina said.

When Elvina halted, Juliet stopped and looked up, her stubbed ears pricked forward. Elvina moved into the shadows with the pug beside her, and watched. A giant man stepped from the front door, stooping to clear the overhead threshold. He took the stairs in one easy leap.

"Lord have mercy," Elvina whispered. She'd seen some big fellows in her time, but this one belonged in the book of records.

He strode to the driveway and crawled into a dark-colored pick-up with a fishing boat hooked behind it. Elvina wondered if he'd even need a pole. The fish would take one look at him and flap into the boat, then die of pure fright.

The engine rumbled. Diesel. Noisy thing. And stinky too. Bet the next-door neighbors hated that. Juliet pulled on the lead and growled. "Shh, honey." Didn't want this man to see them. Doubted the tiny pepper spray hanging from her carabiner would do anything except piss him off. Plus, Elvina wasn't able to haul buggy like she used to.

The truck pulled from the driveway. The boat trailer rolled behind, its safety chains clanging. Elvina picked up Juliet and eased behind a hedge. The truck crept by. She felt the pug tremble. Heck, she was trembling, too.

Seemed as if it took a century for the pick-up to reach the corner and turn. Elvina noted the direction: toward town. Could be headed to the river or the lake.

"Now, why would someone take to the water this time of night, you reckon?" she asked Juliet. She'd bet her bottom dollar he was up to no good.

Elvina waited until she could no longer pick out the sound of the big diesel engine before returning to the road. She set Juliet down.

"Remind me to speak with Chief J.T. about this."

Juliet snorted her reply.

Chapter Nineteen

Saturday, October 17th, early

Jake poured two cups of coffee, added cream and sugar. "Want me to soft scramble some eggs, maybe a slice of toast?" When his partner looked up from his cell phone and shook his head, Jake's chest squeezed. Pronounced shadows circled Shug's eyes.

"What time did you get home last night?" Jake set one of the cups down in front of Shug and rested a hand on his shoulder. "For once, I actually managed a few hours' sleep."

"I'da know. Well after midnight." Shug's voice sounded more wounded than his expression.

"Rough one, eh?"

Shug didn't answer, only stared at the mug in his cupped hands. Jake considered sharing his last few adventures with him, but he'd have to fun it up a bit. Make light of the jolly redneck giant who'd scared him spitless. Anything to see Shug smile. For sure, he wouldn't tell him about the ongoing text warfare.

"I need to go away for a few days." Shug didn't look up.

The lack of emotion in the words sent a chill through Jake. "Okay, so as soon as the festival is over, we can throw some clothes into a bag and whisk off, first thing Sunday morning." Jake slid into the chair at the opposite end of the table and dredged up enough enthusiasm to sound positive. "Maybe Destin? We'll comb the outlet stores together. Walk on the beach." He glanced down at Juliet, who sat at his partner's feet, staring up at Shug as if he was a choice slab of prime rib. "I'll find a hotel that accepts dogs."

"No. Not *us*." He shifted his gaze from his hands to Jake. "Only *me*."

The ground opened up and swallowed Jake's soul.

Shug had found someone else. Had Jake been so busy leading the Parade of Horribles that he failed to notice his own partner's distance?

And why wouldn't Shug want to leave? Poor man might as well *not* have a partner, given the limited time Jake spent with him, especially during festival season. Genevieve was right on one account: they were housemates. Ones that left notes to each other under a refrigerator magnet, or exchanged clipped texts. **Be home late. Don't wait dinner on me.** The **love you** add-ons were automatic and expected, and probably not heartfelt.

If the other sequined pump was going to fall, Jake would push it. Why prolong the agony. "Are you leaving me, Jon?"

Shug's head jerked back. "What? No!" Jake watched Shug comb his hair with fingers that trembled. "It's Genevieve."

Blind fear morphed to blind mad. What had that witchy sister done now?

"She's bad, Jake."

This was a newsbreak? Bad didn't even start to cover it. Jake stuffed down a snarky reply.

"I had a call from Lois last night."

Lois. The baby sister. Jake thought he remembered correctly.

"Gennie's taken a turn. From the sounds of it, she's close to—" Shug's mouth hung open and water gathered in his eyes.

Wow. The man worked with death every day, and he couldn't say the *d* word. "I'm sorry, Shug." No lie. He *was* sorry. Not for Genevieve. For Shug.

"Gennie's been sending me texts nearly every day since she left here," Shug said. "Some days, more than one. Asking me to repent. Telling me how I was going to burn."

The sensation rippling through Jake caused him to suck in air. Why hadn't he seen it? Sure, most of his nasty-grams were vaguely sexual— still figured some numbers-challenged coed had given his name out in a bar—but the others? Some of those numbers weren't from their area code, he recalled. He'd check, but he had deleted most as soon as they came in.

Jake leaned back in his chair. If he could clone himself and sit that clone down next to himself, he'd slap himself silly. He truly had cranked up the Parade of Horribles this time.

Nobody was after him. Not one dang person. He hoped.

"You're going to Alabama, I take it?" Jake asked. "Sure you're ready for that?"

147

"I have to go."

Jake took a sip of coffee to slow his reaction. What was it with family? They could tromp all over you and you were still connected; you'd plant roses by their gravestones and chat like nothing had ever cleaved your soul in half. "You don't *have* to do anything."

Shug stared at him. Those doe-brown eyes. The kindest man Jake had ever known.

"I can't hate Gennie."

He didn't have to. Jake disliked her enough for the both of them. "Oh . . . kay."

"She's being true to who she is, Jake. Don't you see?"

Jake laced his fingers around his mug. Pressed his lips together. Shook his head.

"I am gay. It is who *I* am. As much as Gennie is devout. That is who *she* is."

"Still gave her no right to barge into our lives, into our home, like she did, Shug."

His partner nodded. "You're right. It didn't. And if Gennie were to live to ninety, that would always stand between us." His partner looked at him with eyes so full of sorrow that Jake's chest hurt.

What if Shug got up there and they ganged up on him?

He would change to someone Jake didn't recognize.

Jake envisioned Shug returning to Chattahoochee, ignoring his tears and pleas, packing up clothes, Juliet, and a few personal things not overtly connected to their life together.

Good thing he hadn't completely dismissed the Parade of Horribles. It could well start up again.

Jake reached over and rested his hand over Shug's. No matter what he said, or did, the outcome wasn't up to him. "You'll still go to her? To a family that has shunned you."

"She's my sister."

Saturday, 9 a.m.

Hattie slugged down her coffee. No time to contemplate life. No porch sitting. No guard dogs. She should've been at the River Landing by now, actually a half-hour ago.

"Don't know why Jakey is so insistent that I get there at chicken-thirty," she groused. "People don't flock to our tent until at least eleven."

148

"Have more coffee, Mom." Sarah poured a bowl of granola, added sliced bananas and dried cranberries, then floated it with vanilla soy milk.

Kiddo ate better than Hattie ever had. Sarah Chuntian's first solid English word had been *McDonald's*. She'd screech it the moment she spotted a billboard with those golden arches. As she aged, if given a choice between a French fry and a carrot stick, Sarah chose the latter. Hattie cradled the warm mug in her hands and watched her daughter dig into the cereal. Other than an occasional Big Mac, Sarah shunned typical American fast food.

"You should eat something, Mom."

"Who's the parent here?"

Sarah didn't reply, only pointed to the mantle clock. Hattie snorted out a breath then grabbed cinnamon raisin bagels and cream cheese from the fridge. Minutes later, she joined her daughter at the kitchen table.

The piece of furniture had been the heart of the farmhouse for as long as Hattie could recall. The marred surface told the history of years spent with family: breakfast and supper during the week, and three meals a day on weekends. Tillie Davis would never abide folding aluminum TV trays. No, ma'am. The Davis family ate and discussed life around this simple, pine-plank table. Plenty of room for four, with ample space for another four or five add-ins.

The formal maple dining room table was reserved for Thanksgiving and Christmas. Had to protect it with a linen tablecloth and drag out your best manners. No leaning on elbows. No theatrics. Act right.

Hattie trailed her fingertips across the table's beveled edge. This one, she could pound with a laughter-fist, or slump and cry. Between her family of origin and the one she and Holston had forged, it had soaked up so much drama Hattie imagined it as a living thing.

"Mom?" Sarah's voice jolted her. "Why are you fondling the table?"

A chuckle popped from Hattie, unusual for morning. "I was thinking . . . oh, never mind. You ready to head to the river when you finish your cereal?"

"Sure."

They ate in silence for a beat, until Sarah's spoon clanged against the bottom of the almost empty bowl. She drank the remaining soy milk, using the bowl like an oversized mug.

"Done." Sarah pushed back from the table. "Give me five minutes." She rinsed her bowl and spoon before clattering them into the dishwasher.

Wish I had that kind of energy. Heck, forget five minutes. It'd take Hattie at least fifteen to brush her teeth, do something with her hair, and slip on jeans and a top. Good thing she had packed the portable massage chair and supplies into Bailey last night.

At a quarter 'til ten, Hattie pulled into the grassy parking area reserved for vendors. Maybe if she scurried to the tent and set up fast . . .

"Uh-oh," Sarah said, pointing toward the festival entrance.

Jake crossed the short distance from the admissions booth and met them before Hattie could get unloaded. "Sister-girl, you'll be late to meet St. Peter." He idled by the CR-V's back hatch, tapping his silver-tipped black cane on the ground.

"Chill, Jakey." Hattie handed the supply carryall to Sarah then slid out the massage chair in its case. She swung the strap cross-body, shut the back hatch, and hit the key fob to activate the locks.

"Mom, *chill* and *Unc Jake* do not go together in one sentence." Sarah flashed one of her perfect-teeth grins. Jake pursed his lips, yet nodded agreement. Her daughter could get away with most anything where Jake was concerned.

"Meet me at the booth, baby." Hattie tipped her head in the direction of the vendors. The festival grounds teemed with people. Given a couple of hours, the crowd would quadruple.

Jake watched Sarah walk away then swung his head to refocus on Hattie. "Gah, Sister-girl."

"Don't *gah* me. You know I don't do mornings."

"Not only do you not *do* mornings, you murder them," Jake said. "Your sister has set up her gumbo booth, and Leigh and that sweet little baby doll Amelia have the medic tent up and running." He huffed. "Heck, even Elvina is here. Well, she was. She dashed home to check on Juliet and the kitties, feed the little ones. Then she'll be back."

Hattie felt a flash of guilt. Elvina had to be in her late eighties, with the responsibility of taking care of *her* orphaned cat family.

"Don't go there, Sister-girl."

"What?"

"I saw that look. Elvina is in her element, taking charge. And you're not responsible for everything. If guilt was a drug, you'd need rehab."

"Takes one to know one, they say."

Hattie lifted her nose, testing the air. The usual smell of damp river mud mixed with the faint scent of fresh coffee. Heavenly.

"Stef has her massage table in place," Jake said. "Your brother and nephew have been here since six."

Tempting to reply, *Goodie for all of them*, but Hattie held her lips together. For a moment. "You and Bobby spend so much time together, I'd worry for Shug and Leigh if I didn't know better."

Jake guffawed. She joined him. Most times, she could goad Jake Witherspoon away from a full-flame snit fit.

"Shug coming later?" Hattie asked.

"He's out of town."

She noted the way his face clouded. What was up with this? Hattie opened her mouth to ask, but his eyes warned her silent. Then he resumed his earlier, pleasant expression.

They entered through the makeshift gates Bobby and his crew had constructed the day before. Some people might sneak through the surrounding woods and a few by boat, but most respected the small admission fee and queued up for a ticket.

Jake planned every detail; the numbered tickets doubled as raffle entries. This year, loaded baskets from the Madhatter's Chocolate Shoppe, along with gift certificates donated by local businesses, lined the giveaway table. The grand prize was a queen-sized quilt, hand-pieced by her sister-in-law's sewing circle. Hattie paid for three tickets, not because she had to, but who wouldn't want a chance to win that gorgeous quilt?

"Love that you're helping with the fund-raising, but you might as well save your moolah," Jake commented. "That bed covering is mine, mine, mine."

"You wish." Hattie stopped long enough to shift the case's strap to the opposite shoulder. "You seem like you're in a better mood today."

"I am." His lips lifted on one side, then dropped. "And I'm not."

What was that supposed to mean? She hated it when Jake talked in riddles.

"We'll kvetch later," Jake said before Hattie could pepper him with questions. "For now, get your belated-butt self to your tent and set up." He aimed in the direction of the food trucks. "I'll bring you a monstrous cup of java."

No matter where Jake positioned their massage therapy booth, tantalizing aromas would waft her way. So far, only the coffee and a warm sugary scent—Mary-Esther's beignets? Later, the scent of hot,

151

greasy, blooming onions would drag her to them. Happened every year. Oh, and don't forget the funnel cakes. Jake swore Hattie would eat cow poop if it had powdered sugar dusted on top. He was probably right.

From here, Hattie spotted the peripheral food trucks. Barbeque, burgers, chili, gumbo, gyros! Oh my. Fried *anything* you could dip in batter; if it couldn't be seared in grease in the South, it wasn't worth eating. No small wonder everyone's blood was the consistency of syrup.

Saturday, late afternoon

Jake's cell phone vibrated in his pocket. He paused next to the Pudding & Pastry truck and unclipped it from his belt.

In Ala-damn-bam-er. Will keep you posted. Love you.

Jake *love-you*-ed back. Then he scrolled through the other texts. No nasty-grams. Nothing telling him someone watched or waited.

Around him, his fellow *'Hoochians* ate, sipped tea, soft drinks, and coffee, and shopped. The redneck wind chimes fashioned from flattened beer cans and metal washers were a huge hit again this year.

Folks from surrounding counties mixed with the townspeople. Elvina reported she had met several people from out of state—the farthest, a retired couple, snowbirds from Michigan. Guess they were heading south to escape heavy winter. Who could blame them?

For the first time in weeks, Jake's shoulders relaxed. If it wasn't for the lingering sorrow for what Shug was experiencing—probably a mixture of sadness and the family piling on—he felt peaceful.

Maybe he'd visit the Pet's Haven booth and buy an outfit for Juliet. Something medieval and flowing. Fitting of a Shakespearean star.

Chapter Twenty

Bobby trailed his fingertips along the edges of an oak table Elvina had commissioned for her sunroom. He buffed one ragged spot, felt again.

Between this and the screened gazebo Elvina now wanted, Bobby figured he'd die with a power tool clamped in his rigor-mortised hands, all for the old woman who'd been chewed on by the home improvement bug.

He used a tack cloth to capture the fine, loose filings left by the sander. Ready for the first coat of polyurethane. Best thing: ready to deliver shortly and free up space in his workshop. Yay.

"That dadgum Jake Witherspoon!" he directed to the rug where Stick lay, chewing on a Nyla bone. The hound lifted his head and his tail whumped a reply. "Little dude showed Elvina some magazine spread about functional outdoor living spaces"—he waggled the tack cloth in the air—"and now she's fired up about having an enclosed breezeway leading from the sunroom to the gazebo."

He ran the sticky cloth over the wood twice more. "You'd think having a litter of kittens to nurse might dampen her enthusiasm, but ooooooh-noooo."

"Did you chat with yourself like this back when you used to drink?" a voice behind him said.

Bobby jerked his head toward the opened shop doors. Hattie stood with her hands akimbo, an asinine grin on her face. Captain and Ensign flanked her, tails aloft and wagging. Stick scrabbled to his feet and ambled to greet first Hattie with a hand lick, then the two canines with butt sniffing. Doggie handshakes.

"Sure did. And then some. Did a lot of cussin' to myself back then, too." Bobby stored the sander next to his workbench. "Especially after I fell out on the ground somewhere." He wiped his hands on the rag hanging from his jeans pocket.

Hattie took a couple of steps inside. "That Elvina's?" When he nodded, she added, "Looks good. I should get you to make one for me."

"And put it—?"

"I'd find a bare spot, somewhere." Hattie shrugged. "Maybe not."

"Figured you'd spend the day slung up on your couch, after yesterday. None of us got up until almost ten. Heck, by the time my crew broke down the booths and made sure the fire pit was banked and cool, it was after midnight."

"We all slept in, too. Holston's the one still piled up on the couch. He's wiped out from his trip. But I need to move around a little. Me 'n' the dogs are heading to the pond, to feed the fish. Wanna come?"

"I welcome the break." Bobby dropped the rag onto the bench and slapped his shirt and jeans free of sawdust. "Let me step in and let Leigh know I'm gone, fetch the pistol."

"Gun?"

"Hattie. Think. Know you don't much like fire arms, but we've had two crazy critters in one month. Could be more."

"True." She fell into step beside him. "Sarah went inside with Tank."

"Video games," they said in unison then laughed.

"Why mess up your life by breathing outdoor air and getting exercise?" Hattie commented. "Both of them had *way* too much of that yesterday."

They stopped by the log home long enough for Bobby to check in, and grab the pistol and a couple of soft drinks. He handed one to Hattie as he stepped from the door. Then they walked together up the lane toward the farmhouse.

All three dogs scouted ahead, noses to the ground. Good thing too. The weather hadn't cooled off enough to send the rattlesnakes to ground. Plenty of them out in the piney woods, some as big around as his forearm.

"Rather take the ATV?" Hattie asked.

"Nah. Let's walk."

Passing the chicken yard, Bobby shortened his stride so Hattie could keep up. The Chick Flicks cackled when the dogs gave them

154

drive-by barks. Hendrix charged the fence. The dogs circled back and yapped at the rooster, then caught up to Hattie and Bobby.

A few feet beyond the barn, they entered a grassy, single-lane road between a stand of cultivated slash pines before stepping into a thick hardwood forest where the land had never been timbered. Stick bounded into the woods. Captain and Ensign whined a bit, but stayed near Hattie.

The pines would provide a cash crop in a few years. Still, Bobby preferred the feel of the natural thicket. Some years, given the right blend of rain and cool temperatures, the hickory trees would flash yellow leaves so brilliant they made his breath catch. This wasn't one of those years. A dry and warm fall led to nothing but brown foliage, then barren branches.

Beside him, Hattie kept up a constant line of chatter. Some, she directed at the dogs; some, she aimed at him; some, to who knows. Probably yakking to the trees and calling them by name, a game Hattie and their father came up with years ago.

"And then," Hattie said, "this one really *huge* guy came by the booth. And I mean flippin' massive!"

That snatched his attention. "When was this?"

Hattie plucked a strand of broom sedge as they passed by, snapped off the stalk, and stuck it into her mouth like a long toothpick. "Late, near the end," she said. The straw bobbled with her words.

"Did you get his name?" Bobby asked.

"I'da know." She took a few steps, stopped, her eyebrows scrunched together. "Think I heard him tell Stef. Started with an *R*, I think. Ricky, Randy . . . ?"

Something big crashed through the fallen leaves. Bobby halted and scanned the woods, his hand curling around the pistol butt. A doe leapt from the tree line ahead of them and cleared the lane in one jump. It bounded into the shadows. Stick loped behind the deer, baying. Captain and Ensign dashed for a few feet but returned to scrabble at Hattie's feet. How did his sister garner such blind devotion?

Bobby released his hold on the gun. "That dang hound. Come hunting season, he couldn't scare up a deer if it walked up and tapped him on the behind." Stick's hound yodel echoed, growing fainter.

Hattie ruffled Captain's hair then bent to give Ensign equal time. "I know we have deer all out in these woods, but I hardly ever see one."

Bobby's pulse picked up. Seeing deer did that. Or could it be, he was out of shape? Needed to work out more, maybe jog from his house to the pond and back a few times a day. Easy to grow soft when he didn't make it a point to keep fit. Hated to admit it, but he felt old. He moved ahead. The hell with his heart. It would beat or not.

Hattie caught up. "Did I say something wrong?"

"No."

"Why were you asking about the big guy?"

They crested a small ridge a few feet from a screened, wooden structure. In the valley below, a one-acre fishpond sparkled in the mid-day light. Bobby paused. He loved this spot as much as his father had. Tall hardwoods circled the pond. At the top of the hill, a series of stairs and decks descended the slope to the water's edge. "Think he might be the same dude I spotted at the landing on Friday," Bobby said after he caught his breath.

"Lots of people come and go from there." Hattie led the way down the stairs to the pond. Parallel to the steps, a waterfall cascaded over river boulders. Clearly manmade, but beautiful. The sound of the water sluicing through the rocks lifted Bobby's spirit in ways alcohol or drugs never could.

Hattie picked up a lead pipe next to a rusted barrel and used it to bang one side. Fish dinner bell. She removed the weighted lid, scooped up a can full of commercial catfish food, and flung the pellets into a wide arc over the water. A few ripples showed at first. Then the water boiled with catfish scooping bits of the floating feed into opened, whiskered mouths. No matter how many times Bobby watched this, it still mesmerized him. The catfish fed for a few minutes, until every round pellet disappeared.

"So, did this big dude get a seated massage?" Bobby asked.

Hattie returned the feed can to the barrel and resealed the lid. "Nope. He only asked how much. Then he stood around and watched a few other people get theirs. Kind of creeped me out a little. Stef too."

Bobby followed her up the stairs and back into the screened room. She chose a rocker and he settled into one beside her. He matched Hattie's pace with the rocking chair, as he had during their walk. During the dark times, Bobby had been out of sync with his family, in particular Hattie. Seemed important to mirror her now. He did his best to spend time with Mary-Esther, too, but he had grown up with *this* sister.

Captain and Ensign flopped down on either side of them. "I can see it, years from now. Can you?" Hattie asked.

Bobby waited for his baby sister to continue. Leigh had taught him to listen, when it was important.

Hattie held up her hands, her index fingers and thumbs creating a frame. "Sarah Chuntian and her family, Tank and his . . . even Amelia and hers. One of our kids would have to build another house somewhere, but there's plenty of room out here."

Stick appeared at the screened door with his tongue lolling out one side of his mouth. Good thing the dog always came back. Bobby'd hate to lose him, dumb or not. He let the dog in. The hound nosed Bobby's hand, and Bobby rocked and patted. Multitasking, even in leisure.

"Sarah was so on-task yesterday," Hattie said. "She and Tank both. Helping Jake with errands."

"Jake's good at getting the kids involved."

"For sure." Hattie propped one foot on the chair's crossbeam and used the other foot to push the rocker back and forth, back and forth. "I see flashes of the person she's becoming, between the child and the somewhat annoying teenager. It's going to be okay. We're good now." Hattie sighed. "I feel really peaceful."

Trouble with peace: it came in spurts wedged between chaos. Hattie's blind optimism amused Bobby. She still believed in the spirit of Santa and the tooth fairy, and that politicians served the people, though she had waffled a tad on that recently.

He and Mary-Esther were realists. Happened when a person scraped the bottom then clawed their way back up, one bloody inch at a time.

Given a cup of coffee and time to wake up every morning, Hattie bubbled with positivity. Signs appeared, sent from above. Goodness flowed from everywhere. Guess someone had to believe.

Bobby breathed in the pine-scented air. Easy enough to wrap his mind around peace and positive vibes, seated here in a rocking chair amidst the trees, faithful dogs, and his baby sister. Heck, Hattie didn't give up on him, even when *he* almost had.

His gaze lifted to the tree line above the calm pond. Out *there*, when he factored in the rest of humanity, Bobby found it nearly impossible to believe in goodness and reason.

Peace was the intermission between scenes. Only, nobody handed out a program. Hard to know what act he was in, the influential factors, or the proximity to THE END.

Sunday evening

Elvina settled the calico kitten next to Juliet. The pug talked to the kittens in grunts, a mama dog version of a bedtime story, Elvina figured. Juliet performed the cleaning ritual as she had for the gray tabby and the black and white. Then she nuzzled the calico between the others. Two males, two females, the vet had pronounced when he stopped by the Triple C Friday afternoon. Good of him to make a house call. She'd bake up something and take it by the clinic sometime this week.

So far, so good. Though it had been a juggler's folly between nursing kittens, her front desk duties, and daily visits to chat with Piddie and feed the squirrel brigade. She and Juliet managed with help from Sarah Chuntian, and sometimes Wanda, Mandy, or Stefanie.

Evelyn had cuddled a time or two but worried she'd become too attached, and no, she was *not* going to adopt one, so she said. Piddie once told Elvina that her daughter was far too tenderhearted to own a pet. Evelyn nearly grieved herself to death when one died. Best to let the master seamstress stick to fashion design. It made Evelyn happy and kept the rest of Chattahoochee from an unfortunate encounter with one of her disastrous culinary creations.

In the whelping basket, the runt cried. His tiny round eyes were blue, but Elvina bet they'd turn a different shade in a few days—green would be nice. Gray fur with emerald eyes. She picked him up. Still the smallest of the batch, but by far the most insistent.

The internet articles said some foster parents preferred to sit cross-legged so the nursing kitten could push against one folded leg as it suckled. Heavens above, Elvina couldn't do such. She'd have to call 911 to get help standing up. Instead, she sat in the recliner with a thick, jelly-rolled towel on her lap. Worked just fine.

Tipping her arm at an angle, she held the runt's head elevated and nudged his mouth with the nursing nipple. The bottles and nipples, she sterilized in hot water. The rest was simple: canned kitten formula gently warmed in the microwave then drop-tested on her wrist to make sure she hadn't overdone the heat. The runt latched on, his front paws kneading against the towel. Wasn't the same as Mama, but Elvina hoped she at least approximated the security.

Elvina's chest flushed with warmth. Maternal instinct, at her age? Suppose anything was possible in this life, given enough space to unfold.

She watched the tiny cat feed. Maybe it was selfish to keep the runt. Cats could live upwards to twenty years. Elvina doubted she had that many left. Toward the end, she'd be doing good to take care of herself, bathe and groom, pee and poop, eat: all of the things she and Juliet had to teach the young'uns.

"I'll talk to Hattie," she said in a low voice. "Make her and Holston your godparents." Was that the silliest thing ever? "Meanwhile, you and I will keep good company, Mister R."

Mister R? Elvina gave a head bob. *Perfect.* Mister R would be his new name. If Hattie could have dogs with military ranks, then, by golly, her cat deserved a little respect, too.

In a few minutes, Mister R had downed his ounces. His belly looked like a rounded sweet potato. Elvina held him to her shoulder and tapped gently to expel any trapped air. She kissed him on the head and turned him over to Juliet for his bath and the grunted bedtime story.

Finished dinner with the kids, she texted to Jake. **Will bring Juliet by after our walk.**

No reply. The boy had gotten slack about such. Elvina would fret, if not for the fact Jake looked like death on simmer. Hope he could rest now. Only one more event, the fall carnival, and it didn't require the high level of anxiety. Elvina wondered why Chattahoochee still bothered to have it, but oh my, did she love those Angus beef burgers the Lion's Club grilled. And the cotton candy. Oh, and the caramel apples! Praise be, she still had her own teeth.

"Guess your step-daddy's not going to answer us," she reported to Juliet.

Shug didn't show for the festival. Elvina hadn't the time or brain cells to question Jake about that. Probably work-related. The poor man spent too much time with his patients and precious little at home.

"Oh no." Elvina's spirit tanked. "I hope that's not at the heart of Jake's hangdog face."

Elvina needed answers. Sometimes, it was best not to pry head-on, particularly with matters of the heart. Like any mystery, there was more than one way to ferret the truth.

Jake heard his phone: *Blue Suede Shoes*, an Elvis classic, and the ring-tone for Shug Presley. He pitched the scrub sponge into the tub and dried his hands before swiping the screen.

"Hey, doll," Jake said.

"Hey."

Wow. Did Shug ever sound exhausted. Jake could imagine him pinching the bridge of his nose, the way he did when he hadn't had any rest.

"Sorry I haven't called. It's been . . . Gennie died a couple of hours ago."

"I am *so* sorry." Though he held no fondness for the woman who had caused his partner such pain, he felt Shug's grief. The hope of ever making a relationship work, or at least shift to one less caustic, evaporated as soon as that person died.

"Have y'all made the arrangements yet?" Jake asked.

"No. We'll be meeting with the funeral director in the morning. Probably Tuesday or Wednesday. I'll text you."

"I can come up. I'll leave tomorrow after I finish one last delivery." Jake paused, struck by the fact the order he had to finish in the morning was for a funeral. "I can bring a nice peace lily from us, or silk flowers, so they can be left at her grave."

"Either will be fine, but—"

Jake closed the toilet lid and sat. The smell of bleach, strong, even with the window raised. "But?"

"Best you not come, Jake. Please understand. Things have been . . ."

"I get it. I do." He flipped on the exhaust fan. Wouldn't help either of them if he passed out from bleach fumes and cracked his skull open on the way down.

"I'll stay here for a few more days after the service."

Jake cringed at the thought of more time alone. "Have they . . . been dreadful to you, the others?" He listened to dead air for a beat before asking, "Shug, you there?"

"We'll talk later. Have to go."

"I love—" Jake said as the end-call beep sounded "—you."

He held the phone and stared at Shug's contact directory picture, a face creased with laughter. Jake didn't recall where he'd snapped that photo.

If the other siblings were as adamant as Genevieve, Jake imagined them circling Shug, with interlocking hands. Shug, pacing in the middle like a fox trapped by drooling hounds.

That kind of pressure could break a man.

Jake switched the phone to the text list. Six "hot babe, hook-up" messages. No hate-slinging. He slid the phone onto the towel cabinet and finished scouring the tub before moving to clean the toilet with a brush and flush. He spritzed vinegar water on the mirror and sink, polished the nozzle and controls until the silver reflected light. Cleaning: the one thing that calmed him, no matter the situation.

He toggled the text alert button from silenced to sound, in case Shug texted.

No more Genevieve. No more threats. The others, he could ignore until he had the time and presence of mind to figure it out, or change his number. A hassle, but so was an endless river of texts from horny strangers.

After the fall carnival, he'd contact the service carrier.

Then he'd allow himself the luxury of that nervous breakdown before facing the year-end holiday season.

Jake rinsed and dried his hands, stuck the cell phone in his pocket, and grabbed his cane: today, a drab gray utilitarian walk-aid. No need to squander flash when he wasn't planning on leaving the house. Should go to the shop, get a start on the casket drape and standing sprays for Hildegard James. Rudy had stopped by the admissions table and handed him another roll of cash—fifty dollars this time, mostly ones.

"Nope. Today is *my* day." His voice echoed in the narrow hallway. How empty the house sounded without Shug or Juliet.

The text message alert beeped. He pulled the phone out, swiped the screen.

He is waiting for you.

Unknown caller, blocked number.

Unless Shug's sister had figured a way to get cell service from the great beyond . . .

The floor creaked. He jumped.

Houses settled, particularly old ones like this.

Jake heard the screech of the screened door hinges. Three knocks. He grabbed his chest, sucked in air. Three more sharp raps.

He blew out the breath, chuckled at himself, and walked to the front door. When he opened it, Elvina awaited on the porch. Juliet pranced at her feet.

"What's wrong?" she asked. "You look like all the blood's drained from your face."

Jake held the door ajar. Juliet led the way. The little dog paused for Elvina to unsnap the leash from her belt carabineer, then dashed toward the kitchen.

"Guess I rate top position on her dance card," Jake said. "Want a glass of tea, or maybe water. Guess it's awfully late in the day for tea."

"Water's fine, and let's sit out on the porch and pass a bit of time. It's nice out tonight."

Jake refreshed Juliet's water and filled the food bowl with kibble. He grabbed a tumbler of iced water for Elvina and one for himself as he chatted to Juliet in what he thought of as Olde English. She wagged and licked his hand. Imagine.

"So," Elvina said when he delivered the water. She chose the porch swing and patted the cushion beside her. "Now, tell."

"Just talked to Shug. His sister Genevieve passed away."

"Ah." She took a deep draw from the tumbler. "Not that she made *me* a friend, but I *am* sorry for Shug's loss. I'll pay you to wire some flowers, to honor Shug."

Jake nodded. A car passed, the only manmade noise. A cricket sang near the porch. This was nice. He should sit out here more often, watch the world slide by, without joining the fray.

"Explains why Shug wasn't at the Madhatter's Festival," Elvina said.

"Yes."

"Family's family, I suppose."

The swing's chains complained in rhythm as they swayed forward and back. In the distance, a train whistle blew. The sound made Jake feel nostalgic.

"By the way," Elvina said, "who was that giant fellow I saw leaning over the admissions table yesterday? He seemed a bit intimidating."

"That was Rudy James from out around Sycamore. I'm doing the flowers for his mother's service. He's harmless."

Elvina tapped the water glass with one fingernail. "Miz Hilde. Yes, I read her obit."

Juliet sat at the door, watching from behind the screen. They swung and sipped, quiet for a few minutes before Elvina spoke. "I can take Juliet on back to my house if you'd prefer, since Shug's not home."

"No!" Jake realized the edge to his tone then softened his voice. "I'd rather she be here."

"Alrighty then." Elvina handed him the tumbler and slapped her thighs with her open palms. "Reckon I ought to get on back to the house, check on the kittens."

Jake toe-braked the swing. Elvina stood with a grunt, flipped her headlamp on, and grabbed her hiking sticks. He stood and walked her to the steps.

"Night, 'Vina. Thanks for everything."

"Night, dear." She glanced toward the screened door. "I bid you goodnight until the morrow, sweet Juliet." Then back to Jake, "Don't know what I would've done without her help. The kittens are thriving under her watch. Plus, I don't have to wash cat butts ten times a day. For that, I am greatly indebted."

The old woman descended the three stairs and then turned around. "Occurs to me, Jake. That big fella, one you said was Hildegard's son? If memory serves me, he did some hard prison time."

Chapter Twenty-one

Monday, October 19th, early afternoon

Jake stepped back from his worktable. No matter how often he fiddled with flowers, no matter how diminutive or massive the arrangement, the wonder settled over him. *This must be how an artist feels, facing a blank canvas, paints at the ready.* The image in his mind's eye would unfold in front of him. Given two competent hands, his muses, and quality natural materials, Jake could create a unified piece. The flowers would wilt and die. Everything did, fact of life. But, for a few hours, his artistry would live.

Stripped of spare foliage and thorns, the flowers rested in their buckets. It was an orderly process: cut the ends at an angle, let them drink at room temperature for a couple of hours, and then put them to rest in a darkened cooler overnight.

The specialized holder serving as a base for the full casket drape, the casket saddle, rested on the worktable. Lashed to the saddle's center, a block of water-saturated floral foam awaited its role of keeping the flowers supported and alive. Floral netting surrounded the foam.

Jake placed leatherleaf ferns pretty-side up around the base. He plugged in more fern, clipped in varied lengths, until the saddle wore its green disguise. Next, he inserted the larger blooms. As Jake worked, he bobbed around the worktable in what he and Jolene called "the dance."

If Miz Hilde was here, whispering over his shoulder, what would she ask for? He thought of the diminutive lady and wondered if Rudy would have her laid out in the same rose-printed dress with the thin red belt. Hope he didn't put her in something somber. Based on the times Jake had seen Hildegard, such would not be fitting.

The clothing wasn't his call, but Jake could do right by her with this casket drape, a full-lid arrangement used when the family planned a closed coffin and no viewing. Why had Rudy James opted for no visitation, only a graveside service? His mother's wishes, or his? No matter; Jake would give Rudy what he paid for and then some.

He circled the table, spacing pink and red roses, snapdragons, and bells of Ireland around plump white hydrangeas, building the arrangement to a mound with a peak no more than eighteen inches. Any taller, and the drape wouldn't fit atop the casket when the hearse transported it to the cemetery.

A few white lilies. *Not* stargazer lilies. He wrinkled his nose, thinking of their sharp scent. Sure, they would've provided a stunning splash of hot pink, but Jake disliked them as much as he did baby's breath sprays, for different reasons. Unless a customer specifically asked for stargazers, Jake avoided bringing them into his shop. So many other beautiful blooms were available, without smelling, at least to Jake, like stale cat urine.

Rudy had once been Miz Hilde's baby son. Hard to think of that large man as anyone's infant. Easy to think of Miz Hilde as a mother. Such a sweet, smiling, compassionate woman.

Nothing like Betsy Lou Witherspoon. His mother only smiled if some bauble cost more than what most people made in a year.

Jake had arranged his mother's funeral drape, those many years ago. Home from New York, for the first time since Betsy Lou *suggested* that he live elsewhere. The former owner of this shop had allowed Jake to order the flowers and create his mother's final floral tribute. His mother believed in an open-casket viewing and was as adamant as Elvina Houston about attending others' visitations and funerals, as if they were social soirées. Betsy Lou's would be no less grand and no less costly. No matter how much her son had to scrape together to pay off the debts.

He had saved a smidge, doing the flowers himself. Good thing he had worked in a florist shop in New York to put himself through school.

Jake smiled, recalling that casket drape. Nowadays, people might refer to his combination of flowers as a "riot of color." In honor of Betsy Lou's passion, the drape had consisted primarily of roses in every shade Jake could obtain. People whispered behind their hands about the wild mishmash, shocking for that time, in a small, Deep South town. Of course, Jake's choice made sense. Betsy Lou Witherspoon had been blind to colors, though she would never admit such. Why would her final floral statement be matchy-matchy?

"Don't worry, Mother. I won't make Miz Hilde's more spectacular than yours were."

His phone vibrated. He wiped his hands and picked it up.

Gennie' s service set for Wednesday. The remainder of the message provided the basic information: time, place, and name of the mortuary. No *I love you*. Nothing personal. Hope they weren't slathering Shug with guilt.

Ok, he tapped. **I'll take care of ordering our flowers.** Jake hesitated then added, **Assume it's all right for my name to be on the card?**

Sure.

Jake waited. When no more texts appeared, he moved to the computer, pulled up the search for affiliated florists near Genevieve's address, and started an order.

Well, shoot. He walked back to the workstation, grabbed up the phone, and texted, **Any color in particular?**

Her suit is gray with yellow trim. So yellow is ok.

He idled for a moment, hoping for another text. None came. He lay the phone down and returned to the computer. Jake completed the transaction, hit *place order*. He would've guessed Genevieve's chosen shade to be more aggressive and less cheerful. Red perhaps. A power color. Her matching Vera Bradley luggage had been the color of dried blood, with paisley.

On the way back to his workstation, he grabbed a cola from the refrigerator. Needed to caffeine up. Still two standing sprays to make before delivering Miz Hilde's flowers to Joe Burns. The funeral director would take it from there. Given a pinch of luck, Jake would only have to see Rugged Rudy a few more times when, and if, he paid off the balance due.

A phone vibrated. Good, Shug must be free to communicate now. Something more personal. Jake's cell phone rested on his worktable beside scattered stem shards. *Hmm. Nothing in the queue.* The buzzing continued. He traced the sound to Jolene's bench, where he spotted Hattie's phone. Typical. Sister-girl was forever misplacing her device. Good thing it alerted or she'd be in a high rolling boil when she came out from her massage session. He'd have to stop what he was doing, no matter how important, and help her rummage.

Jake walked Hattie's cell phone over to her side of the business, past the chocolate shop's glass display shelves, and placed it on the small table near her treatment room door so she would see it first thing. No muss, no fuss. Then he returned to his workbench and resumed the flower fandango.

He glanced at the wall clock. Quarter 'til twelve. Hattie would finish the massage soon. The text was probably Sarah Chuntian checking in. Early release day. Jake knew Hattie's family schedule better than she did, most days.

Hattie exited the treatment room and closed the door with a soft snick. She felt the subtle buzz of endorphins: a bonus massage therapists shared with their clients. Practicing a healing art had its rewards.

She spotted her cell phone on the pedestal table. Didn't recall laying it there, but okay. The missed call icon appeared on the black screen, faded, appeared again. Probably a client requesting an appointment. She moved to the small restroom to wash the massage oil from her hands. Hattie picked up the cell phone and walked into the Dragonfly Florist side of the business to retrieve a container of water from the shared refrigerator. No plastic bottles. Sarah Chuntian preached about swollen landfills to her and Holston so often, Hattie wouldn't dream of purchasing bottled water. Parents were *so* trainable.

"Your phone has been driving me nutso," Jake commented when she stopped beside his worktable.

"Some days, I rue ever owning one. *It* can wait." She took a deep drink and wiped her mouth with the back of one hand. "Hey, that's pretty. I love all the pink."

Hattie checked the time. Sarah would be at the library by now, her version of Nirvana. Take Sarah, add books, and time stood still. Then her daughter would be off to the Triple C for kitten duty, her idea of bliss beyond books. One more client, then Hattie would swing by and pick her up.

At least she and Holston didn't have to worry about their daughter becoming bored and *harvesting trouble*, as Mr. D used to put it. Hattie set down the water container and checked the text messages.

Holston. **Elvina gave me some fresh grouper filets, so I'll grill them for dinner. XXX!**

Good. There was stuff for a salad in the fridge. Add a packet of brown and wild rice. Instant meal. She tapped in a reply: **Super. See you in a bit. XXX back at you.**

The next text came from a number she didn't recognize. **Hattie. J.T. here. Trying to reach you. Come by the station ASAP.** Hattie checked the missed call list. Same number.

The Dragonfly's business phone rang. Jake moved to answer it. He spoke a few words then looked at Hattie. "Sister-girl, you need to go to the police station. Now! Something's happened with Sarah."

Hattie's mouth went dry. She retraced steps to her side of the business and grabbed her purse. She scurried past the Madhatter's Chocolate Shop counters and hesitated by Jake. "Can you dismiss my client? Tell her to drop a check by later . . . or—"

"Go. I'll take care of things here. Who's your one o'clock?"

"Um . . . " Hattie searched her memory. "Sheila Burns."

"I'll get in touch with her, tell her not to come, and that you'll call her to reschedule. Now go!" Jake pointed to the door. "Call me later," he said as she dashed off.

If not for that ASAP, Hattie could walk to the station in less than five minutes. She reached Bailey and touched the handle. It beeped twice and unlocked. So glad she didn't have to fumble for keys, thanks to keyless remote.

When she entered the City of Chattahoochee Police Station, the officer behind the front desk glanced up. Hattie recognized him. Most of the local officers came to either her or Stefanie for massage therapy. Between crawling in and out of squad cars, sitting, and wearing heavy gun belts, most eventually suffered back pain.

"Hey, Hattie. Go on back. Last room on the right. Tank and your daughter are with the Chief. Your brother and Holston are on the way."

Hattie's pulse skipped. What the heck? The officer hit a button and the lock released with a loud buzz. She opened the heavy door and started down the narrow hallway. Was this the call every parent feared? What could be so bad that Sarah and her cousin had ended up with the freaking Chief of Police? Drugs? Criminal mischief?

The door buzzed behind her. She turned to see Holston step past the threshold. She hung back long enough for her husband to catch up. "Any clue what this is about?" she asked.

Holston shook his head. "J.T. called the Triple C, and Elvina came and got me on the phone." They moved toward the rear of the station.

The plastic sign read *Conference Room*. Holston opened the door and allowed Hattie to step in first. Sarah sat next to Tank, across the long metal table from the Chief. As soon as Sarah spotted Hattie, she jumped to her feet and rushed toward them.

"Oooph!" Hattie released a huff of breath when her daughter body-slammed into her. Holston wrapped his arms around both of them.

Hattie disengaged from the embrace and held Sarah at arm's length. She looked her daughter up and down. Nothing bruised or bleeding. Nothing obviously broken.

"Mom, I—"

Bobby appeared at the door. "What the Sam Hill is going on?" He moved past them to stand next to his son. Tank looked at his father, his eyes wide.

Chief Mathers stood, motioned to the chairs lining the table. "Why don't we all sit down."

Chapter Twenty-two

Monday, midafternoon

"Take especially good care of these," Jake said to the funeral director. Joe Burns slid the casket drape from the delivery van and centered it on a rolling cart.

"This has to be the most dramatic drape I've ever seen, short of the one you did for your own mother, of course," the funeral director said. "Didn't realize you and Mrs. James were well acquainted, but I'll be extra watchful of them." He tilted his head with a questioning expression. "Don't I *always* take care of your masterful arrangements, Jake?"

"You do, Joe." The funeral director took as much pride in his services for the deceased as Jake did with the floral tributes. "Pay no mind to my senseless prattle, today."

Joe pushed the cart toward the mortuary's delivery door. Jake grabbed his cane and one of the standing sprays and followed him inside. The funeral director set the drape on a long counter then reached for the other arrangement. "This everything?"

"One more upright and two dish gardens." Jake led the way back to the van where he and Joe Burns retrieved the rest of Hildegarde James' flowers.

Not many floral tributes, given that she was a local. Nowadays, many people opted for charitable contributions in lieu of plants. In times past, Jake might make three hauls to deliver the abundance. He wasn't the only florist in close range of the small community Hildegarde had called home. Many in that area used a lady in nearby Quincy. Hope Hildegarde had more flowers show up at the service. To Jake, they eased the harshness of death.

A few minutes later, after sharing a cup of coffee with Joe, Jake checked his phone before starting the delivery van engine. No hate lines. Thank goodness. A few usual text messages about how *hot* he was—old news, now—but still not one peep from Hattie. Whatever Sarah Chuntian had gotten her sweet little self into must be sending his best friend into orbit. Hattie had a tendency to assume radio blackout mode when she was really pissed or sad.

Jake stopped by a convenience store to grab a cola. What could a little more caffeine hurt? He texted Jolene at the shop then drove toward River Landing Road. He parked the van near the park and walked the short distance to the Old Victory Bridge. Might have been better to swap the delivery van for Pearl. The little gray truck would better blend with the scattering of pick-ups and boat trailers. If a patrol car passed by, which he doubted would happen in mid-afternoon, the Dragonfly Florist van would stick out like a drag queen in a cathedral.

Let them come after him. So what? He'd pay the fine for trespassing. For now, he needed a little peace of mind.

Jake understood why they'd fenced off the shattered bridge. Sure would be more convenient for him not to scale a six-foot fence, dragging a bum leg like a lead ballast. He stopped, eyed the padlock suspended from its rusty chain. If he could ferret who was in charge of the key, he might offer free flowers for life, or chocolate. They could trust him to secure the gate, and he'd protect their little shared arrangement. A lifetime of living as a gay man in the straight South had taught him how to keep a confidence.

He hooked the crooked cane handle across the crest of the fence then scrabbled up, careful to lead with his good leg. As soon as he swung over, he transferred the cane to his side of the span. On the way down, a jagged snip of wire caught his pants and suspended him for a moment. He jerked his leg. The wire let go, ripping a gash in the material. He landed on the concrete with a thud and grabbed the fence mesh to regain his balance.

"Well, crapola!" He inspected the tear. His favorite pair of khaki pants, ruined. Close to the inseam, inner thigh. A few inches higher and the rusted wire would've snagged more than cloth, and something far worse than his bad leg would be throbbing. Guess he should be thankful for small graces; the thought of a tetanus shot for torn testicles made him cringe.

Jake retrieved the cane and followed the familiar curving path to the bridge's end. Across the river, a stand of willows concealed all but one corner of the severed cement where the bridge resumed on the Jackson County side. Was that span accessible? Odd, Jake had never questioned that. From here, he could sense the other side, yet not see it clearly. What would he think if he stood on that side, looking back to this section? Remorse? Longing?

Sort of like death, crossing over.

Jake leaned against the chain-link span that blocked the bridge's severed end, felt it give a little. He shifted his weight back. Should never tempt the devil. That grim reaper would as soon allow the metal to release its hold and send him flailing toward the muddy Apalachicola. He was able to swim short distances, and had in Hattie's pool. Could he stay afloat in the swirling current?

Given one useless leg and questionable upper body strength, added to the drag of clothing, Jake doubted he could keep his head above water long enough to battle to the shallows farther downstream.

At least he wouldn't die alone. Plenty of mud cats and bream to witness his spinning corpse.

Jake shuddered. What in the pluperfect hell was *up* with him? Just because some nutcases cyber-stalked him; just because his partner was miles away, in the clutches of a judgmental family; just because he still carted around an envelope bearing his attacker's name; or because his best friend was in a snit-fire, and some behemoth man was burying his mama . . .

Forget the Parade of Horribles. Jake had himself a Fleet of Horribles.

If only pot was legal. And he smoked.

He'd tried marijuana once. The night after he graduated high school. *That* didn't turn out well.

Part of that evening had been wrapped in the happy oblivion only an eighteen-year-old could muster. The majority of his middle school and high school career had seriously sucked. Not the academics—he could ace a test with one glance at a textbook. Jake inherited his late father's near-photographic memory, from what Betsy Lou told him.

The social aspects sent Jake into the separate holding pen, along-side the other misfits and nerds. Back then, nerd was not a fashionable label. Add being an effeminate nerd from an eccentric, moneyed family, and Jake slid to the bottom of the sludge pile.

Even then, Jake didn't feel as if he was a deviant. He was who he was. Many others didn't share his opinion. Except for Hattie. She looked beyond his swish and peacock bravado, and saw the sensitive, often forlorn, Jake Witherspoon.

He closed his eyes and tilted his head to smell the tang lifting from the damp river willows. Some memories stood out in full sensory detail.

●●●

After the graduation ceremony, Jake stands amidst the swirl of his classmates. The football jocks still wear their mortarboard caps, tassels swinging as they swagger and slug each other in their pumped biceps. Other guys tug at ties and group with their families. Girls preen, gesturing toward the males, planning and whispering. In nine months, someone will probably end up with more than a diploma to mark this occasion.

Jake searches for Hattie and finds her across the parking lot, exchanging hugs with her mother and father and Aunt Piddie. Elvina Houston stands nearby, beaming as if her own daughter had walked the aisle. Hattie's butthole brother isn't around; probably already swilling brewskies with his clan of jailbird wannabes.

Jake pivots his head. Betsy Lou's Lincoln sits in the same spot where he'd escaped from her clutches an hour ago. She is inside the gym, wallowing in the fact her son graduated in the top ten percent. Not a huge deal, considering the class numbers less than a hundred students. *He'll be a doctor or lawyer*, Jake overheard her bragging to a crony before he slipped from the gymnasium.

Jake jogs to the car and searches the glovebox for a scrap of paper and a pen. *With Hattie. Home later. Before two.*

That will keep her happy. She has granted him the extra time beyond the customary, acceptable, midnight curfew. As long as he doesn't get arrested or bother her beauty sleep, he can do as he pleases for two sweet hours past normal.

Hattie appears beside him. She jiggles car keys in front of his face. "Got the Ford."

Jake snaps the Lincoln's wiper blade over his folded note. He peels off his gown and pitches it into the back seat. The cap, he casts like a Frisbee. It bounces off the rear window and lands belly up on the crumpled gown.

"Let's ride, Clyde," Hattie says and dashes off. Jake runs behind her. She's been the leader since they could both toddle. They crawl into the Davis family's sedan and pull away from the gymnasium parking lot ahead of many others. Hattie floors it.

"Where're we going?" Jake rolls down the window. Late spring air pushes inside. This is what freedom feels like.

"Lost Landing."

Jake cranks up the radio, beats out a rhythm on the dash. "Good thinking, Sister-girl. Miles from nowhere, USA. Dead in the middle of the woods."

"Big bonfire party. You'll see." She glances from the road for an instant. "Don't worry, Jakey. You are with *me.*"

Maybe they'll all be lit and will lay off the queer-boy jokes. No matter, really. Other than Hattie, whom he plans to keep for life, the others can all go piss up a rope for all he cares. College lies ahead. Florida State University! New faces. A chance to be the Jake Witherspoon he wants to be. Needs to be.

Twenty minutes of winding, narrow county roads lead them to a clearing on Honna Lake, a tiny off-jet of Lake Seminole. More a glorified mud hole than an actual landing, it's been home to countless all-nighters, plus fifty gazillion mosquitoes and more snakes and gators than Jake wants to consider.

So what if he's swallowed by a gator longer than he is tall? What a monumental way to perish. He'd be a local legend, like the parties next to this spot. Hey, he could be the Ghost of Lost Landing.

Hattie parks between two trees and kills the engine. "I promised Dan and Tillie I wouldn't drink and drive. So, knock yourself out."

Jake smiles, loving the way Hattie refers to her parents by their first names. Not to their faces, never to their faces! Fat chance he will get snookered, but stranger things have happened. He never gets to imbibe more than a few purloined sips of Betsy Lou's bourbon. Tonight could be epic.

No food and three beers later, Jake is buzzed. He glances around the fire-lit faces. Most of them he has known since birth. Have to feel a smidge of affection on that account. Where has Sister-girl gotten herself off to?

Someone hands him a lit joint. He stares at the thin plume of sweet smoke curling from its tip.

"Take it or pass it!" a male voice somewhere in the circle calls out.

●●●

Jake opened his eyes. *Take it or pass it.* For years, and still when a situation calls for a snap decision, Jake pulls out that phrase. What if he had passed it on without taking a hit, those years back?

The party details blur in his memory. Fragments remain. How that inhalation scalded his lungs. His body relaxed, yet his skin felt as if it was on hyper drive. He loved everyone. They loved him. Hattie's face swam into focus. Bags of cookies made the rounds, Oreos maybe? He can almost hear the echo of boisterous laughter, but can't bring to mind the tall tales circulating like the booze and pot.

Marshmallows. There were marshmallows. Toasted over hot embers. Thick, gooey yum. Had he eaten one since that night? No. Nor had he touched any more illegal drugs.

Near the opposite shore, a boat motor sputtered to life. Thoughts of that distant party dissipated. Jake watched the man steer the vessel downstream. A gentle whir took the place of the gas two-stroke's rumble. The angler stood and cast his line toward the deep banks shadowed by the willows' canopy. Probably working the electric trolling motor with a foot control.

The image of his mother popped into his mind's eye, clear as if he'd tuned into a cable TV movie. Her hair pulled back tight by a yellow clip. A sheen of cold cream on her face. Hands propped on hips. Pink chenille robe and purple fuzzy slippers.

●●●

Beneath the gooey gloss, his mother's face flushes. She racks up the charges against him: drinking, late, stinking of wood smoke and god-knows-what-else. Did he have sex with some whore, too?

"I may be sloshed, Mother." Jake falls backward onto his bed, still clothed. "At least you don't *ever* have to worry about me getting a girl pregnant. Cause *I* am"—he swishes his arms as if he's making a sheet version of a snow angel—"gay!" He bounces up, wobbles. "Queer. Faggot. Light in the loafers!"

●●●

Jake chuckled. He had never shared details of his fall from Betsy Lou's good graces with anyone, not his best friend or Shug. If Hattie was standing here now, he'd tell her about that scene. Even Bobby—

he'd tell him. It was sit-com material. The one and only time he'd heard Betsy Lou say the F word.

Nobody had witnessed the moment his life pivoted. Only one person besides his mother saw him the next morning. Actress, with her tears drawing lines on her brown, ashen face, didn't have a chance to wrap any cookies in a napkin this time.

Betsy Lou had handed him an envelope of money and told him to "get the hell out of her house."

Jake tapped his pants pocket and heard the crinkle of paper. Envelopes seemed to be an intricate part of *then*, and *now*.

Bet this one didn't contain cash.

Chapter Twenty-three

Bobby stood with his hands propped on his hips, appraising Elvina's back yard.

"Get right on it," Elvina had driven that boat of a car all the way out to his house to tell him, earlier in the morning. "I have a deadline on this, Bobby." She had tried her best to draw him into conversation about the police incident, but he managed to dodge.

Was *this* house going to turn into a never-ending project? Sure seemed as if it was heading that way. Reminded him of the stories he'd heard about that haunted Winchester Mystery House, out in California, where the convoluted construction went on for years, reportedly to keep the Native American spirits appeased, or some such. Who was Elvina soothing, the ghosts of people she had gossiped about? One thing for certain, she'd eventually run out of lot space.

Good as anything to take his mind off the events of yesterday. How he had hoped his own kids would never have any dealings with the dark side, or with anything involving law enforcement. Dash that dream.

He'd built a sunroom for a dadgum alley cat, why not a complex for a kitten, two perhaps? Elvina considered keeping not only the runt, but maybe the other gray tabby as well. She'd even mentioned fostering needy cats for the local vet. Elvina Houston was well on her way to becoming that strange, old, cat lady. He, Bobby Davis, was that strange, old, cat lady's master builder. So be it.

Might not be able to ride herd over his teenaged son but Bobby could tame wood, nails, and glass. He had the specs for this project in his mind. Like Mr. D, Bobby didn't require a set of blueprints. One basic outline sketched on a scrap of paper was all he needed. The rest, his mind stored in a way he could never explain to others. Elvina's gazebo and breezeway already existed; his job was to bring it to life. Suppose that was the way Jake felt when he converted flowers and a handful of ferns into something beautiful.

Believe it then build it, his daddy had often said.

If not for a talent for construction, Bobby wondered if he would've managed to maintain sobriety. Slamming nails into a pine two-by-four vented more stress than a case of Jack Daniels Black, without the hangover, apologies, and guilt.

Preparing the groundwork: the first task. A solid, level base was the key. Get that whopper-jawed and the whole structure was set up for failure. Corners wouldn't be square, gaps would appear like gunshot holes, and worse, the structure wouldn't last. Bobby liked to think something he had a part in would still stand strong, years after they planted him in his final piece of graveyard real estate.

Better get to it. Dirt ain't gonna move itself.

He took a quick *before* photo with his phone and messaged it to Elvina. That woman was a fool for documentation, said she had to scrapbook the stages of her home improvement. Already had one binder half-filled in the sunroom, laying on the table he'd just delivered.

Bobby chuckled and took a cheesy selfie standing in front of the garden tractor. Might as well get his ugly mug in that book, too.

He slid into the seat of the tractor, cranked the engine. Once in position, he lowered the earthmover blade and moved forward. The first slab of grass and topsoil curled into a green and brown jellyroll. His movements were so automatic they didn't stop his tired brain from mulling over the previous day's drama.

He and Leigh had talked about their son's role late into the night. She felt the same way he did: proud and upset at once. Tank had backed up his girl cousin, helped to keep both of them from certain abduction by that sick sombitch. Felt wrong, punishing his son for bravery. What Tank lacked was judgment, the ability to see the possible coincidences, to ferret the boogers behind the bush well before they popped out to snatch you.

Bobby hadn't had a lick of good sense at Tank's age. Surprising that he'd made it past adolescence and his twenties. The thirties and forties hadn't been stellar either, not until he dried up his booze-soggy brain.

But he had to be the father in this situation, stand tall. His daughter Amelia was soaking it all in, watching her big brother's actions and reactions. Bobby backed up the tractor, culled another piece of ground free of sod. One day, that precious little girl, his heart of hearts, would be Tank's age. Lord help him. How would he keep Amelia safe in this scary world?

Family pictures lined every wall of their log home. In the future, Bobby might look back at that project and be as proud and satisfied as he was of his buildings and hand-tooled furniture. Too bad his own parents hadn't lived long enough to see Bobby make the turn, in the end. He glanced skyward. Hope they watched now.

He and Leigh had a son and a daughter to raise and keep from killing their fool selves. Babies were easy. Nobody had prepared either one of them for the stages to come after diapers and midnight feedings. And no book could possibly cover every angle.

Tuesday afternoon

Hattie steered the ATV around a pine seedling, jotted a mental note: bring a shovel and move that little volunteer tree somewhere other than the middle of the road. Beside her, Sarah Chuntian sat—silent, eyes straight ahead, and arms crossed.

Riding with your disgruntled mother for a talk: a teenager's version of walking the Green Mile. Nobody was going to kill her, but Hattie was certain Sarah felt as if someone were. Hattie could recall feeling the same.

Big difference between then and now. Hattie's infractions had been minor, not nearly as life-threatening as Tank and Sarah's latest misadventure. Hattie's stomach roiled, thinking of all the possible outcomes.

Captain and Ensign galloped on either side of the vehicle, alternating between noses-up, noses-down. The scent of deer and wild creatures had to be alluring, but their guard duties trumped pleasure tracking.

Hattie reviewed the two pieces of solid parenting advice passed down from her parents. First, after the immediate threat passes, take a moment to calm down. Approach the problem with a reasonable mind, not one pumped by adrenaline and fear. Second, let the child "pick his or her own switch." The punishment for wrongdoing meant more when the kid had input. Hattie had seen this principle work with Sarah as soon as her daughter was old enough to use reason. Actions, no matter how well-intentioned, produced consequences.

Holston and Sarah had discussed Monday's events later in that day, after they returned to the Hill. Beyond the official statements, the Chief's advice, and the what-happens-now. Florida Department of Law Enforcement would step in, possibly the federal officials. What Jake would call *one hot and hairy mess*.

They reached the gazebo and Hattie parked the ATV. "C'mon, honey." She slid from the driver's side and started toward the building. When Sarah didn't move, she added, "I didn't bring you down here to drown you in the pond, so relax."

Sarah swung her legs from the ATV, stood, and shuffled toward Hattie. *Get used to this*, Hattie told herself. *Drama squared times ten equals teenaged girl.* No matter that Sarah started out more mature than most kids; she still had to navigate raging hormones and the shift from adolescent to adult.

Hattie entered the gazebo, chose one rocker, and pointed to the one next to her before Sarah had a chance to distance herself. The dogs settled into their respective positions. Wonder how Bobby and Leigh were handling things with Tank? Tank's kid sister would have a ring-side seat, maybe pick up clues on what *not* to do when she got older: the second child advantage.

"So, let's talk about yesterday." Hattie pushed the rocker into a gentle back and forth.

"I told it all, with Chief Mathers." Sarah slumped into the chair.

"No matter. I need to understand exactly *how* it went down. Start at point A. Take me all the way to point Z." Hattie held up two fingers as if she physically measured the event chain. "Help me understand why, what, when, and how." She focused attention on the far side of the pond. "Pretend I am *not* your mother."

Sarah sat up a little straighter. "The project for school is where it started." She hesitated. "Sort of." She slouched back into the rocker.

A cool breeze lifted the leaves and sent ripples across the water's surface. Hattie sniffed the air. Could it be, finally, a hint of fall?

"The teacher gave us a list of topics. I didn't like any of them. Dull. So I asked permission to invent one of my own."

Of course she had.

"I decided to write about cybercrime and kids." Sarah shifted to look at Hattie. "I did a ton of research about online predators."

Questions bounced around in Hattie's mind. She forced herself to keep her lips zipped.

"About the same time, Tank and I started to play this online game, where you—"

Hattie held up a hand. "Whoa, Nellie. Remember, this is the un-computer-whiz you are talking to. Still *not* your mother, but leave out the techie parts, please."

Sarah flashed a quick eye-roll. Since Hattie was pretending to be the not-mother, she let the gesture pass. For now.

"There was this one player—greatguy14. He showed up most times we were online. He was really good. Sometimes he even smoked Tank, and Tank is better than me."

Her daughter turned back to face the pond. "It was so wicked to play against him. We, me 'n' Tank, set up times when he'd meet us online. Then we started to team with him instead of play against each other."

Step one: establish trust. Hattie's neck hairs prickled.

"After a while, couple of days maybe, he asked if we were on Facebook. We said yes." Sarah flicked a quick glance toward Hattie. "I mean, what was wrong with that? Not like we were inviting him into our house."

Oh, but you were, my sweet girl. You were.

"Tank friended him first. His name, at least what he told us, was Gerund. I friended him after Tank. Gerund had a few friends on Facebook, not many. Said his dad was strict and that he hadn't been on there long."

Yet he could play online games. Huh. Hattie tamped down her need to interject adult reasoning. Sarah seemed mature, and was for her age, but she still harbored childlike innocence.

Captain nudged Hattie's hand and she scratched the fur around his ears. Ensign propped his front paws on Sarah's legs, eyes pleading. She stopped rocking and picked up the small dog. Ensign settled, content, into Sarah's lap.

"So Gerund, he started messaging us, mostly me. He *said* he was fourteen, from Pensacola, and was a huge FSU fan. Said his mom and dad both went to college there."

Easy to figure that one out, you pervert. All you had to do was take note of the online pictures of her in Florida State garb. Working the familiar.

"I sort of started to tell him stuff."

"Stuff? What kind of stuff?" *Easy, Hattie. Remember, not the mother.*

"About Chattahoochee, what I liked in school, things like that. I told him about shooting the raccoon, and about the fishpond, about the kittens. He liked a lot of the same things."

No doubt.

"When I got in trouble for leaving Olivia's house, I told him about it and he was, like, *oh man, I am so sorry* and how it wasn't fair to someone like me, who was old enough to think for myself, and how I didn't do anything wrong."

Hattie wanted to scream. She chewed the inside of her cheek.

"He knew I liked the library. A lot. He did, too. He practically *lived* at the library when he wasn't at school."

Sarah rocked, silent for a couple of minutes. Hattie took note of the tears gathering in her daughter's eyes, the way her nose had grown red at the tip. *Of course. This guy was her first real crush, and she's hurting.* The deception added to the pain. Hattie wished she could charge into the jail cell where they held that sick creep, wrap her hands around his neck and squeeze until . . . She forced herself to take a deep breath and release it in a slow stream.

"On Sunday, I mentioned about how Monday was an early release day, and how I was so excited 'cause I could spend extra time at the library before going to help Miz Elvina with the kittens." She held up a finger. "He liked cats, too. Has three. Used to have a dog, but it died and that made him really sad."

Probably would've claimed he owned a pack of pythons, if Sarah said she adored snakes. *Step two: draw the person to you.*

Hattie drummed her fingers on the rocker's arm to tamp down the rising anger. "How did you figure things out?" Rushing the subject, but . . . Sarah was usually on task, unlike Hattie. Jake often claimed Hattie could lead him around for hours before centering on the point.

Sarah shrugged then hugged her arms to her. Ensign whimpered and licked her hands. "Something felt weird."

"How?"

"Like, how he *loved* everything I did. Food, school, pink. Didn't matter. And if I said I hated it, he did too. Couple of times, I loved then hated, and he switched it up."

Intuition. Maybe the kiddo will be okay.

"I looked close at the pictures he had posted online," Sarah continued. "Not many, less than ten. There were only two poses, but different backgrounds and the shirts' colors were different. Who looks exactly the same, I mean, unless its Photoshopped?"

Had to give her daughter huge points. Hattie doubted she would've thought of that. At Sarah's age, Hattie's idea of cut and paste involved actual scissors and a vat of glue.

Hattie turned to look at Sarah. Tears gathered in her daughter's eyes. Hattie's head felt as if it might explode. "I know this is a lot for you to handle. It is for me too."

"Can we drop it for now, Mom? Please?"

"Sure, baby."

The time following her parents' deaths came to Hattie's mind, how the mishmash of emotions had threatened to swamp her. Sometimes the bad needed to slip out a little at a time.

Hattie's chest hurt as much as her head.

Chapter Twenty-four

Wednesday, October 21st, morning

Each time he visited the Rutabaga Café, Jake felt nostalgic for the small eateries he had frequented in New York. Unlike those haunts, the charming Chattahoochee eatery outshone any of those framed in his memory. It was located in the place he called home, and the food and atmosphere were uniquely, deliciously Southern.

The café occupied a bungalow-styled house one block off West Washington Street. Jake took a moment to appreciate the flowerbeds that lined the front walkway. Whoever planned the intimate garden with its glass sculptures, pond, and flowering shrubs and perennials deserved an award. If Jake had no idea of the wonderful food waiting inside, he would want to enter based on the décor alone.

Jake opened the front door, checking out the chalkboard specials. They had roast beef and collards today. Oh my. Even on a good day, he couldn't match Chef Billy's collard greens.

"Hi, Jake. Flying solo today?" the owner asked when he spotted Jake.

"No. Hattie's on her way."

"Ah." By the way Billy elongated the single syllable and his empathetic expression, Jake knew he had heard about the arrest. Who was he kidding? Everyone in town had surely known within the hour. Surprised Elvina hadn't alerted the casserole committee to descend on the Hill.

"Why don't you and Hattie sit out in the garden? It's a nice day." The owner leaned forward, added in a low tone, "It's the end of the lunch rush. You'll have it to yourselves. I will make sure of it."

Jake wondered how he could get by without nice people. Easy to believe the world was pure evil, given the terrorists, wack-jobs, and child predators. Good folks were out there; kindness seldom made the network news.

The chef rested a hand on Jake's shoulder. "Go. Sit. I'll send out two tall glasses of iced tea."

"Best bring more than a few slices of lemon. It's Hattie. Her obsession with lemon is legend."

Jake stepped from the front door and chose the bistro table nearest the pond. Perfect. The air wasn't as heavy and the garden might provide a balm for Hattie. It did for him.

A few minutes later, Hattie stepped through the white picket fence gate and walked over to the table. One look told Jake more than her few texts and one hurried conversation.

Jake patted the chair next to his. "Saved you a spot."

Hattie slid into the metal chair and dropped her purse onto the pavers at her feet. "I must be dying, right? I never get the gunfighter's seat."

Jake waved her comment aside. "No bad seat when both of us have a clean view of the street."

The server appeared with two tall glasses of tea and a bowl filled with lemon wedges. "Today's specials," he said, handing each a menu. "We've sold out of the cream cake. But we have hummingbird cake and chocolate with raspberry torte."

Easy pick. He would get a piece of each, to go. Maybe Shug would be home soon. He loved their hummingbird cake.

After they ordered and the server left, Jake said, "Okay, tell."

"I'm not supposed to discuss it." She emptied a packet of artificial sweetener into her glass, then squeezed in the juice from a half-dozen lemon slices and stirred.

"I do wish you'd have a little tea with your lemon water."

Hattie took a loud slurp. "I like lemon."

"Second only to ketchup." Jake added sugar to his glass. Most of it settled to the bottom, undissolved. Should've asked for the sweet tea or used the powdered fake sweetener. The final few sips would be nothing but syrup.

"I feel as if I'm cheating on my relatives when I eat here," Hattie said.

"Don't be silly. You and I have sweet potato biscuits from your brother-in-law's place at least twice a week, and he and your sister both eat here all the time. She and Billy have even discussed joining forces with their catering businesses." When Hattie raised her eyebrows, he added, "She didn't tell you?"

"No."

"Actually, I may be in the mix too, as the event planner." Jake sipped tea. Winced. Added another packet of sugar and did his best to stir it in. "I'd love to get your brother to build a storage house for me. He could make it match the style of my house. But," He drummed his fingers on the table. "Elvina has him bound up. Again."

"Storage. What, for the shop?"

"No. So I can collect props for the joint business with Mary-Esther and Billy. You know, candelabras, serving pieces, things to give a wedding or party that certain splash. Guess I'll rent a storage unit somewhere." He snapped his fingers. "That place between here and Sneads. It'll be a bit of a jaunt, but none of us have extra room."

"Use my extra building on the Hill."

"Your daddy's shop?"

"Sure. Why not?"

Jake fiddled with one of the empty sugar packets, folding it in half, then again, with neat creases. "Last time I saw it, it was crammed to the ceiling. God only knows what's living in there. Could be a possum, like that ornery one that had taken up residence in the smokehouse turned jam and fruit preserves hut. That creature was none too happy about being turned out of his combo home and eatery. Guess we're lucky it wasn't a bad year for rabies."

"There could be a few mice, but it's not full of holes like the smokehouse. We'll clean it out. Most everything could go to charity, or to the dump." Hattie breathed in, blew it out. "It's the only place on the Hill that still has stuff left over from Mama and Daddy. With our old junk packed on top."

It would be a huge amount of work. He could rent a dumpster then have the company haul it away afterwards. Mary-Esther and Billy would surely pitch in since it was for their business, too. He lifted one eyebrow. Hey, he might be able to sneak a few boxes of Christmas decorations into that dumpster. Accidentally, of course.

Jake mentally scolded himself for even thinking about pitching Shug's holiday fluff. If the man came home from Alabama—no, *when*—he could drape the yard in so many colored lights they could see it from the international space station.

"I will talk it over with your sister and Billy. We could pay you rent. Three miles to the Hill beats fifteen one way to the storage units across the river."

Hattie shook her head. "Absolutely no money. Helping us get that place cleaned up will be payment enough."

"You, my dear, are a gem."

"What are friends for?" Hattie studied her hands and picked at a ragged cuticle. "I really need to stop by and see Mary-Esther when I leave here. She called the house, spoke to Holston. I didn't feel like talking to anyone." She let out a long sigh. "I've been so wrapped up in our drama, I haven't talked to my own sister."

"Or to me."

When Hattie looked up, Jake saw the same blend of fear and exhaustion he often noted in his own mirrored reflection, especially lately.

"You know you can trust me. Someone could torture me with non-stop Barry Manilow and I still wouldn't peep." Jake hesitated. "Though, I do like some of his tunes."

One corner of Hattie's lips lifted. At least it was a start. She was a true sap for love songs.

"C'mon. Tell Jakey. You know you'll feel better."

Hattie recounted the bare facts. Jake didn't interrupt. The food arrived: his fried redfish po'boy and her seasonal fresh greens salad with braised chicken. The server made sure the two of them were content then he slipped back inside.

"I'm so freaking scared the media's going to get involved." Hattie flicked the salad greens with a fork and took a small bite of the chicken.

"They probably will. Child predators and computer stalking are hot issues these days."

She dropped her fork. It clattered against the plate. A cherry tomato skidded off the edge of the table and bounced onto the patio pavers. Hattie bent down, picked it up, and added it to the shredded sugar packets. "What if the reporters zero in on Sarah? What if that guy wasn't working alone?"

"Good questions." He knew all about the stress of having the media circus shadow every move. The fact Hattie hadn't ordered a burger spoke volumes, and she usually adored their rutabaga fries. Jake took a moment to choose his words. No need to get her any more riled. "Sarah handled the situation with such bravery. And thought."

He reached over and gave her hand a squeeze. "I know our little china-berry will soldier through whatever comes along." He cocked one side of his lips in the Jakey smile. "Besides, you can always give them a taste of what you did to that rabid raccoon." Neither his touch, his signature expression, nor his clever remark drew any response from his best friend.

Hattie scraped her bangs away from her face then pushed the plate aside. "All of it runs circles in my mind, the *what-ifs*. It could've turned out so horribly wrong." Her eyes watered.

"But it didn't."

"Sarah and Tank could've been abducted, ended up God knows where, or . . . dead."

"But they didn't."

It was a Parade of Horribles. In reverse. Rewound and replayed with different, awful endings. Hattie had good reason to lead the procession.

"You're right, Jakey. I know you are." Hattie propped her chin on one hand. "How do I deal with this overwhelming panic and stay strong? I feel like I can barely breathe. Holston's a wreck, too. He won't leave the house, even to go to his office at the mansion."

"Fear can lock you up inside yourself." Man, did he ever know that. For months after his abduction, Jake fought blind terror each time he stepped outside. He felt safe nowhere.

He felt the same prickly sensation he had experienced lately, with the weird texts and the unopened envelope he carried in his day planner. Not as ramped up. More like the dull, background buzz of a station fading in and out of tune.

Jake's cell phone vibrated. He picked it up to check the sender. Not Shug. Still no messages or calls from him. Did they have him locked up at that de-gay camp, learning how *not* to be?

Dark emotions bubbled to the surface. He willed them down. Later, he could freak out in a grand way. Maybe go to the dump and pitch old china plates at the roaches. Watch them scatter as the porcelain flew into shards. Throwing dishes had a way of making him feel better ever since he had taken it up in his teens. But Hattie needed him *now*.

Jake set down the phone and took a bite of his po'boy. He chewed then nudged his plate to the center of the table alongside Hattie's.

"Not good?" she asked.

"Delicious. Just, not as hungry as I thought I was. I'll have Billy put it in a to-go box."

Hattie sat back in her chair, tilted her head to one side, and gave him *the look*. He had been on her radar since the cradle. How he wished he could open up a portal and let his own Parade of Horribles spurt out.

"Jakey . . . What's up?"

"Nothing for you to fret about."

"Is Shug still in Ala-damn-bam-er?" she asked.

They both smiled. God help them if humor ever evaporated. The sound of her laughter had gotten him through some rough patches. He hoped she felt the same about his.

"Yes," Jake said. "Unfortunately he is."

"Is . . . everything okay with you two?"

The woman could see through his skin. If her own troubles didn't have her distracted, Hattie would surely intuit that more was wrong than he admitted. Jake dabbed the corners of his lips with a napkin. Cloth, not thin paper, another reason he liked the Rutabaga Café. "Now, Sister-girl. Why would you think such? Shug and I are peachy."

"I—" Hattie's cell phone rang. "Jeez. I miss the days when I could sneak away for a few moments without a stupid phone."

Jake flicked a sour glance to his own phone. "Know what you mean." He could silence the text message notifications, but Shug might try to contact him. The slut-mail usually started in mid-afternoon, then accelerated as the day wore on.

Hattie frowned at the screen. "I have to take this one." She answered, responding to the caller in snips. "Yes. No. Yes. Okay." She tapped the disconnect icon. "I have to cut this short. Sorry."

"Problems?"

"Two FDLE agents are at the police station."

Jake reached over and squeezed her hand. "Go. I'll take care of the bill. Consider it a small, belated birthday meal, with a promise of dinner later when things settle down."

Wednesday afternoon

Elvina held Mr. R, formerly Runt; she reminded everyone of the name change. She studied his triangular, tiny face with its dark and light gray lines, the letter M characteristic of a true tabby where the left and right forehead stripes met in the middle. Yes, she had dearly loved

189

Buster, more that he had lodged in her affections after he chose *her*. But this little one, Elvina had selected to become a part of her life.

The veterinarian said the kittens were doing nicely, praised her for keeping them clean and well-fed. No fleas. From the start, Elvina had used a fine-toothed metal comb dipped in soapy water to kill the tiny bloodsuckers. Couldn't use chemical repellants on them until they were ten weeks old.

Mr. R had grown in length from palm sized to reaching the first knuckle of her pinky. With his belly full of formula, he blinked contented, sleepy eyes and kneaded the fleshy part of her hand with his front paws.

No sharp claws. Yet. Elvina refused the notion of declawing, once the veterinarian explained the procedure as an amputation of the last section of bone near each tip. Unlike Buster with his nocturnal philandering and battle scars, Mr. R would live inside. The only things his claws would shred were her couch, chairs, rugs, and curtains.

"Don't you fret, Mr. R. Mama will buy you so many scratching posts and climbing gyms, you won't consider attacking her furniture."

By the time the kitten grew to a more destructive age, Bobby would've completed the gazebo and covered breezeway. A cat's adolescence spanned only a few months. Much easier for her to keep Mr. R out of trouble than what Hattie and Bobby faced with their young'uns. Maybe Elvina could order a set of glue-on nail tips like Hattie had once used on her indoor cat. In blue or green sparkly.

Elvina heard the back door snick shut. Sarah Chuntian walked in. Elvina confirmed the time with a glance toward Piddie's wristwatch. Precisely 2:45 p.m. The piece was so old she actually had to wind it every morning.

"Have you fed them?" Sarah slid her backpack onto the floor in the spot Elvina had designated a trip-free zone. Out of the way of patrons, and her. A broken hip could be the kiss of death for a senior. She didn't have time for that. She had cats to raise.

"I fed all of them except for Patches. Saved her for you."

The teen smiled so wide Elvina saw clean to her molars. Sarah skittered back to the spa's kitchen.

The litter had outgrown the laundry hamper. Now they bumbled between a low-sided box and the confines of the infant playpen one of the spa patrons had donated. Kept them contained yet able to explore. Wanda had come up with the brilliant solution. Give that Jersey gal a star. Soon, Elvina would replace the shredded newspaper with a small box of litter. From what she'd read, kittens were easy to housetrain.

Maybe when Elvina grew too crotchety to head up the Triple C, she could volunteer at the veterinary clinic. *Reinvent yourself*, the oldster magazine articles advised. For sure, she wasn't going to waste away in her own house, waiting to die. Or in some nursing home.

Elvina cupped Mr. R to her heart and the kitten nuzzled into the folds of her shirt.

I'll have to train someone to take charge in this wheelhouse.

Or, as Piddie had done, she could *will* her front desk position to the next in line. That, she'd have to consider long and hard. Wasn't only the schedule to keep up with, but the goings-on in Chattahoochee and much of the surrounding countryside.

Sarah reappeared, a bottle in one hand, a towel in the other.

"You test the formula to make sure it's not too hot?" Elvina asked.

"Yes, ma'am."

Never hurt to review protocol. Elvina watched Sarah remove Patches from the playpen. When the kitten cried out, Juliet lifted her head and whimpered. Sarah patted the pug and reassured her, and Juliet resumed her motherly huddle with the other two kittens.

"Everything okay at home?" Elvina asked.

"Uh-huh." Sarah smiled down at the nursing calico. That little one had finally shucked her reluctance to bottle feed.

Kids nowadays. Had she texted that same inquiry, Elvina might have received a more detailed answer if she could decode the multiple abbreviations. It had taken her some time before she understood that LOL meant *laugh out loud* instead of an insulting *little old lady*. WTF she got right off.

"You and your parents worked things out then?"

The answer: a shrug. *Humph.* Elvina had spent the majority of her life with humans who viewed gossip as a high art form. These fresh generations barely needed mouths. She felt a little sorry for all of them, what they'd miss by not passing time on a porch, finding new subjects to discuss before they wore them out.

Elvina put on what she figured to be her most benevolent expression. "If you need someone to talk to about—"

"Can't." Sarah glanced up, then back to the nursing calico. "Ongoing investigation."

Oh Good Lord Almighty. Life itself was an ongoing investigation. Why was Elvina's less important than the authorities'?

Elvina conceded and shifted her end of the faltering conversation. Additional questions about school, life, and thoughts met with clipped, one-word answers. Had to be the hormone dump of adolescence. Sarah used to babble so much, Elvina wished for a muzzle. She took note of the bluish circles beneath the teen's eyes. More to this than Sarah was telling, Elvina guessed, to anyone.

Mr. R's legs twitched in sleep. Elvina looked down. What did kittens dream? She caressed his head with two fingertips then carried him to the playpen. Juliet shifted to make room and nuzzled him with her nose. After Patches finished nursing, Sarah could add her to the pile of contented felines.

Elvina returned to her post at the reception desk. Sarah sat on a nearby stool, talking to Patches and the others in a low voice. Sheesh, even the animals heard more from the child.

So what if she hadn't needled the details of the big arrest that had the town buzzing? Elvina didn't require news straight from the source. She picked up her smartphone and moved toward the kitchen for privacy.

Nope, she, Elvina Houston, head of the little-ole-lady hotline, had *people.*

Jake pulled Pearl off the driveway close to the edge of his house then went inside to gather the bucket and car grooming supplies. Half of the pick-ups in this part of the state sported so much dirt they appeared two-toned. By Jove, his vehicle was not going to look as if it had competed in a mud-bog. After the carnival weekend passed, he would bring the Dragonfly Florist van home and give it a good going-over, too.

He scrubbed and rinsed, then used a soft chamois to buff away the water beads. A little spray shine for the tires. Then he moved to the inside. Emptied the folding trash bag, rubbed vinyl protector on the dash, and vacuumed the floorboard. The little gray Toyota glowed.

When Jake loved something—person, plant, pet, or vehicle—he took care of it.

The day planner rested on the front seat, half as thick now that the two large fall events were a memory. One corner of The Envelope peeked from the leather binder. After the carnival, Jake promised himself, he would open the thing. Or burn it.

He really didn't need to consult the planner about the fall carnival. The parade consisted of four floats, three high school marching bands, a local children's dance class, and the ROTC squad. The fire department, Chattahoochee Police, and Gadsden County Sherriff's Department would lead off, their pulsating light bars and sirens thrilling the kids. He liked that part, too.

The carnival wasn't his baby anymore, not for the past couple of years. He had turned it over to a committee. They still consulted him. No matter. It was good to feel needed. One huge lot filled with kids' games and food booths. Compared to PiddieFest and the Madhatter's Festival, it was a non-event. Jake could pull it off with his eyes shut, if he had to, which he didn't.

As exhausted as he felt, he might sleepwalk through the rest of this month. The nightmares ramped up every time he closed his eyes for longer than a half hour. Blame it on the ball of worries that had bowled his way from day one of October. Keep this up and he'd have to declare another season as his favorite.

His cell phone vibrated. Jake wiped his hands and dug it out. Finally, a text from Shug! His lips moved as he read. **Need to stay longer. Will let you know.**

Those people had to be tormenting Shug. Monitoring his phone. Jake typed out a terse reply then deleted it. They were probably reading every text. He wouldn't give them the satisfaction.

After he jammed the phone back into his pocket, he glanced toward the street and realized he hadn't checked the mail in a couple of days. What a slacker. Should rip the mailbox down and put a flowerbed in its place. The important bills appeared online; no one penned letters anymore, or bothered with banal communication—he flicked a dark look toward the day planner—except for the sick individual behind The Envelope and the line-up of morons still texting him how hot and cute he was.

Jake grabbed his cane and moved toward the mailbox. When he passed the roses, he stopped to deadhead a couple of spent blossoms. Gosh, he needed to spend some intense yard time. These rosebushes were a disgrace, and him a florist! The plumber always had the clogged sink, didn't they say?

The phone jiggled. Again. Maybe Shug, wondering why he hadn't replied. Suppose that was a tad passive-aggressive of him. He pulled the phone out, tapped the message icon.

Time is running out for you.

He clenched the device so hard, his skin blanched. He should pitch it to the curb, watch it crash and crack.

"I am done, done, done!"

Jake stomped the final few feet, his cane jabbing divots in the grass. He jerked the mailbox lid open. It squealed a complaint.

"Oh, shut up."

A stack of flyers waited, political glossies from the look of them. So many wasted trees. He scooped out the pile and shuffled toward the porch where he sat in the white swing.

A plain legal-sized envelope stood out from the rest. Jake stared at it. His hands trembled.

In the upper left corner: *M. Thurgood*

Wednesday evening, late

Hattie paused outside Sarah's bedroom. This reminded her of how both she and Holston had behaved for the first few months after they returned from China with the then-baby Sarah Chuntian. Up all hours of the night, making sure she was secure and asleep, and still breathing.

The door stood open a crack. Unusual. For the past few months, Sarah had instituted her "closed sanctuary policy." Hattie heard Ensign whimper. Beside her, Captain grunted a low answer and perked his ears forward. He nudged the door with his nose. Hattie reached down and stopped him before he shoved it completely open. The kiddo deserved her space. Hattie understood that. She hated to hover as much as she disliked someone hovering over her.

Dim light from a small plug-in illuminated Sarah's room. Her daughter used to sleep with the light on when she was a child, but hadn't in several years.

When she detected the sound of her daughter's crying, Hattie's maternal instinct took control. Both she and Captain pushed the door at the same time, so hard that Hattie grabbed the knob to keep the door from whamming against the wall.

Sarah jerked upright in bed and screeched. Ensign growled and barked. A flashlight beam struck Hattie in the face, blinding her.

"Hey, hey. It's me!"

"Mom?"

The light flicked to the carpet. Hattie blinked and strained to see past the dance of spots. Ensign hopped to the end of the bed, tail held aloft. He and Captain touched noses. Doggie salute.

Hattie heard a click. Flashlight off. Another click. Bedside lamp on. She moved a few steps and knelt beside the bed. "Oh, my sweet baby." She ran her fingers through Sarah's disheveled hair. Her daughter's nose bubbled and tears carved streaks down her flushed cheeks. Hattie enfolded Sarah in her arms, rocking, rocking. When the sobs calmed to clipped intakes of breath, Hattie shifted away long enough to grab a tissue and hand it to Sarah. The teen blew her nose twice then wiped her eyes.

"Bad dream?"

Sarah shook her head. Ensign wormed between them and Sarah pulled the small dog to her chest. Captain plopped his front paws on the bed and whimpered. "Get down, Cap." She patted his head. "I know you want to help."

Should buy the kiddo a bigger bed. At least a double. Sarah had insisted; the twin was her choice.

"Ready to talk about it?" Hattie said.

"It . . . It . . . I was so scared, Mom." Sarah scratched the fuzz around Ensign's ears. Captain crammed himself as close as possible. Dogs were guardian angels sent to earth. Too bad these two couldn't shadow her daughter's every step.

Hattie waited. When Sarah met her gaze, the child's eyes telegraphed her fear. The brave, in-control, all-knowing, teenaged façade crumbled.

"I'm here, honey. Your daddy is close-by." Hattie tousled Captain's ruff. "And these too goofs. No one would be stupid enough to face down *this* family."

A corner of Sarah's lips flicked up then sank. She inhaled. The breath released in shudders. "I felt okay when it was happening. Like, really calm. This plan was in my mind. Like a movie."

Sarah shifted and plumped the pillow behind her back. She and Ensign settled again. "Tank didn't want to go along with my plan, but I told him he was acting like one of the Chick Flicks, you know, freaking out over nothing and running around like they don't have brains."

Good analogy. Mean, but good.

"All he was trying to do was protect me," Sarah continued. "And I bullied him to play along."

"You have been a strong spirit from the first time we met back in that orphanage," Hattie said. "You'd ball up your little fists and get that look in your eyes, even as a baby. Your daddy and I knew straight away you'd be a force." She smiled, reached for her daughter's hand. "And you are."

"I didn't feel scared at all. Even when I was walking out toward that van. I saw Chief Mather's black car parked near the exit of the parking lot." Sarah flicked her fingers. "I walked across the lot, half hoping my friend Gerund would step out, call my name. The driver's side door opened. I was a few feet away. A man's leg came out. And I knew. I just *knew*."

And your heart broke in two. "And then?" Hattie had heard J.T. describe the scene, at the station, but not from her daughter's lips. Not this part.

"Everything happened at once. The door swung all the way open. That man lunged out and came at me. Then, there was Chief Mathers hollering. His gun was out, pointing at the man. Two other police officers ran up. I don't know where they came from. I heard Tank yelling my name. Sarah! Sarah!"

Fresh tears popped into her daughter's eyes. Sarah reached for a clean tissue before Hattie had a chance.

"What if he had snatched me? If Chief Mathers hadn't come right away when I texted him? What if someone had gotten . . . killed!"

Hattie leaned forward and drew Sarah toward her. Ensign allowed himself to be sandwiched between. Captain nosed his large head into the embrace. Hattie breathed in the combination of her daughter's sweet scent combined with dog breath. The big dog licked first Sarah's then Hattie's face. Then he gave Ensign a sloppy lap. No need to leave anyone out, Hattie guessed.

Sarah giggled. Hattie joined. Captain lunged onto the bed. The absurdity made Hattie laugh harder. Now both dogs wagged tails and licked faces.

When the tumble-fest slowed and Hattie managed to herd the dogs off the bed, she said, "In many respects, you are like me, honey. In a crisis, I am all brave, large and in charge. I order people around. Take action without mulling over outcomes. Like you did with that last rabid raccoon."

"Huh?"

"I know, I know. Don't say it. Everyone swears I take *for-ev-ah* to make a decision. Usually. But when it's a crisis, I act first and freak out later. Not really a bad way to be. Sometimes, if you hesitate too long, a decision is made for you. And not always a good one."

Sarah sniffled.

"Does this whole thing scare the bejabbers out of me? You bet. But, I am also amazed and proud of the way you handled things when you figured out they were heading in the wrong direction. At your age, I don't know if I could've done the same."

Her daughter offered a shaky smile.

"I'm not sleepy. Seems like you and the guard squad aren't either." Hattie stood. "Why don't we move this circus to the kitchen. I'll make us some chamomile tea and get chewy bones for the dogs."

Chapter Twenty-five

Saturday, October 31st, evening

Hattie stood at the periphery of the fall carnival grounds with her arms crossed over her chest and her feet planted twelve inches apart: the same stance she'd seen law enforcement officers assume, only she wasn't packing heat like some of the others on the large grassy lot in front of the state mental institution. Other than a small mention in the *Twin City News*, this event had not been advertised, not like the Madhatter's Festival or PiddieFest. Between her family and Elvina Houston, the chances of spotting an odd character were good.

Spread in front of her like a movie scene of small town Americana, Hattie's neighbors and friends enjoyed the early fall evening. Finally, not too hot, but not yet cold. Perfect, if not for her aura of suspicion. Made her furious, how the innocence of her country carnival could be tainted by out-of-town crazy.

She lifted her nose to take in the same scents she recalled from youth. Grilled Angus burgers and hotdogs. Warm sugar from the cotton candy cart. Hot cooking oil. Brewed coffee. The tang of gumbo from the soup booth. She could lose herself in the wash of pleasant childhood memories evoked by the flavored air. Her stomach growled. Gosh, those burgers smelled good. Make hers with melty orange cheese stringing from the edge of the bun and gobs of catsup. For dessert, a funnel cake.

Hattie scolded herself, drew her attention back to looking for trouble.

Who would've ever believed her family could be in the center of an ongoing federal investigation? If what the FBI and FDLE agents suspected was true, the man they had spirited away from the police station in the back of an unmarked black SUV was one of a gang of international human traffickers. Girls and boys brought hefty profits. Hattie's brain hurt, thinking of it. Across the country, heck the whole planet, how many parents longed for their missing children? She snugged her light jacket to her chest and shivered, despite the balmy temperature.

Sure, those feds had told her and Holston to report anything suspicious directly to them, not to take matters to hand. Screw that.

If this were a cartoon, she would have steam piping from her ears, nostrils, mouth, not to mention the top of her head. Thinking about that, she stuffed down a smile. Probably wouldn't come out friendly at this point.

There had been times when something blew up her blouse in the wrong direction, made her show her Southern redneck, mama-bear indignation. Hattie scraped her memory, trying to pick out a time when she'd felt this pissed. Not since . . . Jake's assault.

Then, she'd had a direction to focus her wrath, at least until she found out the Thurgood teen had killed himself—shotgun to the head. Bobby had found the kid with his brains blown all to bits. Hattie ended up feeling sad for him, for his family, and for the hateful, narrow attitudes that had fueled the attack.

Hattie's jaw muscles pulsed and she willed them to relax. Keep this up and she'd pay the dentist for as many crowns as Bobby had. She swiveled her head in a slow arc, right to left, left to right.

As she aged, Hattie noted more and more of her mother's traits surfacing in herself. Like her mother, Hattie could tolerate a good deal, until she couldn't. Mr. D called it the "toe over the line syndrome."

This close encounter with a twisted man who took advantage of children—*her* daughter, *her* nephew—had slipped Hattie's entire foot over that line. Somewhere deep in the previous night, when every small noise had jerked her from sleep and shadows took on human shapes, Hattie Davis Lewis got white-hot, you-ain't-messing-with-my-people mad. *Oh-hell-no* mad.

It wasn't good and dark yet, still the purpled sky of early autumn, with the promise of the upcoming moon. She could make out details of the milling crowd. The carnival had changed little over the years. The cakewalk game, the go-fish booth, ring-toss, pony rides, and others: low-tech, old-time fun. Kids who normally focused their attention on computer screens darted from one game to the next. Some wore Halloween costumes. Even the lighting was old school: strings of clear, incandescent bare bulbs draped like tinsel between posts.

A toddler dressed as a pirate passed by, holding onto his father with one hand and a tall fluted mound of cotton candy with the other. Melted sugar painted blue rivers down one of his costume's puffy sleeves. Between the candied and caramel apples, funnel cakes, and hot cocoa, there was enough sugar to keep half the children bouncing off the walls for several hours. Bless the hearts of their parents.

A Bluetooth bud rested in one of Hattie's ears, hidden by her hair. Techno bling. So many people wore them nowadays she wouldn't stand out even if someone noted her talking to herself. People who knew her well might wonder; Hattie was infamous for her disdain for cell phones. Even so, most wouldn't connect the tiny device with a covert operation.

The best place to hide is in plain sight; Hattie had read that somewhere, in a spy novel maybe. Plenty of local, uniformed officers walked through the crowd and others patrolled the periphery. Just the thought she was doing something, *any*thing, nipped the edge from her anger.

She shifted her head to view the pony rides where Holston stood, chatting with the handler. Her husband periodically scanned his section of the crowd, pausing when he looked in her direction. How she loved that man. Best thing was seeing that love reflected back at her when their eyes met. Plus knowing Holston was just as vigilant.

Her sister-in-law played her usual nurse role in the first aide station at another corner, keeping Amelia by her side until she could break to accompany the child to each station. Poor kid; she should be running around like the others, carefree as a yard dog.

Though Hattie couldn't see her sister, she knew Mary-Esther observed from the soup booth while her husband Jerry scouted the edges of the gathering. He'd been immediately involved in the plans to set up a safety net for this event.

Hattie watched Elvina, taking her turn from an important position. She had called in favors to have the cakewalk grid moved from one corner to near dead-center of the carnival grounds. The senior guardian of Chattahoochee had a three hundred sixty-degree view. As soon as she'd secured a sitter for the kittens, Elvina had promised to lend her "every last surveillance brain cell" to the mission. Elvina could spot a stranger in their midst better than the local officers. She knew most everyone in a two-county radius by sight, if not by reputation.

Across the carnival grounds, Bobby worked the ring-toss booth. Though he appeared to operate the game, Hattie knew her brother watched, too. His years in law enforcement came in handy. Of all of them, exception Jerry, Bobby was the most adept in undercover actions.

She tried to pick out the plain clothes agents. Oh, they were out here somewhere. Blending in. Sipping coffee. Hattie wished she had a cup.

Maybe one of them wolfed down a burger. People might take a second glance toward the stranger. Perhaps he was an uncle or cousin from out of town. Impolite to ask.

Through the crowd, she spotted Sarah and Tank at the cakewalk booth. Okay for them to be untethered, as long as they stuck together. Her daughter had pitched a fit and fell in it when Hattie suggested she remain by either her or Holston. The teenager had reemerged. Horrors to have your parent by your side. God forbid.

Everyone accounted for. Hattie nodded once.

Though the agents had not asked them to form a family squad, they *had* advised vigilance. Watch for anything out of the norm, someone acting odd or twitchy. *Even a child.* When the federal agent said those words, a gush of emotions bubbled up: anger, sadness, disbelief. To think they would trap and use children to lure other unsuspecting children! There wasn't a layer of hell deep enough for those sick sub-humans.

Someone stepped beside her. Hattie jumped.

"Oh my. Sorry to startle you." The woman, Hattie recognized. Sarah's human studies teacher.

"Guess my mind was a million miles away," Hattie said. She shifted enough to hold a conversation and still monitor her quadrant.

"I haven't returned the graded research papers yet, so please don't breathe a word of this to your daughter." The teacher lowered her voice and leaned forward, though the crowd noise would surely cover any of her words. "Sarah's paper on the unseen dangers of the internet is the best I have ever read, in all my years. Such attention to detail, to grammar and punctuation. She obviously spent a great deal of time with her research."

More than you could ever imagine. "Glad it turned out okay. Sarah wouldn't let me touch it before she handed it in."

"Ah." The teacher chuckled. "That takes it up another notch. Not written, or even edited, by a well-meaning parent."

Hattie flicked a smile, did a quick eye-sweep of the crowd while the teacher continued to talk. All normal, except for . . . who was that huge guy near the coffee stand? Was he the same giant that had stopped by the massage therapy booth at the Madhatter's? Had to be. Hard to believe there would be two men *that* large in this area.

"Mrs. Lewis?"

Hattie refocused on Sarah's teacher. "Oh, I'm sorry. What were you saying?"

"I'd like to enter Sarah's paper in the county competition. I believe it has a good chance of winning, maybe moving on to the state and national levels."

"Wow. Oh, sure. That would be great."

The teacher tucked her hands into her jeans pockets. "I see my husband waving me over. Have a nice evening, Mrs. Lewis."

"Yes. You too." Hattie focused on the teacher. The woman probably thought Hattie an ungrateful cretin. "Thank you for everything you do for Sarah. She loves your class."

"You are most welcome. My pleasure. Truly."

The teacher turned and walked off. Hattie pivoted her head. Where had that ginormous guy gone? She spotted him loping through the crowd. Now there was someone strange, for sure. He walked up to Jake, who stood between the Lion's Club grills and the funnel cake stand. He and Jake walked alongside each other until they reached the far corner of the grounds. Hattie strained to see. They stood, inches apart. The giant reached out a hand. Jake took something from it and shoved it into his pocket. Jake stared up at him. They stood like that for a beat too long.

The giant turned and walked away. Reminded Hattie of a gorilla, the way the man's shoulders tipped side to side with each stride. And what was up with the way Jake Witherspoon watched until the hulk disappeared into the shadows?

Shug, gone for an extended time. Jake sloughing off her questions, looking as if he hadn't slept for months. No appetite. Hmm. Hattie's spirit tanked. Could Jake possibly be having an affair?

Bobby accepted two one-dollar bills and handed three rings to a boy with a green-tipped Mohawk. One day, would this kid see a picture of himself and wonder what the hell he had been thinking? Same way Bobby felt when he viewed the photos of his younger self with punked-up '80s hair, he bet.

Jake sauntered by and leaned over, said something about *redneck ring-toss referees*. Bobby volleyed with a mumbled comment about *flashy festival fairies*. Not so anyone else could hear.

He watched Jake amble off, noting the bright, road-worker orange cane. Where did that man find such? At least Bobby could pick him out in a crowd.

Which he did a few minutes later.

A tall hulk trailed behind Jake, the same dude Bobby had seen stepping from that john boat not long ago. Between his job of watching the flying rings, Bobby took note of the odd scene. The man calling out. Jake freezing, a rabbit caught in the crosshairs. The oaf catching up to Jake, then the two of them continuing to the filtered light at the edge of the festival grounds.

"I'll take three of them rings," a voice said.

Bobby switched his attention to the man next in line and handed the wooden rings over to him. After he accepted money, Bobby took turns watching where the rings fell and checking on Jake and the ogre. Ripped flannel jacket. Stained, worn blue jeans. About six eight. Hair: dark brown and greasy, unkempt. The way he towered over Jake. The way Jake's shoulders rolled forward.

"Hey, lookie there, will ya! Give me my prize!"

Bobby scanned the rows of empty cola bottles, the targets for the toss game. Sure enough, three ringers. He motioned to the array of stuffed animals suspended over his head. The victor jabbed a finger toward a purple dinosaur with green spots. Bobby used a hook to detach it from the wire and handed it over. The guy beamed like he had just won tickets for a Bahamas cruise.

When Bobby searched out the Jake/big dude scene, he saw only Jake facing the shadows, as if he expected the devil himself to sift from the darkness. What was up with that?

Something told Bobby that big fella bore watching, closely. His intuition had saved his ass on more than one occasion, no matter if he had been so drunk he thought a pine tree was a long-lost friend who needed a shave.

Jake paused at the edge of the festival crowd and watched Rudy lumber into the shadows. This time, he had handed Jake a thin packet of folded bills. Had to be getting close to paying off his mother's funeral drape. Maybe Jake should write off the balance and face Jolene's dressing-down. Kindness? Nope. Jake would rather *never* see Rudy James blocking his view of the world. Made no sense. Man hadn't done anything to raise his hackles. But still . . .

He checked his cell phone messages to distract him from Rudy thoughts. Quick count: twenty texts about his cute, hot, hook-up self. One stood out: Shug! He tapped the picture icon with a smile that felt genuine.

I am sorry. I will always love you.

What was *that* supposed to mean? Sorry he had been away so long? Sorry he hadn't called to talk? And that *will always love you* sounded like a wave toward the past, not a promise of a future.

The crowd noise echoed in his ears. Even his good leg wobbled. He leaned on his cane to keep from losing his balance.

The family had done it. Gotten under Shug's defenses. Beaten him down.

The air thickened. Jake took a couple of deep breaths and fought off panic. Every direction he looked, eyes watched him.

Have to get out of here.

Pearl waited nearby, in a lot reserved for vendors and carnival staff. Jake moved as quickly as his bad leg would allow. He unlocked the truck. Got in. Backed out. Put Pearl in drive and accelerated.

What took over at times like this, Jake often wondered, when his mind squirreled with worries and he didn't recall how he had shifted from one point to another with no memory of the road, stop signals, or other cars?

When he became aware of his surroundings, Jake understood why some silent sentinel had steered him to this one place. He switched off the engine. Stuck his cell phone in the glove compartment. Grabbed his cane.

The light from a moon two days past full, a waning gibbous moon, silvered the trees. No need for the compact LED flashlight. The same inner guide that had piloted him here boosted him up and over the barricades and fence. Jake wasn't aware of thinking, only acting.

Elvina had a prickly sensation worm up and down her spine. Couldn't put a solid fingerprint on what rippled her, but it wasn't good.

She packed up her iPod and wireless Bluetooth speakers. Lordy, this was a sight easier than it had been years back when she and Piddie had to cart a portable record player and worry about extension cords. Didn't even have to bring records anymore, or tapes or CDs. Just hit shuffle and the little gizmo did all the work. All she had to do was tap pause, announce the winner, then hustle the next group of players into the circle. Do it all again until the last cake had been claimed.

A few diehard carnival-goers hung on until the last minutes. Supposed to fold up the booths by nine o'clock. Hattie and her family had gone to the Hill, and Leigh and Amelia. Tank helped his daddy break down the ring toss enclosure, and the Lion's Club members had the rolling charcoal grills hitched up to the back of their trucks, thin lines of smoke and sparks still piping from the vents. Good thing they didn't have far to drive, and the woods weren't too dry. The little children had long gone home to sugar-fueled dreams, but a few of the older ones hung around, pretending to help pack away the carnival props until next fall.

Elvina wiped crumbs from the folding table then rolled up the covering drape: fake vintage lace, plastic, two dollars and ninety-five cents at the Dollar Store. She'd learned a lesson from all her years in charge of the cakewalk. Never, ever bring an expensive tablecloth. Linen and chocolate icing do *not* mix.

This year, the ten-layered chocolate death-wish cake from the Borrowed Thyme Bakery and Eatery earned the top honors. Piddie's son-in-law had outdone himself on that one. Took all Elvina could do not to spirit it beneath the table until she could sneak it home later. The cakes were gone now. But not the memory of the flushed, surprised joy of the winners.

She could operate the cakewalk game on automatic. Good thing too. This year, she had to keep an eye out on things for the Lewis and Davis families, all while monitoring the half-dozen contestants making the rounds of the numbered grid. If Elvina ever claimed a surefire talent, it was multitasking. She was dang sure good at it.

Nobody lived to be her overripe age without paying full mind to body sensations. Even a spell of gas had a story to tell. Her gut was telling her Jake Witherspoon was in a bad way. He had crisscrossed the grounds at least a dozen times, an unsettled look on his face. Didn't seem like there was much about this carnival to merit concern. The committee had done its job and it went off without a hitch. Not counting that one little boy who'd screamed like a slaughtered pig when his loose front tooth got snatched out by a candied apple crust, the carnival was one of the best she recalled.

Elvina had caught Jake's expression in those unguarded moments when no one else was watching. Seemed to be a blend of anxiety and something else, something deeply unhappy. He hid it well, but anyone who knew Jake could see beneath the mask of freckles and that lopsided grin of his.

Did no good to quiz Jolene. Elvina had tried that when she took a pee break. All Jolene said was that business had been exceptionally good at the Dragonfly and maybe Jake's mood was the result of October's three events in a row. Jolene's explanation made not a dab of sense. Jake lived for party planning.

As she did with Google searches, Elvina stepped back and revised her parameters. A mystery was like a rotten piece of cloth. Pull the correct thread and the whole shebang would rip wide open.

Wanda, though fast friends with Shug Presley, hadn't heard from him in over two weeks. Odd, since they usually talked every day when Shug stopped by the Triple C for a cup of that spoon-dissolving coffee of hers. Mandy didn't take much note, other than to comment on Wanda's distress.

Shug had been gone to Alabama for quite some time. Jake's gloom grew with each passing day. Add to the list that big guy she'd seen following a few feet behind Jake. Couldn't miss him. Reminded Elvina of drawings she'd seen of Paul Bunyan. Big hulky fellow, looked like he could stomp any of them into the ground, if he took a mind to.

She had spotted Jake talking to him. Then the big man was gone. And she lost sight of Jake.

Come to think of it, she hadn't seen Jake in well over an hour and he hadn't answered any of her texts. Worrisome. It was one thing to know people's business; *that*, the Bible mandated. But interfering in their lives was a stretch of the Good Book, unless it was someone she deeply cared about. Even the Almighty's rules could be curved a tad.

Something was hot-stink and gamey in her corner of Gadsden County. Sure was. Elvina picked up her cell phone and tapped in a quick message. A minute later, Bobby Davis appeared by her table.

"Got your text. Need help loading up?"

"No, sir." Elvina stuffed the tablecloth into her carryall. "I got this nailed down. One of the clean-up boys will pick up this table."

"Seems like our super stake-out wasn't necessary tonight," Bobby said. "Glad of it, too."

"Yes, that's all good. But something else is working my worry radar. I need for you to find Jake, see if he's all right."

"What makes you think he isn't?"

Elvina massaged the back of her neck. All that surveillance swiveling had set a crick in the muscles. "I don't know exactly. Just find him. Then text me. I won't sleep a wink 'til I hear back from you."

Bobby nodded. "Okay. Reckon the rest of these folks can finish up the packing. Did you try calling his cell?"

"Why you suppose I'm involving you if I'da reached him? I've texted him several times. Haven't heard a peep back." Elvina tapped her smartphone screen, frowned, then added, "And *that* is not like him. Even when he's up to his armpits, he'll answer me." She slung the carryall over one shoulder. "I got to get on to my house and check on Juliet and the kittens." She jabbed a bony finger in his direction. "Do what I ask you, son. I *am* your elder."

Bobby pulled a stiff salute. "Yes, ma'am. Soon as I make sure Tank has a ride to the Hill, I'll get right on it."

Chapter Twenty-six

Bobby drove first to the Dragonfly Florist. The front window display light was on as usual, highlighting a grouping of plants and fall arrangements. He wheeled his pick-up onto the side street, then into the alleyway behind the shop.

The delivery van sat beneath the security light Jake had Bobby install years back. No sign of Pearl. Why would there be? Jake *never* entered or exited the shop from the back door after dark, hadn't since the assault. Bobby shook his head, thinking of that little gray pick-up with the human name. He was getting to be as big of a nutcase as Hattie.

Bobby circled the block then headed south toward Morgan Avenue. Two minutes later, he slowed to check out Jake and Shug's house. Porch light on. No inside lights. And no Pearl.

A few clusters of trick-or-treaters bobbed between the houses. Not the small kids at this hour. It *was* Halloween after all. How folks could still allow their children to roam the streets in search of candy, knocking on strangers' doors, defied him. Most had given up the age-old tradition in favor of private parties, or in the case of this year, the carnival.

Bobby idled by the curb for a moment, engaging his bloodhound brain. One good thing had come from those years of tracking no-goods down narrow country lanes and swampy waterways. If he allowed his second sense to kick in, Bobby could find most anybody. He had been the one to locate Marshall Thurgood in that deserted Gulf Power shed, all of those years back. Bobby pushed that thought aside. Best not to go there. His mind would replay the picture of the blood, bone, hair, and gray matter that had once been the teen's head. And the smell of death, piping through the July heat. He flipped a U and accelerated.

After a quick sweep of the major streets and a call to the Hill to check if Hattie had seen or heard from Jake, Bobby completed the circle to West Washington Street where he had started.

One place remained. Long shot, for sure. That trip across the bridge to the deserted Gulf Power plant had been a long shot, too. He turned west, picking up speed in spite of the twenty-five mile per hour limit.

He rounded a curve on the River Landing Road and spotted Pearl tucked between the trees near the entrance to the Old Victory Bridge. Bobby pulled in behind Jake's truck and shut off the engine.

Creepy down here, even with the luminous moon. Bobby rifled in his glovebox for a flashlight. He started to get out then reached back for his semi-automatic. Loaded. He didn't have to check the magazine.

When he reached the barricades, Bobby stuck the handgun beneath the band of his jeans, mid-back, and scaled the cement blocks and fence. Unbelievable that Jake could do it with that wonky leg. He thumped to the pavement and palmed the handgun.

Jake had once mentioned how he liked this defunct bridge. Bobby couldn't recall the context. No matter. The little dude had come out here in the dark, by himself. That alone was enough to cause Bobby to increase his pace.

Bobby held the five-inch flashlight. Not his best, but the LED was powerful for its size. After a few steps, he flicked it off and slipped it into his pocket. The moonlight showed more detail and wouldn't give him away in case someone watched. Might be a peaceful escape during the daytime, but not now. Deserted and decayed structures gave Bobby the crawlies.

Ghosts of his past haunted the Old Victory Bridge. How many times had Bobby driven this span, nearly too drunk to focus? Barely clearance enough for two vehicles to pass, especially if one of them slipped back and forth across the double yellow line. Miracle he was still in one piece, much less the other drivers unlucky enough to share the road.

Bobby checked out his escape options. If someone cornered Jake, or him, on this narrow bridge, there would be nowhere to run. Over the side and drop, hope not to break your fool neck. Or jump off the end and pray you could out-paddle the current.

He went into stealth mode, avoided fallen leaves and limbs, anything that would crackle. Not easy on pavement, in the semi-darkness. He stuck close to the cement railing where meager shadows offered

209

cover. In a few feet, Bobby smelled the river, a scent as familiar as his own sweat. He paused, allowing his ears to search for sound. The wisp of air through the river willows. The low, liquid rumble of the Apalachicola. Cricket song. The bass thump of a bullfrog in the marsh beneath the pilings.

When he rounded the final curve, he spotted a figure and halted again. Jake? He saw the dayglow orange cane propped against one cement side rail. Had to be Jake. No one else. Good.

Bobby approached. Was the little dude sitting atop the fence spanning the drop-off? Any sense of relief he'd felt evaporated.

"Jake?" He kept his voice low and level. "Buddy?" One swift movement and the little guy might . . .

"Who's there!?"

Wow. Didn't sound anything like the Jake that had kidded with him earlier in the evening. "It's me. Bobby." He eased forward a couple of steps.

"Go home, Bobby. To your wife. To your kids."

Didn't take a shrink to pick up on the desolation in Jake's tone. Bobby had heard it before. From himself.

"I'da know." Bobby stretched for an easy-going tone. "Kind of a cool spot to spend Halloween." He inched closer.

"I'm a golden retriever."

The statement flummoxed Bobby. Last thing he thought he would hear. "Ya lost me on that one."

"Loyal, needs to have approval. Everybody's patsy."

"Nah, I wouldn't think of you as a dog." Though if he did, he might see Jake as a poodle or some yappy little ankle-biter. Prissy and cute. Not the time to point that out. "I get the loyal part. But you're no one's patsy."

Bobby heard the fence complain when Jake shifted. Why couldn't he be seated atop one of the cement side rails?

"Really, Bobby?" Jake's voice came out higher pitched than normal. "Shug and I were at this little dive a couple of months back, down near the coast. I'd heard they had good Oysters Rockefeller, made with bacon crumbled on top of the melted parmesan. There was this family at the next table. Four, an older couple and a young couple. The girl was the daughter, from what I could piece together. We had just ordered, sitting there chatting about . . . I can't recall what. Something mundane. The older man started slamming 'those homosexuals,' how Jesus was soon going to 'rid us of *them*.' Told how he and his wife had taken in some young boy who thought he was queer, had turned him around, steered him clear of that life."

Bobby didn't interrupt. Didn't try to inch closer.

"Then the daughter piped up, defending a person's right to choose what they wanted to be as long as they 'didn't bring it into her house so she'd have to explain it to her kids.' I wanted to jump up. Blast them with the fact that the majority of child molesters are white heterosexual males. But you know, I just sat there, frozen. So did Shug. We were silent, except for a couple of banal comments about the weather or some such. The man went on to rail against Jews, blacks, Muslims. Anyone who wasn't exactly like him, he blasted, in a voice everyone in that small room could hear." Jake took a slow breath and released it. "The food arrived. We ate. I could barely swallow, can't honestly say if it was good or bad. We paid. And left."

Bobby heard the sound of deep misery, a choked sob that came from Jake's center.

"Shug and I talked about it later, only once. What was there to say? Both of us had heard that same, worn-out conversation before. So many times. Even if we *had* said something, anything, it wouldn't have accomplished a thing.

"Okay for the man to broadcast his opinions to everyone, but not okay for me or Shug to defend ourselves." The fence creaked. "And why should we have to, Bobby? Huh? Who are we hurting?"

"Nobody." Bobby scrounged to offer some comfort, but had none. He had once been that loud-mouth, shouting out his condemnation.

"You know the funny thing?" Jake coughed out a harsh laugh. "The reason why we don't ever speak up? We don't want to make others feel uncomfortable. In public, we keep a low profile. Try not to offend. Live and let live."

And what gave that blowhard the right to make Jake and Shug feel like pond slime? Anyone could look at Jake and tell he wasn't straight. Shug might pass. But not Jake. Bobby wished he could've been there. He was angry enough now to wipe that guy's face across the concrete if he appeared in front of him.

"I can't do this," Jake said.

Bobby took note of his tone: flat, devoid of emotion. *Shit. Shit. Shit!* Okay, he'd had some training in negotiation. Time to pull from that. "I hear you, dude. You say you can't do this. Can you tell me *what* you can't do? Is there more? Talk to me."

The fence groaned again. If Bobby could get Jake to swivel his legs to this side, away from the open maw over the water, he could reach for him and guide him onto the pavement.

"Shug is leaving me. And crazy people keep texting me. And there are *two* envelopes now. I can't take it. I'm done."

Whoa. This was getting weirder by the second. The little guy was all over the place. Bobby wished Hattie was here. Even Elvina.

"Hey, you and me, we're buds, right? I mean, I kid you a lot and all, but if you weren't around, I would be one lost puppy."

"What." The word came out like a puff of air. But a little hopeful. Maybe. Build on that.

"Like, who can I talk to about all that touchy-feely crap, if not you? Hattie?" Bobby forced out a small chuckle. "I'm still amazed she's speaking to me after what all I put her through." When Jake didn't reply, Bobby continued, "And forget Mary-Esther . . . she's blood, sure. But she didn't grow up with me. We talk about nothing in particular. Leigh listens to me, real good. But I tell you stuff I don't tell anyone."

That fact struck Bobby, mid-chest. No matter that Jake was gay as the birds in May and moved with such flair he left no doubt, he was a friend, a *true* friend.

A boat motor sounded somewhere below, near the landing. People did fish at night on this river. Or maybe something less legal than angling. Not his concern at the moment.

Bobby considered reaching into his bag of gay-boy nicknames to prompt some humor. Defuse the situation. He decided against it. Especially not after that story Jake had told.

"Why don't you come down off that fence? You and me can go back to your house where we can really talk things over." He flicked his hand. "Without the mosquitoes toting us off."

No answer.

"Look how you pulled me away from being such a flaming ass. I was bad as that loud-mouth, every bit as bad. And there're plenty of folks who have changed their way of thinking because of you and Shug."

Still no sound from Jake.

"I'll even let you make me a cup of that disgusting tea you and Hattie rave about." Bobby waited a beat then said, "Please, Jake. You ain't no damn golden retriever, whatever that means to you. You'd fight 'til you couldn't stand up, if one of us was in danger. I know you would." Bobby poured every ounce of feeling into his words. "I ain't got many friends. I can't spare a single one."

The fence wires creaked. Jake's torso swiveled. He swung one leg over, bridge side.

Thank you, sweet Jesus. He was coming around. "Good. Good. One more. C'mon buddy."

Bobby heard a pop. The end support pole jerked. Bobby leapt forward. A second twang, like a snapped spring. One moment, Jake was there. Then he wasn't. That fast.

Bobby heard Jake's cry, a loud whump and splash. *Holy crap!* A boat motor sputtered in the semidarkness.

He didn't hesitate. He shucked off shoes, jeans. Added his gun atop the pile. He vaulted over the sagging fence and plunged feet first toward the river.

Falling. Falling. The impact stung his skin. He sank then battled toward the surface. His head and top of his shoulders cleared the water and he sucked in oxygen.

The current tugged him downstream. Bobby treaded and searched the broken moonlight. There! Flailing arms. The rounded shape of a head. Bobby pushed through the water, swimming as hard as he could toward the bobbing figure.

"Hang on!" he shouted. The river swallowed his words. The head went down, came up again. Bobby struggled to move faster, thankful that the current flowed in his favor.

An elongated shape swept past him, several feet away in the direction of the far shoreline. The motor tone changed from full throttle to the low rumble of an engine sent to neutral. Bobby paddled to keep his head above the swirling water.

A figure stood inside the vessel. Even from the distance, Bobby could make out the silhouette of a large person, bending over, dragging something from the river.

The engine changed pitch again. The boat aimed upstream, nearing Bobby. He pummeled the water, kicking as hard as he could manage. His bum knee screamed.

The boat shape loomed larger. Bobby reached out one arm and clawed at its slick hull. A hand clamped around his forearm. He felt his body lift, higher, higher, until the hand released its grip. He crumpled into the boat, coughing up clots of river water and phlegm.

"Bobby? Bobby?" a breathy voice said.

He pushed his body in the direction of the voice. Two arms reached out, then clung to him. Jake. *Thank God.*

For a beat, Bobby's mind wouldn't focus on anything but *Jake's not dead. I'm not dead.* When they drew close to Chattahoochee Landing's floating dock, the yellowed light from the single streetlamp revealed their savior.

Sombitch.

After the man secured the boat, the three of them walked to dry land. Bobby supported Jake with one arm. His little friend shivered. Water dripped from his face and clothes.

The big man looked them up and down, as if he had landed the oddest catch of his life and couldn't grasp what he'd pulled into his boat.

Had to look weird. Two men. Half-drowned. One with no pants. *Lord.* Bobby cleared his throat. Felt like he'd swallowed half the river. "Thank you."

The man nodded. "Ain't gone ast what you wuz doin' on that there bridge."

Bobby and Jake exchanged glances.

"Like *you two* ain't gone ast nothin' 'bout none of my bidness."

The man stared at them. In that instant, Bobby understood why the huge guy had looked familiar the first time he'd spotted him at this same spot a couple of weeks back. Rudolph K. James. Small-time doper. Caught running his "square grouper" shipment up the Apalachicola from the Gulf of Mexico. Older, heavier. The eyes, Bobby recalled clearly. One lid drooped and the eye beneath it drifted to the side then quivered back to center when he blinked.

"We got us a deal?" the man asked. More a veiled threat than a question.

When Bobby looked at Jake, all thought of alerting the authorities stalled. Too many questions would pop up. This guy would spill what he had seen, *whatever* he thought he'd witnessed. Jake had enough troubles just being who he was. Rumors of some bridge tryst might send him to a bleaker place than the one he already occupied. Bobby didn't care as much about what people might say about him. He was a dark legend already.

"I don't give a rat's ass what you do, or *don't*," Bobby stated.

The man's lips curled up. In the low light, Bobby noted gaps where a few teeth once lived.

"Thank you, Rudy." Jake's voice came out so soft, Bobby thought he had imagined it. How would Jake know this ex-con?

Rudy replied with one head nod. "Need a lift?"

"No," Bobby said. "Our trucks are nearby."

The crickets sang in the willows. Behind them, the river swooshed past. Nobody moved.

"Mama's flyers wuz purty," Rudy directed toward Jake, punctuating the statement with another head dip. He turned and walked toward the moored boat. He unleashed the bow rope, stepped in, and fired up the motor.

Rudy James disappeared into the Apalachicola River shadows.

Elvina's phone vibrated. She stepped close to the curb and unclipped it from her belt. "Sit," she said to Juliet. The pug looked up then tucked her backside onto the grass.

Jake Ok

She snorted. Texting was all well and good, but stingy on details. Bobby wasn't telling Elvina a thing she hadn't already figured out. At least he'd done like she told him and let her know *some*thing, little as it was.

From here, Elvina could see Pearl and Bobby's rattletrap pick-up parked beside Piddie's old house. Had been for the past forty minutes, the length of time it had taken her and Juliet to walk the usual loop.

Thx, she tapped back the abbreviated reply.

"Let's move it." Juliet popped to her feet; her tail wagged her body. "You and I have babies to feed."

Jake was safe as long as Bobby was with him. All that mattered.

The sheets hugged Hattie like a sausage casing. Beside her, Holston's chest rose and fell, his snore a gentle purr. If it wouldn't awaken him, she'd nestle one ear over his heart. She used to do that with Bobby, when she was a little girl. Made her feel protected, hearing the deep thump-thump.

No need to bother Holston because she couldn't sleep. Hattie extracted herself from the covers and eased from bed. Captain met her halfway to the door and she rested a shush hand on his muzzle. Instead of using the master bathroom, Hattie stopped by the one near the laundry room. They'd added the half bath a few years back, to have a place to clean up and pee without trailing dirt into the house. Captain

215

crammed himself inside with her, watching while she used the toilet. No such thing as privacy.

She washed her hands then moved to the kitchen. Nice cup of chamomile tea. Maybe that would buy relaxation. She heated a mug of water in the microwave and gave Captain a dog biscuit and fresh water.

Here it was—she glanced at the mantle clock—eleven thirty and she was wide-freakin' awake. Adrenaline left over from the surveillance gig scrambled her brain. How did law enforcement folks do this all the time and manage to get any rest? Show up to work shift after shift, un-sure if you might get shot, what gore you'd witness, what stupidity you'd have to endure.

The microwave dinged. She removed the mug and added a tea bag.

Good thing she and Holston didn't pull eight to five jobs. Times like this, their professions afforded the luxury of sleeping late, or, like tonight and the past few since Sarah and Tank's misadventure, not at all.

For the length of time it took the tea to steep, Hattie leaned against the center island counter and stared out the front plate glass window. Moonlight draped the shrubs and grass. She dipped the bag a few times, then removed it and added a dollop of honey. Stirred.

"C'mon," she whispered to the dog. Captain answered with a tail wag. She headed toward the back of the house.

The two of them slipped up to Sarah's bedroom door and listened. Captain looked up at Hattie, made a small noise in his throat. She held one finger to her lips. His ears perked forward, but he obeyed the hand signal. Smartest dog she'd ever had. Swear he'd talk if he could.

The door stood ajar a couple of inches, but the night light wasn't on. Good sign. A tad of her daughter's unease had faded. Hattie moved the door enough to see inside. At the foot of the bed, Ensign slept. He lifted his head and blinked. Hattie held out a stop hand to Captain. The lump of daughter under the covers shifted slightly then grew still. Hattie detected the gentle rise and fall of her breathing.

She backed up, reversing Captain with one hand and setting the door to its two-inch-open position with the other. In the kitchen, she stopped in front of the window again. What a beautiful night.

Doggone it! Fear would not keep her from sitting on her own porch. Hattie slipped a small flashlight into her pocket. Just in case. Captain trailed Hattie through the door. He took up guard position by her rocker.

A perfect moment. No human noise. Only the song of the crickets in the velvet shadows.

Captain moved from an alert sit to a lounge. Hattie rocked and sipped chamomile tea. The blended flavor of herb and sweet coated her tongue. Tupelo honey had to be the "Gold of the Gods," like they claimed.

No place on earth she'd rather be than on the Hill, with her people, her dogs, the barn cats, and Hendrix and the Chick Flicks. The spirits of Mr. D and Tillie Davis gathered around her.

The lyrics from a favorite Eagle's song hummed in her mind. The one about every manner of refuge having a price.

What price did this refuge of hers exact?

The answer: they never went anywhere too distant. Only as far as a car would carry them. Never more than a day's journey.

If fear wasn't holding her back, why was she allowing it to tether her and her family? Hattie tried to recall the last time they'd traveled farther than a few hundred miles from the Hill. Every summer, they planned a road trip: St. Augustine, Orlando (theme park world), St. George Island, the Appalachian Mountains, and once to New Orleans with Jerry and Mary-Esther to visit her sister's home city.

Last plane trips? To the West coast for the Alaskan cruise before she and Holston married, then to China to adopt Sarah not long after that.

Easy answer to her fear of flying: Twin Towers, November 11, 2001. That had grounded a lot of people.

Holston flew into JFK International several times a year. To visit his elderly mother upstate. To see his editor and friends in New York City.

What was the nature of fear? It had stalled life, circled it with invisible barricades. At the same time, it robbed her and her family, and others, of experiences. Hattie breathed out a long sigh. Raising a daughter to be strong and independent had always been her and Holston's number one goal. Passing along her own insecurities didn't fit the plan.

"Fear and worry are the two most worthless emotions on God's green earth," Aunt Piddie used to say. She was right.

Hattie reached toward Captain and clicked her fingers. The shepherd rose to a sit and leaned into her hand. She rocked and petted.

She'd talk it over with Holston, first thing in the morning. They could take a family trip as soon as school let out next spring. Fly up to

New York State. High time Sarah saw her only living grandparent other than on Skype. Holston had always wanted to show them New York City. Good for Sarah to see the Empire State Building, the Statue of Liberty, and a Broadway play. New York pizza! Of course, Ground Zero, to honor those Americans who'd lost their lives. Didn't she owe it to them to move forward, shuck off the fear-borne inertia?

Where else could they go? Hattie clicked off a destination with each pitch of the rocker. Grand Canyon, Yellowstone, Niagara Falls. Other than the Great Smokey Mountains, Hattie had not seen the national parks.

She drank a slurp of tea. Oh, and what about abroad? Ireland, the British Isles, Spain, Greece, Italy? The south of France. She'd have to work up endurance for hitting Australia and New Zealand. Hours and hours on a plane. But she could. She would!

Hattie chuckled low. Wouldn't take anything to convince Holston or Sarah to travel. Those two had a bag packed at the hint of a road trip.

Wait. Was *she* the one who had projected fear onto her family?

That was going to stop. Right now.

Hattie ticked off several more destinations. It could take a lifetime to see the best of this world and she was getting a late start.

A *whump* halted the travel bucket list. Hattie braked the rocker with one foot. Captain jerked his head toward the far end of the porch. A low growl rumbled his throat.

Something shifted in the shadows. Hattie could hear the blood whoosh in her ears. If she tried to make it to the door, would it have time to cut her off? Holston slept soundly. Even if she screamed, he might not wake in time. She moved her arm enough to set the mug onto a table by the rocker then slipped a hand into her pocket.

If someone was coming for her, she would at least take a good look at him before . . . She snapped on the flashlight. Two round eyes watched her.

"Stay!" Hattie ordered Captain. The big dog danced in place, but followed the command.

The creature hunkered near the overturned birdseed container. Frozen. Hattie willed herself to remain calm. Observe.

No erratic behavior. It wasn't salivating.

Seemed like fifteen minutes passed. Hattie. The dog. The animal. Then it whirled around and disappeared through the hedges.

Hattie let out the breath she'd held. Her head felt swimmy. The adrenaline she'd tucked down earlier hammered her heart. So much for attaining sleep tonight.

Tomorrow, she'd clean up what was left of the seed and move the canister inside. Away from little beggars.

"It's okay, Cap. It's okay. Settle."

Sometimes a raccoon was just a raccoon.

Chapter Twenty-seven

Sunday morning, November 1ˢᵗ, the wee hours

Jake cracked two eggs into a shallow cup, one at a time, and checked for shell bits, then poured both into a large mixing bowl with creamed butter and sugar. Such a simple recipe, passed down from his beloved mentor. Jake figured every Southern cook had a teacake recipe. The old-fashioned cookies reminded him of his mother's maid Actress, and of Piddie.

The scent of fresh linen drifted up from his shirt and lounge pants. The river-soaked clothes—his and Bobby's—were in the washer. Not that either of them had to hide details from Leigh; she wasn't the gossip-monger type. Bobby had the option of telling his wife about what happened at the river. Shouldn't keep secrets from a spouse, or partner.

Jake added in the milk and the dry, sifted ingredients to the creamed mixture, a bit at a time. He stirred by hand.

He'd tell Shug. He would. *If* Shug ever came home.

Gloom threatened to drape over him again. Jake picked up the cinnamon jar and inhaled. Not as effective as the scent of the amber spice baked with sugar, but sufficient to release enough good to ward off the bad.

Jake recalled Piddie's knurled hands at work, smoothing the flour lumps in the thick batter, her arthritic fingers wrapped around a wooden spoon much like the one he now held. This kitchen had witnessed so many versions of his younger self, Jake couldn't separate the memories. Sometimes, Hattie or Bobby sat next to him at the metal table. Others, only Piddie. No matter what parental misstep Betsy Lou had taken, Piddie's teacakes soothed away hurt.

Jake glanced around at the narrow kitchen barely large enough for the table and a couple of chairs. Had Rudy not been there tonight, or Bobby . . . had the Apalachicola swallowed him, he would've never seen this room again.

"What cha cookin' up there, Martha?"

Jake jerked. A dollop of batter dropped to the tile. He took in the sight of Bobby standing at the threshold.

Had Jake died, he would not have lived to see Bobby Davis in *his* chenille robe, with those hairy, butt-white, banty rooster legs.

He grabbed a paper towel and wiped up the spilled batter, then focused attention on the bowl before Bobby could notice his watering eyes or his smile.

Bobby moved to the end of the counter and poured himself a cup of coffee. Decaf. Both of them were already so hyped up, Jake figured it to be the best choice.

"I'm making teacakes."

"Makes total sense"—Bobby consulted his watch—"at midnight."

Good thing it was waterproof or Jake figured he'd have to buy him a new one. "Washer's on last spin cycle. I'll have your clothes dry soon."

"No worries. Leigh's cool. I let her know I was here."

"Okay."

"I'll tell her as much, or as little, as you want." Bobby pulled out a chair and plopped down. The tufted robe strained to span his shoulders. Shug's would've been a better fit, but it, and Shug, were miles away.

Jake slid a baking sheet loaded with rounded mounds of dough into the preheated oven and shut the door. "There." He set the timer. "Twelve minutes until magic." He refreshed his coffee and sat down in the chair opposite Bobby.

"All right, Jake. Tell me. All of it."

As the timer ticked off the seconds, Jake replayed the Parade of Horribles. With each word, he felt lighter. Guess the old adage held truth: *Misery shared is misery halved.*

When Jake finished speaking, Bobby whistled low. "What a shit storm." He pushed his cup to one side. "Can't help with the family drama, but I *can* lay fresh eyes on the other stuff. Where's that list of texts? Let's start with them."

Miracle both of them hadn't drowned. Miracle someone like Bobby sat at his kitchen table, in a fuzzy robe, after midnight, and at ease.

Everyone assumed a gay man was out to jump on any male that got within two feet. Ridiculous. Jake knew that. He was grateful Bobby understood. Now.

Jake walked to the study where he'd left the planner with the Envelopes and the notebook containing the tome of nastygrams. He returned and dropped both the Envelopes and the list in front of Bobby. "There's probably a fresh load of texts on my phone from earlier tonight. I get at least thirty a day. I deleted a few, early on."

Bobby shifted the Envelopes to one side and lined up the notebook parallel to them, as if he handled case evidence. He picked up the notebook and thumbed through the first few pages. The skin between his eyebrows crimped. "Bound to be a common thread in here."

Jake checked the timer, laid eyes on the rising cookies. He sat down. "I tried to keep up, at first. Then it was all too much. Most are from our area code."

Bobby agreed. "Some are south Georgia and Alabama, I think." He glanced up. "Did you do any reverse look-ups?"

"No." Jake rotated his mug one way then back the other. "Been preoccupied, one reason. And I didn't want to know."

"Why?"

Jake lifted his shoulders, let them fall. "Suppose I was worried I might know some of them."

"May I take this? Make a copy?"

"Sure. Torch it, for all I care. I'll probably end up contacting my carrier to get a new phone number."

"What a flaming pain in the ass. Hold off on that. For now. Has to be a way to get this cleared up." Bobby closed the notebook. "I know exactly the authority to contact."

"Oh, Bobby. I don't know if I want to involve—"

"Elvina." When Jake didn't speak, Bobby added, "That woman could find a cotton ball hidden in a herd of sheep. Should've been a detective. J.T. consults her all the time."

Jake considered. Elvina often said she counted both him and Shug as family. "Think she would do it?"

Bobby stared at him, one eyebrow crooked up.

"Forget I asked that. Of course, she will." Who better to solve this than the woman dead-center of the local nucleus? Nothing could stand up to Elvina when she came down with a good case of righteous indignation.

But she would want the whole story. Jake huffed out a breath. Who did he think he was fooling? For sure, not Elvina Houston. By now, she would've spotted Bobby's truck parked by the house. Had watched the two of them slogging into the front door like half-drowned sewer rats. The pair of field binoculars Elvina kept on the living room table wasn't for viewing finches at the feeders.

Bobby picked up Jake's phone and tapped the screen. "Thirty-two new text messages. Mind if I forward them to my phone?"

"Knock yourself out."

He tapped the screen several times then lay the phone on the table. Next, he picked up the Envelopes, checked the postmarks, and put the one with the most current date back on the table. "Want me to open it? Or would you rather . . ."

"You do it." Jake twined his fingers around his cup to keep them from shaking.

Bobby patted his upper chest, where his pocket would've been. "Crap. Guess my jackknife's in the washer with my clothes. Sorry. Got a letter opener?"

Jake retrieved a butter knife from the silverware drawer. "This do?"

Bobby slid the rounded tip beneath one edge and walked the blade beneath the sealed and taped flap. He inspected the insides of the envelope, then extracted a single sheet of white paper and unfolded it. He lay it face down on the table.

Jake thought this had to be the same way an aspiring film star felt, waiting on the academy awards announcement. A bit excited. More, sick.

"Nothing exploded. No strange white powder. Ready for number two?"

Jake dipped his head down, then up.

Bobby performed the same careful technique, pulling out another folded white sheet. He added it, printed side down, lined up next to the other one. "Want me to read them first?"

"Yes."

Bobby flipped the first letter over.

Jake used to razz Bobby about those retro-nerd, black-rimmed reading glasses he bought cheap at Walmart. Since the cataract surgery, his friend didn't need help to focus. Jake's eyes burned. Needed to remove his contacts, give his river-waterlogged eyes a break.

Bobby's lips moved as he read. Any other time, Jake might have kidded him about struggling with multi-syllable words. He lowered the paper, picked up the second page and read. When he finished, Bobby returned the paper to its spot next to the first. "Wow. Didn't expect that."

The oven timer chimed. Jake jumped up, relieved for a brief respite. He plated several cookies and refilled both of their coffee cups before returning to his chair.

Jake bit into a hot teacake. Seared the roof of his mouth. *Yowsa*. He put the rest onto his plate to cool. Bobby picked up a teacake then dropped it back on his plate. At least *he* had sense enough not to chomp down on one while it was still cooking.

Jake braced himself. "Okay. Tell."

"Both are from Matthew Thurgood."

Matthew Thurgood, Marshall's cousin and partner in crime. Totally wacked, that Jake had expected them to be from the deceased Marshall Thurgood. Been a while since he'd heard either name spoken aloud. Jake recalled the boy. Nearly identical to his cousin because of their DNA, but not as mean-crazy. Matthew had a part in destroying his shop, but wasn't the one who had abducted him, swung the bat. Changed Jake's life. Changed *all* of their lives.

Bobby tapped the first handwritten letter. "This one asks if you'll allow him to see you. Says he *must*." He gestured to letter two. "The other is the same, only sounds more like he's begging." Bobby paused. "Your call, little dude. Matthew's provided his phone number. And his email address."

The teacake threatened to ripple back up his throat. Jake swallowed.

What could the boy, man now, Jake corrected himself, possibly have to say to a gay man he had taunted? Without reading either page, or answering Bobby, Jake slid the papers toward himself, refolded the letters, and returned them to their envelopes.

Bobby reached for a cookie, tested the temperature with his lips, bit down. He moaned. In spite of the tension, Jake smiled. Bobby Davis sat in *his* tiny kitchen, in *his* robe, moaning. Classic. Nobody would ever believe the scene. Especially not Hattie.

"Maybe we should bring the police in on this, Jake."

His amusement waned. "No." Jake stood, used a spatula to scoop the remaining teacakes onto a cooling rack. He turned to face Bobby. "Let *me* talk to Elvina."

"Sure. Whatever you want." Bobby crammed another teacake into his mouth. Crumbs dotted his lips and chin.

A few minutes later, Bobby left, fully outfitted in clothes that didn't reek of mud and fish. Jake watched him back his pick-up from the driveway, gave a wave. He returned inside for his cell phone and tapped a text.

If you're still up, can you and Juliet come over? Need to talk.

The reply appeared immediately.

Put the kettle on. I'll bring my own tea bag.

Chapter Twenty-eight

Jake made kissy noises at Juliet. The pug lifted onto her back legs and danced. He rewarded her with a biscuit. How could he ever have disliked this little angel? Showed how unglued the events of October had made him.

He checked the time on Felix the Cat. Three a.m. November first. Officially, *not* October anymore. Jake took a twirl around his dayglow cane. Not as amusing as Juliet's tapping steps, but good enough.

The back doorknob jiggled.

Jake stood still. Juliet angled her body toward the sound, tilted her head.

Jake heard the door push open.

Juliet yipped. Her nails drilled a fandango on the tile.

Two shuffling steps.

Jake's vision grew dark around the periphery.

Shug stepped into the kitchen. Dropped his bag. Held out his arms.

Chapter Twenty-nine

Monday, November 2nd, near noon

Hattie parked Bailey in her reserved spot behind the Dragonfly Florist/Madhatter's Chocolate Shop and Massage Parlor. Flowers, sweets, and relaxation under one roof. Reminded her of a Gary Larson cartoon sketch she'd once seen, *Fred's fill dirt and croissants*. Nobody could ever say Jake and Hattie's shared business wasn't as diverse as its owners.

Pearl sat in her spot, too. Betty beside her. Wow. Three of her vehicles—past and present—in a row. A family, as much as the people who drove them.

She hit the automatic lock. Bailey beeped once. This new car talked to her more than Jake had lately. Elvina had texted her earlier; Shug was home. Hope that meant something good.

When she entered the shop, she spotted Jolene in the storage room, rummaging through a box of florist Styrofoam. Hattie mouthed the words, "How is he?"

Jolene held her hands, palms up, and shrugged.

That's it. He's talking to me today if I have to hobble his good leg. She spotted Jake standing next to his worktable. The beginnings of a half coffin drape rested in front of him. Too bad it wasn't flowers for a happy occasion, a wedding, a baby shower. She said a quick good morning, though it was near noon, and passed through with her stack of fresh sheets. First, she prepared the massage table, picked out the music for the one o'clock client. Then she walked back to the florist side of the business.

"How are you?" Hattie asked. When Jake's gaze met hers, it provided more information than his words had lately.

"Partly cloudy with a good chance of showers." He picked up a handful of fern and plugged them into the arrangement.

"That is clear as mud." She pulled up a stool and sat. "I know Shug's back. Totally expected you to be chirping this morning. You're not. I'm not budging from this spot until you talk to me, Jakey."

He lay the ferns on the worktable and walked to the cooler. "Want a diet cola?"

"No. I do *not* want a cola. I want you to sit your fancy pants down and tell me what's up."

Jake screwed off the cap and pitched it into the trash. He took a long draw, wiped his mouth. He stood, facing away from her long enough for Hattie to study his posture and clothing. Not the usual pressed and pleated Jake. Shoulders slumped. If she could see his aura like some of her New Age cohorts claimed they could, Hattie bet it would be gray.

He turned, shuffled the few steps back to the workstation, dragged out a second stool, and sat down. "Yes. Shug is home. Suppose everyone knows that fact by now."

"And?"

"And what? He's at the house. That's all I got."

"You didn't talk to him?"

Jake shook his head. "He walked in. Gave me a hug like I was the last life preserver on a sinking ship, said he was too ragged to talk."

Hattie stood and walked to the cooler, pulled out a cola. Maybe a little more caffeine was a good idea. She removed the cap, returned to the stool. "Find it hard to fathom that he didn't say anything. What did those people do to him?"

Water rimmed his eyes. He blinked. "Sister-girl, you ought to have seen him. Looked like a prisoner back from the trenches. Face sallow and sunken in, as if he hasn't had a decent meal since he left." He breathed in, out. "I helped him to bed. He asked that I sit beside him and hold his hand until he fell asleep."

"And he told you nothing, nothing at all?"

"Only that he had to get home. Needed some peace. Some space." Jake raked a sprig of hair from his eyes. "I offered to take today off, stay home, maybe cook him a good meal. He told me to go to work. He was still asleep when I left."

Hattie fiddled with the stem of a fern. Twirled it around in her fingers. "Shug never has been one to keep things bottled up. I'm sure he'll tell you as soon as he feels he can."

The bell on the front door clanked. They looked up to see Elvina Houston, decked out in an eye-popping shade of red, with a purse and shoes to match.

"Mornin' glory," Elvina said. She walked up to the worktable. "Popped by to let you know, think I have some good leads on that little issue I'm helping you with. Stayed up the rest of the wee hours."

For the first time since she'd arrived, Hattie noted a spark of interest in Jake's expression.

"Appreciate your immaculate discretion, but you can talk freely." He glanced toward Hattie, then back to Elvina. "Sister-girl will drag it out of me eventually, anyway."

Elvina sniffed, adjusted the clutch purse nestled beneath one arm. "I used my reverse look-up app on the threatening texts. Some were from up in Alabama. But four came from right here in town."

"Wait. What threatening texts?" Hattie frowned in Jake's direction.

"I told you about this," Jake said.

"No sir. You did not. Only about some goofballs telling you how hot and cute you are."

"Thanks for that," Jake fired back.

"You know what I mean. You *are* striking and wonderful, but you told me nothing about any threats." Would the drama never end? Hattie longed for one truly boring day, where no federal officer left her a message, where she didn't freak every time she heard the Chick Flicks upset, when she didn't study the face of each person she passed.

Well, okay, so this wasn't the all-about-Hattie show. She waited for Elvina or Jake to elaborate.

"I think I've yanked that one thread and the whole shebang is fixin' to unravel." Elvina bounced her head once. The mound of curls barely moved. "I have enlisted a friend of mine over in Tallahassee to help with the others."

"Thanks, 'Vina." Jake's lips quivered.

"My pleasure. Least I can do, given how much Juliet has helped me raise those kittens." She pivoted toward the door, turned back to add, "I'll report back soon. Hope to have this mystery wrapped, sealed, and stamped before the end of the week."

After Elvina left, Hattie gave Jake her most intense *give-it-up* look.

He finished the last of his cola, picked up the fern cluster and studied the drape, then resumed work on the arrangement. "Sure you want to hear about my Parade of Horribles, Sister-girl? You've had one of your own, lately."

"Yes, and don't you dare leave anything out."

Elvina greeted Chef Billy and seated herself at the garden table reserved for her party. And it *would* certainly be a party. Inside, the Rutabaga Café bustled with patrons. Suppose she could've chosen the Wild Rose Diner for the showdown. Mary-Esther would've gladly roped off a private table for her, but *The Rousting at the Rutabaga* had such a ring to it. Besides, they had fresh carrot cake today. She told Chef Billy to set aside an ample slice for her. Elvina didn't care what anyone said, carrot cake counted as a vegetable serving, two if the hunk was large enough.

The cake wasn't the only thing delicious about this little soiree. Elvina loved it when power and knowledge dined at the same table. Especially when both belonged to her.

She ordered coffee, the high-test version. Might as well get a caffeine jolt before the others arrived. Keep her edge.

A few hours ago, after she had gathered intel on the phone numbers, Elvina wondered why, and how, all four ladies fit into the picture. *Look for the common denominator.* Piddie reminded her of that. Whispered it in her ear this morning as she tended to the kittens. They were eating a slurry of formula and cereal now, and growing like ditch weeds.

The women were from Chattahoochee. About the same age. Knew each other, of course. But what would motivate them to harass Jake Witherspoon? The answer popped to mind when she settled the final well-fed kitten into the box with Juliet. All four clumped together, making soft mewling noises, and Juliet whimpered back: different from them, yet she fit herself into the group, clearly in charge.

Elvina recalled how the women in question had gathered around Genevieve at the PiddieFest event. They'd been doing more than swapping recipes and banging their lips together. The four women whose names she'd connected with their phone numbers were like those kittens. Genevieve Presley Alcott, God rest her conniving, sanctimonious soul, was Juliet, though she disliked comparing the pug to Shug's sister. Juliet was by far superior.

The conspirators arrived in a clump. Elvina spotted their car vulture-circling for a close parking spot. Must've burned up the phone lines calling each other as soon as Elvina had contacted them. One thing to talk to her in passing at the Triple C, quite another to be summoned.

"Over here!" Elvina called out in sing-song before they reached the picket fence. She imagined her smile resembled the Cheshire cat's.

They flicked nervous glances at each other, practically shoved one woman through the gate. Ah, there was the spokesperson and ringleader. No surprise. Elvina often used Bernice to spread the word when time was critical.

"Isn't this lovely," Bernice said. She took the power seat directly opposite Elvina. The others jostled for positions. Reminded Elvina of a game of musical chairs. Used to play that as a child. She always won then, too.

"Spontaneity is delightful, I believe." Elvina forced herself not to smirk.

Bernice flipped a napkin open and settled it onto her lap. The other three mimicked her actions. "This is nice and all, but is there a reason for such short notice?" the spokeswoman asked.

"Can't we gather for a pleasant lunch at this special spot for no reason at all, except to catch up?" Elvina paused for that to sink in. She took a sip of coffee. Rich, like she liked it.

The covey tittered approval. More relaxed now, they perused the menu, discussed the specials of the day, and negotiated who would get what, and might they share to get a taste of everything?

Forty minutes later, Elvina pushed back from the table. The swordfish with lemon caper sauce had been worth every bite. And, oh my goodness, those mashed sweet potatoes and collard greens! Add two more vegetable servings to her daily tally. And fish, not read meat. Elvina gave herself a mental pat on the back. Keep this up and she might well live to be over a hundred. Even if reincarnation proved true, it seemed such a bother to have to start from scratch.

"The oddest thing happened," Elvina stated. The women stopped chatting and looked her way. "I dropped by the Dragonfly to see Jake on the way here. Seems he's getting mean little text messages from someone, here in our area code. Imagine."

They looked like Lot's wife, turned to pillars of salt. Sweat popped out on one woman's upper lip.

"Suppose the authorities will figure out who sent them, if Jake decides to turn matters over to the police." Elvina relished the moment. "Can't imagine why in the world anyone would hassle that gentle, kind man. Can any of you?"

It was a choreographed dance, the way they clucked disapproval and shook their heads in unison.

"Jake does so much for this little town. Why, Bernice, he did those lovely flowers for your husband's retirement party." She fixed her gaze on the next in line. "And such a sweet memorial for your sister." Next, "He carried food to you after you had your hysterectomy. That was golden." Last, "He organized your daughter's baby shower and made the decorations."

Elvina dabbed her lips. None of the women made a sound. "Such meanness in this sad old world. Wonder why anyone would want to add suffering to someone who's already had more than his share."

A party of five exited the café. The door banged shut. Elvina waited for them to pass by.

"I told Jake he should let it go. That whoever sent those texts might have been influenced by the devil. They'd come to their senses and stop. No need to hand it over to the police. Why, it would be considered a felony, don't you think? Harassment at the very least. Maybe a more serious charge, given that Jake is a former victim of a hate crime. Shame to have that big dark mark on anyone's record. Bad enough they will have to answer to their maker, in the end."

For a beat, no one spoke. A stream of lunch patrons left the café, heading back to work.

Bernice cleared her throat. "We'll ask around, see if we can find out who might've done such a horrid thing." She appeared two shades paler than the linen napkin clutched in her hands.

"I knew I could count on you all." Elvina lifted her hand to summon the server. "I know so much about everyone in this town. You'd think I could figure it out myself. Guess mothering a litter of kittens has gotten me sidetracked."

Bernice held up a hand so filled with rings it reminded Elvina of barnacles crusted on a boat hull. "Don't concern yourself with that, Elvina." She shot meaningful, shut-your-mouth looks to the other women. "We will certainly keep our eyes and ears open."

Too bad you can't open your minds, too, while you're at it, Elvina wanted to say, but didn't.

The server appeared with Elvina's to-go box of cake. "Y'all best get a slice before it's gone." She let a slow smile lift her lips. "If I was in jail, I'd have someone slip me a piece of this."

The word *jail* hovered in the air. Elvina noted how Bernice coughed to clear her throat then snatched up her water glass.

Heaven forgive me, Elvina sent up the request. Relishing one's talents was surely a sin. Add it to her column.

"Hey, I'll be back in a few." Jolene filled the rolling cart with five red hats, upended and filled with clusters of scarlet roses and purple status. Puffy silk ribbons added the flourish to the arrangements.

"Those Lady-Hats turned out nicely." Impressed Jake how his business partner could create magic in the most unlikely containers. If it could hold a chunk of floral foam, Jolene could use it.

"Thanks." She added her purse to the cart. "These are for the Red Hat Society Meeting tomorrow at the Wild Rose Diner."

"Thought they met at the Rutabaga."

"Not always." Jolene fluffed one bow. "They're making an effort to support all local restaurants." She drummed a finger on her chin. "Next one is a brunch at the Borrowed Thyme Bakery and Eatery."

A mental image of sweet potato biscuits from the small bakery made Jake's mouth water. First time in a while he'd had an appetite. Influence of those teacakes, and Shug coming home.

Jolene wheeled the cart from the back door. He heard the lock click at the same time the front door opened.

Rudy James stepped inside.

Jake instinctively shifted a couple of steps to position the worktable between them. As quickly, he realized what he'd done, grabbed his cane, and ambled into the open part of the room. This man had saved his and Bobby's miserable hides. Least he could do was show some respect. Didn't he berate others for judging him and Shug? *Shame, shame.*

"Afternoon, Rudy."

The big man mumbled a sound Jake took as a greeting and pulled a fold of bills from his shirt pocket. "Oughta square us."

Jake accepted the money then shuffled to the counter to deposit it into a metal lock box. He scribbled a quick receipt, stamped it paid in full.

"Ain't cha gone count it?"

Jake handed over the slip of paper. "I'm sure it's correct."

"Ahh-iight." He put the receipt in the shirt pocket.

All right, Jake interpreted. Add that one to his growing list for the guidebook.

Rudy dipped his head once. When he didn't make a move to leave, Jake asked, "Something else I can do for you today? Perhaps"—he glanced toward the upright display cooler—"a cluster of sunflowers for Miz Hilde's grave?"

Rudy shoved his hands into his jeans pockets. "Them's purty. I best not spend the money right now."

Rudy stood, watching Jake. Not scary. Awkward. "Last night, at the river. Wuz you gone jump?" He extracted one hand from its pocket and held the palm toward Jake. "You don't got to tell me. I just been ponderin' on it. I know we had us a pact."

Jake inched backward until his backside bumped into a stool. He lowered himself then motioned to a second seat. "Please. Sit. My leg's complaining."

When Rudy put his weight on the stool, Jake hear the wood groan. He prayed it would hold up.

"To answer your question," Jake said, "I don't know. I was in a bad spot. I don't remember crawling up there, honestly." He shifted his gaze from Rudy and twirled a scrap of Jolene's purple ribbon around his fingers.

"I seen you up there after I put the boat in the water. I got a trot-line up that way, wuz gonna work it before I went downriver."

"Things piled on." Jake couldn't fathom he was confiding such personal things to this guy. "One atop another. Until I couldn't feel my way out."

"Reckon I get that."

"It gets blurred when I think about it, and I have been for hours. I remember looking up at the moon then down at the water, how the light sparkled. Thought about drifting downstream, how peaceful it might be."

"Uh-huh." Rudy's brow furrowed. "Didn't take that other fella to be . . ."

"Bobby is my friend," Jake stated. "If he hadn't cared enough to come searching for me, I might have leaned over and let the water snatch me. Instead of falling."

"We wuz both at the right place." Rudy slapped his knees with his meaty palms. "Best I get on out of here."

Jake held up a finger. "Wait. Tit for tat. Why were *you* there . . . fishing?"

Rudy squinted one eye, the one that didn't tend to wander.

"What is said here"—Jake indicated the room with a head swivel—"stays here."

"I wuz supposed to meet a fella downstream for a . . . package."

"Ah." Drugs or guns?

234

"Man's gotta make a livin'. I got bills to pay. Can only sell so many fish or do so much yardwork." He paused before adding, "And nobody wants to hire an ex-con."

Rudy pulled out a frayed toothpick and stuck it into one corner of his lips. "You ain't the onlyest one got spared last night."

Jake cocked his head to one side.

"I wuz supposed to hook up with this guy at a private landing, 'bout three miles downriver. I wuz to pick up a package and bring it back. Then another guy'd call me and tell me where to deliver it. Them handful of minutes I stopped to snatch you and . . ."

"Bobby."

"Yeah, Bobby, from the river, saved my bacon. I couldn't go too fast to make up time. Supposed to cut the motor and drift the last quarter mile, so's nobody could hear me." Rudy crossed his beefy arms over his chest. Perched on the stool, he reminded Jake of a circus bear.

"I stuck close to the river willows, last part, like I's told. When I cleared the last curve, all I saw wuz spotlights and boats gathered around where the landing road met the Apalach. With the moonlight, I wuz able to see they wuz law enforcement."

"Ah."

"I turned my boat upriver and paddled for a good while, careful not to bang the oar against the sides. When I figured I wuz out of ear-shot, I cranked the electric trolling motor. Ran for a good mile with it before I fired up the outboard."

"Wow. Had you been on time . . ."

"I would'a been smack dab in the middle of the bust. With my record, and me still on probation, I'da been bound for prison. Again."

Jake remained silent. What could he say?

"I made up my mind right then and there, if I have to live in my truck and eat roadkill, I ain't gonna go down that road no more." Rudy shook his head, moved the toothpick to the other side of his lips in one smooth gesture. "No more."

The big man hoisted his bulk from the stool. "Reckon I'll get on out of your way now." He glanced around. "You is lucky, you know? Ain't ever'body gets to work around all this purty stuff."

Even the hulk recognized the need for beauty. Jake smiled.

Rudy tipped his head, moved toward the door.

"Rudy. Hold up."

He turned.

"You up for a little part-time work?"

"I'll do anything." Rudy held up a finger. "Almost anything."

Jake chuckled. The big guy was growing on him. "Occurred to me, you'd be an asset for this shop, making deliveries. I struggle with some of the larger arrangements because of this bum leg. Jolene does what she can."

Rudy remained silent, watching Jake with a flicker of interest.

"Chef Billy told me recently, he and Mary-Esther at the Wild Rose need some muscles to help with the catering business. Toting coolers, supplies."

Rudy flexed one bicep. Looked like a volleyball with tanned leather stretched over it. "I'd be obliged for the work." His features darkened. "They ain't gonna hire me."

"Helps to have someone vouch for you."

Rudy's face went from solemn to shocked. "You'd do that?"

Jake looked Rudy up, then down. Buy him a pair of decent pants, a shirt with sleeves, maybe trim that hair. "You aren't half bad, Rudy James. Call me tomorrow or drop by. I'll see what I can drum up."

Chapter Thirty

Tuesday, November 3rd, afternoon

Jake positioned four buckets of fresh flowers into the cooler. First thing tomorrow, he'd create yet another casket drape, this one for a twenty-year-old FSU student who had sent that one last text, going seventy-five miles an hour on Interstate 10. Her subcompact had been no match for the semi she'd met head-on, after she overcorrected, lost control, and rolled across the grassy median into opposing traffic.

The family ordered a full drape. No viewing for this young woman.

Jake shut the cooler's sliding door. At least she hadn't suffered. Wasn't that what people said to make themselves feel less awful?

He couldn't fathom the timing. Her accident had occurred close to the moment he had fallen from the Old Victory Bridge. "Why?" he said aloud. "Why does one person live and another die?"

No one replied. Hattie was in the massage therapy room with a client. Jolene had left earlier for a dental appointment. And the powers on high might know the reasons for the random things that happened on this earth, but didn't give up the inside scoop.

He had survived a horrible assault years ago and recently a—what to call it?—oh, go ahead and own up to it, a suicide attempt.

And in Chattahoochee, a family would hold a funeral for a sweet young woman who'd died because of one bad decision.

Jake shuffled back into the public end of the shop and poured a cup of fresh coffee. Fifth one today, but who was counting?

The past Saturday evening wasn't the first time he'd danced with the idea of ditching life, only the first he had stretched his toe so far across the start line. Years back, as he fumbled his way through the grueling depression in the wake of the assault, he had coined a secret term for his delicate condition: *passively suicidal.*

Jake couldn't count how often he'd driven with the collected sadness clenching his chest, thinking how he wouldn't care if another vehicle cruised through a red light and smashed into Pearl hard enough to eject his spirit.

Too many.

How often had Piddie and Hattie, then Elvina and Shug, urged him to continue seeing a counselor? Deal with the stale leftovers of a damaged childhood, the collected scorn of society for his obvious homosexuality, and the mental and physical pain that had been his constant companion since the assault.

His text alert chimed. Elvina, or someone, had worked a miracle. Usually by this time of day, the nastygrams stood in their line-up of cuteness, hotness, let's-hook up-ness.

As if some force had yelled STOP! and they had.

One message: Shug's. **Picked up Juliet. Going to the river. Don't wait dinner on me.**

The river. Why not the park, or anywhere else?

When he pulled away from the Dragonfly at a quarter past five, Jake intended to head home to Morgan Avenue. Tidy the house. Air out Shug's stuffy bedroom and change his sheets. Put on a pot of that cheesy potato soup both of them liked. Short of chicken and rice, the best and quickest comfort food in Jake's treasure box.

Instead, he steered Pearl west and turned onto the River Landing Road. When he passed the entrance to the Old Victory Bridge, Jake stared straight ahead. If he looked, he might see the ghostly image of his vehicle still parked between the trees.

One disadvantage about living in one place so long: scenes from his life lay atop each other like layers of puff pastry—good, bad, good, horrible. Turn too fast and he'd catch sight of an earlier version of himself plodding down a sidewalk with outdated clothes and horrid, spiked hair.

Jake accelerated to put the past in the rearview mirror. He spied Shug's Prius parked beneath a live oak at the edge of the landing parking lot, and pulled Pearl alongside. A sturdy metal gate blocked his way, lashed shut with a thick, padlocked chain. Jake would dare Shug to give *him* a ration of grief for bypassing barricades once he finally told him about the bridge and the Parade of Horribles.

Jake reached for a thin, gilded walking stick then set it aside in favor of the aluminum cane he kept in the truck. Ugly. Utilitarian.

But sturdier. No need to chance a broken ankle when he only had one leg he could count on.

The gate blocked vehicular traffic, but not pedestrians. People defied it often, to visit favorite fishing spots along the bank, or to sneak into the Madhatter's Festival via the woods. Jake ribboned through a hardwood thicket then resumed his walk along a narrow strip of paved road, once open to the public. A quarter mile later, he left the fissured asphalt for a dirt trail barely wide enough to pass.

He looked down, saw the tread patterns of Shug's favorite Merrill sandals. Here it was, first week of November, and Shug still wore those rat-butt shoes. If Jake could ever catch them unguarded, he'd escort them to the county landfill.

Jake heard Juliet's staccato yips before he spotted Shug seated on a crooked tree limb. The knurled branch dipped from a century-old live oak near the bank and lowered parallel to the ground. The people who visited the clearing called it *God's Bleacher*. Beyond, the Apalachicola spread out, still in a hurry, but not as frantic as below the Old Victory Bridge.

When Juliet spied Jake, she directed one last yap toward the leopard frog she'd cornered next to the tree then hop-stepped toward him. The little princess didn't like getting river mud between her royal toes. Jake leaned over and gave her head a pat. Shug swiveled then went back to his river watch.

Maybe it was a mistake to intrude. But weeks of wondering and two days of nothing but short answers had worn thin.

"This seat taken?" Jake asked.

Shug patted the trunk beside him. Jake sat and stretched his bad leg out in front, propped on the shaft of his cane. Juliet studied them for a beat before resuming frog patrol.

For a few minutes, neither spoke. Then Shug said, "I hate the months before a big national election."

Two days without one complete sentence and he sniped about politics? Jake squelched the urge to shoot back a sarcastic comment. Instead, he opted for simple humor. "If we didn't have politicians, where would the comedians get fresh material? You're nobody 'til somebody loathes you."

Shug answered with a short chuckle. Something besides catatonia. A start.

Jake studied Shug's profile, so familiar after the years. The man could've been in pictures, with that strong chin and tousled hair.

His partner gazed across the river at the opposite shore. Jake followed his line of vision and saw a floating log. Then he took note of how the log moved against the current. Alligator. Big one, judging from the distance between the rounded nose and the twin lumps designating the eyes on its partially submerged head. Couldn't pass a mud puddle in Florida without seeing a gator, or at least a snake. Jake scanned the nearby ground. Probably some reptile within a few inches. Jake shook off the creepy feeling. His special haven on the old bridge was constructed of concrete. The pavement felt safe. Or it had.

Jake breathed in the scent of damp earth and fish, let the air release in a slow stream. Might as well cut past the politics, weather, and any other banal chatter. "Jon, are we splitting up?"

Shug jerked to face Jake. "What? No!" He swung his head toward the river and called out, "Juliet! Come!" The pug scuttled to stand at Shug's feet, her round eyes intent. Shug bent down and scooped up the little dog.

"Good move. No need to bait any gators lurking on this side." Jake reached over and noodled the wiry hair around Juliet's ears.

"We used to come here a lot in the evenings. Sit, watch the river roll by, remember?" Shug asked. "Why don't we do that anymore?"

"Jobs. Life. Lack of extra energy? Hattie asked me that same question not long ago. Suppose we're all guilty of bogging down."

"I love my hospice work. But I spend so much time away from home. All that's happened, all of this . . . I've realized I need to find *my* life again."

Juliet sprawled on Shug's lap, content. Would she miss the kittens when they no longer needed their nurse? Maybe he and Shug should adopt a second dog to keep Juliet company. When Shug didn't speak after a few moments, Jake led, "You said, *all of this*? Can you talk about it?"

"I don't know where to start." Shug's voice was so soft, Jake leaned in to hear.

"Wherever you can."

"I've never been through anything so . . . brutal." Shug shifted position. Juliet readjusted. "Torture. It was torture."

This, from a man who had survived cancer and witnessed suffering and death every week.

Jake's knee-jerk reaction: screech, rail against what and whom had harmed Shug. Instead, he clamped his lips together and dug his nails into his palms.

"So many things." Shug's voice faltered. Jake saw his Adam's apple lift and fall. "Awful, hateful words. And then, the texts."

Wait . . . "Texts?"

"Drumming in their message. *Repent. He is watching. No time left for you.*"

Truth settled around Jake. Had his own Parade of Horribles been an eddy in Shug's parade? Anger mushroomed until the tips of his ears burned.

When Shug turned to face him, Jake's blind rage folded. Never had he witnessed such bleak despair.

"Jake, the family didn't allow me to attend my own sister's service, the one *inside* their church, unless . . ."

"You gave in. Repented your sin of loving me." No doubt, Brother Jessup had put in his recommendations.

Shug's head dipped down, up. "To be taught, no, to *understand,* that God is love. That He sees each of us as the imperfect beings we are." He hesitated. "Each of us shall answer for the life we've led, the kindness, the times when we fell short. I strive to treat others with gentle care, to love them at a time when they aren't always easy to love. Yet, if I am true to myself, true to God, I am doomed?" Tears cut lines down his cheeks. "In my soul, I don't believe that, Jake. How is it good to lie to God, or to myself?" He brushed the moisture from his face. "I attended Gennie's graveside service. Stood far back, away from them all. Lois left the family tent and walked over to stand beside me."

Jake thumbed through the sibling line-up. Lois, the baby sister.

"The next days, I—" Shug raked fingers through his hair. "I have no words."

Jake draped his arm around Shug. The brown river rippled past. Jake cried. He heard Shug snuffle and did his best to suck his own tears back in place. If he let himself go, he might not be able to stop.

God wasn't cruel. People were.

Juliet licked Shug's hands. The universe sent dogs to cushion the world.

Jake believed in God. His faith had kept him alive when all he could see were tubes and bandages. Without the strength of his conviction, he would not have clawed his way back from a hatred that had almost killed him.

Did Jake believe in self-appointed henchmen? No.

241

Shug broke the silence. "Sometimes, when I am out in nature like this, listening to the birds, the river passing by, the wind in the trees . . . I wish . . ."

Jake waited.

"Being human gets so tiresome at times. Does that make sense?"

"Absolutely." Jake took a shaky breath.

After a bit, Shug said, "Let's go away for a few days, Jake. You, me, Juliet. The kittens are old enough now."

"Where?"

"Paris." Shug pulled a tissue from his pocket and blew his nose. Gave a little chuckle. "Or anyplace more than two hours from here. No matter. I don't care."

Wednesday, November 4th, morning

Bobby judged the window ledge with a level. Perfect. Why did he bother to double-check himself? His eyes knew.

"Knock, knock!"

He turned to see Jake standing at the doorway to Elvina's latest addition, grinning. For once, no gay jabs came to mind.

"Heard *El Gato Gazebo* was coming along nicely," Jake said. He stepped into the room. "Had to pop by and see for myself."

No redneck references? Guess that part of their relationship had gone all fuzzy. Careening from a bridge could do such, he supposed.

"Yep. Another few days and I'll be free to design your storage building, or my baby sister's screened front porch. That one, also for the benefit of a cat, I might add."

"When I die, I'm coming back as a house pet."

Bobby grinned, held Jake's gaze for a beat before he cleared his throat and plucked a rag from his jeans pocket. A little too soon to be joking about death. At least for him. "How's that business with your cell phone coming along?" he asked.

"Elvina Houston is incredible."

"Roger that."

"You won't believe the root cause of the majority of the nastygrams."

Bobby pulled two canned drinks from a compact cooler and handed one to Jake. They popped the tops and drank.

Jake belched, deep and long.

"That was well brought up. Too bad you weren't," Bobby said.

"You're just jealous."

Bobby took a slug of cola then pounded his chest to let loose his own baritone burp. Good thing they weren't cramming down pork 'n' beans, or the expelled gas contest might deteriorate to a lower level. "So . . . Tell."

"'Vina turned things over to a female police sergeant friend of hers, over in Tallahassee," Jake said. "She's in the cybercrime unit. Here's what broke the mystery. One text said, *Saw your ad, call me.* Then the one shortly after said, *Caught your ad on Backdoor. Interested.*"

Bobby scratched his chin. "Back door. Why does that sound so familiar?"

"Maybe because it was on the news recently. Some state government muckity-muck got caught hooking up with an *escort*"—Jake pulled air quotes—"he met on an international website called Backdoor. The police sergeant told Elvina it's a hotbed for prostitution and all kinds of illegal trafficking. Well known within law enforcement communities."

"I don't get it. Someone playing a joke?"

"Probably not. Basically, some young woman put her totally adorable picture on the website with *my* cell phone number."

Bobby guffawed. Jake joined in. Felt good, hearing the little dude laugh.

"Yep. Leave it to me to cross digital paths with the only dyslexic hooker on the planet."

Bobby rubbed joy-tears from his eyes. "Did you see the ad?"

"Oh no. I would've had to put my contact information on the sign-in page and I didn't want to do that. No telling what kind of trash I'd start getting in my email." Jake sipped his cola. "And that's not all. The officer told 'Vina that she found a similar ad on Craigslist. Took that one down, too."

"Unreal. Have to feel a little sorry for the woman. She was missing a boatload of business." Bobby laughed again. "Probably thought her picture wasn't cute enough."

Jake shook his head and Bobby mirrored the gesture. Some things were so bizarre, he couldn't imagine even the most talented fiction author could dream them up or make them remotely believable.

"Wait. You said 'majority of the nastygrams.' Is there more to this?"

Jake looked away. "I'd rather not go there."

Bobby could get it out of him eventually. Then again, maybe Jake needed *some* privacy. "What about the Thurgood letters?"

"Haven't decided yet what to do about those. *If* I do anything. Why add any more drama. I have had quite enough."

Yes, he had. They both had. "Thanksgiving's almost here. Wow. Time is skiing by, ain't it?"

"Yes." Jake's lip lifted on one side. "Then there's Christmas."

Bobby motioned to the overhead beams. "Elvina wants me to line the inside and outside with rope lighting. She's going to give you and Shug a run for your money in the holiday light division."

"Unless she's adding yard décor, she won't. I'm buying Shug a bizarre new piece that will have everyone talking. Going over to Lowe's to pick it up when I leave here, matter of fact," Jake said. "Which leads me to beg a favor. May I store the box in your shop for a few weeks, until I gift it to Shug? I don't have one place that Mr. Snoopy Butt won't find it. I'd ask Hattie, but she has a hard time keeping her trap closed when it comes to surprises."

"Sure." Bobby started to ask the particulars then stopped. Life was better with a few nice surprises.

Chapter Thirty-one

Friday, November 6th, morning

"Won't be long until I bring your poinsettias, Betsy Lou." Jake used a hand broom to whisk the clumps of dried dirt from the marble head-stone. "I think I'll order the variegated pink and red this year." More for him, not to honor his mother's preferences. No telling how the flowers might appear to a colorblind person, though he could pick up some for Rudy's mother. She would like the combination.

He traced one fingertip over the Colonel's and his mother's engraved names, then across both birth and death dates.

His parents. Life hadn't turned out exactly as they planned. Finally able to settle down, build the impressive showcase mansion, birth a baby son, then boom. Daddy keels over in the kitchen while drinking his first cup of black coffee, so Betsy Lou told it.

Then his mother: the poor, dear, loaded widow.

Jake lingered over his mother's name, retracing the letters. BETSY. LOU. WITHERSPOON.

Betsy—Hebrew for *oath of God*. Lou—French for *famous warrior*. He'd googled it once. His surname, Scottish for *an unidentified place*.

Jake fit it together: a *bullish woman from an unidentified place, who even made the Almighty swear*.

According to Urban Dictionary, *Jake* meant "amazing guy that is really funny and adorable, and you can't help but love him." Perfect for his golden retriever self.

He straightened up and stretched his back, then pulled his cell phone from one pocket.

"As you know, Mother, I am big into symbolic gestures." He tapped the first saved text message. Read it aloud, with flair. Deleted it with flourish.

Jake tapped, read, deleted, until the last of the remaining nastygrams floated into nothing.

"Time to let that shit go." A gust of wind pushed the hair from his eyes, his mother admonishing him for cursing, though she could, and had done, far worse.

He lifted his face to the early November sun.

Stop that. You'll freckle. He could hear Betsy Lou's words, recall the concern in her voice. Almost maternal.

Jake stepped back from the headstone and looked down. His father and mother lay six feet below. At rest.

He reached in a pocket for a pebble he'd found near the front door of the mansion and balanced it on top of the marble.

Might be time to let them go, too.

Chapter Thirty-two

Friday, January 1, 2016

Jake watched a tiny anole lizard leap from the mansion's back door column onto a potted spider plant, still dew-damp. The reptile froze in place for a moment until his lime green skin blended with the foliage. How unusual and telling of climatic changes, the facts nobody in power liked to admit. This time of winter, the lizard might appear later in the day when the sun reached its zenith, the only time to soak up warmth. Christmas had been short-sleeve weather. Everyone he talked to longed for at least one cold snap. If not, come spring, the mosquito population would be legend.

The lizard stretched its neck to sip pearls of moisture from the narrow fronds. Jake made no sudden moves. In less than a minute, it lunged onto a nearby woody shrub. Its skin morphed to a dusty brown. Had Jake not witnessed the landing, he wouldn't have seen the creature. Nature, so freaking cool.

"What cha doing, Jakey?"

Jake turned to see Hattie studying him with the same intensity he had trained on the common garden lizard. "Marveling, Sister-girl. Marveling."

"Me too. Marveling at this whole shebang you've pulled together." Hattie motioned to the mansion's rear grounds. At least fifty people milled through the landscaped acreage, oohing and ahhing over the new walking paths and series of what Jake labeled *serenity spaces*.

"And the food! Wow." She held a plate loaded with finger sandwiches, assorted canapes, and traditional New Year's Day dishes. "Mary-Esther and Chef Billy are a perfect match. Southern *and* Cajun." She popped a mushroom stuffed with cream cheese and bacon into her mouth and moaned. "Plus, it kept Evelyn from cooking that horrible green casserole she swears will bring good luck in the new year."

"Amen on that. Only good that dish can bring is good riddance." Jake chuckled. "Mary-Esther used Piddie's chocolate cake recipe for one of the desserts. Don't breathe a word to your misguided cousin. All in all, this gathering has turned out well," he said. Especially the focus for today's celebration on the first day of a new year: the dedication for The Fountain of Forgiveness.

Using the same type of river boulders as he had for the pond waterfall, Bobby had taken Jake's rough conceptual sketches and constructed an eight-foot pyramid. A strong pump sent water up through a hidden center pipe, to cascade over layers of rock and into a holding pond surrounding the base. Jake designed the landscape around the periphery to appear natural, not manmade. The Fountain of Forgiveness echoed the same mood of tranquility as the mansion's gardens.

"Aunt Piddie would have approved of the fountain next to her memorial patch," Hattie said. Barbeque sauce from one of Mary-Esther's short ribs glistened around her lips.

For now, Piddie's plot remained fallow, a patch of rich earth blanketed with pine straw. In a couple of months, less if the weather stayed balmy, Jake could set the bulb garden: tulips, daffodils, and irises. He'd make a grand gesture of tilling in Buster's ashes soon, too. Elvina had reminded him at least a dozen times since the old Tomcat died.

Jolene passed by, saluted the two of them with the hand holding a tall mimosa cocktail. The orange juice added to champagne made the drink healthy, his business partner had adamantly stated when she grabbed the first filled flute. How many had she consumed? No matter. Someone would drive her home. She'd left Tizzy at her house. True to his name, the black and white kitten, now three months old, was a manic terror, regardless of Jolene's attempts to train him to a gilded collar and leash.

Elvina's two tabby fur babies, Mr. R and The Madame, had it made, with full run of the sunroom, breezeway, and gazebo. Oh, and the three-tier, carpeted scratching post, bird-feeder viewing platform Elvina had summoned poor Bobby to build. Hattie and Sarah had already spoiled Patches rotten, but not nearly as much as Elvina's brood.

"How're things going with—" Jake started.

"Let's limit talk of freaks and Feds today, okay? Enough to say, my daughter continues to fascinate me." Hattie popped a tiny meatball into her mouth, chewed then added, "This business could go on for a while. The creep's turned state's evidence to lessen his sentence, I suppose. He's chirping names and contacts." She dragged a fried scallop through catsup. "At least some good may come from it. If even one kid is spared from harm. I bet Sarah's sixteen by the time it all settles." She ate the scallop, licked catsup from her fingers. "And I believe it may change Sarah in the end, too. She's hot on the trail of pursuing cyber-crime as her profession."

"With her knowledge of computers, she'll be a natural. But she's a teenager. Things could change. Next week, she'll want to be a brain surgeon." Jake located Sarah Chuntian in the crowd, near the soda fountain stand. Tank and his kid sister Amelia stood beside her. The two teens gestured and talked to Rudy James. Rudy, that big lug, had agreed to don a striped apron and cap for his soda-jerk role.

Rudy must've said something amusing; all three kids laughed. If Jake never did a good thing for the remainder of his days, he could count the redemption of Rudy in his win column. Not much for words, he was a hard-working man, grateful for every job Jake, Mary-Esther, and Elvina cast his way.

Mandy pattered by, tugging Stefanie, Wanda, and Melody behind her like a conga line.

"Glad you decided to have black-eyed peas, greens, and corn-bread," Wanda said to Jake. "Tradition means everything."

"We'll make you into a Southern gal yet," Mandy aimed at Wanda.

"Might as well give that up. Been too much blood under that bridge." Wanda grinned, proud of her quip.

"That's *water* under the bridge, Wanda. Why in the world would you add *blood* into the saying?" Mandy shook her head and added, "Besides, even that makes no sense in this discussion." Melody giggled. The nail specialist had obviously visited the open bar, too.

"Aw, cut Wanda some slack," Stefanie said. "She's had a glass of Merlot. You know she can't handle alcohol."

"Another reason to get food." Mandy tugged. The Triple C's dance team lurched forward.

Elvina stepped from the back door and trailed behind the others, pausing only to nod and smile. It pleased Jake, seeing the cat-print cane in her hand, his Christmas gift. Wasn't the only new thing in Elvina's life, along with the house additions and two cats. She'd shocked everyone by selling the Delta 88 to some man up in south Georgia. Didn't tell a soul. Pulled up to the Triple C a couple of days after the holidays in a brand spanking new Toyota Camry. Red. With a sunroof. And a killer stereo. Full wi-fi connectivity. Cameras at every corner. Crash avoidance. Named her Stella after Hattie insisted the vehicle had to have a proper title. Elvina was in techno-geek heaven: her words. Claimed to love Stella more than her smartphone, but not as much as she adored Mr. R and The Madame.

Jake prayed he didn't catch the new car fever that had overtaken both Hattie and Elvina. Elvina had told him she planned on tossing an old key to the Delta into the fountain. What was that all about? Jake figured, a way to set the past to rest, too. He didn't grill her about what she had to forgive. Or what the vintage car had to do with it.

Elvina's beehive bobbed through the crowd, conspicuous now that it was the only one. Someday, he'd miss her as much as he did Piddie. Had to face reality; the head of the little-ole-lady hotline was getting old. Heck, they all were. Who would take Elvina's esteemed spot when that sad day came? Jake took stock of the crowd, mentally tabbing through his intel on the potential candidates.

He had as much insider information as Elvina.

Happened when you were present for the worst and best times. No one took much notice of the floral designer. Like the staff of his beloved *Downton Abby*, Jake blended into the background, a great position for observation.

Yes, I can be the Hooch Hotline Headliner. Where is it written that the position must be held by a female?

Soon, he would plant the idea in Elvina's mind, offer to adopt the two cats at some point when she moved on to be with Piddie, hopefully years into the future.

"Bobby told me he'll be freed up to start your storage building next week," Hattie commented. She nodded in the direction of the fountain where Bobby held court with several women. All vying for a spot in his construction line-up, Jake figured. As if Bobby sensed their scrutiny, he lifted his gaze and gave a what's-a-guy-to-do shrug.

Suck it up, dude, Jake shot back in his expression. From the way Bobby grinned, Jake figured he got the gist of his facial reply. Bobby was no longer just the legendary, ex-drunk, pissed-off guy.

The other woman magnet, Holston, manned the dessert table. Young and old, the females fluttered around him. Wasps drawn to watermelon rind. The best part of Hattie's good-looking husband, his oblivion to the effect he had on women.

Jake spied Shug ladling black-eyed peas onto his plate. Had to pat himself on the back again, this time for the surprise he'd pulled on his partner at Christmas. That four-foot-tall lighted Eiffel Tower he'd found at Lowe's was the perfect announcement of his gift to Shug: two weeks in Paris, in April no less.

Paris in springtime, what a cliché. He and Shug had longed to go for so many years, often sang the lyrics in true Sinatra style any time the newscasters mentioned France. Jake hadn't minded that the new piece of gaudy Paris-inspired yard art still stood near his dormant rose garden. Shug swore he wasn't ever going to take it down, or at least until after he saw the real thing.

"Love your shirt, by the way. Perfect for you." Hattie motioned to Jake's long-sleeved T.

White. With black lettering: **Think. Rethink. Overthink.**

"Thanks. Shug came up with this, designed it himself." And it *was* perfect. It took a true over-thinker to conjure a Parade of Horribles.

Beside him, Hattie rambled on about this and that. Her voice calmed him. It always had. Jake allowed his gaze to drift across the grounds. One invited guest hadn't showed. Ah well. He'd cast his concerns into the Fountain of Forgiveness as he'd already seen others do.

"Where'd you come up with this idea?" Hattie asked.

Jake tugged himself from crowd watching. "Appeared to me in a dream."

For once, not a nightmare. He'd stopped having the tortured night visions. For now. They might resurface, probably would. The mind seldom truly released the memory of fear. PTSD, his counselor dubbed it. Giving it a label honed his focus in a way he hadn't experienced.

Jake fanned out the fingers on both hands, like twin peacocks. "I saw all of this . . . the rock pyramid, the waterfall, the reflecting pool. A place to cast aside grudges and old hurts. To forgive. Yourself. Others."

Hattie held her lips in a thin line. "Hmm. Some things, I may not be so ready to forgive."

"Doesn't mean *forget* or *condone*, Sister-girl. Humongous difference." He stared at the cascading water for a beat. "Everyone has something to forgive. Something they've been hanging onto. Even if it's to forgive yourself for not being the best person . . . or parent . . . or friend."

"That new therapist has turned you into Mary Poppins."

"Hardly." He gifted Hattie with a purposeful eye roll. He knew she detested that. Claimed she got enough of those from mothering a teenager. Hattie play-punched his arm. He feigned agony.

"Holston and Sarah are doing research for a book. He's allowing her to coauthor this one. They already have a working title: *He's Not Who He Claims; A Parent's and Child's Guide to Combating Cyberstalking.* Holston's editor is very excited. Says the dual viewpoints should prove interesting."

"Using their knowledge to help others avoid trouble," Jake said. "To quote your dear Aunt Piddie, *deep-frying negative until it's a positive.*"

Hattie took a deep breath and released it. "May be as close to forgiveness and closure as Holston and I, and Sarah, can come. For now."

"When you get ready, no matter what *it* is or how much you wish to leave behind"—Jake presented the fountain with a flourish—"I have provided a suitable spot."

He and Shug had talked long into the previous evening about what each would leave at the fountain. Forgiveness for any pain their families had caused. Jake's mother. Genevieve. Shug's other siblings. Except for his baby sister Lois. The only one who didn't view Shug or him as Satan with a swish.

Hattie and Jake stood side-by-side, taking in the jovial gathering. Must be a heap of forgiveness happening; the party had taken on a country carnival atmosphere.

A thought gonged Jake. It could be a new event for Chattahoochee! Held every year on January 1ˢᵗ. The Forgiveness Festival. No other purpose than to eat traditional New Year's food, chat with neighbors, and dump your bucket of moldy troubles in the flowing waters.

Bet Piddie Davis Longman had sent down *that* inspiration, too. She had been as fond of loaded gestures as Jake.

"Who's that?" Hattie pointed to the corner of the yard near the gravel parking lot where a man stood, holding the hand of a little boy.

"Oh." A mishmash of leftover fear, misery, and anticipation overwhelmed Jake.

"You okay? You look greenish."

Without taking his eyes from the man and child, Jake said, "Do you know who that is?"

Hattie squinted in their direction. "Looks a little familiar. Sort of like . . ." Then, "Oh dear God, no." Her voice came out flat. She jerked her head to face Jake. "What is *he* doing here, in *this* town?"

"Chill. I invited him."

Hattie looked as flummoxed as he'd ever seen her.

"I talked it over with my therapist. It's time, and it's right, for *me*." He took his best heart-friend's shock as the opportunity to vacate the porch.

She'd be hurt. He hadn't mentioned his plans. To Hattie, or to Bobby. Or to Elvina, for that matter. Having a trained professional to guide him through the graveyard of his past was the best move he'd made in years. Friends supported, loved, mirrored. But he told the therapist things about Betsy Lou, the assault, and his angst that he had never shared with anyone. With every visit, the vise around his heart eased.

Jake threaded his way through the crowd. Toward the spot where Matthew Thurgood—he now called himself Matt—waited as if he'd pulled up short of a protective force field.

A few feet shy of the two, Jake stopped. The child, obviously the son, was the innocent, smaller version of his father.

"Hello, Mr. Jake." Matt glanced down at the child. "Say hello, J.W." The little boy, J.W.—for Jake Washington Thurgood, Matt had shared that in one phone conversation. Named after Jake and the Chattahoochee street where life had changed for all of them.

The child tucked his face behind his father's arm. Jake heard a muffled *Hi*. Jake took note of the boy's attire. Dark gray dress suit. Blue buttoned shirt. Striped tie. Shoes shiny with polish. Hair parted and combed into place. Probably only forced into this outfit for church. Poor kid, sweltering in this warm-for-January weather.

Jake shifted his gaze again to Matt. The likeness to Matthew's dead cousin Marshall stalled Jake's brain. It was one of those cinematic freeze frames Hollywood did so well: the air went still, the crowd noise faded, the area around the scene caught lemony light.

Matthew. Not Marshall. Marshall was *dead*.

Jake had shared several long phone conversations with Matt. This man had paid for his part in that night with prison time, and with years of regret. Had reached out to ask for forgiveness, any that Jake could and *would* offer.

Jake's cell phone dinged four times. He held it up. Four messages, similar. From Elvina, Hattie, Holston, Mandy. **You okay? You amaze me! What's up? WTH?**

Another text message alert chimed. Jake wondered if the sound would ever be ordinary again. This one, from Shug. **Here if you need me. Love you.**

His tribe. His own personal pack of timber wolves. Standing behind him. They weren't with him on that horrible night so many years ago, but had traveled every step of his journey since.

"We should go," Matt said. His son looked up at him, questions in his eyes.

"No. Please. Stay." Jake shook off the lethargy and took a few steps to extend his hand to first Matt, then J.W. "You are *both* welcome here."

THE END

Aunt Piddie's Artichoke Dip

This recipe belonged to Piddie Davis Longman, the best Southern cook I have ever known. I use the lighter versions of the cream cheese and mayonnaise, to save a few calories.

Jake Witherspoon

1 (8 oz) package of lite cream cheese, softened
2 cans artichoke hearts, drained and chopped
1 cup grated Parmesan cheese
1 cup lite mayonnaise
1/4 stick margarine or butter
2–3 dashes Worcestershire sauce (Piddie called it *"what's-this-here"* sauce)
1/2 tsp. lemon juice
1/4 tsp. garlic powder

Mix softened cream cheese and mayonnaise. Add Parmesan cheese and melted butter, garlic powder, lemon and the Worcestershire sauce. Fold in chopped artichoke hearts.

Bake uncovered at 350° for 25–30 minutes until lightly browned on top. Serve with crackers or toasted bread squares.

Country Grits and Sausage Casserole

This is my go-to dish for Christmas morning, or anytime I need a quick yummy breakfast that can be prepared ahead and popped into the oven. The cheeses make it gooey and oh so decadent. The recipe serves 10–12, but can be easily halved for a smaller pan. To die for!

Jake Witherspoon

2 cups water
½ tsp salt
¼ cup uncooked quick grits

● ● ●

4 cups (16 oz.) shredded cheese (I use half cheddar, half mozzarella, 2% reduced fat)
1 cup milk (I use 1%)
4 eggs, beaten
½ tsp dried whole thyme
1/8 tsp garlic salt
2 lbs sausage (I use 1 lb. turkey sausage), crumbled and cooked

Bring water and salt to a boil. Stir in grits and cook for 4 minutes.
Combine cooked grits with cheese and stir until cheese melts into mixture.
In separate bowl, whip together eggs, milk, thyme, and garlic salt. Add the warm grits mixture, a little at a time, until all is mixed in. Do this slowly, so that the eggs don't "cook" and clump together. Blend in the cooked sausage and mix.
Pour into a 12 x 8 x 2 baking dish (spray with cooking oil for easier clean-up), cover, and refrigerate overnight.
Remove from the fridge and let stand for 15–20 minutes. Preheat oven to 350°. Bake for 50–55 minutes. Let stand for a few minutes before you cut and serve.
Garnish with a dollop of sour cream or plain Greek yogurt, if desired.

Genevieve's Pumpkin Muffins

Everyone thinks these are the best in the world, and they are! I never let on that I use a box mix. Heavens no! I make them both with and without the topping. Very scrumptious with softened cream cheese.

Genevieve Presley Alcott

Muffins:
1 box spice cake mix
1 small can pumpkin – 15 ounce can (not the pie blend, just pure pumpkin)
½ cup water
¼ cup dried cranberries
¼ cup chopped pecans (optional)

Mix these ingredients together until well blended. This will make 12 muffins. I like to use paper liners sprayed with Pam to make clean-up easy. Fill each to the top, as they don't rise much. The mixture will be thick. Sometimes, I add about a ¼ cup of chocolate chips to the muffin mix for a different taste.

Top with streusel topping if desired. Bake at 350° for @ 23–26 minutes until toothpick inserted in center comes out clean. The muffins will be very moist.

Streusel topping:
1 stick margarine or butter
1 cup brown sugar
1 cup flour

Use fork to incorporate the dry ingredients into the butter. Mixture will be crumbly. Sprinkle on top of unbaked muffins and press gently to set the topping into the muffin. Save extra topping in fridge.

About the Author

Rhett DeVane is a true Southerner, born and raised in the muggy, bug-infested forests of the Florida panhandle. For the past forty years, Rhett has made her home in Tallahassee, located in Florida's Big Bend area, where she splits her workdays between her two professions: dental hygienist and novelist.

Rhett is the author of seven published mainstream humorous fiction novels set in her hometown of Chattahoochee, a place with "two stoplights and a mental institution on the main drag": *The Madhatter's Guide to Chocolate, Up the Devil's Belly, Mama's Comfort Food, Cathead Crazy, Suicide Supper Club, Secondhand Sister,* and *Parade of Horribles.* She is the coauthor of two novels: *Evenings on Dark Island* with Larry Rock and *Accidental Ambition* with Robert W. McKnight. In addition, Rhett has released two books in a series of middle grade fiction, *Elsbeth and Sim* and *Dig Within.*

Suicide Supper Club won first place in 2014 for fiction from the Florida Authors and Publishers Association.

Rhett uses her writing to remain balanced in an unbalanced world.

To learn more about Rhett and her writing, visit her website: www.rhettdevane.com

Book Club Discussion Points

1. A number of lessons about judgement appear in the story. What characters are judged *and* act as judges?

2. In one scene, Jake recounts an unsettling incident in a small eatery. Do you feel as if either Jake or Shug could've done anything differently? Have there been times when you witnessed hatred or discrimination such as this, and how did you handle it?

3. Every person reaches a tipping point. In which spots did you note a character reaching his or hers? Looking back, has there been a time in your life when you can identify a tipping point?

4. Jake is one for grand gestures. How do you feel about his idea of forgiving vs. forgetting? Are there situations you couldn't or wouldn't forgive?

5. How might Jake go forward and cope with his PTSD?

6. Did this story make you question any of your beliefs about hatred based on differences between people? If so, why?